THE PLATTE RIVER WALTZ
(Orphans in the Storm)

BY KEN CONSAUL

ACKNOWLEDGEMENTS

Cover design by Aerolyn Consaul

Cover art:

Surveyor's Wagon in the Rockies
by

Albert Bierstadt

#

CHAPTER ONE
#

May 30, 1848

Dear Uncle Virgil and Aunt Martha,

I write to you from four days' trek west of Fort Kearney. I am in the Indian Territories now, near the Platte River. It is better this sad news come from me than by a traveler from these parts. I have to tell you of the death of Mother and Father. It was from the cholera, which was present in St. Jo when we left and has been with many emigrant parties on the trail. Father showed first signs about the time we made afternoon camp on Saturday the twenty-fifth and was quickly consumed by fever and the purging of the sickness. He was gone before the sun arose on the Sabbath. Mother tended to him well during the night and was with him at the end. On Sunday afternoon, Mother became ill and I feared the worst. Mrs. Gresham, who you may know, tended her along with a Dr. Bingham from a Missouri train encamped nearby with sick people of their own. He gave her barberry and an opium pill, and it seemed she rested comfortable and that the malady would spare her. Our party remained at camp as two other wagons also took sick with the cholera. Mother stayed quiet till Monday afternoon when she awoke in a delirium for about an hour and then quickly slipped back and soon died. I was with them the whole time but thankfully am not sick. Mr. and Mrs. Hampton along with their boy James died from the disease, too. I didn't know this until they were gone. I was with my own kin, as would be fitting.

They was buried near a cold water spring next to the river along with the Hamptons. All except the father from a family of the Missouri party, name of Cooper, perished. There was a mother, a daughter, and a baby boy. All were given Christian rites by a Missouri Methodist preacher name of Clark. It was as pretty a resting place as any at home. There were some willow trees within a glade where we laid them down and green grass all around.

Elizabeth Hampton survived without affliction. She will travel on with the Clark preacher and his wife at least as far as Fort Laramie 'cause there is no one on the trail going east who she could safely travel with.

The Hamptons were from south of town near you, and you may know their people and can tell them of their loved ones' passing. Please let the Greshams of Cairo know that theirs are all right and how Mrs. Gresham was an angel to all the stricken. Mr. Gresham was not so Christian as he feared for the cholera coming to him and his. Their people maybe shouldn't know this as he was always liked about town but is much changed after only a month on the trail to Oregon.

I am left now with our hand, Jubal, and our stock and wagon. I have thought this well and have chosen to stay on the path to Oregon. I do not want to return to Cairo and be the orphan Bonner boy. My Father said this trip will make a man of me and that is a part of my reason for going on. I want to make my fortune like my brother, Ned. Perhaps I will meet him in Oregon as he has shipped on a steam packet out of New Orleans and is destined to stop for trade in California and Oregon.

I send this back with a family who has also suffered and has given up. I hope this letter reaches you, and I will try to write again from Fort Laramie.

Your nephew in sorrow,

Josh Bonner

Josh Bonner wasn't tired of walking. He was just tired of looking. For over an hour, he had been staring only at his feet as they trudged through the new grass of the plain beneath him.

For the last ten minutes or so, he had been concentrating on a white pebble picked up between the sole and toe of his boot. It wasn't that his boots fascinated him; it was just that he dreaded looking up again at the endless vista of shifting green buffalo grass against the constant horizon and eye-stunning blue sky. Nothing ever seemed to get any closer.

It had been seven days since he had buried his parents near the spring on the Platte. He was glad for the copse of trees near the gravesite. It was a peaceful place and made a landmark in this changeless sea of waving green and the occasional stunted tree. It was almost time for the afternoon camp, and he would be grateful for the respite despite how despondent his evenings had become.

The dreg ends of the days were the worst. With them, he had the dragging hours of the evenings to think about his parents and to entertain doubts of his decision to push on. Sometimes, it seemed every step was a chance to turn about.

The mornings, strangely, made everything seem right. Each day, he was thrilled by the bustle of having breakfast in the open and by the breaking of the night's camp. Packing, getting the mules from the picket line, and helping Jubal hitch the team to the wagon renewed him. Best of all, the affairs of the new day took him away from off his misery and his doubts.

Jubal watched Josh from his perch on the wagon. He held the reins loosely and let the mule team plod along. The river was just out of earshot to the right, and Josh walked aimlessly abreast the wagon about five rods distant. There wasn't much for Jubal to do in driving the wagon. The mules had steadied to their task in the past few days. Still, at night he picketed all the animals lest they get a notion to return to their old homes along the Missouri River. Other than an occasional flick of the reins he had little to do but watch the miles roll under the wheels and wonder about the young man pacing alongside.

Josh Bonner had changed more in the past month than in the seven years since Jubal fled slavery and become a part of the Bonner household. When they first set out for Oregon from their home in Cairo, Illinois, Josh had been just a boy, all full of himself and brimming with jump for the venture ahead. Since the deaths of Mr. and Mrs. Bonner he had seemed still a boy but one changed beyond the pain he must feel. Jubal was surprised that Josh decided to continue on.

After burying his folks, Josh sat for nearly a whole day by the bank of the river and wouldn't brook any company. Everyone knew he was crying but striving to behave as what he thought a man should. He wouldn't let anyone see his grief and turned away if any of the party tried to approach.

At that day's end he returned to the wagon camp to eat a sparing meal in silence. After an hour or so of poking the fire with a stick, he quietly announced they would go on. Surprisingly, neither the captain nor any of the other emigrants questioned Josh nor tried to dissuade him. They just passed glances around, shuffled about, and that was it. Nobody looked to Jubal, as they wouldn't pay any attention to a black man anyway. Even if anyone had bothered to ask for his opinion, he probably wouldn't have been able to tell them how he felt about the casual way the whites allowed even a boy to decide what to do with his own life. Perhaps it was the offhand way Josh spoke up or the determined set of his features that discouraged comment. As for Jubal turning back on his own, that wasn't even a consideration. Jubal had nothing to return for or go back to. Worse, some of the emigrants were from slave states and might not take well to him walking away like a free nigger.

A flicker of movement ahead brought Jubal back to the moment. Shading out the sun with his hat, he saw amidst the glare the shimmering form of a rider approaching at a fast trot. As the dust rose around the rider, it was a few moments before he could pick out the scout returning on his roan gelding. He sure was coming back at a faster gait than he had left with that morning. Something had happened on the trail ahead.

"Mr. Bonner!"

No response.

"Mr. Bonner! Lookit! It's Monsoor Delcroy a-comin' back!"

Josh had heard Jubal the first time but didn't register it was him he meant and not his father. At the second hail, he realized he was the only "Mr. Bonner" here. The thought crossed his mind that besides Ned he was the only "Mr. Bonner" that ever was going to be. He looked to where Jubal was standing and pointing, then stared off in the direction he was gesturing. He could only see a wispy cloud of dust he guessed to be about two miles distant. He ran to the wagon and vaulted up for a better vantage. Jubal halted the team and moved over as Josh stepped onto the wheel and into the bench box so he could see.

Closer than he'd thought but still some distance away, Josh saw the rider and could tell by the horse and outfit it was the scout, Delacroix, returning with some bit of news. He was moving at a fast but comfortable gait. Evidently, he had seen something worth tiring his horse for but not riding so fast as to alarm the train.

Josh's wagon was in the fore this day, and he decided to halt and let the others draw up. He raised his hand in a signal and stopped.

7

Their original party of three wagons from Illinois, the Bonners, the Greshams, and the Hamptons, had joined up with the Missouri party led by a Captain Metzger. In this party were Dr. Lemeul Bingham and his wife, Hattie, the Parson Clark and his wife, and six other wagons of people he hadn't met yet. It seemed to Josh that one of the names was Oroville.

Altogether there were about fifty people including the Missourians' half dozen or so slaves and about eighty head of mules, horses, cattle, and oxen. Elizabeth Hampton's wagon was being driven by one of the parson's slaves, Ely. Another of their slaves, a woman named Dinah, helped with the camp chores.

The men had all gathered and stood shuffling about, speculating on the news the scout was bringing. Most huddled around Captain Metzger and many brought their guns. They were checking their priming as they talked. In these parts, any news or change carried the prospect of danger. Josh carried no weapon, as the carriage of the scout didn't seem to indicate any threat was close at hand.

Josh sidled up to Mr. Gresham, who stood slightly away from the group, enough that he didn't seem a part of it.

Josh asked, "Mr. Gresham, what do you think the scout has seen?"

"Either Indians or buffalo, I reckon, Joshua. The weather's clear, and I expect we would have smelled a fire on the wind."

"Well, we ain't seen sign of either so far, but I expect we'll have our fill of both afore we get to Oregon," said Josh.

"Reckon that right enough. I wonder what Metzger's plans are."

Gresham's remarks about Metzger's as yet undisclosed plan seemed tinged with some hostility. Mr. Gresham apparently felt he should have been the captain, but the others had already elected Metzger their leader before the Cairo party joined them.

Delacroix rode up to the milling group of emigrants and they crowded about, all probing him with their questions. The scout could see they were on edge, and it would do no more good talking to them than to a jabbering flock of crows.

"Nothing to worry about, men, but I'll need to talk to the captain," he said.

This didn't do much to quiet them but did give him the opportunity to take Metzger by the arm and lead him aside. Metzger saw what the scout was about and raised his hand to quiet the others.

"Hold off, boys. I'll talk to Delacroix and then we'll see what's to be done, if anything."

He strode away a few paces with Delacroix and turned his back to the group.

"Well, Delacroix, what did you find up ahead that's worth lathering that fine horse of yours?"

The scout replied, "'Cap'n, I espied some Indians up ahead." He slapped the brass spyglass he carried on his chest. "I didn't bother to make their acquaintance, and I saw but two. However, they was travelin' in a peculiar manner."

"Thunderation, Claude, I've never been in the Indian Territories, so maybe you better explain 'peculiar' to me," Metzger retorted.

"I means peculiar in that they was bein' watchful but movin' too fast to be scoutin' game. I think they was runnin' from something."

Metzger asked, "Are they headed this way?"

"*Oui*, there is a place about a mile ahead where one could ford horses, and this, I think, is the place to which they ride," replied Delacroix.

"And do you think there are more than the two you saw?"

"I believe so, *Capitaine*. If there were just the two, they would travel close together. They were some distance apart and one seemed to be watchin' the land about while the other scouted the river. I don't think they saw me."

The captain thought a moment. "We'll stop here, then. I don't want a party of Indians able to come up behind us where they can run off our stock." He spoke loud enough for his voice to carry to the milling settlers.

9

All the men had been straining forward, trying to overhear the scout's report. The mention of Indians didn't do much to placate them.

"He still didn't tell us what's come up. He ought at least to do that much," Gresham muttered, mostly to himself.

Josh made no comment. He knew Gresham resented Metzger's being captain. When they steamed up the Missouri, the three Cairo families had chosen Gresham as their leader. He had been a selectman up until the last election, and it had come natural to pick him. As near as Josh knew, none of the people emigrating had been any farther than Cincinnati except his father, who had been to New Orleans as part of his steamboat enterprise. Josh figured floating to New Orleans on a boat didn't qualify. Josh hadn't voted. Gresham seemed as good as any other to him.

When the two parties allied at the camp where his parents died, Metzger had already been the elected captain of the Missouri families. When they joined up, no one had asked for a new election. They had just been soaked up, Gresham's captaincy and all. It was a risky thing, asking a group with disease to come on with them. Metzger could have been voted down then, but he hadn't. Josh was grateful but a part of him wondered at the wisdom of such a decision.

"We'll stay below the ford where we can keep an eye on them till they pass. Thank you, Claude," Metzger announced.

Dismissing the scout, the trail boss wheeled back to the anxious faces awaiting him. As the throng parted, he strode amongst them and began to outline the situation.

The guide watched Metzger being surrounded by the nervous greenhorns, like chickens to a housewife with corn. While they were distracted, he ambled up to retrieve his horse. He softly stroked the horse's nose and led it away to the riverbank.

Kneeling by the horse as it drank, he commenced to refill his canteen, keeping his eyes westward toward the distant ford. The roving band wouldn't be any bother, but it was always wise to keep your eyes and ears open in these parts. The two he had seen looked from their topknots to be Pawnee, and while it was not unexpected to see Pawnee so near the Platte fords, the Sioux considered this their land. From the way these two were behaving he reckoned them to be scouts for a raiding party looking to put some distance between themselves and a pursuing party of Sioux, probably Oglala. He sure couldn't begrudge them their haste. The Pawnee and Sioux were hereditary enemies and they wouldn't be just touching with coup sticks if they met up. Revenge for old murders, stolen horses, and stolen women would turn any meeting between those two into a hair-lifting party, certain as sunset.

He surmised it was just plain orneriness that sent the Pawnee this far north. There were plenty of *buffle* for them all, and there was water and land enough on these prairies for all the tribes. Old habits didn't die easy, he figured.

It was good for the emigrant trains that the Lakota had pretty much driven the Pawnee south near the Kansa River. As long as they were busy cutting each other up, they generally left the trains alone. The Sioux, while more numerous and therefore potentially much more dangerous, seemed to abide the whites who just passed through their lands. As long as they could trade for blankets and knives and be allowed to steal a horse now and again, they remained tractable enough. Sure, they would probably kill a lone hunter or scout, but as long as the whites traveled in groups and didn't wipe out more game than they needed, travelers were tolerable safe.

Delacroix walked the gelding up the short embankment and back to the train. He saw the men had gone back to their wagons and were commencing to form into an open corral where the animals would be protected. Metzger had gotten them doing the right thing without much of a fuss, and the scout was grateful the crisis had been averted with no further bother. So far, Metzger had been an easy man to lead. These people were fortunate to have picked Metzger as their headman. He had a natural ability to command but was smart enough to know he didn't know his way past St. Louis. He usually listened to Delacroix's advice, even beyond which direction to go.

The year before, he'd taken a party of fifty-five from Ohio to Oregon who had picked a rich farmer as their wagonmaster. Even when they had gotten as far as the Salt Lake, he still thought he could buy his way across the country. Worse, the skunk—Perkins his name was—turned out to be a Mormon hater. Not that Delacroix knew or even cared much about the Saints' religion, but he did know they would need their help by the time they got far. Blowhards like Perkins were dangerous on a journey like this, and it was asking for disaster to have one in charge. In spite of the rich Ohioan, the scout led them through. At least he led forty-nine of them through. Of the six that had died, three probably would have anyway.

11

Two others had died needlessly, and one more had died viciously because of their damnfool captain.

The only real complaint Delacroix had about Metzger was that he let the Illinois group join up with them. Delacroix didn't know anything about treating cholera, but he did know it best to keep your distance from any fever or disease. However, the malady seemed to have passed over them. He surely hoped so. One of his bonuses as trailblazer was to be fed at each wagon in turn. Today he was to eat from the camp of one of the *morte* wagons, the one in which the steamboat mechanic and his woman had died.

He had been watching the boy and the black for signs of cholera. There didn't seem to be any, and he did admire the boy's pluck for going on. The black seemed like he could handle himself in a fix. All told, though, he would rather camp with the red-haired Hampton girl. She seemed a likely wench to take care of a man on a lonely night. And her breasts! *La Tetons Grand*, he joked to himself and smiled.

Leland Metzger was pleased with the train's progress so far. Except for forming up into a U-shape with the livestock picketed within its confines, this day's camp was much like any of the previous ones. He was glad a potentially dangerous panic had been so easily thwarted. His people settled down after the first talk of the Indian sighting. The news sent the menfolk scudding to drive the women and children to the wagons. Now that the task of corralling up was complete, the usual routines of the afternoon camp were commencing, albeit with an air of nervous anticipation.

While it would have been pleasant to congratulate himself on his own handling of the crisis, he knew he was as green as any of the rest. Visions of a butchering party of savages had raced across his vision when he'd first learned of the nearby Indians. However, the quiet confidence of the pilot quickly settled his nerves and let him think clearly about what was to be done.

When he accepted the captaincy of the expedition prior to leaving St. Joseph, it was the reputation and the qualities of the Western guide that had inspired him to service. He now felt this dangerous journey could be completed. After all, Delacroix had led three other groups through to Oregon City, and they should consider themselves lucky they were able to hire him for the trip. Although he had heard good things spoken of him in

St. Joseph, he didn't really know much about him. He had been told he was the son of a French *voyageur* trapper. Delacroix told him he had been to Oregon and California before with Fremont in '43. He sure looked and smelled like a trapper.

It was good luck they had a surgeon amongst their group of farmers, merchants, and clerks. He guessed he had old Doc Fletcher to thank for that bit of luck. If he hadn't had all the birthin' and buryin' business in Monroe County sewn up, Doc Bingham would probably still be at home settin' busted legs.

Home! That was somewhere ahead of him now in Oregon; unless he wanted to consider the wagon he and the missus and their young'uns slept under as his home. Rough as that might be, it seemed to him better than the shabby rented house they had back in Monroe. Being the constable in Monroe hadn't been half-bad, but the townsfolk sure begrudged him his keep. Most of his job was keeping drunks off the street and transient scalawags moving on down the road. It had surely been a thankless job, but lately it seemed there were plenty of other men who wanted it. Chief amongst these was the cousin of the county sheriff, Bill Archer. Archer was about to put him out of the job anyway and the hundred dollars in gold he had offered him for an early retirement was all the convincing he needed to move on. A hundred dollars! That, and the guff his wife had to take from the wives of the other town officials who didn't think Claire Metzger was quite good enough for their parlors. Hell, they had been about ready to pack up and git even without the ten gold eagles Bill Archer had slapped down on the constable's scuffed desk that Saturday morning in March.

Delacroix wasn't around when Metzger stopped at the Bonner wagon.

"Where's Delacroix? Ain't you supposed to feed him today?"

"He be on the rise on t'other side of this wagon here. 'Spect he'll come for his supper when he's done Injun watchin', Cap'n, suh," Jubal replied, indicating where with a swing of his head.

Metzger noted Jubal was fixing two sleeping places under the wagon. True, it was on the ground, but a nigger shouldn't ought to bunk up with a white man, even out here. People sure got some strange ideas from living across the Mississippi in Illinois.

Josh stepped around from the other side of the wagon. One forearm was dusted with flour and held a canning jar dusted white.

"I suspect he'd rather watch for Indians than spend much time down here with us. I'm hopin' some of Ma's put-up peaches with his bacon and potato might friendly him up some." Josh held up the floured jar.

"Mebbe' you ought to pass some out to the other wagons, too. I don't see anybody crowding your camp here," said Metzger.

He paused to see how that set with the boy. Asking to hook up with them hadn't been received well by the rest of the Missourians. He had, however, elected to let them come on after Doc Bingham assured him once the cholera had killed whom it might there was no further danger from it cropping up again. It was like the pox. After you were once exposed to it, you were safe in the future. Even now, he was considering sending the Hampton girl back to Fort Kearney with the boy and his nigger as escort. He couldn't care what the others might say about the arrangement.

As though Josh was reading Metzger's mind, the boy spoke up.

"Captain, if there were still cholera about, Jubal and I would both be dead. The rest'll see so in a few days, but I don't expect any of the womenfolk to be bringing over any pies. I mean to press on, be it with you or alone."

"You all are getting by, then?"

"We're gettin by. Jubal helps fine," Josh answered.

"Now, you be tying off your stock to the wheels tonight. A picket stake might pull out if there's any excitement. I'd just hobble that sorrel of yours. You might need to saddle up right quick-like if there's trouble later," Metzger cautioned.

"You 'spectin' trouble later?" Josh asked.

"Just putting careful ahead of wishing, you see," he replied.

"I'll be ready if you need me," Josh said assuredly.

14

"Good thinking, boy. Now, I've got to see the Frenchy."

As Metzger turned, Delacroix appeared from in front of the wagon.

"Our company's come," he stated evenly. "Don't raise any call. They are at the ford and just mean to pass, I'm sure. Come have a look."

Without waiting for comment, he slipped away back the way he had come. Metzger stepped off after him, and Josh, unbidden, followed several paces behind.

As Josh got to the base of the knoll, he saw in the failing sunlight that Metzger had taken the spyglass the scout produced and was looking toward the ford about three-fourths of a mile distant. Using his hat as a shade, Josh could make out four horses in file crossing the whirling river. The horses were sunk to their chests and seemed to be losing some ground to the frothing current. Each horse appeared to have a rider lying low on its back. As the horses emerged from the water onto the sandy bank, he saw two of the animals had swimmers hanging to their tails. When all were ashore, the two extra swimmers leaped up behind the riders who had swum them across and all six immediately rode off through the knee-high grass.

Metzger peered through the glass until the Indians disappeared behind a low rise. He handed the glass back to the scout, who turned and proffered the telescope to Josh.

"Ever seen an Indian before, boy? Take a spy through this," the scout offered.

Josh accepted the battered instrument, put it to his eye and scanned about until the party reappeared in the distance. He had seen Indians before, mostly as they traveled up and down the river on steamboats, probably to trade. Other than their long hair and dark complexions, the ones he had seen before could as well have been white men. Close up, one could see the medicine bags and beaded ornaments they wore around their necks, often in addition to the cravat a white would wear. His father had pointed them out as tame Algonquians or Kansa, who years before had treatied with the government and had taken on the white ways.

When Josh focused the spyglass he had his first gaze upon wild Indians out in the territories. The sight more thrilled him than terrified him.

Mounted on calico ponies smaller than the draught horses he was accustomed to, they seemed fleet of foot even under the extra burden half of them bore. Patched with white and tan, they gracefully carried their riders. As they emerged suddenly back into view, the Indians' ponies struck off directly across Josh's vista. The riders were intent upon their course, never even glancing toward the train or the watching men. Josh was certain they were aware of the emigrant party. How could anyone miss the wagons and eighty head of livestock? It was puzzling to Josh why they wouldn't even look over. Did they hold the whites in such disdain, or were they hoping to remain invisible to the surveying eyes?

Josh recalled hiding from his father in the boatshed for some misdeed and squeezing shut his eyes as his father peered over his hiding place. A child's reasoning told him he couldn't be seen if he closed his eyes.

"Guess those gents didn't do their chores," Josh remarked absently.

"What are you saying, boy?" Metzger said, turning his gaze on Josh.

"Nothin', sir! Just thinkin' out loud."

"Hrumph," snorted Metzger.

"Them rascals be Pawnee, sure," broke in Delacroix. "You can tell by their leggings and their hairpieces. They stick part of it in the air with paint and bear grease and shave off the rest. Maybe they feel it makes their scalps less appealin'."

Delacroix could see the greenhorns were impressed with this bit of plains knowledge. Of course, he could tell them that buffalo came from mating horses and bears and they'd probably sell the story to a newspaper. What the hell, let them think he was Kit Carson hisself.

"They're sure movin' like the devil's come for supper," said Josh.

"If the devil had Sioux on his trail, he'd be making quick time, too," Delacroix retorted.

"What're we seein' here, Delacroix?" interrupted Metzger.

"It appears, *Capitaine*, those Pawnee came up north for some fun and got a taste of Sioux hospitality. T'would expect they left some of their companions behind to pay the bill," the scout replied. "We may see some Oglala if they don't pass us in the night."

"Does that mean trouble for us?" inquired Metzger.

"Not likely, but they will steal something if they can just to say they did it. They see it as a point of honor to be able to come and go without us knowing. Stealing something would just go to prove it."

Metzger motioned them back and nodded toward some approaching men. "Let's head back to camp. I'd best be tellin' everybody their scalps are still safe." Metzger left the scout and Josh to themselves.

"Mr. Delacroix, we've some fine peaches to liven up your supper. Hope you'll like 'em," Josh invited.

"Mighty fine, boy—and I'll bring something to the fire to liven yours."

The scout untied a sack from his saddle pack, reached in, and with a glint in his eye, produced a rattlesnake as thick as his wrist and about five feet long. He held it by the head, pressing down so the fangs dripped yellow venom. It was hideous.

"Always happy to share with those that haven't any. Let's go eat."

"Oh, sir! I couldn't eat snake any more than I could eat crow," Josh squeaked.

"Can't blame you to that point, boy." Delacroix was warming to his fun. "Crow meat cooks up a mite too strong for good eating, but a baked rattler is as sweet a plate as you'll find." He looked at the stricken young man and added, "Don't get smarmy there. After you eat nothing but bacon and hard biscuit for two months, you'll be looking for snakes and such and a-licking your lips."

When they arrived back at the wagon, Jubal was crouched at the fire tending some biscuits in the collapsible tin oven and had a bacon slab sizzling on a skewer over the low flame. Josh pulled up a crate, sat down, and casually turned the bacon spit.

"We saw some Pawnee Indians, Jubal, on the run from a scalpin' party of Sioux."

"Everybody else see'd 'em, too, Mr. Bonner. That's as close as I ever want to be to Indians if they cause as much carryin' on as they did here.

You'd a thought a circus was passin' for all the ruckus," Jubal replied, winking.

Suddenly, Jubal's mouth fell to his chest, his eyes bugged out, and he fell on his backside. Silently working his mouth, he peered over Josh's shoulder. With feigned disinterest, Josh nonchalantly turned to look behind him.

Delacroix cut the snake's head off and tossed it near the fire. He planted one foot on the tail and had the snake stretched out like a washtub banjo. Beginning at the tail, he slit the snake along its length and proceeded to gut the carcass with a callused thumb.

Josh finally found his tongue. "That's a right big snake, mister. Is there more on the road ahead?"

"Been seeing 'em regular now for two days," Delacroix replied. "This one about threw himself at me, so I couldn't refuse. But, *oui*, there are more. It's spring and they are out of their nests. We'll see many more than you will like. I wouldn't worry much, though. They will git quicker than they are likely to strike—and they always shake their hips first."

With that, he picked up the rattle and shook it mischievously next to his face. The image of the slick gutted snake looping below the Frenchman's creased face was eerie in the gloaming light. The scout set the carcass at the edge of the coals. Josh squinted his eyes shut for a second, hoping the disturbing vision would vanish.

Josh could see, short of convulsions, he was in for a taste of snake. He looked toward Jubal hopefully to see if he had any ideas. It appeared, for a black man, Jubal was a little green about the gills. His return glance didn't seem to hold any promise of escape, and Josh reckoned there was little hope of avoiding the tracker's preparation. Picking up the dishes, he handed them around.

"May as well have some sowbelly whilst we're waitin'," he said. Josh picked up the cup that had been catching the drippings of the sizzling slab bacon and mixed in some flour to make gravy. Jubal handed around biscuits from the tin oven and began slicing the meat.

"Don't get full bound. There will be plenty of *serpent* for everyone," Delacroix admonished as he accepted his plate.

Delacroix peered over the rim of his coffee cup at his dinner companions. While rattlesnake was not his favorite meal, the amusement it afforded him with the greenhorns could soon make it one. Those who had never traveled the Oregon Road departed with the impression they would eat fresh antelope and *buffle* throughout the journey. There were buffalo to be had, surely, but farther west. The antelope, however, had become skittish with so much activity, as had the birds. Only a skillful and patient hunter could bring in fresh game and then only from far afield of the road. Coffee, bacon, and hard bread were the fare for all until the buffalo herds were discovered.

The tracker, upon finishing his dish, set it down. "Dinner's ready," he said, lifting the carcass gently from the coals.

Jubal sensed the guide was having his fun at their expense. He knew Josh and he were going to eat snake tonight, or the Frenchman would brook them no peace all the way to Oregon. Well, he could try it once, but he wasn't about to take up any foreign habits.

"Mr. Del'croy, let's serve up that thing and be done with it. I want to turn in and dream 'bout sweet tater pie."

Delacroix replied, "Any preference for which end we start on?"

"The end without the poison will suit me," Josh piped up.

The scout drew his knife and sliced portions of the snake onto plates.

"It looks and smells better than I expected," said Josh, "though I have no standard to rally to."

He watched as Delacroix fingered loose a chunk, blew on it, and dropped it into his mouth.

"Don't let it cool too much, boys. It loses some of its flavor."

Gingerly, Josh slipped loose a morsel, lifted it to his mouth, and cautiously took a bite. The texture was firm like channel catfish back home, and the flavor was mild. Josh snuck a peek at Jubal and hoped his own face didn't look at all like what he saw.

"Welcome to the trail, *mes amies*," chuckled Delacroix between bites. The scout rose and strode away from the fireside, licking at his fingers noisily. He would leave them so they could spit the meat out beyond his seeing.

"Damn him," Josh growled. "I ain't about to let that blasted Frenchy make me for a fool. I'm gonna eat at this snake until that trapper thinks we have it for Sunday supper twice a month."

"But, Mister Josh, the Frenchy ain't here to see us eat it," said Jubal meekly.

Josh grinned. "I'm glad you said 'us,' Jubal. Let's split up this worm and have at 'er."

"Mister Josh!"

"And don't be sickin' it up, neither," Josh admonished. They began eating.

As they were collecting the dinnerware and finishing up with the coffee and the peach preserves, the scout returned and helped himself to a cold biscuit and some peaches. The fact the snake was mostly gone didn't escape him. Josh was leaning back and wishing he had saved a bone to pick his teeth with. The trapper squatted at the fire and waved his cup at them offhandedly.

"You are lucky, *mes amies, Le Capitaine* Metzger is posting extra guards tonight but is sparing you two. Perhaps you are too young and you are too dark, eh?" He pointed at each in turn.

"Probably he doesn't want any snake eaters pokin' about his wagons," Josh snapped back.

Josh and Jubal rolled their gear out under the wagon. Each had a buffalo robe, bought in St. Joseph, for a ground cover. They pulled blankets up over themselves and balefully stared at their guide, who was laying out his own worn robes.

Delacroix smiled to himself. He was beginning to like these two. The boy had sand, and Jubal seemed an able and willing hand. They had taken the edge off his joke by finishing the snake, but he had enjoyed himself. One had to make do for pleasantries while on the plains. The trapper banked the fire and began to uncoil a stiff rope around his bedding. The inquiry was only moments in   coming.

It was Josh who asked, "Now, why would a man make a rope circle around his bed, I wonder?"

"The snake, she hunts at night, but she won't cross the rope because it smells of man," Delacroix explained seriously.

"Snakes be damned! You must think me a fool fer 'em!" Josh snorted, turning his back to the fire and his tormentor.

"Durned French beaver skinner," he muttered to himself. He did, however, plan to get up and grab a rope out of the wagon as soon as the camp grew quiet.

#
CHAPTER TWO
#

A pale quarter moon rose over the tailboard of the wagon as Elizabeth Hampton watched from her makeshift cot. In this wilderness, even the quarter moon's watery light illuminated the interior of the wagon, giving a pallid sheen to the household objects within. The faded quilt covering her cot had looked just this way in the moonlight as it had streamed through her bedroom window at home in Illinois.

Now this reassuring glow was the only remnant of home she could cling to. There were other everyday things around her as she gazed about: her parents' bureau, the mantel clock, even her own wall mirror and chest of drawers. They afforded little comfort. There was no touch of home from her past. All of these familiar items were stacked, bound, and tied to the wagon body. Crates, sacks, ropes, harnesses, and cooking utensils were piled or hung willy-nilly about her everyday memories.

Now, it seemed, all of the familiar trappings of home were hers alone. With her parents and brother dead from the cholera, and whatever other family she had scattered throughout Indiana and Ohio, she could conclude she was now this branch of the Hampton family. More so, this branch of the family was headed west, box and baggage. She was going on, at least as far as Fort Laramie. To her mind, even the name sounded distant and dangerous. All she knew about the outpost was that it had been built as a show of protection for the emigrants moving west over the past seven or eight years; as protection for them and as a trading post for the fur trappers and hunters that roamed the empty plains.

She had been told by the barrel-chested Missouri captain she would be sent back with an eastbound party when they arrived at the fort. By his estimate, that was still some two weeks distant.

It all seemed so discouraging and pointless now. She could recall how excited they all had been as they had begun preparations for this journey last fall. How wonderful her parents' plans to homestead a farm in the territory had seemed. The things they had sold, the gear they had bought—all were part of a dream vanished in one ghastly day of suffering and death.

22

Since that day, Elizabeth stayed on her narrow bolster in the wagon bed. Tonight was the first meal she had taken by the fire and the first she had helped to prepare. Without the help of Reverend and Mrs. Clark, she would probably still be keening at the gravesite. The kindly Mrs. Clark, besides tending to Elizabeth like a daughter, had given her slave, Ely, the task of driving her wagon and managing the mule team. And every morning and evening, Mrs. Clark herself or her woman slave, Dinah, brought meals and solace to the distressed young woman. Elizabeth thanked them every day for their generosity. What spirit she had left was sustained by the two women's efforts.

Elizabeth wished she might feel as warmly for the Reverend Dayton Clark. He had, after all spoken the words over the graves of the fallen. Since then, although his words and actions were of Christian force, his nature was troublesome to Elizabeth.

He seemed more interested in her in the way of a man who wished to possess a woman than in the way of a preacher to a stray orphan girl. Perhaps it was unkind to think so, but there was no mistaking the way his gaze wandered over the set of her figure. She was used to those types of looks, had even encouraged them back home. Her fanning of such attentions was largely the reason the Hamptons had left their farm for the distant promise of Oregon. The regards Elizabeth coveted from the young beaus of the town had not gone unnoticed amongst the matrons of the river town.

The putty-faced old biddies. They might be content to cling and to grovel before their wooden husbands. Not Elizabeth Hampton. She could not imagine her lot in life as a gossipy servant for some thick-headed bumpkin, beholden to him for her very food and shelter. Elizabeth had her own course to set.

She had heard their whispers, had seen them talking behind their hands about her and her "brazen" way. They would probably faint dead away if they knew how bold she could be when it suited her fancy or furthered her wishes. Let them wag their tongues. Let them bleat.

Her parents, although they had not said as much to her, heard the talk of the townsfolk. To escape the gossip circulating around their only girl-child had been one of the primary reasons for the decision to go west, that and the hope of establishing a small cattle ranch to trade with the ships that called along the Pacific coast.

The Hamptons had not been the only townspeople captivated by the dream of a new life in the Oregon territories. The Greshams and the Bonners, minus their older son Ned, had packed up their lives in high-sided wagons and set out on their common path.

Elizabeth knew Mrs. Gresham had not been one of those to pass on the tidbits and conjectures that were the chief entertainment of the married women of the town. Miriam's taciturn nature was legend in Cairo. Elizabeth suspected it stemmed from stories circulated about Custis Gresham and the seamier side of his hostelries. Besides being a town selectman, he owned two hotels. One that catered to the genteel travelers on the Mississippi and one at the landings that counted transient gamblers, boatmen, and soiled doves amongst its guests. Many supposed it was Custis Gresham's discretion about some of the doves' town clients, as well as his financial acumen, that led to his appointment as a selectman.

The Bonners, she supposed, may well have heard the tales of Elizabeth's exploits. Whether Joshua and Ned's parents repeated the chatter, she didn't know. She had never spoken to the mister and had only seen the missus on a few occasions. She had given no indication in their meetings that she had given any credence to the rumors.

It didn't matter much now, she imagined, as both the senior Bonners were laid out alongside her own kin by the quiet pool alongside the Platte. Only Joshua remained, and she was certain that Elizabeth Hampton had been a delicious topic of speculation amongst Joshua and his fellows. Of course, he may have heard all from his brother, Ned. His handsome brother could certainly lay to rest any imaginings of the awkward young man. She had selected Ned as much for his quiet ways as for his charming appearance. Her memories of their secret moments together recalled their first intimate encounter.

She had gone to bathe in the stream that ran along the south end of their farm. As she was undressing, she heard voices from down the bend where she planned to swim. Dropping down and clutching her clothes about her, she crouched behind a large limestone outcropping. As the voices got no closer, she decided to investigate. Creeping up the bank, she parted the milkweed and peered toward the sound of the voices.

Her heart came up in her throat as she filled her eyes with naked manhood for the first time. There, perched on a log and smoking a pipe, was Ned Bonner. He was chatting amiably with his chum, Neville Winton, who was lazily treading water in the deep pool. Elizabeth felt herself flush with excitement. Never before had she seen so much flesh. The sight of their lean physiques, wet from their plunge, thrilled as much as startled her. She couldn't seem to fill her mind as fast as her eyes could see. This was a far cry from the young boys she often spied cavorting at this secluded hole.

She could see Ned's manhood as he lolled on the log. She had talked with some of her married friends about this mystery, and they had blushed as they told of how a man looked when aroused prior to the act of love. She could not imagine the flaccid, dangling thing before her eyes could ever be as she had heard it described when it was "angry." Elizabeth believed such an opportunity was at hand, and she would make the most of the moment.

Blushing excitedly, she quietly retreated down the grassy bank. She finished disrobing and strode into the steam. Stroking placidly through the sluggish current, she headed upstream and around the bend where the young men were relaxing. Her plan was to flip onto her back as she came into view. This would support her claim of an accidental intrusion and afford them a good look before her "modesty" overcame her. She grinned impishly to herself at the commotion about to occur.

Just as she planned, as she rounded the turn in the stream, she heard splashing and a warning.

"Look up, Ned! Somebody's a-comin'."

Elizabeth continued paddling on her back as though she hadn't heard.

"Lordy, Ned! It's a girl!"

At the sound, Elizabeth turned and stood, her breasts exposed. Slowly, she raised her hands to cover herself and proclaimed her "outrage."

"What are you two doing here? This is my father's stream!"

Neville Winton was blushing furiously and had sunk to his nose in the pool. To her genuine surprise, Ned Bonner hadn't moved a muscle and was still casually puffing away.

Conversationally, Elizabeth said, "Why, Neville Winton, you're flushed fair hot enough to steam the water. What's come over you?"

"I shore wasn't expectin' anybody to come floatin' by," Winton replied, turning his eyes downward.

"Certainly not someone so pretty as you, Miss Hampton," Ned spoke up.

Elizabeth gawked at the naked form as long as she dared before casting her stare into the treetops.

"Why, you snappy rascal! You came up here hoping to catch me at my bath." Elizabeth put on her most indignant tone.

"No, ma'am, I didn't. But I believe I'll bathe with more frequency from now on. Perhaps I should ask permission of your father for use of this hole?" Ned replied.

Elizabeth, now flustered, exclaimed, "No! You may not speak to my father."

She stared boldly at the naked man, hoping to rattle him. With some satisfaction, she noticed he was now puffing quite avidly at his pipe. With even more satisfaction, she noticed his other "pipe" was seemingly growing and twitching with a life of its own. Under her stare, Ned sat down, consciously aware of her and the involuntary goings-on between his legs. Instinctively, Elizabeth knew this scene had carried as far as it could for the moment. She now wished Ned had been alone, for she knew Neville would have the incident spread throughout the township before sunup tomorrow. She had to end this most exciting encounter now.

"I'll thank you to keep on this side of the bend. I'm going back, and I'll never forgive either of you if I even think you'd peep over at me." With that, she swung about and stroked away, giving them a good look at her rump as she departed. It was in her mind to bathe here more herself. Ned would certainly return, and she found herself wanting more of this bold riverboat man.

Around the cutoff, Elizabeth shampooed her auburn hair while perched on a boulder at the stream's edge. She was half hoping they would try to peek at her, and she looked out of the corner of her vision for any movement that would betray their presence. At the same time, she luxuriated in the carnal tensions coursing through her. The feelings of arousal were not new to her, but the fresh recollections of her encounter had raised them to a new peak. The talk of her married friends was titillating but was nothing compared with the thoughts and visions racing through her mind.

The memory faded as Elizabeth brought herself back to the present. She felt shamed and frustrated. Here she was, alone in a wagon, a thousand miles from anywhere, her family dead just seven days behind her. How could she be in such a dilemma and still have her mind consumed by such wicked thoughts? She must not think like that again, ever. Ever. She grabbed a twist of flesh from under her arm and pinched herself hard to clear her mind.

Outside the wagon, silhouetted by the firelight against the canvas, was the figure of a man. The form seemed to linger as though listening for movement inside. Oh God! Had she been talking as she recalled those wicked memories? The figure stopped, hesitated, and then moved to the rear opening of the wagon. Reverend Clark peered into the dim interior.

"Are you able to rest well now, child ?" he asked.

"Yes, Reverend," Elizabeth replied. "You and Mrs. Clark have been so kind to me. I don't know how I would have gotten on without your help."

"It is a fair part of our Christian work. We could have done nothing else."

"Still, I want you to know how grateful I am to you," Elizabeth said.

"For your gratitude, then, I thank you, child. We will need to speak some of your future. Do you feel able?" asked the reverend.

"Yes. I suppose."

"When we reach Fort Laramie, the captain, as you know, plans to send you back. You are aware of that?"

"Yessir, I am."

"When you reach St. Joseph or St. Louis, do you have family that can care for you?"

27

"I have family in Indiana and up the Ohio River," Elizabeth replied.

"Do you have means by which to reach them?" Clark asked.

Elizabeth thought, then answered, "My father sold everything and bought this wagon and team. He said he had almost two thousand dollars left."

Looking directly into the gloom at her, he asked, "And do you not have it?"

Elizabeth sprang bolt upright. She had not thought of the money since her parents died and little enough before that. "No!" she cried out. "I haven't thought of it at all." She paused as a grim thought crossed her mind. "You don't suppose my father was wearing a money belt when he was—?"

Reverend Clark held his hands out palms forward. "Child, no, he was not. We would have seen it as we were laying him out. Your stake must be here, somewhere in the wagon. Are you telling me you don't know where?"

In a sudden panic, Elizabeth groped wildly about at everything she could reach.

"I have no idea!"

The reverend held out his hand and grasped her ankle through the quilt. "Be still, child," he commanded. "There is time enough to look. You will have no need of money until we reach the fort." He paused. "That is what I wish to speak to you of."

"About the fort?"

"Mrs. Clark and I want to ask you if you would consider going on to Oregon with us. We have but recently married and are determined to start a school for the children of the settlers. You could help us teach at the school or perhaps start some small concern of your own. Would you think about staying with us?"

"To confess, sir, I do want to go on. There is nothing left for me in the East and I haven't seen any of my other kin for over two years. I don't know if they would welcome me or   take me in," Elizabeth confided.

28

Soothingly, Clark said, "You are still in distress, girl, and no decision is needed now. You let us know before we reach the fort. In the meantime, Mrs. Clark and I will continue to aid you, and, if you are concerned, we will help you to find your cache—if you wish," he added.

"Thank you, Reverend. I have been thinking about Oregon, and I will think about your offer," said Elizabeth.

The preacher patted her ankle. "You brave child. God bless you."

"Good night, Reverend Clark. And thank Mrs. Clark for me."

Without another word, Clark turned and faded into the evening. Elizabeth lay back and covered her eyes with her hands. The money was just too much more to think about. What was she to do? The Clarks' offer of an escort to Oregon would well fit her plans, but she couldn't see herself as a spinster teacher in some backwoods settlement. Her parents' plan of starting a cattle ranch had been an accepted conclusion, but what sort of a "concern" could she manage on her own? And what about the money? Hopefully, it was hidden in the wagon somewhere. She tried to put it out of her mind, but she couldn't dismiss the reality of its importance. It was going to be crucial to find, as having it would determine whether she could even consider going on. Elizabeth lay in the milky moonlight thinking until she fell into a fitful sleep.

Across the encampment, Josh Bonner was wide-awake. At least both of his dinners had settled nicely, and he was free to visualize stalking Indians and striking rattlesnakes. Under the blankets, he loosely held the Colt Walker revolver his father had managed to purchase from a Texas captain whose boat he had repaired. His father had told him civilians were not ever supposed to own one, and they were fortunate to have it. His father had taken great pride in its ownership. Now it was Josh's, contraband or not, and he felt the same pride his father had. Holding it somehow felt like the only secure thing he had in life. Its iron and nickel weight was a comfort to him as he lay wrapped in his bedroll.

He was upset he had not been considered for standing a watch over the sleeping families. Here he lay, with probably the best weapon for three hundred miles, expected to sleep under the protective eye of men who thought him a boy. It rankled. If he could not stand apace with the other men, they might veto his decision to move ahead and send him back in company with the Hampton girl in the tow of some frontier vagabond.

Picking himself off the ground, he stuck the pistol in the back waistband of his trousers. He didn't want to walk around with it openly displayed, and should it go off, he would rather take his chances with a ball in the butt than somewhere more personal. Stepping out, he snagged his foot in the rope laid on the ground around the bedrolls. Shaking it loose from his boot, he stalked heavily through the wagon encampment.

A few other overlanders were still about, tending to small tasks or staring dreamily into the weaving flames. To each he mumbled a greeting and received a muttered reply or a nod of the head. Several yards ahead, another form patrolled slowly with a carbine or shotgun cradled in his arms. A farmer's rumpled work hat was pitched on the back of a shaggy head. His gait was pronounced, like someone who imagined how a sentinel should walk. He wheeled at Josh's approach.

"I heer'd ya walkin' up! I guess if I heer'd ya, ya couldn't be no Indian!"

Josh offered his hand. "No, I guess not. Josh Bonner's my name. I'm not ready for sleepin', and I thought I'd have a look about the camp."

"I've been lookin' since right after supper, and there's nothin' to see but dark, I reckon," said the watchman.

Josh's new companion was well over average height, with such a long upper lip his nose seemed lost on his face. The man's eyes were overhung by bushy eyebrows, so the eyes appeared deep in their sockets. He looked to be in his late twenties.

"Josh Bonner," Josh repeated, still clasping the man's hand.

"Henry Shearwood. Sorry if I forgot m'manners. This Indian business got me wound up tighter than a broken clock," Shearwood said.

"I'm a mite spooked m'self," Josh admitted. "Though the guide seems to think naught of them." Josh hoped this might relieve some of the man's jitters.

"That do settle me some. Now I guess I don't mind I can't see a damn thing," Shearwood remarked in mock relief.

For the first time in days, Josh felt the corners of his mouth pull back in just the memory of a grin. It felt new. He welcomed the sensation.

"What finds you here on the road?" Josh nodded generally westward.

"Land! One hundred sixty acres of prime land is what I've read. Free to any who will settle it. M'wife and I have been workin' an eighty-acre plot in Samuels County. The idea of that much land unbeholdin' to anyone is all we've been dreamin' about for the past year. Hell, it's more than two folks can work, but jist the idea . . ." His voice trailed off as his thoughts captured his tongue.

"If it's as fertile as the ground we're passing over, a hundred and sixty acres under the plow would be somethin' to see. Knowin' it's your own, even better," Josh said, although he doubted Henry Shearwood even remembered he had company.

Josh was glad he had met the spellbound Shearwood, not only for the memory of a smile but for the ambition that finally removed the last doubt in his mind about his own destination. Without people like Henry, and, he guessed, himself, America would just be some Atlantic trading posts on the edge of a wild and forbidding interior. He was sure he was in the right place.

"Henry!" Josh nudged his new friend.

The lanky man, released from his daydream, regarded Josh with a grin.

"That's another reason I had to leave. People began to poke fun at me fer all my talkin' and daydreamin' about Oregon. I guess I had to go or be laughed at all m'life. You understand, though, don't you? Else you wouldn't be on this road yourself?"

"Indeed I do, Henry Shearwood. I guess it's Oregon and not Indians keeping me from my rest. Good night." Josh clapped the man lightly on the arm as he departed.

Continuing his patrol, he quietly stole in amongst the picketed stock. Padding as noiselessly as he could, Josh sought out his riding horse, Natchez. The seventeen-hand sorrel nickered and fidgeted as he recognized his master's approach. Josh murmured back softly and stroked the horse's muzzle. He swung the great head about and blew gently into the horse's nostrils as a greeting.

31

The Bonners had acquired Natchez as a two-year-old. Now, his dependability and steady nature had made the horse almost a part of the family. Checking Jubal's rigging, he found the hobble secure but with sufficient length to allow Natchez enough motion to ensure balance. The bridle picket, however, was too short and kept the sorrel's head down uncomfortably. For the future, Josh resolved, he must check his stock nightly; those who had been tending his animals since the burial were not as conscientious as they might have been. All of the animals were irreplaceable and demanded constant attention. Josh tugged gently at Natchez's mane and stroked his flanks as he sought out his string of mules.

Upon finding them, he noted the four that had pulled the wagon had been brushed out. Their coats shone faintly in the wan moonlight. Jubal must have done the currying after cleaning up the supper gear at the river. Jubal took pride in "skinning" the team, and Josh knew he need not worry about them. They had been purchased only the month before and had no names. Naming them, Josh decided, would be Jubal's province.

Next, he sought out the two oxen, Banner and Flag. They were a matched span, colored with russet saddles and flashes. Docile and powerful, oxen were indispensable for the long, hard pulls up the mountain passes yet to come.

The question of mules versus oxen was a never-ending debate in St. Joseph. Those favoring oxen argued the cheaper cost and superior strength of the great beasts, discounting the slower pace. Some even advocated using cows as draught animals, citing they would provide milk on the trail. Not many agreed, the Bonners among them. The convincing argument in favor of mules was that they demanded less water and could thrive on the forage of the trail.

The departure of wagons from St. Joseph, or any of the other debarkation points, had to be well timed in the spring. Passage was impossible until the thaw-soaked ground firmed up and there was enough new grass for the animals. Too long a delay and the grasses would dry up or be consumed by preceding trains. The spring floods of the rivers were also a consideration. There were several early fords to be made. Most had to be made without the assistance of portage or ferry. However, waiting too long meant the possibility of little or no water when reaching the borders of the deserts in high summer.

The Bonners had opted for mules despite the high cost of superior animals. Most of the best mules were of Santa Fe stock, fattened in ports along the Mississippi and shipped upriver by steamboat. A healthy mule could bring as much as seventy-five dollars and there were stories of some going as high as a hundred dollars. They considered themselves lucky to have gotten theirs for sixty dollars a head.

The wagons in Josh's train were about evenly divided, mule and oxen. The pace seemed compatible for both. Many of the pioneers drove small herds of cattle, and this fairly dictated the progress of the train.

Josh wound his way through the sleeping forms around the firesides back to his own empty bedroll. Casting his eyes back at the banked fires within the circle, Josh assured himself of his direction. He felt more confident in his decisions and in his companions. He stared vacantly at the glowing fire. Embers, lifted on the night wind, drifted toward the stars, seeming to join with the heavens.

#

CHAPTER THREE

#

Dawn came, but not with the swift clarity that had announced a new day thus far. The prior mornings had commenced with a band glowing orange on the horizon, quickly spreading to pink, dispelling the shadows of the night just past. By the time the sun had whitened, the soft veil of the pre-dawn sharpened to quick brilliance and the hard defining edge of the day. Today was the first variation in this routine.

Dawn on this day brought no orange glow or radiance. The sun arose as if in combat with the elements of sky and earth. The orange sparring of the morning was replaced by a turbid glare of light that merely paled the murky sky. The sun appeared, indifferent and ringed. At best, it could only manage a harsh illumination on the windless prairie.

Delacroix, upon rising, immediately cast his attention to the western horizon. No clear vista appeared across the plains, only a gradual easing of the smoky gloom that gave way to a still and folded blanket of low cloud cover.

The first critical determination of the migration was upon him. Before the train was a useable river crossing, swift and broad, but with a firm, even bottom shallow enough not to threaten the wagon bottoms. Should they not cross immediately, rain in the threatening weather could swell the river, making the ford impassable for weeks. A delay now entailed losing several days' travel or continuing on the south bank. While still passable, the southern bank turned away from their destination and was cut by numerous creeks and tributaries. The cutoffs would mean many detours and chanced possible breakdowns. He must convince Metzger of the urgency of crossing in tumultuous weather. He hoped the emigrant leader would heed his warnings.

His camp companions were up and standing groggily about the fire, stretching and gaping. The pilot secured his blanket and bedroll together with rawhide thongs.

"*Mes amis*! Perhaps only coffee this morning. Pack swiftly and put my saddle and guns into your wagon for me, *si vous plait*." He hurried away, searching for Metzger.

34

Josh and Jubal squinted sleepily, watching the guide depart.

"What is a 'see view play'?" wondered Jubal.

"I shore couldn't tell you, Jubal, though I think he wants us to do it right now, judging by his haste. You grind the beans, and I'll hang out the pot to boil. I'll not be fair awake till I've some coffee in my belly," Josh said.

Meanwhile, the plainsman had sought and found the leader, awake but sitting with a blanket over his knees. He was watching his diminutive wife stirring some life into the coals in preparation for the morning meal. Delacroix summarized the situation, more than once emphasizing the need for haste.

Metzger agreed with Delacroix but ventured one objection.

"Hell, Delacroix," he protested. "I can't see as that weather's in any hurry to get here. Besides, by the time I've made the rounds of all the wagons, most will have their breakfasts half-cooked. I think we'll just let them all eat. It's that or ask them to toss out their vittles."

Delacroix saw Metzger had an eye to his own upcoming meal and was not to be dissuaded.

"*Mon Capitaine!* Perhaps the men could sort out their stock and harness their teams while the women are making the meal," suggested the scout.

"Why don't you join us for breakfast, Claude? The fare out here's plain enough without inviting the mules and a dust cloud for company. Besides, breaking camp with the wagons already hitched is asking for an accident, what with these women and the young'uns about."

The pilot could see some sense to the argument but declined the invitation. "*Non, mon ami.* I shall tend to my possibles. Then I shall mark the crossing with a rope. I shall need more than one. If I might borrow one from you?"

Returning to Josh's wagon, he retrieved a horsehair hackamore from his saddlebags along with four sturdy wooden stakes. Jubal poured hot coffee into a mug he offered to the plainsman. Delacroix laced it heavily from the sugar supply and stirred it with one of the stakes. He squatted by the fire and addressed Josh.

35

"Yesterday, son, yours was the point wagon. Today, yours will be the trail one. We are going to ford the river, and I pray all can cross before the weather strikes." He pointed back over his shoulder at the threatening horizon. "Yours will be the last across, so pay attention to those before you that you may learn from their mistakes." He looked at Jubal to include him in the caution.

Josh asked, "You're expectin' it to be dangerous?"

The scout studied the youthful face, looking for fear and finding only curiosity.

"There is always danger out here. But there is less for the man who watches and learns." He wagged a callused finger at Josh. "*Fete attention.*"

The phrase was foreign to the boy's ear, but the intent was clear.

"We'll pack up. Then what shall we do?" Josh asked purposefully.

"Go fetch your horse and saddle him. Leave your bags in the wagon. You will come with me." He tossed the dregs of his coffee into the waning embers. Delacroix had taken a liking to the teenager.

Josh sprang from his seat, the promise of camp-breaking forgotten. He ran to retrieve his horse. The frontiersman grinned at Jubal.

"It appears the young master would rather swim a cold river than pack the camp. *Non*?"

Without awaiting a reply, he began laying out the collected ropes and joining the loose ends, which he then hung over his horse's rump. While Jubal rummaged for a mallet from the wagon, Delacroix slid the stakes into his baggy shirt and mounted up. Taking the mallet from Jubal, he cantered his horse toward the riverbank and headed slowly upstream, his focus on the bank and shingle.

After a dry winter on the prairies, the Platte was well below the embankments as it coursed its way to the east. It was uncommon for the south fork of the river to be this narrow, about four hundred yards. In a normal spring, the river could lay out over a mile in width but seldom managed enough depth to discourage fording or ferrying at numerous locations. The fords had to be carefully chosen as sections of quicksand made for a treacherous crossing. Here would be an opportunity for crossing on a more easily traversed bed, and the plainsman hoped the chance could be easily exploited.

As Delacroix plodded along, he looked for a graveled approach with a minimum of slope. Finding such indicators would suggest a shallow ford with solid bottom. He did not glance up as Josh drew up alongside and reined in.

"We must find a firm bottom without deep holes that will catch the wagon wheels," the scout explained. "If the water reaches above your knees as you ride, the wagons may well float. Stay to my right side. We shall not want to fight the current, but to strike across with the flow." He pointed, indicating a shallow angle. "If it should be too deep or too swift, you must get off the horse and let him swim freely. Hold him by the tail or the saddle horn. Do you understand?"

Josh nodded and followed behind Delacroix as the scout reconnoitered the shoreline. Josh scanned the sandy bank but could not discern what sign the scout sought. Josh was accustomed to a real river, the Big Muddy. Looking up and into the river, Josh noticed a long line of flat current with a trench of muddy froth before it. He caught himself up with the scout and pointed to the danger.

"That's overfall there. You'll find a ditch in front of and an undertow t'drown anyone caught in it." Josh spoke loudly over the rush of the river.

Delacroix looked at Josh, perplexed.

"How do you know this?"

"I've lived on rivers all m'life. It's probably a snag, catchin' trash and sand all spring. When the water flows over, it digs a hole, and the river just churns away at it. We should find a crossin' downstream of it."

Delacroix replied, "I fear we will have to go above. It will be too deep below for the wagons."

Fording rivers was not a new experience for the pioneers. Upon leaving St. Joseph, they had had to ford two rivers, the Big Blue and the Little Blue. Although both had steeper approaches, they were mere streams compared to the South Platte. The duration of this fording offered many more opportunities for catastrophe. Here was the first danger of an overturned wagon or a broken axletree. Because of the previous crossings,

37

all of the wagons had additional bolsters inserted between the beds and the axletrees. Additionally, the bottoms and sides had been caulked with pitch and cloth strips or with oakum. These precautions and their previous experience would have to serve for this first major test of the emigrants' resolve.

Delacroix halted and wheeled to face the muddy flow. Dismounting, he pounded a stake into the gravel.

"We shall try here. Stay abreast of me but about ten feet distant. Do you remember all I tell you?" He looked intently at the young man.

"I remember. Let's go," Josh said pointedly.

Delacroix took the lead and Josh followed, splashing the big sorrel into the current. He watched the scout for his cue. Delacroix veered back and forth in a course about six yards wide, searching for rocks or depressions in the riverbed. They progressed in this manner until the water rose to the hocks of the horses at about a hundred yards from the shoreline. As they neared the middle of the channel, the bottom became more uneven. The horses hesitated, unsure of their footing, sometimes halting and seeming to prance in place. In some places, the horses plunged in to their shoulders, water foaming momentarily over their withers. Other than these few instances, the horses were in only to their bellies and Josh was never threatened with being dismounted. His boots soon filled, and he held his feet tightly in the stirrups to prevent their being swept away.

It was impossible to speak over the tumbling river. As they neared the northern bank and the water receded, Delacroix recommenced his zigzag exploration. The chill morning air cut through Josh's sodden clothes and he shivered, as much from the release of tension as from the brisk morning.

Dismounting, the pilot handed Josh the reins to his gelding and pounded one of the remaining stakes in near the water's edge. Tying one of the rope ends to the stake, he ran, uncoiling line as he went. At the rope's end, he pounded another stake, stretched the rope, and made it fast; thus marking a pathway to the cut bank. Upon returning and mounting up, Josh noticed the scout was shivering, too.

"I think the river will feel warm after being in this cold wind, eh? Come. We must go farther upriver to cross so we will return from where we left." Delacroix headed his horse upstream and trotted away

38

Snapping his reins, Josh set Natchez in pursuit. Josh, too, anticipated shelter from the breeze in the river's flood. The exhilaration returned. As Josh caught up to the plainsman, he observed he was not looking back across the water but upstream.

Fixing his gaze upon the younger man, Delacroix shouted over the cascading water. "Ride slowly with me, boy—and keep quiet."

The sudden, sharp edge of his tone startled and puzzled Josh. What did keeping quiet have to do with fording the river? He looked blankly back at his companion. Quickly and without comment, Delacroix seized Natchez's bridle, turned the horse away from the river, and started both horses forward at a slow walk.

Peering ahead, Josh felt his whole body start. Just cresting the embankment were about a dozen Indians. They paused as a group, then effortlessly descended the crumbling bank to approach the pair of sodden white men.

Terrified, Josh realized he had no weapon, not even the sheath knife he had left at the campsite for fear of losing it in the river. Josh could see no weapons visible on the scout, though even a brace of pistols would be of little account against the advancing troop. Josh held still the reins in his hands as his companion was clutching Natchez's bridle and was leading them slowly toward the Indian party. Both groups halted, some yards apart. The plainsman released Natchez and displayed both of his hands palms open to the Indians, indicating he was unarmed.

Josh reckoned he had been holding his breath for some time and he released it, consciously trying not to be too obvious. His hands and feet told him to wheel his mount and dash for the river and safety. His brain fought back the impulse, and he followed the guide's lead, displaying his hands in supplication. Beneath him, he could feel Natchez twitch, sensing his fear.

None of the Indians were more than of average height, though they seemed much bigger, perhaps due to the small stature of their ponies—perhaps then only in Josh's mind's eye. All seemed lean and perhaps a bit thin. Some wore only breechclouts and leggings of buckskin. Two wore buckskins painted with strange devices and festooned with bone and beads. A few wore a type of chest armor that appeared to be of bone or shells strung together with thongs and decorated with strips of braid. These had beaded and painted martingales for their mounts. By their demeanor, the two decorated warriors appeared to be the leaders. All had deep burnt complexions with wild black hair. Taken as a group, they were both terrible and magnificent.

The older of the two clad in buckskin made a series of hand signs, gesturing across his mouth and chest. These were answered in kind by Delacroix, who spoke several words, apparently having some calming meaning for the savages. The buckskinned old one and one of the chest-armored warriors, a man Josh guessed to be in his thirties, separated from the group and approached the two whites.

On Josh's left, Delacroix continued speaking and gesturing to the advancing pair. Josh could only sit his mount quietly and take his mark from his more experienced companion. Josh became aware the younger warrior was studying him with a sullen curiosity. His demeanor expressed only a casual, cruel indifference. He felt himself being scrutinized like one would stare at a signpost on the roadside. Josh sensed he was being subjected to some sort of a test, perhaps as ritualized and prescribed as the exchange of the two older men. This realization clear, Josh felt he understood his role in the unfolding drama.

Often at social events back home, Josh would encounter a rival in a position that necessitated restraint. In the company or presence of his elders, Josh and the rival would eyeball each other contemptuously. It amused Josh to encounter this stylized confrontation here in the wilds. The younger of the two Indians, although much older than himself, had to defer to the elder much like he had to respect the scout. Josh hoped his careless inspection of his counterpart was as studiously casual as the look he suffered.

Josh noticed the younger Indian sat his mount with the easy grace of a born rider. Upon self-examination, Josh discovered he was standing in Natchez's stirrups with both hands locked around the saddle horn. As Josh relaxed, he could detect no change in his adversary's disposition. The warrior's eyes stared pointedly through the young traveler. They were so piercingly dark that no pupil could be discerned.

Josh's attempted nonchalance corroded completely as his eyes wandered down to the withers of the mottled Indian pony. There, encrusted with blackened blood and a slab of flesh, hung one of the decorative scalp locks such as the ones worn by the fleeing Indians of yesterday afternoon. Large blue and green flies crawled on the dark crust. Josh couldn't tear his eyes from the gory trophy. A macabre fascination seized the young man; fascination and an appreciation that his Indian adversary was quite distinct from the town toughs back home in Cairo. Josh no longer wished to raise his eyes and encounter the stare of a man who, perhaps even this very morning, had killed another man and peeled the scalp from his victim's skull.

Josh felt Delacroix's hand on his shoulder and heard his voice speaking his accented English.

"What!" Josh exclaimed.

"Have you any whiskey in your wagon?"

Trying not to stammer, Josh replied, "Yes, I'm sure we have some."

Soothingly, the scout drolled, "Relax, boy. They aren't going to hang your hair alongside that Pawnee scalp. They just want us to pay them for crossing their land and using their ford."

Looking at the veteran plainsman, Josh could tell there was still some danger, but not to the degree he had feared. Delacroix was trying to calm him. It let him know what was due of him, and he was able to relax considerably.

"Whis-ka," interrupted the younger brave.

Delacroix explained. "This bunch is after those we saw on the skedaddle yesterday. I guess we can find enough mash to pickle 'em all."

Josh smiled, confidently, he hoped.

Delacroix indicated to their hosts they should follow along and he would get them some "whis-ka." As they turned their horses back across the ford, Delacroix instructed Josh, "When we touch the far bank, you trot on ahead for the jug. Make sure you get back with it before we get too close to camp. I don't want them to look us over."

Josh nodded his assent.

"Go easy, though. Don't make it look like you're going for help. Now, git!"

More welcome words had never passed his ear. Still, even as he trotted off, he didn't like the idea of leaving his new friend with a dozen armed warriors at his back.

Minutes later, Josh returned with a gallon jug of riverboat whiskey. As he cantered up, Delacroix was engrossed in an animated "discussion" with the Indians. Josh took the jug, pulled the cork, and handed it to the elder leader. Seizing the jug, the Indians began whooping it up like this would be their second jug of the day and galloped off. They quickly disappeared behind the next rise, the jug perhaps becoming an aid to their quarry's escape.

Josh tossed the top in his hand. "I kept the cork so they would have to finish it."

As Delacroix watched the departure of the war party, he was thinking perhaps he had underestimated the mettle of the young emigrant.

Josh, in turn, was amazed at how coolly the scout had behaved, unarmed, against a pack of savage warriors on the hunt for blood. He hoped someday to measure up to men like this grizzled trapper.

As they made their way back to the train, Josh asked, "How come they're after those Pawnee?"

"Son, Pawnee and Sioux been fighting over this grassland since there was *buffle* to hunt. Those p'ticular Pawnee killed two women and a girl that were out hunting for berries. Just being in Sioux land is enough to get them killed, but murder like that will get them hunted down," Delacroix explained.

"How come they let us pass, then?"

"You ask too many questions, boy. We got a river to cross." Delacroix spurred his gelding and left Josh alone with his question and his sodden clothes.

CHAPTER FOUR

The first wagon rolled off the short bluff and down the incline excavated to allow an easy access to the river. Where the scout intended the wagons to enter the stream, he had strung a rope between two stakes to mark the spot. On horseback, Josh, Henry Shearwood, and two other men were hock deep in the shallows awaiting the first crossing wagon.

"This first one is my rig. So I'd best take the lead," shouted one of the newly met pioneers.

His name was Wallace McCardle, a stockman from Lafayette County, Missouri, who was traveling to Oregon with his brother, Ethan, and their neighbor, Lewis Petry. McCardle dropped a loop over the horns of the lead oxen in his team and held the coiled rope slack in anticipation.

It had been decided to take the more tractable oxen teams over first in the hope the still fractious mules could be tempted more easily into the torrent. Henry Shearwood tied the bitter end of his rope to the rear hook of the wagon; should it begin to float, he could prevent it from drifting downstream long enough for help to arrive.

During the preparation, Josh had been introduced to the elder McCardle and to his own work partner, David Oroville. They would team together like McCardle and Shearwood. Beyond a brief introduction and a handshake, Josh knew nothing of Oroville's background, and the middle of the Platte River didn't seem like the place for an exchange of pleasantries.

The ropes stretched on the far bank were there for the driver to use as a target to shoot across the planned route. By driving for this mark, an even progress could be made without fighting the current while lessening the risk of heading too far downstream and losing control in the deeper waters. That was the plan. It was the job of the outriders in the stream to steward the wagons across without mishap.

Oroville rode up to Josh, shouting through cupped hands. "How deep does the river run?"

Leaning toward him, Josh called out, "Not much more than three foot in the middle. The noise spookin' the teams is most to fear."

Together they watched the advance of the first high-sided wagon, which was now nearing the middle of the river. The water level was above the hubs, and muddy wavelets lapped and splashed against the caulked wagon body. As the wagon entered the deepest section, the waters rose menacingly up the wagon's side and rocked it to and fro. There was no tendency for the burdened wagon to float. Henry Shearwood, at the rear station, had no tension on his line. His mount strode easily, following the team across. McCardle, with his rope about the lead oxen, did not appear to be in any difficulty. He did, however, have his end secured to his saddle horn and was using his horse's pull to keep the oxen from turning their heads too far downstream and into trouble.

Oroville motioned toward the next team just entering the stream.

"This one's ours. I'll take the rear."

He splashed away, leaving Josh to muse about his new partner. He had some doubts about his abilities, but so be it, Josh thought. He had already been across the river and he had helped his father use their oxen team, Banner and Flag, to launch boats into the river at home from their draught wagon. Josh might have doubts about his own abilities, but he would give it his best.

Warily, he looked to the west. The dark clouds of the dawn were still ominous in the distance but had not moved appreciably in their direction. It looked like any weather would hold off until late in the afternoon. He uncoiled his rope and moved to the head of the approaching team.

Crossing the first team and wagon had been relatively easy. With his rope around the horns of the lead oxen, Josh used Natchez's weight and strength to keep the oxen's head pointed in the right direction. It was the natural tendency of the placid beasts to turn their heads away from the oncoming riffles. Fear was present in the animals' eyes, and they protested mightily being in the current, bellowing constantly.

Each of the mule teams had one or two experienced animals in the traces with the balance only recently broken to their trade. These were not docile nor would they pull as a team. Many seemed content to just kick at the mule behind. Others seemed intent on making the crossing with dry front feet. None, thankfully, elected to bathe in the swift flow.

David Oroville, after overcoming his initial fear, proved to be a capable worker, keeping the wagons in line and dismounting into the chill to help move a mired wagon. Several times, he had disappeared under the surface to wrestle a recalcitrant rock out of the path.

Sipping scalding and heavily sugared coffee from a hot mug he could barely feel, Josh cast a weather eye to the blackened western horizon. The wind had picked up noticeably in the past hour, and still three wagons remained on the far bank. These three belonged to Reverend and Mrs. Clark, Elizabeth Hampton, and, of course, Josh's own. Peering across through the haze, Josh could make out Jubal standing anxiously in the driver's box. Jubal had noticed the freshening wind and the approaching tempest, too. His very stance alerted Josh of the need for haste. Josh flipped the dregs of his coffee into the blaze and made for the river, signaling the remaining three to start across the ford.

Claude Delacroix watched from astride his roan gelding as the young emigrant waded back into the Platte River ford. He noted how Josh had signaled for the next wagon to come ahead, unaware of his leadership in the task at hand. Delacroix dropped a loop over the lead mule's head and took his position ahead of the Clark wagon. He looked to the rear of the wagon where Leland Metzger had stationed himself. The wagon and its escorts commenced the crossing.

Josh, standing thigh deep in the stream, watched the proceedings. He strode forward to meet them and assist. The water seemed much colder now, but he attributed this to his fatigue and his spell at the fireside. He could see the Reverend Clark snapping the reins, urging the team to pull. Mrs. Clark huddled inside the wagon and clutched her husband's burly shoulder. Their team eagerly responded to the urging of the driver.

Josh wished he were on Natchez's strong back. The current frothed about his legs, pulling tenaciously at his feet. As the escorted wagon entered deeper water, walking became even more difficult. Josh stopped stepping and went into a shuffle, leaning into the current with his arms outstretched for balance. At the deepest part of the ford, it was apparent the water had risen noticeably. It was high enough now to continually buffet the wagon, resulting in a constant tremor in the oilcloth cover. It seemed to vibrate and rattle to the whim of the river's hand. The water sucked about the team of eight, and while they labored with the burden behind, it was not possible to make a harmonious effort. From wheel mule to lead mule, the team was bowed in an arc downstream. The short legs of the middle mules were losing their footing across the swift, stony bottom.

A pair of riders plunged past Josh, hooking their ropes to the lead mule and the wagon gate to keep it from foundering.

As the team breasted the flood, Josh seized the trace chains of the second pair and added his own weight in an effort to control the nervous animals. Now, from his position down current of the struggling beasts, Josh became aware of the animal hooves scratching the bottom for purchase; the team was in a near panic but fortunately was well harnessed. A misstep by man or beast could result in a crushing injury or worse.

Distracted by the sound of a voice, Josh looked over his shoulder. The scout was pointing to him and indicating he should go to the upstream side of the wagon. He reckoned he was serving no purpose clutching the tackle and thus impeding the team. He began working his way down the mules' flanks, ducking under the rope about a mule's neck, and made his way back to where Reverend Clark was urgently beckoning. Although he was yelling, Josh could understand nothing over the river's chaotic voice. Indeed, he could only tell he was speaking because he could see moving teeth and lips within the bearded face. It crossed his mind that for a preacher Clark didn't have much of a voice. Fire and brimstone wouldn't be much of a peril if you had to strain to hear about it. As Josh waded to the wagon, he climbed the spoked wheel. Clark gripped his upper arm and easily lifted Josh up to where he could bellow directly in Josh's ear.

"The rear wheel is hung on something. See what you can do to free it."

Josh looked him in the face. The reverend's eyes shown with the same near panic he had seen in the mules' bugged-out eyes. He nodded vigorously to show he understood. In climbing down, he had to wrench his arm from the man's grasp.

The water flashed past him as he handed his way to the rear wheel. In the lee of the wagon, the water flowed smoothly by and did not reach up to wash his chest and face. Once he crossed to the upstream side, he was pressed against the wheel. The wagon was sitting level, so the iron tire had not dug into a soft spot on the bottom. It must be hung behind a rock. Gripping the spokes with both hands, he poked about with his feet, trying to identify the obstruction. He couldn't tell a thing by touch. Without hesitating, Josh ducked under the surface and below the wagon bed, where the current pressed him bodily against the spokes. With his body firmly anchored, he groped about for the impediment. There were only pebbles and sand in front of the rim, and Josh was startled not to find anything like what he expected. Feeling next up and down each spoke, he soon discovered the hindrance. A branch from a buried stump, as thick as his forearm, had hooked one of the spokes and brought the wagon up fast.

Pulling himself from behind the wheel and from under the wagon, Josh burst to the surface. His legs were swept from under him, and only his grip on the spokes kept him from being carried away.

Looking about, he saw men on the near bank wading with their arms outstretched for balance making their way to assist. Reverend Clark's head appeared around the edge of the cover, and his mouth moved in his bearded face. The words, however, spun uselessly away.

Gulping a breath, Josh ducked back under. After a moment's struggle, he managed to brace his feet against the spokes and pulled mightily back and forth on the stickup, arching his back with the effort. It was of little use. He could barely move the obstruction. At the peak of his striving, Josh relaxed his hold. He stopped straining, realizing Clark was urging the team forward for all they were worth. If he was successful in breaking the branch, the wagon would lurch forward, probably entangling him in the wheel as well. Just as he realized he could easily get wedged up under the axle and drown or be crushed in the muddy torrent, he felt a strong grasp pulling him to the surface. It was Captain Metzger.

"What're you humpin' under there, boy? We got wagons to cross before you have your fun."

Regaining his footing, Josh gazed about at the grinning faces of Metzger, Wallace McCardle, Custis Gresham, and several others. Josh could imagine how his underwater gyrations with the branch must have appeared to the company. Momentarily struck dumb with embarrassment, Josh managed to splutter.

There's a big branch stickin' up in the spokes. It won't be broke." Slapping the wheel, he added, "We'll have to back her up and go around."

Turning to the task at hand, the grins vanished, replaced with the looks of men falling to work. Metzger barked orders. McCardle relayed instructions to Clark in the wagon seat. The outriders pulled the team backward to counter their struggle against the snag.

Together, the balance of the men lifted and half pulled the wagon back off of the snag. The team was then headed sharply against the current until the obstacle was clear and soon found a firm foothold in shallow water, moved forward, and the crisis was past.

Now, only Elizabeth Hampton's wagon with Ely as driver and Jubal in Josh's wagon remained on the south bank. Elizabeth sat perched on the wagon seat. Distressed, she watched the travails of the wagons crossing before hers. The cresting water, the gloaming sky, and the anxious moments of the men in the river heightened her anxiety. Dispassionately, she had watched the first couple of fordings with not more than a woman's merest technical curiosity. As the number of wagons on the southern shore dwindled, her disquiet rose with the river's crest. From her high roost on the plank seat, she saw the stewards wave her ahead. Ely snapped the reins across the mule team's backs. Their ears flattened and they trudged forward.

A hundred yards, two hundred, and Elizabeth began to relax. Her concerns now were those of a coach passenger on a steep decline. She knew she was in capable hands but would feel better if she could do something besides sit. She became conscious of her hands gripping the seat and studiously placed them in her lap like errant pups. Her seat began to seem more that of a boat than a wagon. Water surged past the team and the outriders. It flumed through the wheel spokes and buffeted the wagon sides. The tarpaulin cover trembled and shivered with the passage. Elizabeth tried to relax in her seat and resolutely held her hands in her lap. *Appearing calm will keep you calm,* she repeated. Now she could feel the wagon just begin to float and drift slightly with the current, its bulk and weight resisting the flood. She watched the riders strain at the tethers holding the team and wagon in tenuous control. Slowly and inexorably, the river began to assume control.

Ely had relaxed his urging of the team, the middle pair of which was now afloat. Nothing could be done until the guides dragged the team to ground. The drift increased, and the wagon began to jackknife in the stream. She mustn't panic. There was nothing to be done.

A rush of help appeared. Men with ropes on horseback and men on foot, barely able to keep afoot themselves, added their weight. All slid and were bounced over the rocky bottom as they struggled to break the drift.

There was a staggering halt as one of the wheels found purchase. Suddenly, they shot forward and the danger was past. A vast sigh of release overcame the work party. Some cheering could even be heard over the torrent. Looking up, Elizabeth saw they had been swept forward and downstream. She was only a few hundred yards from the northern shore and safety.

Suddenly, the left front wheel under Elizabeth rose, out of step with its mates, reached its zenith, and crashed down on the far side of a sunken log. Elizabeth was pitched headlong over the front of the wagon box.

She felt her seat rise, saw the wheel climb, and peered curiously over the side. As the wheel plunged downward she experienced a moment of weightlessness, her fingers slipping over the rough wood. She fell headfirst, glimpsing the swift brown flood, then tasting it as she struck and was swept under the running gear.

Elizabeth felt no panic. She had fallen into rivers and ponds before— had even fallen in fully clothed. She would float and pop up downstream. This time, though, something was amiss. She was not flowing with the current. It rushed past her, buffeting her and filling her mouth with water and sand! And fear! She could not move. She could not rise. She struck out with her arms, craving the surface. She could feel her hands in the air; could feel them splash but could do no more. Opening her eyes she saw only the swift, light-filled brown that would drown her.

When Elizabeth was slung from the wagon, she had fallen before the wheel, between the mule team and the wagon. As she hit the water, her gingham dress had snared the doubletree and its chains. She was carried under the tongue and the hounds. The river roiled her body in its embrace, wringing her dress like a washerwoman wrings a towel. She was trapped under the wagon, under the water, her dress fast becoming a sodden, winding sheet.

Hands gripped her, reached around her chest, pulled and tugged at her. They became arms, lifting her bodily toward the surface. The dress and the running gear maintained their grip, forbidding that desperate taste of air or view of sullen sky. Elizabeth could contain her breath no more. The crushing hollow inside burst from her mouth. She was dimly aware of bubbles instantly swallowed by the torrent. Her lungs, like countless breaths before, drew in. Gritty water rushed in. She choked, sputtered, gave up.

She was shocked to find that she could gasp. Air, sweet air, was filling her. A wind blew the dim feeling away. She could see the scowling sky again. Hands clutched her head, the thumbs digging under her chin, forcing her face above the gushing river that spitefully relinquished its spoil. At Elizabeth's feet, other arms cut and shredded at the hem and skirt of her dress, freeing her legs.

As the panic subsided and Elizabeth organized her senses, she saw it was Josh Bonner who held her head above the water. He was straddling her across the chest. The river bucked and cascaded about his back; he was sheltering her in his lee.

His face had the most curious look she had ever seen. The features were startled, fearful, shaken. His teeth pressed deeply against his lower lip. His eyes, however, were anything but frightened. They were intense, penetrating, and of a hazel that should have been warm, but they were too focused for emotion. She felt safe but strangely unhinged by his stare. She vomited up the invading brown water. It washed away instantly.

Amid the tatters of her dress, her legs were free. She regained her feet, and Josh clutched her to his chest and half dragged her to the shoreline. She felt capable of walking alone; the jitters were past, but he was holding her with such a desperate ferocity she had to abandon herself to him.

They were on the dry bank now. Other people circled about, but none approached. They were somehow aware this episode was not concluded or open to others. This moment was for these two alone. When Josh released her, both staggered back. Elizabeth steadied herself and dragged her hair from her face.

Josh tottered back several steps and pitched backward, sprawling himself on his butt and knocking almost all the wind from his exhausted body. The surplus energy caused his feet and thighs to jitter. He drew them to him as he envisioned what a spectacle he must be. Elizabeth stepped to him, knelt, and embraced him around the arms. She laid her cheek on his shoulder.

As if by signal, the gathered throng rushed to them. The men whooping and backslapping, the women wringing their hands and reaching out to each other. Tears of joy and relief streaked their cheeks, mixing with the first drops of rain from the   approaching storm.

With the sodden girl draped about his body and the milling crowd jostling him, Josh became aware he was being treated as some sort of hero. He felt his face flush and his ears heat up. He hid his face with mortification. When the people had quieted and he felt he could look at them, he lifted his gaze and inquired,

"How's m'wagon?"

#

CHAPTER FIVE

#

The Bonner wagon and all of the stock were fine. With Jubal driving and with the river crew helping, they had, with the sole exception of Elizabeth Hampton's wagon, crossed without major incident. When the left front wheel of her wagon had pounded down off the submerged log, it had split the hounds, the horizontal member that strengthened the front axle of the wagon. But as a whole, the train was in better shape for having crossed. The immersion in the river had swollen the wooden wheels and secured the fit to the iron tires.

The question to delay another day for this repair, to leave someone to do the work, or to arrange an escort back to Fort Kearney was an issue to be addressed by the captain and the members of the train. The debate, however, would have to wait. The storm from the west was nigh, and preparations for its onslaught must be made.

The swath of the vast plains the pioneers traversed in their journey west was the meeting ground of three great weather sources. From the west, the winds that had blown across the unbounded Pacific Ocean found their way over the Continental Divide. These were the most prevalent and consistent as they swept eastward, roiling the grasses and spreading seed to the Missouri and Mississippi Rivers.

From the north, cold and dry Canadian winds collected from the Arctic and Hudson's Bay. The effects of the meeting of this frigid, dry mass with the Pacific air brought great windstorms. In winter, drifting snow made the topography much like the Asian steppes.

In the late spring and through the hot summers, tropical, moist air pushed its way up the Mississippi Valley from the Gulf of Mexico. The collision of any or all these massive fronts created some of the most spectacular and destructive weather in the world. As there were no high hills or even trees, with the exception of cottonwoods along the riverbanks, these colossal aerial battles surged unimpeded over the naked prairie. Huge thunderheads arose, providing fierce spectacles of rain, wind, and lightning. Warm, humid air masses rose against the colliding fronts. The moisture was sucked into the high, lofty sky where it froze and fell back to lower altitudes. This cycle would be repeated many times, adding layer upon layer of crystals to the seed of ice within. Finally, the sheer weight of the crystal would cause it to fall to earth as hail.

It was one of these black tempests descending upon the emigrant train now. It was this front's arrival that caused the river to rise, nearly engulfing the tail of the Missouri train.

In preparation for the gathering squall, the wagons had huddled closely together. Rather than the loose horseshoe encirclements of the previous daily bivouacs, the wagons clustered in rank and file, facing the wind. This way the foremost wagons would break the onslaught, acting as buffers for those sheltered behind. All of the stock had been corralled within the confinement and were fettered and lashed to the wagons. Horses were hobbled and tethered to stakes, hopefully preventing any escape or stampede. The wagon covers were lashed and tacked. If any wind were to get inside a wagon, the cover would easily be ripped from its hoops and sail away.

Now, it was late afternoon. The temperature was slipping rapidly, and the wind began to freshen as a premature nightfall slumped over the weary camp. The earlier light sprinkle had turned to fat drops, then became a steady shower.

Josh hunched up in his wagon. Bolsters had been placed over the trunks and crates of his equipment, making a level enough platform for a bed. Cowled over his shoulders was the buffalo robe he had been using to sleep on outside. At his feet were several blanket-wrapped rocks heated in the campfire to warm him through the chill night. A hot potato slipped into a sock warmed his hands.

Jubal was curled up at the front end of the wagon, encased in his assortment of quilts and blankets. He wondered what the other travelers might think of a colored man sharing sleeping quarters with a white. He understood most of the others were from Missouri and were pro-slavery. They had their own ideas of a black's place in the scheme of things. To his manner of thinking, it seemed if some were house servants, the proper place for them was in the house. Such as it was, this was his house. However, back in Cairo, Jubal had slept in a room fashioned within the barn. On the other hand, Jubilee was an employee, not a servant or slave. So what was proper? Damn! There was too much to think about there. He was sorry he even had to think about it. For now, it was more pleasant to let his memory slip back and bask in the attention he had received as the afternoon's unlikely hero. He had been escorted to his wagon amidst a chorus of huzzahs and backslapping. The men had pitched his campsite, and the women had pampered him and pressed hot, brandied coffee and buttered biscuits at him. Fortunately, the first fat drops of rain had sent everyone scurrying for their own wagons.

For his own part, he couldn't see what all the fuss was about. Certainly, he had kept the girl from drowning in the river. Anybody, though, could have and would have done the same thing. He had been quite content sprawled on the pebbly beach with Elizabeth hanging all over him. If they had left them alone, he probably might still be sitting in her embrace, rain or no rain.

A strange girl, that Elizabeth. Back home, she had quite a reputation and was a constant source of gossip amongst the townswomen. No one had ever spoken of any specific wickedness, but they all implied she would come to no good end.

As he was two years younger than Elizabeth, he had never been the subject of her flirtations. It had been his brother, Ned, whom she never failed to tease. Most likely because he never was affected by her. She was not like the other girls in town who would glance at you and then look shyly at their feet or look over their shoulder as they passed you in the street. Elizabeth would look you, or at least his brother, boldly in the eye and always seemed to be in a posture displaying her figure to its best advantage. She surely was a spirited girl, and if her spirit bordered on the immodest, so much the better. Besides Delacroix, who didn't count, there were only three unmarried men on this trek; as he was the youngest, and her current hero, he figured he was a far crack ahead of the others.

That made him wonder . . . where was Delacroix? When everyone had been treating him like a barleycorn candidate on the campaign trail, he had looked for the scout, but he was nowhere to be seen. If he could garner some praise from the plains veteran, that would be something. As it was, Josh felt somewhat like a cheat getting recognition for doing something he really didn't have a choice about. Something had needed to be done. He had just stepped in rather than look on and have to call himself a coward.

As the rain and wind began to lash at the train, Elizabeth was curled up in her own wagon. Characterizing Josh Bonner as a coward was the furthest thing from her mind. She could still picture his face above her as he held her head out of the water, saving her life. Now, with the mental retelling, his expression became less strained and more valiant. Perhaps not valiant like in the books of Sir Walter Scott she liked. Perhaps more like she pictured John Fremont or some of the resolute explorers she had read accounts of.

Back in Cairo, Josh had just been the pesky younger brother of Ned Bonner, the steamboatman. Josh had always seemed to be in the way when she could have contrived a way to be alone with his older brother. She would never be able to see him again as one of the nervous boys in town who would dog her as she shopped or peek at her on the streets—the same ones struck dumb if she spoke to them.

Well, hero or not, she was not about to let herself be treated as a prize he had captured from the river like a catfish. If he commenced to strutting about looking for her to throw herself at him, he would be wearing out his boots first. Just imagine that impudent boy all full of himself. She couldn't wait to take him down a peg.

Conversely, she thought, as they had clung to each other on the strand, it had seemed he had pulled in on himself and was grateful to be able to hide in her arms. What a curious boy he was!

Elizabeth became aware of a change outside the wagon. The sound was different. The wind had seemed to lessen, and the pinking of the rain against the oilskin covering was now punctuated with harder blows. These were more intermittent but quickly intensified to a constant hammering, overpowering the noisome stirring of the tethered animals. The pummeling soon set up a tattoo that shimmered the cover and created a din in the confined space.

Unwrapping herself from the stack of quilts which warmed her and clutching her wrapper to her chest, she crawled to the rear of the wagon for a peek outside. Unlacing the draw, she peered into the dark. Hail had come. Appearing magically from the dark overhead, the bird's egg-sized stones bounced along the wet ground and ricocheted off the backs of the agitated mules. Already she saw men running bent over to shelter their heads. They dragged down their fractious animals by the bridle and tied blankets and scarves over their eyes in an effort to calm the terrified brutes.

Ducking back inside, Elizabeth soon reappeared. She bounded down to the puddled ground and seized the halter of her nearest animal. Laying on all her weight, she dragged down its neck, and with an effort, threw some toweling over the animal's head. Finally, she succeeded in tying on the blinder that immediately calmed it. She left the mule trembling and turned to the next. Remarkably, this mule had managed to stick its head under the wagon and was partially sheltered. It stood calmly, or at least resignedly, and made no protest about wearing a scarf. She soon completed shrouding the balance and returned to the shelter of the wagon feeling satisfied with her accomplishment. Gripping the tailboard and preparing to hoist herself up, she halted at the sound of a voice calling out.

"Miss Hampton!"

It was Reverend Clark. His left hand held down his broad flat hat. Several hailstones rolled round and round the rim. Two more were slowly melting in his great beard. Barring the funereal night and the imposing size of the preacher, it would have appeared quite comical.

"I came to see if you needed help with your animals," he brayed, leaning close to be heard.

"Thank you kindly, sir, but I have already attended to them," she replied. It was difficult to speak over the drumming of the hail.

"That should not be the work of a young lady."

"We had draft animals at home, sir! I've had an occasion to tend to them."

"Still," he stammered.

She felt no need to explain herself twice.

Clark offered, "That was a close call today. Providence must have been at your side."

She was losing patience talking to this man in a hailstorm.

"Perhaps so, Reverend. But it was Josh Bonner that got to the job first."

Clark stared blankly at her heresy.

56

"I must go now," she said flatly, gesturing at the hailstones pelting about her. "Good evening."

The reverend nodded an acknowledgement as she turned to climb into her wagon.

From over her shoulder she heard, "May I assist you?"

At the same time, she felt his hands low on her hips and felt herself borne up effortlessly to where she could hook a foot over the tailboard. He released her.

Chagrined at his renewed familiarity, she said her "thank you" and fell unceremoniously back to her pallet. As she relashed the drawropes, she could see him sprinting away, splashing through the flattened grass.

She undressed and dried herself for the second time and slid under the now clammy covers. She hadn't meant to be rude; it just seemed foolish to be having a how-de-do in a hailstorm. No, it wasn't just that. It was all the condolence. If one more person tried to comfort her, she would just shrivel up like an old leaf.

From a sandy rise near the encampment, the scout turned over in his robe. He lay under a small oilskin shelter and on a rubber groundsheet he had acquired long ago at a Hudson Bay Company post on the Snake River. HBC—Here Before Christ, they called them. Back when he was young, the Company had already been in the Oregon Territory for nigh on forty years, and as far as whites went, they were the law, commerce, and militia in the territory. Now with all the emigrants headed out there from the States, it would be interesting to see who won out, the Company and the English or Whitman and the Territorial American government. Others had coveted Oregon, too. The Spaniards, but they seldom ventured out of the south and California. Nor could the Russians seem to stay very interested in their far-flung station. Least of all the French, from whom the early *voyageurs* he was himself descended and who he had followed from his home in Montreal so many years gone.

The scout burrowed down in his robe. He was mostly dry, which was better than many nights in his memory. His rifle, pistol, and powder shared his bed.

The period after the storm would be crucial. There was bound to be some damage, and this would be the next test of the emigrants' resolve. The cholera outbreak had strained them but this was the first ordeal to confront everyone. From experience, he knew some would want to push on, leaving the battered to fix and repair. Those left behind could labor to catch up or hook up with a following train. He hoped Metzger could hold them together. He seemed forceful enough when the mood was on him. His fear would be up, and he might have trouble keeping the dissenters in check. Delacroix would support him as far as he could, but there could be some malice to come his way, as though by leading the trail, he had led them into the storm. After all, he was the one who had been so insistent on the river crossing.

The hailstorm quickly passed, but the rain and the wind intensified throughout the night and into the next day. Great forks of lightning ripped the sky and the thunder boomed. A watery sun did little to lessen the gloom. The tenebrous morning, while making the storm less terrifying, only made the tempest more awe inspiring. While all the travelers had seen thunder and lightning before, they were all farmers and townsfolk. Their previous lives had been hemmed in by trees and hills and buildings. Here, the vast prairie made for just too much sky. As far as the eye could survey, thunderheads towered and climbed to the heavens. Within them, balled lightning rumbled and flashed. The growing reports of the thunder following the flashes illuminated the clouds from within like a lantern glimpsed in a fog, occasionally leaping from one roiling brume to the next. The constant wind beat the rain to a drumbeat against the wagon tops and pelted the puddles to a brown froth.

To those few souls about this morning, running or crouched over on some task, the ravaging of the wagons appeared far worse than it really was. The damages were mostly superficial and only inconveniences. The animals had resolved themselves to their fate and stood stoically, heads down. Two oxen had somehow broken or slipped their tethers, wandering off to the meager shelter of a sandy depression. Fortunately, they had not made their way back to the riverbanks, where they surely would have drowned. One wagon was sunk halfway to the hubs and would have to be extricated. It must have parked in a spot where the water ran off. The water eroded the sand from under the wheels until it sank, leaning to one side. The cover of another streamed in tatters from the hoops. The owner, who had lashed a canvas over his possessions, cowered underneath where he could better survey the spoilage.

The Greshams, better off than the rest, had pitched a tent as they had on previous stops. They, too, were sequestered in their wagon. The tent was gone, torn from its stakes and sailing back to Independence. All that remained at the site were flailing ropes, staked at one end with dancing grommets flashing at the bitter ends.

The next afternoon, the storm abated. The sun shone hotly, sucking clouds of mist from the cold ground. The puddles began to vanish, absorbed into the sandy washes. The emigrants stirred.

Numbed, they wandered about the wagons, peering at the majesty of the endless sky, mentally cataloging their damages, and counting their good fortune as they viewed the more serious casualties. Most suffered dissolved salt, sugar, or coffee. Sodden bedding and creeping mildew would accompany them and add to their miseries on the trail.

There would be little in the way of hot meals. The brush and grasses were soaked, and the plentiful buffalo chips had regained too much of their fragrance to be of use. Some wagons had supplied themselves with firewood and tinder along the way, and from these meager stores cautious fires heated coffee and warmed damp hardtack.

Leland Metzger crouched by his fire, musing over his coffee and formulating plans for the day. He had always been a phlegmatic man, content with a routine and peevish when the situation allowed. The daily regimen of the train had settled comfortably about him. The storm and its consequent problems had soured his mood. He stood as a group of men approached.

"G'mornin', Cap'n," offered Henry Shearwood. He was accompanied by the McCardle brothers, Lew Petry, and Custis Gresham. Each added his regards.

"Morning, Gen'nelmen. I hope none of you have fared badly from the storm."

Each offered a small litany of troubles, the most serious of which was Gresham's tent. Metzger felt little empathy for the townsman. He had the best team, wagon, and equipment of them all. The loss of his tent, which was a luxury none of the others could afford, gained little solace from his fellow travelers.

As the elected captain, the men had naturally gravitated to Metzger. The position of train captain carried little real authority. While it was an honorific title, the real purpose was to cohere the emigrants into a unit and to execute the plans for their common goal. Metzger recognized many of the people only wanted a leader to serve as scapegoat, someone they could blame when things went wrong. As a constable, Metzger's best attribute was an ability to defuse confrontation. At home, he had been expected to clean up the town's messes without involving any of the citizenry. Here, it would be the same.

"Well, men, it appears we've had some bothers. I suggest we take today to make things right, and then move on tomorrow. Those of you who haven't a fire can send your women to mine to make coffee. Then we'll get to what needs doin'."

"We shouldn't a crossed the river yesterday. There would have been better fords ahead," piped up Lew Petry.

There is always one who won't leave done as done, Metzger thought. The rest of the men had joined the first enclave, and a murmuring of assent made itself known.

Metzger looked about for the scout. Damn his eyes! He should be here. The crossing was his idea.

"The scout said we should cross here. He reasoned there were too many gullies and streams we would have to make around if we stayed on the south bank."

"We shouldn't have tried the ford in the face of that thunderstorm," a voice from the crowd threw in.

Wallace McCardle spoke, "It was a-blowin' and a-rainin' just as bad across the river as here, I expect. Anyways, we're here now and I'm glad it's behind us."

The facts of their situation couldn't be disputed, and this turned the discussion to other matters, specifically Elizabeth Hampton.

"We'll all be able to move on tomorrow except the Hampton girl! What are we to do with her?" asked Gresham.

"She shouldn't ought to be here with us all on her own. We've already lost time what with her folks dyin'," added Lew Petry.

Reverend Clark stepped forward. "That's not Christian. We that are strong ought to bear the infirmities of the weak."

Small bickerings broke out.

"We can't just leave her!"

"Another train will be along soon!"

"S'posin' it was you? Would you want to wait out here for the next wagons?"

Delacroix had sidled up to the group and spoke out loudly. "It will be you. Maybe not today, but out along the trail every one of you will break down or lose a mule or run short of food. What will you do then, *mes amis*? If you won't stick now, you had just better all go on your own."

"That's foolish talk, Delacroix. The Indians would have our hair in two shakes," said Shearwood.

"The Indians is the least of what would happen. This last was the easy part of the trail. It will be much more difficult as we go on," the scout retorted. "There are miles of desert and mountains with little or bad water. Each of you will suffer and must have the help of your *companions* or none of you will reach Oregon."

These sobering thoughts quieted the throng as each envisioned their own nightmares of disaster. Before anyone could offer dissent, Metzger sealed the argument.

"By Thunder! He's right and you all know it. If we can't hold together, we might as well head back and go on with our old lives. Now, let's patch up and then we'll see about fixin' that wagon."

With that, the group dispersed and set about their tasks. In another circle, listening behind the men, stood the women. As the men moved out, those without dry fuel made their way to the Metzger fireside, coffeepots in hand. Mrs. Metzger made them welcome, although she fretted to herself about their small cache of firewood.

Soon, camp life was in full swing. Clotheslines were strung from wagon to wagon. Damp bedding flapped and popped in the gusts. Animals were tended to, minor chores completed, and the youngest children and the dogs explored under the watchful eye of their elders. All

of the repairs were quickly made with the exception of the split hound on
the Hampton wagon. Men set their hand to assessing the damage while
others busied themselves with unmiring the wagons that had sunk in the
night. Speculating on the repair to the running gear was cleaner work and
drew the bigger crowd.

For a while, Elizabeth listened to the men argue about the best way to
fix the damage. As soon as it became apparent none of them was certain
how to proceed, she decided to join several other women rather than get
discouraged by the men's ruminations.

The women, as women will over their chores, gossiped and chatted.
Those who had suffered little in the storm embellished their ordeal and
commiserated with their sisters who had fared worse. The youngsters
explored near the encampment and searched for combustibles that might be
dry enough to burn. One or two of the idle men mounted horses and went
in pursuit of an antelope that wandered into view. The chase was over
before it started as the antelope sprang away before the hunters had cleared
the remuda.

The Hampton wagon was levered up and braced so the wheel could be
removed. A quick inspection revealed no damage to the wheel or axle.
The hounds were another matter.

The river accident split the forward bar that distributed the loads on
the axle and wagon tongue so seriously it would require the dismantling of
the entire front axle. Not repairing it correctly would quickly lead to the
complete, sudden destruction of the entire running gear. Damage of this
extent required a blacksmith or wheelwright, a trade none of the wagon
crew possessed. The only person with the tools and the fundamental
mechanical skills required was Josh; his apprenticeship with his father as a
riverboat mechanic could be adapted to the scene at hand.

"Pa and me, we was always able to jimmy up something t'work," he
stated confidently. "Boats was always gettin' fouled up off Willow Point
or Cash Island. We fixed 'em up."

With that explanation, the others demurred and Josh began his
examination. The member had split about halfway along the grain of the
piece and was torn raggedly along the length of the rent. The repair
commenced with Josh crouched in the mud. Using a breast drill, he bored
several holes of graduating size perpendicular to the cleft, starting at the

apex. As each hole was drilled, it was fitted with a wooden peg. Other men fashioned the pegs from wooden sticks to the right size. These, in turn, were driven through a serrated hole in a metal plate. What emerged from the other side was a fluted dowel corresponding in diameter to the drilled hole. By drawing the split together from the narrow end, the driven dowels secured the break. Hide glue bound it all. Next, strips of leather were soaked. These were then carefully braided around the repaired assembly. Finally, a slow fire of shavings and the meager available fuel was built under the axle. Additional fuel was placed near the fire to dry out before being added to the embers.

At this point, after the bustle of activity, the crowd of assistants and lookers-on dispersed, leaving Josh to tend to the smoking fire. This was probably the most demanding part of the chore. Besides the irritating smoke and the obvious caution to prevent catching the wagon afire, it was central to the purpose to ensure the braiding dry evenly lest it pull the repair apart. Once dried properly, the leather would shrink tightly about the mend, making it sound and secure.

The day dwindled away, and Josh was left to his task and to his thoughts. He poked absently at the embers and let his thoughts wander over recent events. He snapped back as he became aware of someone approaching.

Craning about, he saw Elizabeth drawing near. Her auburn hair, though tied, fluttered about her face and trailed in the breeze. The wind billowed her dress about her, revealing from his low vantage point trim legs and an occasional startling glimpse of thigh. She made no effort to contain her clothing. Settling herself beside him, she presented a tin plate with a pair of browned turnovers.

"One is tinned beef with some carrots and onions. The other is apple with cinnamon. They are dried apples, I'm afraid, but I'll bet you like pie as much as I do," she offered.

"Well, I expect I do, Miss Hampton, and both are welcome changes from the bacon and fried bread I've been gettin' by on. Thank you most kindly," Josh said brightly, conscious of his neglect of his belly. His mouth salivated at the sight and smell of the unwonted delicacies.

"Won't you have some, too?" He proffered the plate.

"Thank you, Josh. I've eaten."

She scooted a little closer to him, the wind at their backs. "It appears you have become my benefactor now that our folks are gone." She dropped her eyes and spoke before he could offer her condolences. She said, "I welcome the chance to attend to some of your needs as return for your kindness and daring."

Josh bridled at the mention of his 'daring'. He didn't care for this new mantle of hero, or more to the point, the role that title would require he play. Studiously, he sought to find another topic.

"'Spect you'll be goin' on?" he inquired.

"I expect I shall. There isn't anything left for me back home," she affirmed.

"Don't you have family could take you in?" queried Josh.

"I don't want anyone to 'take me in.' I can make my own way," she replied, stiffening some at the affront.

Josh didn't reply, thinking she had needed his help twice already. Although he had his doubts about a woman on her own, he could see Elizabeth was determined and probably as qualified as any man in their party with the exception of the scout.

Noting his silence, she challenged, "Don't you think I can?"

After a moment's reflection, Josh replied, "We're all pretty green at this," indicating the prairies and all before them with a sweep of his hands, "an' we've all a lot of learnin' t'do."

Another pause.

"But I'm thinkin' you seem the sort gets what they set their cap to." He added cautiously. "I wish'd I was as certain about myself."

Touched and a bit startled by this admission, she reached over and touched his knee.

"Josh! How can you doubt yourself so? Riding out to meet those Indians and how you saved me yesterday."

Josh snorted. "Hmmph. It's not I'm afraid of doin' things. It just seems I've taken to running to where the trouble is. That's what has me worried."

"Was it any trouble to hold me yesterday—and to save my life?" she asked in a flirting lilt.

"No! Durn it! You know that's not what I mean. I liked that." Nervously he added, "I'd like to do it again someday."

Teasing, she laughed. "What? Save my life?"

Now he was embarrassed at his own boldness and how easily she had turned aside his gambit. He faced away from her. Quickly turning his attention to the neglected fire, he saw his negligence had not caused any singing of the repair. He poked listlessly at the embers.

Regretting she had hurt him and rueful of how easy it had been, she tendered, "I would like that, too."

Awkwardly and somewhat inquisitively, they leaned against each other and linked their arms across the other's neck. Uncomfortable as it was in their sitting positions, it still felt like the place they both should be. They turned their heads and kissed, at first innocently, then with more vigor.

Elizabeth's thoughts and emotions bounced inside her, raced in her mind. The familiar emotional response of tenderness quickly succumbed to a physical passion she could barely restrain. This feeling competed with the knowledge she was kissing a man in public, and she didn't care a whit, although it was unlikely anyone could see in the gloaming dark. Thirdly, she couldn't understand how she could feel this way over a boy who had to be at least two years her junior. She had always thought of him as a pest, someone that had barely existed for her.

Josh felt her lips on his, full and yielding, then her mouth mixing with his own, the taste sweet and new with its shot of excitement riveting his body. Through his fingers, he felt her back, her muscles vibrant under the flesh. He was aware of her breasts where they pressed one on either side of his ribs. His thoughts raced away, overpowered by the carnal urges let loose within his body. For endless minutes, they explored each other with hands and mouths and tongues. Calmer thoughts returned just as quickly as they toppled over backward and fell entwined. He rolled apart from her, his limbs flung to his sides. The stars overhead welcomed him back to the world, winking conspirators to their tryst.

Quickly propping himself up, he looked around to see if they had attracted any onlookers. No one was about, though they would have presented a spectacle for any one who had cared to look.

Elizabeth still lay on her back, as if to welcome him to an unfinished task. Her eyes glittered back at the stars as they collected the glow of the fire. She mustered herself and sat up. Neither spoke, overcome with the almost instant seizure of passion aroused, then suddenly arrested.

Conspicuously poking at the low fire Josh mumbled, "I can't see to tend to this. I'll finish up tomorrow." He was painfully aware of how oafish he must appear.

Elizabeth was confused. She was almost certain he must be talking about the fire he was attending. She hoped otherwise but chose the less ardent alternative.

"Josh, it's good to know we will be together on this trip."

It was Josh's turn to stiffen some, though he hoped it didn't show as he stood. He clasped her hands and helped her to her feet. He searched for the words he needed to say. When they got to his mouth it felt as if his tongue was bound with twine.

He managed to gulp out, "'Lizabeth, I'd as soon they all went on and we just stayed here." In speaking, he realized how obviously smitten he must appear. He half expected her to laugh at him for his temerity, dealing him a mortal blow that would cause him to splinter and sink into the ground with her ridicule. Instead, her hand slid along his cheek, the fingers lightly caressing his nape.

"Josh, that would be lovely, but you know we must go on. We have new lives ahead of us as long as we keep moving."

Almost as confession, Josh said, "'Lizabeth, it may not be so simple. When the men were talking today, there was some don't think you should be allowed to go on just by yourself. I reckon they'll speak on it again tomorrow when they are all fixed to roll. This mend won't be ready, and they'll be wantin' to get a move on."

She withdrew her touch, and as he spoke, he could see her mood change. She seemed almost to simmer, then to bristle as her words escaped.

"Let them have their talk. They think I'm of no account because I'm female. If my father were here, there wouldn't be any discussion. Most of them are Missourians and not our people anyway." She stamped each foot for emphasis. "Damn them! If I want, I'll ride right around and they can follow me all the way to the Pacific Ocean!"

"But—you don't know the way," he stammered, needlessly stating the obvious.

"Lordy! I didn't mean I was going to lead the way. I just meant if I see fit to travel this trail, I'll do just that! I don't give a bird's nest whether they like it or not. There ain't any one of 'em any better at looking at a mule's butt all day than I am. Damnation!"

She seemed to relax, her gall vented.

Josh was stunned, not so much by how her genteel manner had dropped away, but at how volcanically her anger had erupted and as quickly subsided. He had to admire her pluck. She seemed, unlike himself, to have no doubt about herself and obviously wasn't about to let anyone decide her path for her.

"'Lizabeth, I reckon there isn't a man here could stop you from goin' to Oregon or anywhere else you please. Durned if I won't stick by you. Just see if I don't."

Calmed, she leaned against him affectionately and lightly kissed his cheek.

"Thank you, Josh. I know you will. We'll make it to Oregon together. Good night." She walked to the rear of her wagon and went inside.

Josh squatted, banked the coals for the night, and speculated for the first of many times on the ways of women.

When Josh had looked about to see if Elizabeth and he had been observed, he hadn't seen anyone. This didn't mean their gropings had gone unnoticed. Jubilee had meandered over from the camp to see if there was anything he could do. Somewhat guiltily, but with an envious longing for his woman back at the Pooles' in Missouri, he had watched almost the entire encounter. He grinned at their young fumblings and had crouched in anticipation when he saw them fall over together, embraced. Watching the coupling of others was not new to him. There was little privacy in the slave quarters at the Pooles', and the spontaneous ruttings in the night had attracted little attention. Other than the overseer's visits, he had never seen whites in lust before, and his anticipation turned to mild disappointment as Josh interrupted the tryst to spy about.

He was glad he had concealed himself under a nearby wagon and hadn't been revealed, not knowing how Josh would have reacted to his watching. As quietly as he could, he stole away into the taller grass north of the camp. It was nice to be alone with his thoughts. He would have liked to have had some talk with the slaves belonging to the Missourians, but he doubted there would have been much to talk about beyond his escape and freedom seven years earlier. It was a tale he had told many times, and he had exhausted his own interest in the retelling. It was surely not best to be talking about free darkies in the midst of slaves and slaveholders. While they must know he was a freedman, the circumstances of his freedom were best left unbreached.

He lay back looking at the envelope of the heavens and was surprised that the familiar stars of home were still visible, albeit in a different region of the sky. Josh's brother, Ned, had tried in frustration to point out the constellations to him on a few occasions, and he could recognize the dippers and the belt of the hunter. It seemed far more interesting to just accept the night sky in its entirety than to cut it up into pieces like butchering a hog or a cow. Sometimes he likened the pricks of twinkling light to pinholes in an old curtain with a strong light behind it. He could almost imagine God whipping away the curtain and grinning down at all the people below. He came close to chuckling aloud at the vision.

Lost in these thoughts, he didn't at first notice that the pinholes above his legs had been blocked out, and he stared intently as the black shadow rose over him, amazed at what was happening and searching his imagination for the cause. As he gaped, the shadow assumed the outline of a human form standing at his feet.

Delacroix spoke softly. "If I were an Indian, your nappy hair would likely be on its way to my lodgepole. I expect it would be considered quite a prize."

"Mr. Delcroy, you likened to scare this ol' nigger outen his skin."

Jubal wasn't sure of his ground with the scout. Deference was always the best policy when dealing with strange whites, and this white was way beyond his experience.

"I don't think you scare so easily as that. You don't seem as cowed as the other coloreds. What're you doing out away from the wagons?"

Jubal couldn't tell from his tone whether the scout was angry with him for leaving the encampment or if perhaps he felt he was trespassing on his wilderness. He replied cautiously.

"Nothin' perticular. I just wanted to be away from people for a bit."

Delacroix inquired, "You don't seem to be running away, but I guess your young master treats you all right?"

"Mr. Delcroy, Mister Josh isn't my master. I am a free man. I worked for his father, now him."

"Is that so?" puzzled the guide. "I've seen a lot more reds than blacks, but all those I have seen have been slaves. You are the first I've met who claimed to be free as a white."

The course of the conversation was taking just the turn Jubal wished to avoid; not answering the Frenchman's inquiry could lead him to asking others. He thought carefully as he framed his reply.

"My, didn't you know that part of the United States is slave states and t'other is free states?"

"And you're from the free part?"

"Yessir! I am," decried Jubal.

"I have never been much into the United States. I only make it down to the river towns to trade and lately to guide the trains to Oregon. Those parts I've been near to all had slaves."

"That depends, I guess, on where you go. If you were in Illinois or Ohio or Indiana and such, they all be free states, but goin' down or across the big rivers, them be slave states."

Delacroix asked, "Then, if you were to go to those places, you would be a slave?"

For all their matter-of-fact way, the scout's questions chilled Jubal. This talk was getting far too dangerous, and Jubal wished he could think of a way to end it.

"I 'spect then I would be," Jubal answered, hoping his voice portrayed the nonchalance he was trying for.

"Then, what are you out here?" Delacroix asked candidly.

"I don't know what you mean."

"What I mean is—we're not in any state now, free or slave. This is Indian territory. So does that make you slave or free? How about the other darkies?"

Those two questions, put forth so mildly, shook Jubal like a storm's first thunderclap. His own thoughts, perhaps, had danced around the subject but had never become clear. He had been free a long time, and thinking like a free man, had never dared ask this of himself. He knew it would dog him from now on, and the realization gripped him like the old memories of bondage. With as much conviction as he could muster, he answered, "I am a free man."

Delacroix seemed to mull over his reply, and after some moments' consideration replied, "I'm thinking a man that thinks himself free will be a lot more help on this trek than a man thinks he belongs to another. You just keep thinking like a man with all his liberties."

He stretched and added, "You had best be getting back to the wagon." He turned and walked silently back into the night.

While it was good advice, Jubal could no more have gotten up than he could have floated away. His body seemed struck dumb. His mind was half-relieved at the conclusion of the interview and half-paralyzed with the reality of his situation. Jubal's eyes still stared at the stars, but any carefree thoughts of God and his blanket were wiped away. It was some time later, on leaden legs, that Jubal made his way to bed.

#

CHAPTER SIX

#

As per the routine, the dawn brought back the usual breeze that soon would freshen to a light and constant wind. The emigrants, now a part of the pattern of the prairie and accustomed to its ways, awoke and started their daily regimen with the same regularity as the sage hens, hawks, and gophers whose home they traveled through. Gear was checked and the livestock inspected for ticks and cracked hooves. The animals were collected, children's heads counted, meals prepared and eaten.

As Josh made his way to Elizabeth's wagon, tin coffee mug in hand, he noticed the captain and the scout, along with several other settlers, milling about her wagon. Elizabeth stood on the wagon bench embroiled in an animated exchange with the crowd. As he drew to its fringe, he could discern several boisterous arguments in progress. He feared the topic was whether Elizabeth was to continue.

Metzger was gesturing for order as the small arguments drew their own circles of spectators and ralliers for both sides. He could gain only momentary control before another wildfire broke out. Elizabeth was trying her best but was failing to maintain her composure. She was engaged in a heated debate with two or three adversaries at once. She pointed accusingly at Custis Gresham.

"I would have expected more from you, Custis Gresham. You know there is little for me to return to."

"That's not it, missy," he replied. "How many more times will you be the one to hold us up? Maybe make us get caught in the snows?"

Gresham's wife, Miriam, pulled at his sleeve, trying to restrain him and obviously pleading on Elizabeth's behalf. Gresham was worked up and noticed his wife's entreaties not at all.

Lew Petry spoke up. "It's hard enough takin' care of our own without haffin' to watch out for you as well."

Elizabeth retorted, "And so you would force me back or maroon me to wait for the charity of some other train?"

Josh watched the goings-on with deepening despair. He hated to hear shouting like this and wished Metzger would make a decision and hold the rest to it. The scout sidled up to Josh.

"How near is that wagon ready to travel, Josh?" he asked.

The boy brightened at the explorer's familiarity.

"That mend will take this day to set up. It will roll tomorrow, good as new."

"Then listen up. This argument is going nowhere, and Metzger won't be able to resolve it without some real hard feelings all around. It will just pop up again and again. Can you stay with her, fix the wagon, and then catch up on the trail?"

"Yessir. Jubal can go ahead with my gear, and we will catch up in a day or two."

"I thought that would suit you," he laughed. "A good plan, don't you agree? It will probably be only a day at best. We will be coming to Windlass Hill tomorrow or next. The train will be backed up there for a full day, or at worst you can catch up with us at Ash Hollow, shortly beyond the hill. Most trains hole up there for a day or two."

"I can do that if I can follow the way," Josh offered.

"*Mon ami*, the trail is well worn, but I will leave markers along the road to show the way. I must go now and tell the others."

Delacroix stepped up on the wheel of Elizabeth's wagon and spoke loudly to the throng, finally corralling their attention. He quietly explained his proposition. With the attention diverted to the guide, Elizabeth searched the faces for Josh, and on finding him, rewarded him with a look that spoke of more than relief.

Delacroix explained about Windlass Hill and Ash Hollow and seemed to gain a consensus from the group. At least the discussion had gotten orderly, which salved Josh's mind.

The rumination of the emigrants was interrupted by the appearance of a team and wagon. The wagon was a large and roughly used teamster rig

73

with high slatted sides drawn by eight handsome mules in polished harness. Two men perched on the bench. The larger and older of the two was dressed in dirty leather pants and shirt, shiny with grime. He wore a full brown beard that hid most of his face and was the driver of the team. Seated next to him was a scruffy thin man in corduroy trousers, a red shirt, and dark vest. A thin face was highlighted by a badly set broken nose. His thin mustache struggled under the misshapen nose.

Riding before the wagon was a medium-sized man in black frock coat and pants. He wore a clean but faded blue shirt and wide suspenders. A short, well-trimmed beard framed even features. His hair was hidden under a broad-brimmed hat. He was mounted on a spirited chestnut mare, whose reins he constantly attended. Approaching the group, he halted as best he could on the nervously prancing horse.

"Hello, friends! Oregon bound, I'll venture."

Metzger stepped forward, removing his hat. "That we are, sir. I'm Leland Metzger, captain of the train and bound for the Dalles in Oregon Territory. Might we have the pleasure of your name?"

The stranger replied, "I'm Jerome Gates of Council Bluffs." He pointedly ignored his two companions in the wagon.

Dr. Bingham spoke up. "There aren't many folks would head for Oregon with an empty wagon like yours, sir."

Gates laughed, robustly and with the air of a man sharing a joke with himself.

"It won't be empty for long. The trail ahead is heavy with sand, and Windlass Hill's not far. As people empty their wagons, I'll fill mine and then my store in Council Bluffs."

"Why should people be emptying their wagons?" asked Wallace McCardle.

"Because they try to bring too much with them and soon decide there is a lot of truck they can do without. Why, I recall an iron stove I've sold and collected three times now. There are supplies for the picking on the road ahead."

Gresham, ever the merchant, said, "We've seen no other wagons. Are there enough goods to be had to warrant such a dangerous trip?"

"Like you, sir, it was only dangerous the first time out. The Indians know me. I bring some trade items, and they thieve a little from me. It's expected and we all get along. As for plunder to be had, there are two trains, larger than yours, one and two days back."

He turned to look behind, then pointed. "There—you can see the dust from the foremost in the distance. It seems when it rains out here everything gets wet but the dust." He chuckled at his own jest, then remembering his task, signaled the two teamsters to move out. Turning back to the attentive crowd, he spoke.

"We will probably meet again at Ash Hollow. Most folks like to lay up there a spell. There will be broken wagons after the Hill for firewood and a clear, cold spring at the Hollow. Godspeed to you all."

Everyone, of course, had questions for him. Knowing this, he spurred away, only turning to wave farewell.

It was true a thin cloud of dust stained the distant sky. The storm that had left them wallowing in mud must have been very localized. The knowledge that a train behind was approaching cemented the solution to Elizabeth's state of affairs. It was quickly resolved Josh would remain as her protector while the rest went on.

Josh wondered at how the rules changed here on the trail. At home, it would have been unheard of to leave an unmarried man and woman alone for such a time. With good cause, too, he added. With the exception of Gresham, who was for marooning Elizabeth anyway, the rest were from Missouri and had their own loyalties to family and friends. Not that he was complaining. This was just what he had wanted and wished for last night. Sometimes, a man just got lucky.

Back at his own wagon, he gave instructions to Jubal. He would keep the two oxen with him in case the road got too heavy for the Hampton team. He also would keep the Walker Colt, the shotgun and the Hawken rifle with him. He figured Jubal was with the protection of the train, and it was unlikely they would trust a colored with a gun on any account. Gathering the weapons and his bedroll, he lugged his burden back to Elizabeth's site. On the way, Captain Metzger halted him.

"Now, boy, I want you to pay attention to me. You stay away from that girl. We'll all be on the road together for a while, and if she got with child the women will know right off. If that happens, they will have your balls. You just keep your pants buttoned and my job will be a lot easier. D'you understand me?"

Attentively, Josh answered, "Yes, Captain. There won't be any trouble on my account."

"That's good, boy." He relaxed his vigor some. "You've kept yourself well. Better than most really. I'd hate for you to go wrong. The Frenchy's told you about leaving markers on the road?"

"Yessir."

"Then we'll be seein' the two of you tomorrow late or next day. Good luck." Without further ceremony, Metzger turned back to the chores of getting the train rolling.

Delacroix and Metzger leaned forward, their hands bunched on their saddle horns, and quietly watched the train parade slowly past. Delacroix gazed off in the distance to the faint trace of dust rising in the morning sky. This proclaimed the passage of a train—coming down from Council Bluffs, one of the other jumping-off towns into the territories. While this was not a rare occurrence on the plains, he knew it was important to keep a plentiful supply of the new grass and meager forage available. If too many teams passed before them, they would find no fuel and would discover the grasses gleaned to stubble far along the breadth of the trail. Those expeditions that started later, while avoiding the likelihood of flooded rivers and hub-deep mud, assured themselves of hard forage across a baked and trodden landscape. Delacroix was familiar with the importance of passing the Sierras before the first heavy snow and insisted on the early, if wet, departure.

Metzger chimed into his thoughts.

"Was that trader feller tellin' the truth," he paused, "about fillin' his wagon?"

"That he was, *mon ami.* You could pretty well outfit yourself for free between Windlass Hill and Fort Laramie, 'cept for victuals."

"Why not vittles?"

"It just seems there is something *contrariant* with people. They will leave their marriage bed or their fine china along the road for someone else, but when it comes to food, they break jars, kick sand in flour, and pour coal oil on side meat. I can't figure it myself."

Metzger puzzled. "How come you didn't warn us about carrying so much?"

Delacroix chuckled. "It would have been *futilite*—useless. These people are headed into the unknown. They want to bring as much of their old world with them and buy as much provision as they can carry. No one will change their minds but themselves. Perhaps they discard the valuables with care in hopes they will be preserved and destroy the food because they are angry with themselves."

Orneriness in people was something Metzger could understand, being a lawman. His own mind had turned to what he could discard from his own wagon should the need dictate.

The thoughts of Custis Gresham were of an opposite bent than the captain's. He was coveting the varied treasures lying ahead for the picking. These visions and his position as lead wagon cheered him considerably. The contention over the Hampton girl was forgotten. Perhaps he was just indignant his own wife was spending more time attending to the orphaned girl than attending her duties to him.

Josh crouched by the fire drying the wagon repair and watched the train slowly disappear over a low hillock. His anticipation of being alone with Elizabeth almost, but not quite, allayed his concern of being marooned by his party. He couldn't feel completely abandoned as there was another train approaching that might well arrive by nightfall. The dust plume seemed ever closer. That set well with him. He would have at least all day alone with probably the prettiest woman on the path to Oregon. The possibilities flew across his imagination, all with fanciful and satisfying conclusions. He smelled breakfast and turned to watch the girl poke at the food in the iron pan. The repetitious meal of bacon and biscuits never smelled so good.

She stood, bent, one slender hand against her legs, holding her dress from blowing in the breeze. Her face was partially hidden from him by her gathered chestnut hair, worn loose at the neck, billows of it draping and half concealing her features. Josh could see her mouth moving, singing softly to herself. The words were lost as they drifted away on a skim of wind. As he gazed at her, she looked up at him and rewarded him with a placid smile. All was right in Josh Bonner's world.

David Oroville strode next to his oxen team, giving them an occasional "gee" or "haw," emphasized with a prod or pull from his hooked staff. It was sure a fair stretch of the imagination calling these critters oxen. They were a far cry from the sleek and well-rounded beasts he was accustomed to back home in Morse Hill. It seemed in St. Jo, any animal with hooves that could be yoked was deemed an ox. Probably by the end of the trail season, someone would cut the beards off some goats and pass them as "Carolina" oxen.

The two yoke he had bought, judging by their longish horns, belied a Texas background and were little more broken to the yoke than the range cattle they had formerly been. They had tamed some, but the recency of their schooling was apparent. While they had seemingly lost the tendency to bolt at every bit of windblown trash, they still refused to pull together, creating a jerky but improving effort. At least he had had the sense to insist on watching the team broken to the yoke instead of accepting some intractable beast at the word of a trader.

For training, each animal had spent the day starved and snubbed up tight to a post. The next day, they were fed and made to wear a wood yoke while they were snubbed. Finally, upon being freed, each "ox" was yoked to a trained animal and given a rudimentary lesson in left and right and a chance to get used to trace chains as regular adornment.

A hail and a half-seen motion came from his left. He looked to his brother, Daniel, who was driving their stock of cattle between the train and the river. Several other drovers rode amongst the common herd. Daniel cupped his hands and shouted toward him. The words slipped away in the tramping and lowing of the herd. Daniel grinned and thumbed back toward the lone wagon falling behind on their trail. Again he thumbed, grinned, and hailed. The meaning of his gestures was not lost on David, who grinned and acknowledged the joke with a lascivious rotation of his hips. He liked his new friend, Josh, disregarding the few years difference in their ages. He had shown his mettle as an equal to all but the rough and ready scout. He was sure the Hampton girl had noticed, too.

Although well content with his own woman, Sarah, there was something disturbingly arousing about that Hampton woman. She was obviously aware of her attraction to men, and she was smart, a certain dangerous combination for the inexperienced or unwary. What was even more hazardous was the almost feral allure about her that made even a man like himself, who kept his chin in, go all moonheaded and randy.

At the lone wagon left behind, Josh settled himself to his task and to his imaginings. He watched the herd and train diminish in the distance.

Elizabeth watched the departing wagons with more contentment than did Josh. Being alone on the vast prairies only stimulated her. The romance and the freedom only whet her appetite for more. She dug desultorily at the smoky fire. She was well pleased with herself. She was on her own and alone with a young man who was obviously smitten with her. Objectively, she admitted she was more than a bit taken with Josh, too. She had already been in his arms twice already, if for two different reasons. The memory of both instances provoked and stirred a hunger she constrained only with some reluctance. It was easy to deduce what this day could lead to, and she was poised to let her impulses free to swell this newly discovered sensation of liberation.

Fixing a plate of side meat and biscuits with preserves, she brought them to where Josh was aimlessly staring at the repair he had fashioned. His gaze turned to her as he surveyed her from hem to crown. She had felt men's appraising eyes on her before and let Josh drink her in.

Josh was taking a long draught and recalling home. On the streets of Cairo, she had never failed to capture Josh's attention or feed his adolescent desire. He'd never spoken more than a casual greeting or a fare-thee-well to her. His reluctance to approach her wasn't from an innate diffidence with women. He had flirted and danced, kissed and fondled his share of the maidens since he was fifteen. Once, in the company of Hugh Duncan, the town's budding rake, he had paid a visit to Sally Cash's crib. She was a well-kept, thirtyish woman who entertained the town swells and initiated young men into the intimate ways of the flesh.

Josh's previous adversity to Elizabeth stemmed not from a fear of rejection but from his observation of the antics of other potential suitors. He smiled to himself remembering the clumsy and contrived means by which the local swains placed themselves in her path and the bumbling manner in which they played out their rehearsed strategies. Unfailingly, Elizabeth found the single phrase that unraveled their simple intrigues and left the unfortunate suitor stammering and defeated. It was his scorn for these sidewalk lotharios that revolted Josh and turned his pursuits toward simpler and less disdainful females.

For a time, like all young men, Josh had tried to emulate his older brother, Ned. His dark good looks and heedless attitudes were the envy of all the callow youth of Cairo. The impetus for this admiration was the constant parade of pretty girls that swarmed about his older brother.

While Josh's motivation was purely carnal and therefore compelling, he quickly abandoned his mimicry. First, he didn't feel the intrinsic confidence to carry off the charade. Secondly, and more importantly, the type of girls and companions that were attracted to Ned soon came to unsettle him. They all seemed so craven, toadying up to him and relinquishing parts of themselves to bask in his glow. The girls particularly seemed to be those that became their own worst enemy, entering passionless marriages with men whose own spark flickered only when drunk or in the company of their oafish friends.

"What are you thinking about?" asked Elizabeth.

Alerted to her voice, Josh found he was still staring at her. He hoped his woolgathering hadn't left his face too vacant.

"Back home, mostly—and some of the people there," he quietly replied. He poked at the embers to emphasize his reminiscing wasn't as deep as it appeared.

"Anyone in particular?" she teased.

"Some 'bout you. Some 'bout Ned," Josh answered and immediately regretted it. Mentally, he had always paired his brother off with Elizabeth. Their independent ways had matched them up in the minds of many back home; the studious way in which they had avoided each other somehow lent credence to a mutual attraction. Worse, he couldn't picture either of them within the frame of the disenchanted people he had been moping over.

"Ned! Why, I haven't seen him in ages. When last did you see him? What is he doing?" she asked, her face brightening.

"He's a mate on a packet out of New Orleans that runs from there to Galveston and to Veracruz in Mexico. I haven't seen him myself for nigh on eight months," he recollected.

To change the subject he asked, "Do you miss Cairo—and home?"

"No! I don't. I love it here."

She turned about, one hand in the air, as though to suggest all of the expanse about and the trail before them.

"Cairo was so small and stifling. I could barely stand to watch the riverboats steaming to St. Louis and New Orleans and Cincinnati. I wanted out, and this is as out and as glorious as I ever imagined."

She knelt by Josh, facing him.

"Don't you just adore the freedom?"

"Yes, 'Lizabeth, I do. I just wish it hadn't come to us the way it has. Our folks wanted to see the new countries as much as we did, and I'm grieved they never got any farther than they did," he said somberly.

"Oh, Josh, I know. After Mama and Papa died, I just lay there fit to die myself. The more I thought about it, the more I knew if I returned, leaving them out on the prairie, I might as well be dead myself. At best, I'd end up as a soiled dove on some riverboat or married to some lout who would think he was my lord."

Tears streamed down her face as she leaned toward Josh, the crown of her head under his chin. She wept silently. He felt her tears spatter his chest and stain his shirt.

81

Soothingly, he lifted her face and traced with his finger the tracks of her tears. He pressed his lips to her cheeks and then to her mouth. He could feel the tears on his own cheeks mingle with hers and pool about their joined lips.

The natural course of their embrace continued. The memories of the previous evening's foray combined with the intimacy of their shared sorrow, intensifying the emerging lust they willingly kindled.

They rose to their knees and crushed themselves together. Their hands caressed each other, finally resting on each other's hips; a slow melding of their loins began. As he grew aroused, she worked her knees forward thrusting herself farther into his embrace.

Slowly, but with promise, she ended their kiss. He looked at her face. Her eyes, as his must also, glittered with desire. The rest of her face seemed pensive, indecisive.

She stood, taking his hand in both of hers. She beckoned wordlessly, leading him to the wagon bed. Josh spoke not a word, fearing any spoken thought would break the enthrallment which had seized them.

As they lay entwined on the wagon bolsters, they began to grope blindly at each other, stripping away clothing with fervent abandon. As each new bit of shoulder, haunch, or breast was revealed, it was caressed, sampled, revered.

He marveled at the wonder of her; so much more than the fantasies that propelled him onward. More than he remembered of his gropings with other girls inside their bodices and petticoats. The stolid frank image of Sally Cash dimmed in the presence of Elizabeth's feral vitality.

Her hand cupped him; her fingers stroked his manhood, drew him down upon and into her. Their twisting and fondling rapidly became more focused. Their union quickly turned their random clutching into a primitive grappling, then into a timeless and wild rhythm that captured the lovers completely and swept them to a frenzied climax. Josh heard Elizabeth gasp as he carried her desperately over the top of her passion. He quickly followed her as he spilled himself within her.

Josh rolled them both over so she lay upon him, her chestnut hair masking his face, her panting breath in his ear, on his neck. Neither spoke, each afraid words might dispel the magic. Each lay stunned by the reckless ferocity of their lust. In abandonment, they slowly rocked together, then lay still.

Gradually, the everyday sensations of winds, warmth, light, and sound reclaimed them. They uncoiled, relaxed.

"Lordy, 'Lizabeth! I never meant . . ." he blurted out, hopelessly flustered. "We should never . . ." Her fingers pressed against his lips.

"Don't try to say anything like that. Why should we want to be ashamed of what we've done? It was good and right. You felt it, I know," she spoke huskily.

"Elizabeth! What will people think?"

She had had enough of his foolish protesting.

"What people?" she laughed mockingly. "There are no people here, no one for miles and miles." She opened the end covers of the wagon, as though inviting him to confirm their seclusion. "Don't you see? This is what I mean by being free. We don't owe any explanations or excuses to anyone. Don't you understand?" She almost pleaded her enthusiasm.

Archly, she looked at him. "You don't mean to go bragging to everyone that you had me, do you?"

It was Josh's turn to laugh. "Brag to who? There's no one about here. 'Sides, I figure a fella that kisses and tells only gets kissed but the once."

"I shouldn't bet that would be one of your worries," she teased.

Brazen in her nakedness, she stepped down from the wagon and pranced about the campsite. Captivated but frozen in his berth, Josh watched as she dipped a towel and swabbed herself. Soon, she returned to their bed with the damp towel, straddled him, and began to bathe him. Josh felt stirrings anew as she groomed him.

Coyly, she whispered, "Not just now. You've got other chores to do." To emphasize her point, she squeezed him somewhat sharply.

"There'll be time for loving after this wagon is ready to roll."

#

CHAPTER SEVEN

#

The fire, though unattended, had finished drying the repair while Josh and Elizabeth finished attending to each other. Time for further trysting was lost as the train under the floury dust pillar approached in mid-afternoon. Drawn to their campfire, the scout from the other party arrived about lunchtime. He was followed closely by a sinister-looking Indian tracker afoot.

Like their own scout somewhere to the west, both the visitors wore scuffed and stained buckskin pants; the seat and knees shone with wear. The scout was an assured-looking white with long brown hair, cut raggedly and tied at the nape with a wide thong of hide. He wore no true shirt but rather a vest-like garment fashioned from a colorful trade blanket. It was laced loosely, and underneath his chest and neck were tattooed with native designs.

His Indian companion, who spoke neither to the scout nor to the couple, was a broad-chested, squat man with a large pocked nose that was flared and dominated an otherwise handsome face. An old scar ran upward from its tip and gave his face a sinister cast. His head was shaved except for a greasy scalplock. He knelt at the perimeter of the campsite and watched in silence.

Josh had been watching them draw near for some time. The manner in which the Indian paced tirelessly before the scout gave Josh the impression of a man out with his rambling and loyal dog. This was reinforced by the way in which the man squatted at the edge of the campground as the scout approached.

Nodding to Josh and tugging at the brim of his hat, the scout spoke first to Elizabeth.

"Every spring, it seems I discover a new prairie flower and each more striking than last season's. This year has proven no exception," he offered. "Will Lacy is the name. I am pleased to make your acquaintance, Miss—?"

"Elizabeth Hampton, bound for Oregon, as you must be yourself, Mr. Lacy." She curtsied to the stranger briefly but a-might too saucily for Josh's fancy.

The scout should have spoken to him first and then Elizabeth. Here she was, with his spunk inside her, almost flirting with this stranger in greasy skins. Josh fairly seethed with resentment and jealousy. He avoided speaking out of cussedness and a fear his mouth might get the best of him.

"Are you and your brother here in a fix with your wagon?" Lacy inquired. "You could join up with this bunch I'm bringing up." He turned back to look at the approaching wagons.

"Blast it! I'm not her durned brother!" Josh's mouth ran away. "I'm her . . . ! She's my . . . !"

Now what? He had jumped in without his wit at the intruder's provocation. He couldn't say Elizabeth was his woman. That sounded like she was a head of livestock. It would be equally devastating to say he was her lover. Whatever the word needed to save himself, he was certain it hadn't been invented yet.

"We're . . . !" he stammered once more, then judiciously silenced himself.

Sensing the source of his vexation, Elizabeth drew close and took him possessively by the arm. He had never felt more immediate gratitude. She placed her hand over his and leaned close to him. Her actions perfectly said what he had failed in words to do.

"This is my dear friend, Josh Bonner. Without him, I would be dead twice over or surely a captive of the savages," she explained.

Josh had never liked stretchers but felt he could except this one.

She added, "He volunteered to remain with me and repair my wagon."

"That must have been some free-for-all when the call for volunteers went out," joked Lacy disarmingly. "I'm proud to meet the man that won out."

Lacy leaned from the saddle and offered his hand.

"You must be a man of some mettle, Josh Bonner."

As flustered as he was, Josh couldn't help basking a bit in the offered praise. The stranger's commendation seemed heartfelt, and Josh allowed he was a bit more disposed toward the man. He fought back his jealousy, managed to relax some, and sought a more neutral topic.

"Our party went on. We're to meet up with them at Ash Hollow."

"It seems most everyone meets up at Ash Hollow. Good place for it. It's got the only shade for a hundred miles and good water, if it's not muddied," Lacy added.

"I propose to lead my train up here to pass the evening. The road is a bit heavy with sand and best met with a good rest. You wouldn't mind sharing your estate here with some weary travelers, would you?" Lacy proposed.

Josh would have preferred to decline the proposal as company didn't mesh with his own plans but knew he couldn't.

In a somewhat waspish tone, he answered, "I would expect not. Ash Hollow doesn't sound like a trip I'd make afore dinner."

"Then I'll just leave Two Noses here with you while I strike back to my charges. I expect he'll prefer his own victuals, so it won't be necessary to set a place at table for him," Lacy replied good-naturedly.

Those were his parting words as he reined his horse over to his brooding companion. They exchanged a few words and signs, and Lacy galloped away eastward. The wagons were now clearly visible but still miles away. Josh and Elizabeth watched Lacy ride back to them.

Neither spoke, and Josh wondered if Elizabeth was as disappointed at their arrival as he was. He was getting to know her and recognized her silence as intentional and a means by which she kept him at a distance. Or perhaps he didn't probe because he didn't want the answer. Josh was relieved they would be safer within the circle of the new settlers' wagons and welcomed their company accordingly. The regret at a night of lovemaking lost diminished slightly with each yard the newcomers drew nearer. The sensation of the touch of Elizabeth's arm on his, while not as intimate as his desire, would have to suffice.

Lacy's Indian companion pulled at some dried meat and paid little attention to the couple. The meal of bacon and biscuits being prepared didn't seem to tempt him. Josh and Elizabeth ate, readied the camp, and prepared to turn in. Elizabeth retired to her wagon. Josh rolled out his buffalo robe and rubber groundsheet under the wagon. Two Noses had slipped away during the course of the evening. Both the young lovers pondered the proximity but unavailability of the other until sleep overtook them.

The next day found Josh and Elizabeth at the tail end of the new procession of wagons. It had come to seem they would make their way to Oregon always at the tail of someone else's progress, enjoying the film of dust on their teeth.

This new outfit was much larger than their own, consisting of some sixty wagons. Most of the new emigrants were from two small towns in Ohio and Kentucky bordering each other across the Ohio River. All told there were probably two hundred people and their stock. The departure of such a large group must have seriously depleted the two small villages.

Clearly, most were following the fortunes of the captain of the train, Jakob DeKop, an ambitious and ebullient Dutchman. In the East, he was the owner of a shoe and boot factory employing most of the fellow travelers. His plan was to resettle his factory in Oregon, obtaining hides from the trading ships sailing the Pacific coast. Most of the party shared his enthusiasm. The rest needed the employment DeKop had packed in wagons and pointed to the Pacific Northwest.

DeKop himself traveled with nine wagons—three conventional wagons and six huge freight wagons carrying the tools and machinery of the factory. Each of these massive conveyances was drawn by six yoke of oxen and tended by a trio of drovers who paced alongside and ministered to their charges.

Those traveling behind were in an assortment of wagons ranging from specially built Conestogas to jury-rigged farm wagons. All referred to DeKop's factory wagons as the "glory wagons." There was a world of envy, resentment, and respect in the way "glory wagon" was spoken and never within their employer's hearing.

As the group broke camp and started the day's march, Josh was impressed by the efficiency and purpose with which they made ready.

Unlike their own entourage, where each wagon and family had their own agenda and cooperated more out of necessity than strength of purpose, the DeKop train was united behind the employment they dragged with them.

DeKop was undoubtedly in command here. The caravan was comprised of his employees and hopeful employees. Each had an assignment and a common itinerary. Their fates were tied to the Dutch bootmaker, and he used his position with complete impunity. There was no petty bickering of place or position. The entire group left Josh with the impression of an army on the march, even though he had never seen an army on the move.

Lacy's description of the road ahead as "a bit heavy with sand" was no short shrift. At one time long ago, the river's course must have followed the current road before settling in its present bed. Their general direction veered north away from the river, and the going was slow and arduous. Traction for the draft animals was unsure as they plodded along, forced to step high to avoid dragging their hooves in the soft, damp sand. The bawling of the oxen's protest brought no relief and was rewarded only by loud cries and rude prodding of the teamsters.

The huge wagons of machinery had the worst going. Even with their wide tires, they continually sank into the soft but abrasive sand. It poured through the spokes and piled before the iron tires. At some junctures, the wheels refused to turn, dragging and slipping their way through the sand. Through particularly tough stretches, teams were yoked and unyoked, added and replaced to add enough muscle to slog on. In some places, men added their backs to the load, rocking and lifting bodily the wagons from the deepest of the gritty mires. Others were employed with shovels, clearing drifts accumulated before the great wheels. It was backbreaking labor, and the men openly cursed and reviled the work. None had figured they would have to shovel their way to the Promised Land.

Progress for the smaller wagons behind DeKop's van was equally tedious. While the path before them had been cleaned and somewhat compacted by the passage of the mighty wagons, the ruts they left were wider than the tracks of the lighter drays. In following DeKop, they were forced to navigate on the slopes of their furrows. If one side tracked in the wheel rut, the other side became buried in the soft mound left in the middle by the larger wagon's passage. This caused the wagon to tip precariously or to slew about and stall. Additionally, the passage of the large wagons had mounded up the middle of the road, forcing the teams to pull to the left or to the right. The mounds, in some places, would drag on the running gear of the wagons. To Josh's thinking, the narrower wagons should have gone ahead. But he was a guest. It wasn't his place to say anything.

By the time the difficulty of the roadway had become so pronounced, it was too late to turn the wagons off the trail and cut a new route. The depth of the ruts forced the train into a single file. They really had become a train. Any attempt to divert from the track was met by sloughing of the sides that buried wheels to the axle hubs and threatened to pitch the would-be trailblazer on its side.

Josh had hitched Banner and Flag in front of the Hampton mules. He hoped their great strength and stoic patience would make up for their naturally slower pace. So far, his plan was working. The pace before him was slow going anyway. Unfortunately, he would have to follow in the track of the other wagons.

He walked along beside the oxen, encouraging them with "gees" and "haws," accented by judicious strokes to their flanks with a switch. Elizabeth remained in the wagon and with reins and carriage whip inspired the efforts of the recalcitrant mules. The outside lead mule, in addition to its constant braying, continually tried to nip at Banner's haunches. The resultant bellow brought quick reprisal from Josh in the form of a swat across the offender's snout.

As the outfit distanced itself from the Platte, the going became marginally easier as the depth and softness of the sand diminished. By noontime, they had passed the worst of it and now made a fair advance up a gentle but persistent incline.

Josh and Elizabeth, as outsiders and at the tail of the caravan, received little aid except in the worst of mirings. Josh's introduction to the family before him, the Hodges, came as he assisted them in their travail. As they became stuck, he pitched in with spade and back. He received their reinforcement through his own most difficult passages. It was an acquaintance borne of necessity and nurtured by mutual support.

Norman Hodges, his wife, Marion, and their two sons had worked for the bootmaker and enthusiastically pursued their livelihood westward. The covenant with their employer measured equally with the excitement of

89

seeing the new reaches before them and the commitment to a life anew in Oregon.

Here in this demanding stretch, they saw the first evidence of the discard described by the merchant from Council Bluffs. Kegs of nails, boxes of books, items of furniture and kitchenware began to litter the roadside. Necessities that had become extraneous luxuries joined articles of clothing, mirrors, and soon, foodstuffs.

Curiously and unbelievingly, they saw all of the food had been despoiled. Barrels of flour had been split open and strewn into white smudges. Handfuls of sand, like cinders on a snowy sidewalk, blotched the pristine white. The air was pungent with the myriad sweet smells of poured molasses and broken jars of preserves. Slabs of bacon and jerked beef were rank with the stain of kerosene and coal oil.

"Josh, I can't believe the waste. It all seems so mean somehow," Elizabeth decried.

"It surely does. Looky there, 'Lizabeth. Some cuss burned his for trash!" Josh exclaimed, pointing to a smoldering pile of bacon and meal. "Doesn't seem right, but I guess it's like that Gates feller said?"

"Do you think we'll have to lighten my wagon?" Elizabeth asked. Her look pleaded for the answer she wanted to hear.

"I'd reckon not. We seem to have passed the worst of this road," he reassured. "Though it probably wouldn't hurt to consider what you could do without."

"Oh! I'd hate to have to leave anything at all . . . but I'll think of something."

He laughed. "I don't think you are beholden to leave something behind just 'cause everyone else seems t'be."

It was true. The road was improving. The heavy sand they had been coursing was getting shallower, and in only some short swales was the passage a struggle. They had a good team, and the patient efforts of Banner and Flag maintained the steady effort required. While the surface of the road was improving, the grade was steadily increasing. They must be on the approaches of Windlass Hill.

It was peculiar even to think of hills and grades in this land of rolling prairies. A traveler could see in the distances bluffs and outcroppings where the land had eroded away. However, the immediate view was of a series of low hills, about five or six to the mile, rolling away like long combers on an ocean. The wagons ahead would dip into a trough and disappear until only the arch of the cover could be seen, only to rise up like a lifeboat on the next crest. If one set their sites to one of the decaying escarpments with an eye to a new view, they were always disappointed. Like being in a huge bay, the distant scene would always be the same as the one just left behind. The headlands in the clear distance remained the same, seeming no closer or attainable. Nevertheless, this steady rise of the terrain was not lost on the voyagers, nor was its portent.

Up ahead, on the left of the trail, Josh saw a chilling site. There, blowing away its final breaths, lay an ox. Its flanks bore the harsh marks of a last and futile caning. Too exhausted and worn, it must have collapsed in its tracks. When the savage efforts to revive it failed, it had been rolled out of the roadway and discarded like the other goods that had spent their utility.

What was most disturbing to Josh was not the site of the dying animal. He had seen such before. It was the knowledge of the utter dependence on the animals pulling their homes and the haste compelling someone to drive an animal to its death. What sense of urgency propelled these people? What dispatch would not allow someone to put the beast out of its misery?

He pictured his own or Elizabeth's teams blown and dead. Neither had replacements, and the importance of their health was nearly on a par with their own. Looking at Elizabeth, he could tell her thoughts were akin to his own.

"Hand me that pistol behind you, 'Lizabeth. I can't let that animal suffer to death," he said.

"Wait until I've passed, will you? I don't want to see."

She handed down the Colt. Josh checked the cylinder and rotated it until a live chamber would fall under the hammer. He strode to the prostrate animal. Its eyes were beyond pleading and stared vacantly, already clouding over. He placed the muzzle behind the ear, cocked, and fired. The ringing percussion shivered the still air. The weapon's recoil lifted his arm. Its job was done. He felt the weight of the pistol hang on his arm, and although he felt badly about killing such a helpless thing, he knew he had but little choice.

The shot had halted the train, and people peered back to investigate. Those at the nearest wagons could see what had happened and only looked in his direction. Those farther ahead had hastily grabbed their own weapons and were rushing to the sound of the commotion.

Lacy, who had been at the head of the train watching its advance, soon galloped back. From his vantage point, he could see what the ruckus was about and turned the nervous men back to their task.

Josh was reloading the gun when he rode up.

"Did you think that was necessary?" he inquired, gesturing to the dead animal.

"I couldn't go by and let it broil to death," Josh said, already starting to bristle.

"I can't abide seeing either man or beast suffer myself. You will find there will be suffering enough out here. You may as well steel yourself to it."

Josh's bile rose, and he started to tell the scout both his and the girl's parents had died on the trail but checked himself because it would require disclosing the cholera as the cause. There was no sense riling up their fellow travelers, so he kept his peace.

Lacy said, "The natives surely know we're passing through, but there is no sense calling attention to ourselves. They might become contrary if they thought we were hunting in their backyard."

"I'm sorry," Josh replied, chastised. "I just wanted to put it out of its misery."

"Powder and ball are dear in these parts," the scout replied in a tone suggesting he was not criticizing so much as informing a novitiate. "You might better have cut its throat. It would still have been a charity."

"I didn't think I could do that," Josh admitted.

"That's good. Killing is often a necessity, but the more personal it is, the less the attraction becomes for it."

Josh sensed the man spoke from an experience more intimate than dispatching oxen and again realized he had much to learn.

"Thanks for your advice, Mr. Lacy. It seems sound, and I'll pay heed in the future."

"Well, pay heed to the trail behind us. You may have attracted visitors. So keep your eyes open—and put that hogleg away. I don't want someone nervous back here with a gun in his pants."

The implication he was unreliable affronted Josh. He stared coolly back at the scout.

"I've never reckoned m'self to be the nervous type. I'm not about to start shootin' if company comes callin'."

Lacy looked appraisingly at Josh. Lightly, he said, "I don't suppose you are. Seems there is something about you that says you know your own limits."

Josh wasn't sure whether this was intended as compliment or criticism. Rather than find out, he let the statement dangle.

The migration continued up the long, rolling incline, marking its advance with a trail of litter. Ancient heaps of clothes, desiccated piles of food, and other discards evidenced the passage of the trains of past seasons.

Presently, Josh and Elizabeth halted behind the line of stalled wagons. Walking ahead to investigate, Josh came upon a flurry of activity at the crest. He was immediately impressed by the fact that beyond the next hilltop there were no more hillocks to be seen, only a line of pale empty sky. They were at the top of Windlass Hill.

The bustle of activity, Josh discovered, was the preparation for the descent of the first of DeKop's six huge factory wagons. The lead team was reduced to two yoke while four yoke were hitched as trailers to provide braking down the steep grade. Handle extensions were fixed to the brake staffs, allowing extra leverage. Each of the rear tires was rolled up onto a flat iron skid, which was shackled around the rim. This skid was then fastened by a chain to a stout timber athwart the undercarriage of the wagon. This arrangement prevented the rear wheels from turning while the friction checked the momentum of the descent, albeit considerably reducing the amount of control. It was not only the task of the trailer team to act as brakes but to keep the load before it under steering control.

The preparations were extensive, and the teamsters discussed contingencies in careful detail. An examination of the perilous descent made their vigilance apparent. The angle of the grade was not dangerous of itself, although it was far more precipitous than any encountered so far in the journey. No. It was the length of the decline that was intimidating; a long defile, probably close to a thousand feet, faced the teamsters. This would test the preparations of both men and teams. While each trip down would become less terrifying with renewed acquaintance, the toll of endurance and strength would keep the chore fraught with difficulty.

The road was essentially straight, but the track had several places where the path was narrow and plunged sharply enough a mistake could not easily be redeemed. Once control was lost, only quick, decisive action would prevent a disaster.

The first of DeKop's wagons slipped past the crest and began downward. Two teamsters in the wagon bed manned the long brake handles and used them to steer as best they could. Drovers on foot near the lead yoke helped to maintain direction with proddings from wooden staffs. The trailer team, unused to being behind a wagon, controlled the pace. They had their own drovers. The first part of the descent was uneventful. Minor slippages or changes of speed were easily corrected by the skilled teamsters. However, the second part of the slide, for that is what it was, saw control slip slowly away as the teams tired. The brakes, as they overheated, became of little use, and the effort to control momentum superseded direction. The lead teams began to speed up in an effort to keep the wagon behind from running them over. It was primarily the success of the chain brakes and the trailing teams' desire for self-preservation that kept the procession in check. Finally, the troop reached the bottom of the hill amidst the cheers of the emigrants at the summit and the self-congratulatory backslapping of the successful teamsters. The rear yokes were led patiently back to the top to rest, to await another journey down.

Elizabeth left the wagon to join Josh at the crest of the hill. Together, they watched the descent of DeKop's wagons. Three went down and awaited the balance of the long train still at the top. As she watched, her heart was heavy. Dread hung over her like a cloak. She had already lost her kin and her home. Everything she had left in the world was in her wagon and would soon be in the hands of her young companion and the strangers from the East. She pictured ruination in her mind and foresaw all that was left of her life spilled and irretrievable at the bottom of this remote bluff, miles from anywhere. She began to comprehend how much she depended on this lanky boy from home.

"Josh. Is it going to be all right?" she pleaded.

"Shore. I've helped my father put boats back in the river with rigs somethin' like this," he reassured.

He added, "And there is no current here."

To lighten the moment he threw in, "I might feel a bit better if we was to go down backward, like t'home."

"Don't tease! I'm afraid of this and more afraid these strangers won't care so much for my wagon as they would if it were one of their own."

"Well, I 'spect that's just natural. But I'll be helpin' them, and we'll have had so much practice by the time your turn comes it won't be any chore at all."

While they were talking, DeKop's fourth freight wagon had reached an impasse. The lead team was straining ahead, trying to escape the wagon looming behind. Meanwhile, the hind team, having made the first trip down, was feeling the effects of this second journey. Try as they would to control the efforts of the pulling team, their exhaustion was beginning to tell, and they bleated in protest.

One of the oxen faltered, stumbling to its knees and tripping the one behind. This caused the heavy load to surge ahead and slew to the right. Once the inertia was gained, the game was lost. The rear oxen shambled ahead under the jerk, survival their only and immediate concern.

Tenaciously, the drivers fought to regain control. They lashed at the beasts. One even grabbed hold of the two hindmost's tails and pulled mightily. The only reward for his effort was to have his own feet skid out from under him, skipping him along on his rear. The jerking wagon caught up and backsided the wheel team, rushing them forward until they yanked at their traces. This sent the wagon careening into them yet again. This time, it slewed off to the side, skidding and pitching up on the one side, hurling one of the brakemen out of the bed, lever extension still in hand.

On this lurch, the rear halters parted and the wagon righted and began to chase the fore teams down the slope. It jounced forward and leapt on and off the course. Within a hundred feet, the outcome could not be in doubt.

With a crash, the front axle gave way, slinging out the last brakeman, which is all that saved him. He landed astraddle the back of an ox and fell off standing, running in full flight for his life.

The wagon skidded sideways and toppled over, spilling the machinery inside to be plowed under by the sliding wagon. The four remaining oxen were dragged along in a tangle until the crashing gear freed them. The teamsters on foot scattered; one leaping off a short bluff in an attempt to save his hide. The skidding wagon, its front wheels gone, pitched off the roadbed and rolled, shearing itself to pieces in its demise.

Much of the contents remained in a lump, captured by the tarpaulin cover. This bundle remained together until it, too, spilled its load, like a tablecloth ripped from its place. Tools and machinery were scattered, demolished, and half-buried over fifty yards of hill and gully.

DeKop, at the first sign of trouble, yelled epithets downhill enumerating the ineptitude of his teamsters. As the situation worsened, these became curses in Dutch, and the bootmaker launched himself down the grade as though to rescue the situation. All he managed to gain from this rush was the first view of the havoc and ruin below.

Upon his arrival, the teamsters were up and brushing themselves off and had managed to rescue their companion who had leapt off the bluff. Other than a fair assortment of scrapes and bruises, the only injury was a sprained ankle suffered by the leaper, who hung grimacing painfully between two of his fellows.

The Dutchman, in an impressive mixture of English and his native tongue, alternately cursed the teamsters and bemoaned the fate of his goods. Occasionally, he stooped to retrieve some broken handle or lever from the debris of his cargo, then cast it away into the dust.

The witnesses still at the top of the hill had curiously mixed reactions to the debacle. There had been a general uproar of shouted instructions when the first control was lost. Women began to scream, and the men fell silent as the runaway developed. All fell silent in the throng as the wagon spilled. Every sound of the mishap carried to their ears. The rending of metal and the splintering of wood added to the imaginings of those gathered above, who pictured their own possessions scattered and destroyed. It was when the bootmaker commenced his own careen down the grade that reactions varied. There were some who cheered, not at their employer's misfortunes but at the miraculous survival of the teamsters. The differentiation might have been lost on the bootmaker had his attention not been distracted by the disaster unfolding before his eyes.

Elizabeth and Josh looked about in surprise when the cheering started, and for an instant, mistook the motive behind the huzzahs. They realized it was for the providential safety of the teamsters. A closer look, however, revealed in the eyes of some onlookers a grace of satisfaction. Both were disturbed in seeing this and wondered at the character of those who would find reparation in another's misfortune. When the Dutchman commenced his fitful tirade, more than a smattering of laughter, mostly suppressed, broke out. This grew as the antics of the stricken man became more fierce and animated. There were no harangues cast down the hill at the poor man. No one was that callous or felt that secure in their future employment. Certainly, no one would have ever laughed had they been closer to the scene of the tirade. It was the security of distance, and perhaps as a relief of tensions, that sustained the laughter. The tableau of the distant figure, leaping and frothing at the downfallen teamsters, was somewhat comical. Even Josh and Elizabeth turned, smiled at each other, then burst into snickering. Despite the calamity below, the ranting figure did appear buffoonish. Fortunately, the laughter had subsided before the employer regained his senses. Ah, yes, these people were well acquainted with their boss.

The crowd dispersed to their various tasks. Josh and Elizabeth ambled back to their own preparations. Elizabeth spoke first.

"I feel so awful, laughing at that poor man."

"Me, too. It sure don't seem right, but I couldn't help m'self. He just looked the clown, carryin' on like a scalded cat," Josh agreed.

They looked at each other, and their memories provoked another round of cackling.

Josh changed the subject.

"C'mon. We've got work to do before our turn comes."

The descent of the balance of the train, including DeKop's remaining two freight wagons, came off without incident or injury. Josh made three trips down the grade before taking Elizabeth's wagon down. Banner and Flag, practiced in such routines, performed well. The mules, though at times fractious, were easier to direct than oxen. A plus for choosing mules, Josh noted to himself. During the trip down, he also noted two of DeKop's oxen, injured in the accident and beyond redemption, lay dead at the roadside with their throats cut.

Getting all the wagons to the bottom of Windlass Hill exhausted the rest of the day. It was nearing dark before all were settled for the night's needed rest.

During the night, the wooden remains of DeKop's wagon were cannibalized for firewood. By dawn, only the metal fittings remained at the wreck site. Josh had scavenged for wood and observed the metal remains of other wagons scattered about the slope. DeKop's loss was not an isolated incident. Wood was too scarce to be left lying about. The scorched and rusted nuts and bolts testified to the efficiency of the passing expeditions. Still, it was sad to imagine the misfortunes of past emigrants, their plans ruined alongside the treacherous slope.

#

CHAPTER EIGHT

#

After supper, Josh had intended to remain awake while the others slept. He wanted to creep up to the comforts of Elizabeth's bed. The labors of the day's work soon overpowered him. He drifted off in his robes under the wagon and slept dreamlessly.

When he stirred awake, he discovered DeKop and several of his workmen were probing the wreckage in an effort to salvage what could be had of the tools and machinery. If DeKop cared that the wooden remains of his wagon had gone up in smoke, he didn't make it known. A calm had returned to the man, and his energies were directed toward gleaning what he could from the destruction of the accident.

A small pile of lasts and twine, hammers, and awls was gathered at the road's edge. One man had gathered an assortment of nails and tacks and was attempting to salvage some kegs. The heavier machinery was a total loss. Frames and arms of the unfamiliar equipment lay twisted and bent beyond recovery. Gears with broken teeth and bent shafts poked out of the dirt. One large machine had twisted itself into the ground as if in an attempt to bury itself. A brigade of workers carried the small salvage down to camp where it disappeared not only into DeKop's other wagons but was distributed into some settlers' wagons, too. Whether this was managed through coercion or commerce, Josh couldn't decide.

Soon camp was broken and the migration continued. As each wagon took up the trailhead, they passed DeKop and Lacy. From their horses, the pair watched the progression, occasionally commenting to someone about a minor defect in their outfit. Loose straps were tightened and harnesses adjusted without delay or rancor. Josh was again impressed by the military efficiency of the DeKop party. He couldn't help but compare this with his own band. Delacroix was usually gone before first trail, and Metzger paid little attention to the individual wagons.

After all the wagons had passed, the two commanders sped to the head of the column. The Indian, Two Noses, was nowhere to be seen, and Josh presumed he had preceded the party to probe the trail.

The morning passed uneventfully with the small exception that no nooning stop was made in anticipation of an early arrival at Ash Hollow. Josh and Elizabeth foresaw the rejoining with their own people.

99

Because yesterday's path led away from the South Platte, there had been no water at hand. Reserves had been tapped for replenishing the dray animals hauling the wagons, but none could be spared for the herd livestock. These animals kept up a constant low complaining for relief.

Shortly into the afternoon, the animals picked up a scent of water. Their stride lengthened as the foretaste of the thirst-quenching source beckoned them. As the migration approached, the loose livestock began to overtake the train, and as they mingled amongst the wagons, the drovers found themselves with not one herd but several small clans milling in and out of the path. There was no stampede, just a determined traipsing to the source.

In the confusion, Josh had difficulty controlling the normally tractable Natchez. The sorrel rigorously insisted on following the herd. Josh had to constantly rein him in, keeping the wagon between Natchez and the unruly mob of critters. At the same time, Elizabeth hauled against the jerk line of straining mules. Fortunately, Banner and Flag were leashed to the wagon and could only protest the tether.

Again bringing up the rear of the train, Josh presently came upon the source of the commotion. At the head of a gully, Lacy and the herdsmen faced off against the loose stock. The other wagons had already passed. Scattered forays by the bolder beasts were headed off, and dominance was being restored. On the ridge of the gully stood Two Noses, who, being on foot, had wisely chosen the high ground.

Elizabeth, the anxiety high in her voice, exclaimed, "Mr. Lacy! What has happened to the animals?"

"Nothing to be concerned about, missy. There is a spring down this arroyo, but it is poison. The animals made for it when they got a whiff of water on the wind. We just had to keep them headed on down the road."

"Who could be so mean as to poison water out here?" Elizabeth asked. She was thinking of the vandalized food along the roadside.

Lacy smiled. "God is your villain in this case. The spring is alkaloid. It leaches into the water from the earth. A taste might cure a sour stomach, but more than that can kill."

"How far is there until we come on good water?" she asked.

"Just on down the road about three, four miles. That's Ash Hollow, and you will find your people there. Two Noses stole a peek at them awhile back and they seem well settled. I expect you will be anxious to see them."

"That we shall, Mr. Lacy. Thank you."

As their wagon passed on, Lacy said to Josh, "Two Noses tells me Travels-in-Winter is with your party."

"Who?" Josh puzzled.

"Your scout, Delacroix. The Crow call him Travels-in-Winter."

"That's some name. Why would they call him that?"

"He used to winter with the Crow, show up in a blizzard sometimes. He would stay holed up with a pair of Indian sisters he provided for. Except for when he got hungry and had to hunt, he would stay bedded up, fucking those two squaws. I couldn't blame him either. They were both comely girls," answered the scout.

"When you see him, tell him Will Lacy has some of the brandy he likes and will call on him."

"I'll do so, Mr. Lacy," Josh said. "I'll expect you'll be welcome."

Ash Hollow was a series of brushy hills and ravines grown over with stands of ash trees interspersed with some struggling cedar. The road passed through the southern side of the hollow and intersected the northern trail at the western end. There were several small springs toward this end with good, if cloudy, water. It was evident that it was a well-used resting place for the road-weary emigrant trains. Even this early in the season, the grass was grazed away in places and numerous experienced campsites were available throughout the groves. Messages had been left on boards, and names had been carved into tree trunks or painted onto rocks. Josh and Elizabeth found their party camped at the mouth of one of the larger arroyos. The herd was grazing on the hillsides above the hollow, tended by the younger boys.

Lemeul Bingham was the first to spy the returnees. He nudged the missus to alert her and waved a welcome. He strode to meet Josh as his portly wife fairly flew to Elizabeth, her arms outstretched in welcome.

"Glad to see you back, boy," he exclaimed, clasping Josh's hand. "You look about packed in."

"I reckon so," Josh replied. "There's a shoutin' hard stretch of trail behind me."

"Don't I know. Providence must have made this glade here to reward the weary traveler."

They slipped into a discussion of wagons, hills, and teams while Elizabeth stood clamped in Hattie Bingham's fervent embrace. Elizabeth was fully a head taller than the doctor's wife, but she found herself being nearly lifted off the ground by her exuberant welcome.

"Lordy, child. I've done nothing but fret about you for two days now," she cried, her eyes brimmed to overflowing with tears. "I am so glad to see you again."

"Thank you for your concern, Mrs. Bingham, but there was little more danger than you yourself faced. Still and all, I am grateful to be back with you," Elizabeth answered.

Hattie Bingham did not have any children of her own to smother. She had, apparently, adopted Elizabeth to fill the vacancy.

"My land! I should say. That hill was a terror. I've never had such a ride in my life! Let me look at you." She held her by the sleeves and looked her up and down.

Elizabeth couldn't take much more of this fawning. Her own mother, while loving, had treated her sternly. She had been aware of her only child's headstrong ways and had rigorously exacted chores from her, suspicious perhaps of the thrall she had over men. Elizabeth leaned down and kissed the woman's broad forehead.

"It's good to be amongst friends again. The people we came in with were kind enough but a mite stiff in their ways."

By this time, others had noted their arrival and had gathered about offering their greetings. Josh sought and found Jubal at the fringe of the crowd. He pushed his way over to him, answering the welcomes and questions as briefly as could be considered polite.

"Jubal, is everything right with the gear?"

Jubilee feigned a hurt look. "Mister Josh. You don't think I'd let your outfit get away, do you? Everything is fine. Would you like somethin' t'eat?"

"I'd like a fresh chicken, stewed with onions, and a piece of apple pie. S'pose you could rustle me up a plate?"

"Finished up the last chicken while you was gone. Might be able to scare up some bully beef and soda bread. Might even be able to wash it down with some hot coffee," Jubal replied with a wink. It was good to have his young friend back.

"Lead on, then. That sounds like welcome palaver."

Josh squatted by the wagon, leaning against a wheel. He reflected how just being near his own gear was beginning to feel homelike. It was kind of reassuring having everything to hand. Things seem to find their places in the course of travel, either put away or stored handy as needed. The same formula applied to himself, he considered. He had put away parts of himself and distilled himself to the skills he might need right away. He considered how his life had become simpler, or at least better suited to the task at hand.

Back home he was always misplacing things. He would set something down without mind. Knowing it would at least be somewhere close by when it was needed had made him careless. Many, almost countless times, he would wander around in frustration seeking the whereabouts of something. It was somehow settling to know the axe was stashed below the wagon seat and the lantern swung from the middle canvas hoop. It was something that just came about. Maybe knowing something carelessly laid about meant a good chance it would never been seen again. What really astounded him was the changes in himself that hastened the transition from feckless to disciplined traveler so unremarkable. He liked how more reliable he felt to himself, but he fractionally longed for the opportunity to resume his lackadaisical ways.

"Has Delacroix stopped by here much in the past couple of days?" Josh asked. He had to repeat himself. Jubilee was entranced in one of his frequent reveries.

"Only to spit m'good coffee into the fire and jabber a bit. He don't make much a-talkin' lest there's somethin' on his mind."

"To look at the man you'd suppose he never spoke a'tall," Josh crowed as he spit his mouthful of coffee into the fire. They both chortled at the jest and frequently revived the laughter by spitting coffee onto the coals.

Josh thought how relaxing it was to laze about with Jubal. While the time with Elizabeth was probably the best he could recall, there was an unsettling tension being with her. He constantly had the feeling the bottom was going to fall out with her. He was conscious of his wariness when he spoke to her. It seemed the wrong words or a misstep would crack them asunder like scalding water poured into a cool pitcher. What had been whole and vital moments before would lay broken and useless at his feet. Truth be told, he felt she sustained the tension by intent as if it was a kind of game.

Somehow, this made him recall that his weapons were still in her wagon, and he felt foolish after complimenting himself on his new powers of organization and attention. It was galling, more so, that he viewed the guns as items of such necessity as to require always being within hand's reach.

"I had better find Delacroix. I've a message for him from t'other scout." He stood up, kicking the stiffness from his knees.

"You go on, then. I'll just finish off the last of the apple pie," Jubal drawled.

Josh found Elizabeth taking supper with the Binghams and paused to make the necessary pleasantries before excusing himself to go and retrieve his guns. As he dug in the box for his weapons, a figure emerged from the shadow of a tree and spoke.

"What goes here? This isn't your wagon to be poking about in," the voice challenged. As the form drew near, it became the Reverend Clark.

"I've just come for some of my gear I left behind." It pained Josh to have to admit his oversight, but there was no point in trying to conceal the arsenal.

Clark noted the guns with a nod of his head.

"So I see, son. I didn't have the chance to praise you for guarding Miss Hampton while she was indisposed," offered Clark. "Nor to thank you for the repairs you made." He extended his hand in congratulation or gratitude, but it was left hanging. Josh was too adorned with weaponry to return the handshake.

"Thank you, Reverend. There wasn't much guardin' to do as we fell in soon enough with the Dutchman's train."

The parson withdrew his hand without taking affront. However, his brow knitted and he leaned over Josh to emphasize his next point.

"I'll trust you were as attentive in preserving the lady's chastity, as well. Some of the ladies have been talking. You can well imagine."

Here was a subject Josh didn't need to be brought up. In spite of the necessity, he couldn't bring himself to lie to a preacher man. He formed his reply mentally and listened to his answer as he uttered, "The lady's chastity is for her to preserve, Reverend. I would never impose myself where I might be unwelcome."

Josh was amazed with what he heard himself saying. It sounded so high flown and breezy. He supposed it must have come off as a little peppery. No matter now, it was spilt.

The preacher unknotted his substantial brows but maintained his stance, studying him for a moment before replying, "I hope my praise wasn't unwarranted. The virtue of our womenfolk is not a matter to be taken lightly. You may bear some watching."

Josh knew anything he might say would come out as a challenge. He wisely kept his tongue quiet.

Clark rocked back to a normal distance and cautioned, "Heed my words, son. The people will be keeping a watch on you two." His point made, the preacher retired, leaving Josh alone with his armful of ordinance. Josh watched him fade back into the shade of the grove.

The man had too much of the smell of bully in him, preacher or no. Josh had the feeling he had been lurking, keeping watch on Elizabeth and her wagon even before his own arrival. The thought made him shiver, but he attributed that to his own guilt at the half lie to the minister.

"Here comes the militia now. I've been wondering when they would catch up," Delacroix greeted Josh.

"Sentry duty must be serious duty in this outfit," added Lacy.

"Fortunately, they're allowed to keep the artillery entrenched," Delacroix chimed.

Josh was aware he must cut a pretty comical picture with his armload of weapons. He had wanted to find their scout and hadn't stopped at his wagon before seeking him out.

"It appears you preceded your invitation, Mr. Lacy. Sorry I wasn't more prompt in delivering it," said Josh.

Lacy was reclined on one elbow by Delacroix's campfire.

"No matter, m'boy. It's been a sore spell since I crossed paths with this varmint. I thought I'd hurry over before he skulked away," Lacy

105

joked. His words were a little thick with the brandy he'd been drinking. It was apparent both scouts had been tipping their elbows at the jug.

"Set down your burden and join us, *mon ami*, I trust all is well with you and Miss Hampton," Delacroix exclaimed, beaming with good cheer.

"'Pears good as new. It worked out better than I expected," Josh replied, taking a seat by the fireside.

"I figured you'd service her well," Delacroix offered with a sly look to Lacy. Both men guffawed at the joke.

Josh felt his face redden and hoped it wasn't apparent across the fire.

"Set down your arsenal and join us for a pull." Lacy offered an oblong stone crock, wiggling it by the handle. "I expect there will be plenty of warning before the siege commences."

Without hesitation, Josh flopped into a reclining position, emulating the two scouts. He felt honored to be included in their circle. He expected some laughter at his expense would be the price of their companionship. It appeared good-natured, and he felt it a fair tariff to be a part of their roistering. With some misgivings, he reached for the jug. He had had only a sip or two of spirits previously and one or two adventures with small beer. Before he could lay hands on the prize, Delacroix put his hand on Lacy's arm and pulled back the brandy.

"Do you think it wise to give a *blanc bec* any of this buzzard choke you call brandy? It could make his knees watery."

Lacy affected an astounded look. "Why, you're right! I wasn't thinking. A man not accustomed to this juice could become permanently addled." He clutched the jug protectively to his bosom.

Josh, in a way, was relieved. He had tasted whiskey before while trying to build courage enough to go to Sally Cash's crib. The memory of the fiery liquor lingered as strongly as his other memories of that night.

"What is a *blanc bec*?" he inquired.

Lacy answered. "A greenhorn, boy. It means 'white face' in Frog talk, though I've never cared enough to ask why. In general, it means someone who has crossed the Platte for the first time."

Delacroix piped up. "Then we owe our young friend an apology, Will. He has been twice across. It was twice in the same day, but we have to abide by the rules. Pour a cup of that stomach robber for a veteran *voyageur.*"

Josh found himself holding a tin cup under the mouth of the jug, which Lacy shakily spilled half-full. The air was filled with a liquor smell which even overpowered the wood smoke. As Josh put the cup to his lips, the raw brandy instantly numbed his mouth. His tongue went cold.

Seeing Josh's expression, Lacy explained, "That's barrel proof brandy you've got before ye. The weaker varieties don't preserve well north of the Platte." For emphasis, he spat a mouthful into the fire, raising a whoomp and a flare.

Lacy raised himself as far as his knees and slurred a toast, "Here's to the rendezvous—Where tattooed gentlemen gather with noble *voyageurs* to indulge their hellion natures." The scout spread his shirt collar to reveal another collar of decorated flesh. Lacy and Delacroix clinked their tin cups and drank deeply, seemingly with little effect.

Josh was dazzled to be welcomed so readily into the circle of the veteran plainsmen. He would have liked to think it was because of his own attainments on the road but suspected the liquor's influence was the prompt. Seemingly forgotten, he sipped away at the fiery potion and listened to the talk of his new companions. They garrulously recounted tales of the colorful people they had known and the places they had seen. Names like Yellowstone Bob, Jim Bridger, his fort, Soda Springs, and the City of Rocks paraded through their conversation. As Josh drank more, he would, from time to time, toss out what he thought were vastly clever comments. Mostly, however, he was ignored except for the occasional jibe at his expense. The scouts' bantering became more buoyant as they outdid each other with the most outrageous lies. Occasionally, they became subdued and reflective as they remembered some fallen comrade or long forgotten incident. He was content to listen and work slowly at his cup. The taste wasn't now so half-bad, and he felt loose and content within the circle.

About halfway through his second mug, Josh became aware of a still presence standing at his feet. Two Noses had silently approached and stood waiting for Lacy to notice him. Finally, it was Delacroix who marked the Indian's presence and nudged Lacy, interrupting a rambling tale. The scout exchanged some signs and spoke some short phrases of some unintelligible language. Lacy struggled to his feet and excused himself.

"The fool Dutchman's making ready to head out in the morning. He'll end up pulling those barges of his himself after he blows out all his teams. I guess the best I can do is plead I'm too drunk to break trail. Then again, maybe his temperance lecture will sober me up enough to go. I must state I have my reservations about that.

"It was grand to see you again, Claude," he added. "If your party will wait for a couple of days, they can discharge you, follow a trail of dead animals, and smell their way to Oregon."

Lacy bent and offered his hand to Josh, almost stumbling into the fire.

"You'll do well, greenhorn, it appears to me. Glad to have shared a cup with you."

Josh, with glazed eyes, peered back at the rangy scout. "The honor was mine, sir. I hope we'll meet many more times on the road."

Lacy smiled wistfully at Josh. "I hope we do. Next time, we'll dirty your parlor."

After Lacy and Two Noses had departed, Josh commented, "Mr. Lacy and Two Noses don't seem to hanker too much for each other. How come they travel together?"

"It amounts to an obligation on the Indian's part. He's a Blackfoot from north of the Yellowstone River, but that don't mean his sort of debt isn't common amongst lots of tribes."

"What sort of debt?"

"Well, it seems Lacy saved old Two Noses from drowning in a quicksand bog some years back. Now, to an Indian, getting killed in battle is just the most glorious way to go out. But to get yourself killed from a simple mistake in travelling is just about the worst. So when Lacy dragged Two Noses out of that mire, he sort of owned his life."

Josh wondered if there was slavery even out here in the wilds. "Then Two Noses is his slave?"

"Indians have slaves, yes; but they are captives from other tribes. In a manner of talkin', Two Noses is his slave, though."

Delacroix was warming to his tale. Drink had loosened his tongue and he was glad for the palaver. "Two Noses is free to leave anytime—but he can't go back to his people 'cept in shame until he pays back the life he owes. The peculiar part is probably no one of his own people even knows of the debt. Just Two Noses himself. That's enough, though. He would be less than a warrior in his own mind, and to live like that would probably kill him."

He added, "I expect when he does get his debt paid, he will probably kill Lacy his own self at the first chance he gets."

Josh was enraptured with this strange tale of honor. "Why would he do that?" he wondered.

What Josh was learning about these strange plains dwellers, white and red alike, was so different from his imaginings or his experiences with "tame" Indians. The Indians he had seen on the river were mostly beggars or drunks or traders. The fierce concepts of territory and morals were difficult to grasp.

Delacroix answered, "Well, even though Lacy saved his life, not giving Two Noses the chance to get even has kept him away from his kin for nigh on five, six years now, and he's itchin' to get tracks made for home."

The scout held up a hand to indicate he wasn't finished with his tale. "Not having the chance to save Will Lacy's life is a peculiarity of itself. There's plenty of folk have pulled Lacy from a scrape, but Two Noses always seems to be a few paces back of the crowd and always misses his chance."

Delacroix sat quietly for a few moments, then began to chuckle to himself.

Josh knew he was being toyed with but couldn't resist. "Are you going to let me in on the joke?"

"I was supposing whites had the same sense of honor as the Indians. I was just picturing Lacy dogging around after one of his saviors, waiting for his chance to repay a life with Two Noses after Lacy looking for his prospect to own up. That could get to be a lengthy procession." He brightened at the image.

"Can't you just see it?" He made a series of leapfrogging gestures with his hands and laughed again at the vision he had conjured.

"So . . . does Lacy need that much rescuing?"

"*Sacre bleu!* Yes!" he whooped. "Will may be the luckiest man alive when it comes to outlasting his own carelessness. I've seen him ride his horse and pack mules right over a frozen lake without even a whit of thought for breaking through. Some of the tribes call him Greasy Foot 'cause he can trip or stumble it seems even when standing still. He's been on his luck for so long he doesn't even give it a thought anymore. It seems like he thinks he is on some grand tour." He paused. "I guess that's what he may be doing."

Josh had been sampling at his cup and noticed it was empty again. He felt contented lying about the fireside with the experienced guide. Hearing the gossip about the intrepid Lacy made him feel he belonged. The scenery glowed in the blur of the liquor.

"Well? He's the scout for the DeKop train . . ." He could hear his words come out thickly and too loud.

"This season he is, and I hope it is his calling. He's been over this country before, both with Sublette and Fremont. If he was paying attention, he could be a fine scout," commented Delacroix, adding with a grumble, "I doubt he had his eyes open much, though."

Both gazed stuporously into the embers. Delacroix, not wishing to abandon his tale but not receiving a prompt from Josh, resumed. "You see those tattoos round his neck?"

Josh's head snapped up as he replied. "Yes. I've never seen anything like that afore. Is it Indian?"

"*Non, mon blanc bec.* Indians set great store by scars and such but don't go in for permanent decorations. They prefer paint so they can change their style as the mood strikes them. That design of Lacy's is from the Sandwich Islands. To hear him tell it, it's a reward for bedding all the womenfolk of one family and being adopted into the clan for his accomplishment."

"Notice how he talks," Delacroix tried to emulate his friend's dialect, "like he's trying to push some of his words out of his nose, sort of."

"I have heard that before. He sounds like he's from New England, though it's diluted some."

"That's where he's from in the original. The story I hear is he's from the East and shipped out on one of his family's whaling ships, 'sposedly to escape some gambling debts. He jumped ship in the Sandwich Islands and made his way to California some eight or nine years back. I've known him four, five seasons now. Every time I see him it's a wonder to me he's still alive."

"How long have you been in the mountains, Mr. Delacroix?" inquired Josh.

"If we are going to be traveling together, you'd best be calling me Claude. It's easier for the American mouth to say," offered the scout.

"To answer your question, I have been wandering across the plains for fifteen summers now. I used to trap some in the mountains, *Le Grand Tetons* mostly, but I've taken a liking to the flatter lands. I like the open sky. Or perhaps I have just grown more cautious. It is easier to see your enemies on the plains. Also, it is easier to hunt than to trap *castor*, and there aren't so many now as in days past."

Josh was curious. "How did you happen to leave the towns?" He paused and tried out the new familiarity. "Claude."

"It was *mon pere*. He was a trapper and *voyageur*. We lived in Detroit. I got the word he had been killed—frozen, and I was to come to collect his traps and furs. I traveled to a Crow village near a river they call the Milk.

"They had honored him by placing his remains on a burial platform. I remember thinking he would have liked that." He paused, reflectively. "So I returned to my *maman* and *soeurs*. But I left again to trap. I would return each spring to my family in Detroit. When St. Louis began to get most of the fur trade, I began going there. My family moved to Montreal, and I haven't seen them since."

Josh asked, "What is it like—?"

"Enough," Delacroix cut him off. "I speak too much of things that sadden me." He waved his hands as if concluding his tale and settled back against his saddle, shutting himself up in rumination.

Josh wanted to revive the evening's pleasure but could sense that his new friend no longer wanted to talk. He was afraid, from the guide's sudden withdrawal, that he had offended him. Quietly he sat, hoping his new friend would return. Presently, Josh reasoned their talk was over. Indeed, the scout seemed not to notice him at all. He wasn't sleeping, though his head was sunk to his chest. The glitter of the fire in his blank eyes belied the notion of stupor or sleep.

Josh reflected on his own circumstances, without family or any real roots. Would it be his lot to wander as a man lost in the wilderness, seeking something he couldn't define or even recognize? The thought of a life of pointless meandering terrified him.

With sights set on Oregon, he was only following his departed father's wanderlust. It was easier, and seemed more aligned with his nature, to just act. Compelling himself to consider motives and consequences, he became doubtful of himself. As he contemplated his motivations, he realized that now he, too, had withdrawn into thoughts much like Delacroix's. The right and easy thing to do was to retire from the fireside.

Dragging himself to his feet brought instant cognizance of the effects of the raw brandy. His first intimation was that he almost pitched headlong into the dying fire. The second was he found one boot partially in the fire. Mumbling some words of departure that received no reply, he lurched homeward. After a few unsteady steps, he remembered his weapons and returned to scoop them up.

It took only a few paces to comprehend how addled he had become. With each jarring step, the ground heaved up at him and the horizon bobbled and rocked. He began to doubt whether he could navigate his way to his bed. Comically, however, the importance of finding his bed seemed of little relevance. He had wandered down one of the ravines a short distance before realizing it was the wrong one. It seemed unoccupied so he looked for a convenient place to relieve himself. He blundered toward the embankment, leaned his head against a convenient tree trunk, and began to unbutton himself. The task became more urgent the more he fumbled. As he at last managed to retrieve himself, the stream came. He thought he had never felt such welcome relief. Finishing, he took two steps backward and collapsed onto his butt. Encouraged by no longer being responsible for walking, he pitched slowly backward to rest, looking at the stars through the branches of the stunted trees.

His peace lasted only a few moments until the sky began to blur and rotate and he discovered he was lying in the dirt, drunk as the village lush. The effort to rise to one elbow was too much. While thinking he should have just fallen asleep next to the scout's fire, his stomach flopped over. The evening's entertainment came up in a sour gush.

Now, the idea of attaining his own buffalo robe under his own wagon became supremely important. Almost as important was the need to escape the scene of his crime. Josh concluded it might be opportune to throw up one or two more times before he departed. No sooner had the thought crossed his mind than the task was accomplished.

He drew himself up as rigidly as he could, becoming aware of his wayward and seemingly independent limbs. By an act of supreme concentration, he locked them willfully to his bidding. It occurred it wouldn't do for someone to spy him out staggering through the camp, drunk with an armload of weapons. He was confident he could assume a normal gait if he was not interrupted. With a few false starts and guided by the familiar sound of Jubal's snoring, he found his own wagon. There, he fell gratefully to the ground, carelessly throwing a corner of blanket over his shoulders. He was instantly oblivious, waking only briefly to notice that it was raining lightly in his face. With an effort, he slid himself and his guns farther under the wagon and passed the rest of a drizzly evening unaware.

#

CHAPTER NINE

#

Elizabeth awoke to the sound of rain spattering lightly on the canvas bonnet. She was muffled to the throat in her mother's patchwork quilt. She pulled her arms free and laid them on top of the covers. In the chill of the dark morning they goose-fleshed over, and she delighted in the contrast of her cold arms with the rest of her, snug in her cocoon of warmth. A person could better appreciate warmth by realizing the proximity of the cold.

Lately, much of her life bore similar comparison. She had often heard people saying you didn't appreciate something until it was gone. The old saw, in respect to her parents, was painfully true. She thought now of how she had taken the sounds of their sleeping for granted when she would awake in the wagon. How she longed for the familiar concert of her mother's regular breathing and her father's dreamy mutterings and sputterings. He had never discussed the dreams that chased through his sleep and she now regretted never asking. Her eyes flooded and her throat choked up with grief. They were gone. She was alone and knew she had to put grieving away until she could recall them without the memories melting to affliction. She couldn't deal with despair for a companion.

Shuffling sideways on the bolsters, she soon lay on a spot chilled clammy by the night. She didn't miss the vacated warmth as much as she relished the idea of making a new one. Probably there were greater implications in this philosophy, but she soon tired of the exercise. Elizabeth's mind turned to more immediate and pressing matters.

The strength of sudden and intent resolve to continue to Oregon had surprised her as much as it had startled the other travelers. Elizabeth was honest enough to recognize a good part of her decision sprang solely from the opposition thrown in her face. Being told she wasn't competent enough to continue had fortified her, but she realized that situations would require the enlistment of aid from the others. All considered, that was the reason they were traveling as a group. Even discounting the threat of Indians, no single wagon could make such an expedition without help. The uncertainties of water and road and weather dictated so. To balance the ledger, she conceded she might well be drowned, or at best be wagonless without Josh.

Smiling to herself, she thought about the boy—no, man—who had now seemed to become both her defender and lover. The romance of the idea was appealing. To think that Josh Bonner, who had always lived in the shadow of his more glamorous older brother and who had struck her as a recalcitrant, almost painfully shy boy, had been thrust in the midst of his own loss as both her savior and the first to share her bed.

It seemed remarkable how quietly he had asserted himself and how quickly the other, even older men recognized his quality. Even the grizzled scout, who seemed to hold this collection of farmers and merchants in disdain, even as intruders into his domain, had taken a shine to Josh from amongst all the more mature men.

If she had to make a list of all her suitors, the likelihood of those to be the first to enjoy her intimacies, the name of Josh Bonner would never have appeared. Even naming him as a suitor would have been a vanity. He had treated her always like some mystery beyond his knowledge. The few times she had caught him watching her, it was never with the desire with which other men regarded her. Josh had always seemed to just observe her as though seeking some clue to be held for future reference.

Perhaps it was because they shared the same loss and the same set of circumstances that somehow affixed them together in a bond neither anticipated or sought. Regardless of the motive, comfort, lust, or some fashion of seedling love, she would accept him. It was apparent she was going to need his help to make her plan work, and his attentions were welcome.

Just, however, what were her plans? After arriving in Oregon, what was she going to do? Originally, she was just going with her parents to reestablish the same life in a new place. It wasn't necessary to set a goal or plan for a living. She possessed no remarkable or marketable skills or a trade. Never was she expected to. True, there was an offer of a position as teacher in the Clarks' proposed school. The idea of trying to educate a roomful of squalling, fighting children until spinsterhood arrived had no appeal. The vision made her shrivel up a little inside.

What was clear was she would have to find her father's cache of money. Amongst his clothes, there was a small pouch containing forty dollars in gold and some little more in "shinplasters." This, she supposed, and hoped, was their traveling purse. Such was a necessity for ferrymens' tariffs and to replenish stores at Forts Laramie and Bridger. Somewhere in the tumble of her accumulated inheritance was the money for a future with some degree of security. There must be a tidy sum even after paying for the team and equipage for the trek. Theirs had been a prosperous farm, and she prayed that upon finding the sale proceeds there might be enough to open a small café or hotel. The picture of endless kitchen drudgery or emptying chamberpots with an armful of some stranger's soiled bed linen dashed the vision from her mind. She strained for other possibilities.

However, first things first. She would have to use the stopover at the Hollow to search through everything. She would start at daylight. The rain was light enough to do it without much ruin. She hoped a wind would rise with the sun to dry things out.

The rain continued lightly into the dawn. The new sun quickly warmed through patches of ground mist and low, tattered clouds. A rainbow formed, but no wind came up to blow the rainbow away.

Josh stirred in his bedroll. The punishment for last evening's escapade was a head that felt like it had been tightened securely into one of his father's wooden clamps, then turned another squeeze to keep the clamp in place for the night. The taste of bile in Josh's throat was awful but not comparable to the raw scouring of his nose from vomit. Please, he thought, give me some coffee, then let me hide under the wagon for a couple of days.

A watery, reddened eye peered out from under his blanket. Even squinting, he spied a bustle of activity from the area of the DeKop encampment. People were scurrying about at the mouth of the hollow. There was no mistaking their intent. Dekop and his group were foregoing the stopover opportunity at Ash Hollow and pressing on.

Metzger, McCardle, and a few others from Josh's group huddled together and sipped at mugs of coffee. They watched the restive emigrants discharge their chores. Certainly, it wasn't from curiosity of how to pack up for a day's trudge. The routine was second nature by this point. Even these neophyte migrants sensed the regimen they were witness to was perilous in its determination. As conditioned to walking and trail mending as they had become, they knew that unrelenting travel took a grievous toll on feet and legs. Their own strains and aches and blisters could well testify. The farmers among them measured the wear on the teams. Harness sores and swollen hooves could easily progress from minor debility to serious scourges that could maroon them far from any relief.

Evidently Dekop, used to running these people like the machines in his factory, didn't recognize the frailties of flesh and muscle. Even he, nevertheless, must realize that the steel and iron of his machines could fatigue and fail. Even machines had to stop. While the engines of industry could halt momentarily for the replacement of a sprocket or bearing, it was soon able to rejoin the cabal of its monotonous task. Dekop couldn't, or wouldn't, acknowledge that flesh and spirit needed a respite, a healing time.

People to him were like replaceable cogs. A workman with crippled hands could be replaced from the stockpile of his town. No such resource lay ahead. Whether from insensitivity or grim determination, he should see or be told that the price may be too dear. Were his people so cowed they feared to speak up their own interests? Lacy, the guide, should speak of prudence. Perhaps his own fecklessness, described by Delacroix, blinded him to the peril of the driven road. The spectators watched their departure with concern, though not enough to intercede. They then dispersed to their own agendas.

Josh hauled himself from the tumble of his bed, stood on watery legs, and spied about for Jubal. He wanted breakfast. Jubilee was no where about but graciously had left the coffeepot perched on a flat rock at the edge of the fire ring. The trudge to the coffeepot touched off new miseries. Josh doubted whether breakfast was the priority he had at first thought. Coffee heavily sugared . . . that was a necessity. Grateful he had enough wit to hand to use a towel to handle the pot, he poured a mug. He could feel the heat of the metal through the cloth. Transferring the cloth and cradling the cup, he basked his damaged senses in its keen aroma. The first tentative sip, though scalding, was already sweetened, almost syrupy with age. Jubal must have been aware of last night's spectacle and, recognizing his condition from his own experience, anticipated his need. It was too bad he couldn't thank him for the consideration without revealing his debauch. Hopefully, Jubal wouldn't be in a teasing mood and would leave him to a solitary misery. It probably would be too much to hope for. He conjured up some disarming retorts as prospects.

Metzger strolled up to Josh's camp, interrupting his contemplation.

"A fine morning, wouldn't you agree?" he hailed loudly. Knowing the effect of his booming voice, he grinned as Josh winced and shrunk his head turtle-like into his shoulders. Josh growled slightly and looked up at the captain, with menace, he hoped. At the sight of two bloodshot eyes,

Metzger guffawed, "Get in a fight with John Barleycorn?" he inquired innocently.

"No, just a little poorly this mornin'. Mebbe a touch of the ague."

"Glad you could get the worst of the 'ague' out of your system last night lest you suffer the more today."

Josh could only look at the burly man, content in his role as plaguemaster. Josh feared his secret was open talk around camp. Silence would be his best bulwark against the assaults to come.

"Ease up now, boy! You can't tell me you weren't in your cups last night. In my lawman days, I've locked up pretty near every man in the county at one time or t'other. Should have turned the key on myself more than once. There's no shame in an occasional howl, though it does rankle some to see so young a squirt as yourself take to the bottle," Metzger said lightly but with a tone of reproach.

"Was I so obvious?" Josh asked. All pretense was useless.

"Obvious to me, experienced as I am in the stride of the besotted," he joked. "You might have kept your secret amongst just us two but for your croaking."

"My croaking?" His breastwork of deception was bested.

Metzger mimicked throwing up, flat tongue distended. His body heaved and jerked in gross pantomime of Josh's stomach's revolt. The captain fell back, rejoicing at the young man's crestfallen reaction to his mime.

Finally, the big man's merriment subsided enough for him to regain his composure. Restored, Metzger fished a cup from the mess equipment and poured himself a cup of coffee.

Josh hoped he wouldn't have to endure further lengthy ribbing in addition to the unbidden draining of his coffeepot.

"We're stopping over here for a day to rest up. You look like you can use it, but you ought to be tendin' to your gear, just checkin' it over." Metzger was still snickering but in moot sympathy, the tone of chastisement gone. He laughed. "You look worse beat then a rented mule. I hope you learned a lesson here."

"I believe I have, Captain. You won't have to worry none about me."

Metzger squinted at him as though the squint should emphasize the weight of his statement. "I don't believe I will. You will do all right."

Standing, the captain threw the dregs of his coffee at the ground. He flipped the mug offhandedly to Josh, who fumbled it into the dirt.

"No, don't expect I shall."

He pointed his chin over Josh's shoulder.

"Here comes your nigger with some game. You two take care now and be ready to roll come morning." He took his leave, nodding recognition to Jubal as he departed.

"Mornin', Jubal. Where did you get the hare?" inquired Josh.

"Oh, there's plenty of rabbit runs hereabouts. I set a snare and bagged some breakfast. Are you feelin' fit 'nuff for some?"

"I'm pretty certain not. Coffee will do me fine. Thanks for leaving me a warm pot."

Jubal smiled back warmly. "I figured you'd need some. Me, I need some rabbit roast. Sure makes a body tired eatin' sowbelly and johnnycake." He began to dress out the rabbit carcasses. Josh, feeling queasy at the sight of the gutting, crawled back to his bed.

Jubal spitted the skinned animals and began roasting in the coals. After a few minutes, he spoke.

"Josh, you still awake?"

"I am, but not by choice."

"I run into that Injun, Two Noses, while I was out this mornin'. He spooked me some, I don't mind sayin'."

"How's that?"

"Well, I was a-settin', tending my snare, when I looked up and there he be, not twenty paces away, jist a-watchin'. I thought I was being close—y'know, so's not to spook the rabbits, and there he was. I never heard him come up on me."

Josh came up on one elbow. Talk of the strange red man had piqued his interests even through his hangover. "So what happened?"

"Damn nuthin'. We jist stood there a-lookin' each other over like a pair of tomcats. I never seen a wild Injun up close. I couldn't talk his talk and don't know any of the sign words. I didn't 'spect he could talk like

119

regular folks. So we just looked one another over. I didn't know what else to do."

"He probably had never seen a wild black man afore neither, Jubal. I reckon you gave him quite a start your own self," Josh speculated.

Jubal rose to the banter. "Lordy, Josh! I ain't no wild African like you seen in the circus. I'm jist Jubilee, a regular darkie."

"How would he know the difference, Jubilee? There's no circus come out here to educate the Indians. Did you see Lacy or Delacroix while you were out?" inquired Josh. He wondered if the two scouts were as ruined as he.

"Saw Mr. Lacy, but not up close. He was sittin' his horse watchin' them Ohio folks pack up."

He held out the roasting spit. "You shore you don't want some of this hare?"

Elizabeth had already searched through the trunk of her parents' clothes but had not found the money cache. Trying to search systematically was frustrating in the confines of the crowded wagon. It would have been easier, of course, to take the canvassed articles outside, but she didn't wish to draw attention to her endeavors. Most of the people in the train were strangers, and she didn't feel like parrying their inquiries or rebuking offers of help from the curious. It was better to shuffle about in the privacy of the wagon, even if the work was much more trying.

Initially, she had looked in what she felt to be the most obvious places and, finding nothing, went to the less accessible. By the time she had explored and shunted half of the contents about, she began to feel anxious about her efficiency. She began to feel she had overlooked something and twice found herself rummaging about in boxes examined earlier before realizing the repetition.

Frustration set in, then the fear that there was no secret stash or that it had been lost somehow, perhaps in the river accident. Pausing with an armload of clothes, she set them down, deciding she had best collect her senses before pawing around willy-nilly in desperation. Needlessly adding to the anxiety was the repeated discovery of some trinket or memento of a life now past. Uncontrollable weeping drove home to her the solitude and peril of her circumstance.

Casting her eyes about, it appeared her organized examination was taking on the appearance of pillage. What had begun as a disciplined inquiry had turned into a scattering of heaped boxes and ransacked trunks. She'd been attempting to keep items she just couldn't part with. Not for their intrinsic value but for their essential attachment, she culled out what could be disposed of. As she sat, forlorn, in the midst of the jumble, Reverend and Mrs. Clark appeared at the tailboard. The diminutive missus could only be seen from the nose up while her formidable husband loomed behind her.

"My dear, you've made quite a mess of things," remarked the scant woman. She appeared even more frail in the severe gingham frock she wore. "Have you lost something?"

"No," replied Elizabeth. "There may come a time when I will have to lighten the burden, and I am making certain I don't throw away some family keepsake whose comfort I might regret being without."

"That's a nice thought. Memories of home and family can be important in a new place. I've kept some foolish little things of my first husband's to keep his memory alive."

"Oh, I didn't know you had been married before."

"My first husband, Reverend Witcher, died last fall from infected blood. He'd hit his foot with the axe while chopping firewood. The Lord sent me Reverend Clark here soon afterward. He was passing through and came to comfort me in my loss. He stayed on and now we carry the Good Work to the new lands," Mrs. Clark explained, running out of breath.

Reverend Clark continued, imploring heaven with his upturned eyes. "It appears our paths were meant to be as one. Regretfully, it took a tragedy for us to meet. The Lord's ways are indeed beyond our poor reckonings."

Elizabeth reflected to herself it seemed the Lord's way was often most unnecessarily cruel. Even trying to explain their vagaries could turn the most devout from their faith. The temptation to speak aloud was almost irresistible.

"His will be done," she commented lamely.

"His will be done," the Clarks proclaimed together, then looked at each other, pleased by their common expression.

"We know not what you may hold dear, but perhaps we could assist you in your sortings," offered the Reverend.

"Thank you for your kindness, both of you. I don't rightly know what I plan to keep until I lay my hand upon it," rejoined Elizabeth.

"This may take most of the day. We will retake our journey in the morning. Perhaps I could offer to look over your stock and wagon for you. I am handy with a wagon and could maybe spot a weakness that bears attention."

Plainly they were determined to find something they could do for her and Elizabeth knew her gear needed some attention. She acquiesced, figuring his help outside would give her more searching time inside.

"You have been so kind to me already. I hate to impose myself on you any more than I have. I will confess, though, I haven't been able to look after the animals properly."

"Say no more, girl. I shall minister to your team as sinners come to salvation." The Reverend grinned, his teeth white in the midst of his dark beard.

Elizabeth cringed at his smile. Kind as he was, his grin lent an air of piratical ferocity to his countenance. No doubt his smile had chilled many a sinner into seeking grace.

As the pair departed to tend to her mules, Elizabeth undertook to check through her father's toolkit before they returned. The reverend might have need of tools and, preacher or not, she had better check there. If the money was there, she smiled to herself, there was no sense in laying temptation before a man of God.

The chest revealed nothing more than the expected wrenches and hammers along with an assortment of well-worn tools she couldn't begin to fathom their use. The homely assortment of mundane implements drove home her dependence upon others.

These unfamiliar implements would probably be needed somewhere before the trail ended. More to the point, someone who knew how to use them would be needed, too. Unbidden, she thought of Josh and the tool he possessed. She intended to make use of that tool when the opportunities arose. She determined she must put such wicked thoughts away.

Back inside, she set herself to thinking as her father might. It would be unlike him to leave all his small fortune in a place where he could not check readily on its security. Was there any part of the wagon he paid particular attention to? She racked her memory and tried to picture their journey before the epidemic struck down her family.

Probing under the improvised bed and in the more handy cases and drawers had been a waste of time. Father would have thought these the most obvious. Her mental search turned to the more obscure but accessible places. He hadn't paid an inordinate amount of attention to the wagon's supplies. There was a gutta-percha box which held his powder, ball, molds, and cleaning equipment. While that would appear secure, he had not opened it to her recollection. No, not there.

Pensively, she considered other possibilities. It didn't seem he would employ somewhere on the outside of the wagon for a cache. Someone would surely spy him checking and discern the reason. It could easily be stolen. Perhaps it had been stashed outside and the thief had already struck.

She remembered then that her father would help her mother with some of the meal preparations on trail. He would gather wood, stoke the fire, and bring her the implements she requested. Finding nothing amongst the pans, she looked with no result among the spices and other utensils. Straining her memory, she recalled him dusting off his hands after retrieving a jar of preserves or crock of butter. She remembered how he would wipe the flour that had spilled from the barrel of the staves and the wagon body, this although the wagon wore a solid film of road dust.

She thought now she knew the reason why. If he had secreted his money belt, along with the breakables, in the flour barrel, this could explain the constant cleaning. Anyone disturbing the belt in its couch of white flour would raise a telltale cloud that would reveal the larceny. It was so simple. He would have been able to check on the safekeeping every day, and his slapdash vault had a built-in burglar warning. Perhaps it was time to make some biscuits for the days ahead.

Prying off the wooden top with its India rubber lid liner, she rummaged her arm in up to the elbow and swam about with her hand. Finding the expected canning and jelly jars safe in their nest of flour, protected from the jolting of the rough road, she descended into the keg. Finding nothing untoward, her rifling became more frenzied. The rim of the barrel was chafing her armpit painfully when the tips of her fingers brushed against something yielding. Standing on her toe tips, she stretched her fingers farther and brought the object to grasp. It was leathery and bulky and difficult to bring up through the layers of flour and containers. Finally, in a spray of dust, it came loose.

She staggered back from the wagon with her prize. She quietly laughed, not only with the satisfaction of discovery and relief but with amusement at her late father's acumen. The front of her smock was sprinkled with flour from neck to hem. A circle of white lay at her feet and the side of the wagon wore a fine white patina. No one could get to the cache without prominently announcing their visit. She picked up the hem of her dress and plopped the money belt into the hammock she had made. Slipping over the wagon board, she began feeling already like a covetous miser.

She had never before seen a money belt but she liked the look and feel of it. Its heft implied the wealth within. The belt was of leather with canvas pouches sewn into its face. Each of the pouches had a flap wrapped about the belt and bound the poke into a compact, secure reserve.

Opening one of the pockets, she drizzled into her palm thirty or so gold eagles, ten-dollar pieces with the profile of Liberty engraved on one side and a warlike eagle on the obverse. Another pocket spilled out copper Spanish *reals* and several large silver British crown pieces with a picture of a mounted man fighting a dragon. There were also some large irregular gold coins so worn as to be unrecognizable. A fourth pouch contained a fold of banknotes, some crisply new and other tattered with their passage through many hands. There was over five hundred dollars in paper bills, large and ornately engraved to lend authority to their statement of worth. Mostly they had been issued by the Bank of New York and the City Bank of New Orleans. While impressive and supposedly guaranteed to be of full value, the paper money did not have the complete trust of the people on the edges of the country. They relied on gold, silver, or copper coins for cash transactions. More heavily, they depended upon crops or livestock for tender. These could be readily bartered and their general value was recognized.

Elizabeth wondered if the paper notes had any value at all in the wilds of the Indian territories. She supposed they would be recognized as tender in the new settlements, where trade goods still remained scarce as a means of commerce.

Five hundred dollars in various denominations made a hefty roll of both crisp new and tattered bills. These she folded and replaced back in the poke. Exploring further, she found more of the little sacks filled with various denominations of silver coins—dollars, half, and quarter dollars. There was also a double handful of dimes and half dimes. She poured the small silver coins through her hands, enjoying the sound and feel of them as they cascaded, splashing into her lap. She turned her attentions to the worn gold coins. None even appeared truly round, and the etched figures they bore were so worn only the shadow of a portrait or seal remained. These appeared to be of great age and were probably gold doubloons or Spanish gold *reals*. These old Spanish coins, hoarded over the years, had probably made their way up the river with the traders and gamblers. Here was a gold French Napoleon that probably reached American shores after landing in New Orleans. There were likely minted silver Mexican *de platas* mixed in amongst the silver coins. She hadn't counted or even looked at the silver as yet. It was the gold, especially the newly minted U.S. eagles gleaming in sharp relief with a dull glow, that mesmerized her. When she held them stacked in her fist, the weight and power of them seemed to carry up her arm. Delighted, she peered at the various images visible between her clutched hands. She had never had more than a half eagle of her own, and she could understand the avarice gold inspired in men. Women, too, she realized.

Lying back on her rough couch, she let the coins drop singly to the bare skin of her throat, cold at first, then warming to her skin. She arranged them into a necklace and dreamed of such extravagant luxuries.

A sound outside changed the dream of luxury to visions of suspicion. While almost certain the sound was incidental, or even imagined, a more basic instinct took over, convincing her she was being spied upon—plotted against. She raked up the empress's necklace, her misgivings stirring a need for rapid concealment. With stifled breath, she listened for further sign of the intruder. Nothing more than the sighing of the wind and the everyday clatter of distant neighbors.

The botheration passed on amongst the familiar sounds. She understood she must replace the belt in its hiding place. Leaving it accessible would be too much temptation. If it were within reach she would constantly need to verify its safekeeping. Elizabeth began replacing the coins in their leather homes, not bothering with more than a rough tally that told her she had near to two thousand dollars and credibly more. Certainly, a satisfactory amount with which to start a life anew.

Josh was hunkered down on his bedroll, sipping at coffee and choking down a stale leftover biscuit. His hangover, thanks to the resiliency of the young, was fast diminishing, leaving only a few sand-filled cobwebs in his head. Through a film of dusty motes, he was watching the tail of the DeKop party wend its way out of the Hollow. The Dutchman's large dray

wagons lead the way, followed like a brood of chicks by the remainder of
the expedition. Reflecting, it seemed foolish to have the large wagons,
with their wider track, in the fore. They disturbed the trail and made the
passage much more difficult. He didn't think it wise for DeKop to
continually assert his position. He noted his gratitude for their more
democratic arrangement, bothersome as it had proved so far.

As the last DeKop wagon trailed dustily away, a solitary team and
wagon bore into the gully from the west. Emerging out of the shadows of
the stunted trees was the freight wagon of the trader, Gates. Perched on the
wagon board were the same two scruffy teamsters, followed by Jerome
Gates on the chestnut mare. They described a wide arc about the just
abandoned site. Gates rode ahead, pointing to articles left behind. The
wagon halted and the two teamsters descended and began to scavenge the
leavings.

As Josh watched the salvage operation, an idea came to him and he
hailed to Gates. His attention arrested, the trader gave instructions,
unheard by Josh, to his helpers and trotted over the where the young man
waited.

"A fine morning to you, laddie," the trader beamed, a merchant gleam
in his eyes. Perhaps he detected a chance at commerce.

"And mornin' to you, too, Mr. Gates. Your wagon seems more laden
than last I saw of it. Have the findings been good?"

"Aye, they've not been bad at all. I swear I get more enjoyment from
picking about than I get from the sale of the goods themselves. Maybe the
fun is being out of the store at home. I suspect, though, that there be a
touch of pirate in my woodpile that enjoys the treasure hunt," Gates
laughed.

"The pirate of the plains," Josh ventured.

"That has a nice ring to it. I doubt, however, I'll be adding that
honorific to my window signs in Council Bluffs." Laughing, the merchant
seemed amused by the image.

In light of his own concerns Josh felt compelled to ask him about the
danger from Indians.

"Ain't you a-scared of the Indians? The one's we've seen seem a
world different than I'm accustomed to. Wilder, I mean."

"The wester, the wilder, I hold. As you press on farther into the territories, the more rascally they become. Out here, they see us as the intruders and levy a heavier toll for the passage."

"How so?"

Jerome Bates considered his point. "As I see it, as the Indian goes east he becomes more beggarish, more in awe of the whites and their machinations. As you move west, the beggar becomes a thief, then he becomes master and demands his toll."

"I seldom go past the Chimney, and when the Indians seem riled, I turn back here from the Hollow. Much farther on and you get into the Cheyenne lands, and I've no desire to meet up with Cheyenne braves with but Hand and Arlo to watch my backside." He thumbed back at his companions.

"Are they that savage?" asked Josh. The Sioux at the Platte crossing seemed to Josh as wild a red man as he ever wished to encounter.

Dismay must have been apparent on his face, for the buoyant expression of the merchant pirate mellowed to a more concerned air.

"Lad, I don't want to spin you tales of butchery. Your road is difficult as is. What I meant is, the more natural the Red Man is, the more unpredictable he becomes. You can't ever tell what may be a mortal offense to him while seeming as nothing to yourself. Me, I've met few of the true aborigine, and those have kept me walking on eggshells. My feeling is to give them what they want and to see them on their way, quick as can be."

Josh explored. "Have you had any troubles?"

Gates snorted. "Not enough to keep me to home. I'm always ready with some small gift, and usually I'll leave them an opportunity to steal something rather than have to beg for it. I guess any man would rather steal something than have to ask alms." He wore a self-satisfied look, as though he had just imparted some wise insight into the root nature of mankind.

"Will you be traveling as far as Chimney Rock this season, Mr. Gates?"

The trader came out of his reflections and smiled. "No, this trip I'll be turning back home after your party leaves." Gates watched Josh's face, anticipating his crestfallen reaction. He got what he was looking for.

He smiled broadly, pushing his beard up his cheeks with the effort. "It's not what you're thinking, son. There's no more than the usual rumors with the Indians. It's just I expect to have a full load with what I pick up from your people. That's my reason."

Josh felt almost re-inflated at the explanation. He turned now to his original reason for hailing the pirate of the plains. "D'you 'spose, if I paid you, you could carry a letter back to town?" He realized as he spoke "back to town," it sounded like he was implying that town was just a jaunt away rather than three weeks' travail.

"Now, that's a service I've done before. We ought to be able to do some trade along those lines. For just fifty cents, I'll see your letters stamped and put safe on a downriver packet. I'll carry yours for free if you'll collect the others in camp. And if you'll offer me a cup of coffee, I've something to liven it up."

Josh was already sloshing full of coffee but was willing to brew a fresh pot to maintain the hospitality and to get his mail done. He offered, "I'd be pleased to brew some up fresh. That one's just dregs from this mornin'."

"You start it and I'll watch it brew while you tell your neighbors of my proposal as courier. Run on back when you're done."

After grinding and starting the coffee, Josh set off on his errand while Gates went back to the scavenging site. Josh received an enthusiastic reception to the trader's scheme. He was himself eager to write to his brother and to his aunt and uncle. Upon his return, he found Gates settled comfortably on the tailboard of Josh's wagon. This seemed like an improper familiarity with his property, but he chose not to make any comment.

"Were you well received?"

"I 'spect so! You should have twenty or thirty letters to post by the afternoon."

The trader fished a worn brass watch from his pocket and consulted it.

"It's nigh on two o'clock now. But never mind. I'll be pitching for the night anyway. Come have a cup. You deserve a treat for your enterprise—after all, it's your own grounds."

Josh, more from civility than want, as his nerves were already jangling, accepted. Gates retrieved both cups and the pot. He poured, then set the enamelware mugs on the tailgate.

"I promised a treat and we shall have it." He revealed a small tin and punctured the rim twice with the point of his sheath knife. "This is something new—tinned cream, sweetened, too." He lifted it over his head and indicated with the point a small spot on the tin's bottom. "They put it hot into the tin, then seal the bottom with a dollop of lead. I sell this by the case in my store. Might even have sold this one."

Gates poured a healthy measure into both cups. Stirring with the knife changed the black brew to a golden ocher. A sweet aroma rose to bathe Josh's nostrils. Taking the proffered cup, he inhaled deeply of the fragrant, rich smell. He sipped and delighted at the sumptuous concoction.

"Oh, but that's lightning good," he spoke in praise. "The only treat we've been able to have is some lemonade, and the juice for that won't last much longer."

"You keep the rest of the can. You'll have to use it up right fast. Otherwise, it will spoil just like regular cream." Gate's face glowed beatifically with the simple pleasure he had wrought. The pleasure in Josh's expression was plainly obvious.

"Wait till Jubal, my hired man, gets a taste of this. It'll be like Christmas." His enthusiasm for the new drink bubbled up. He felt like drinking another whole pot.

"Well, young man, I'll be parked over under the shade of those trees, such as they are. You collect the mail, and I'll reward you with another tin for your industry. I'm off now. Good luck and Godspeed."

The afternoon shadows were long on the dusty ground before Jubal returned. Josh had written his letter to Ned. He had struggled with the words, wanting to tell of his feelings but not being able to pen the right phrases. He wanted to tell of the joy he felt at being in his own command but could not express the grief he felt at the circumstances that provided his independence. Electing to stick to plain fact, he simply wrote what had happened and what his intentions were.

Impulsively, Josh had poured the balance of the tin directly into the remaining brew and kept it warm in the embers. He watched from his eye's corner as Jubal poured out a cup, then stopped in mid-pour to dart a suspicious glance at his companion. Josh broke up in gleeful laughter.

"What you done to my good coffee? It looks like I ought to use a fork in it," Jubilee cried in mock outrage.

"Taste it! Taste it! The trader gave me some tinned cream for it. You never tasted the like."

Jubal peered over the rim at Josh, ready for some prank, but enticed by the sweet fragrance, he took a tentative sip. The look of suspicion dissolved into one of delectation that brought more raucous crowing from Josh.

"Lordy, that's good. I swear I'm spiled already and won't be able to drink coffee no other way," Jubilee proclaimed.

"I'm afraid you'll have to." Josh managed to speak through his mirth. "We'll have but one tin to last us through to Oregon. I thought we'd save it until we make the Pacific slope."

"Then I think we'd best pack up and get movin,' pass them Ohio folk right up," suggested Jubal, joining in the spirit.

"Say, Jubal, you've been gone all day. Where have you been?"

He explained. "I seen how you come home t'other night. Figured as I been in the cups a time or two m'self, you'd probably not want much for company. I been tendin' to the critters, checked 'em all out fine, brushed and curried 'em till they shone. They all look fit 'nuff to be in a parade."

"That took you all day?" Josh inquired.

"'Course not. I like to be off by m'self some, so's I went up on the bluffs for a looksee. It was nicer knowin' I wouldn't run into that Two Noses feller. Is that his real name?"

"Don't know for sure. It could be, but I reckon that's what Lacy took to callin' him and it just got stuck to him."

The pair sat in silence for some time before Josh announced he was gong to retrieve the mail and departed.

Without exception, each of the emigrant families had penned letters to loved ones and associates in the East. Many remarked at the high tariff but, recognizing a seller's market, parted with the charge. Josh's pockets sagged at the weight of the coins he had collected along with a hefty bundle of correspondence. He plied his way up and down the winding shallow gullies and spent some few minutes with new friends making idle conversation of the road and weather. Of course, he tarried overlong at

Elizabeth's and quickly, during the course of small talk, led the conversation toward a more personal and intimate turn. When their eyes met, even more was exchanged. Only with difficulty could he refrain from hurling his embrace at her. He left, not only with her letter but with an invitation to return after the fall of full dark. His assurance that he would indeed fairly jumped from his mouth. He made his way scudding along like the clouds his head was in.

His stop at the Binghams' resulted in a bundle of half a dozen bulky packets to be bound over for delivery.

"Dr. Bingham, you must have spent the whole afternoon writing," Josh said in amazement.

"Not so, Josh. I have been keeping a journal of our crossing and had already made some copies of parts to send home. Dear me, I guess it's not home anymore. We seem to have no home at present. In any event, I had transcribed some anecdotes and medical notations for the attention of family and colleagues. I had been waiting to send them when we arrived at the fort. Do you think they will be safe with Gates?"

The surgeon seemed flustered about entrusting his work with the roving merchant. Josh, flustered himself with talk of "transcribing" and "anecdotes," tried to reassure him. "Mr. Gates seems square enough. I feel better with his word than leaving them at the fort." Josh explained, "What I mean is, later they might be sent on with some traveler or trapper who can't even read. I think a man who can read and write would better know the value of our mail—not just seein' them as bundles of paper."

Bingham quickly grasped the reasoning. "I hadn't looked at that aspect. It makes sense. I'd hate to think of my letters being used to wipe some illiterate hunter's behind." He laughed at the thought.

"Dr. Bingham, I was pretty mopey while my folks were sick, and—well, after. I'm not sure I thanked you for your help the way I ought, and I know I haven't paid you for your time."

"Now, son, our time is all the same on this trip. It's the skills we bring that set our value. I may purport to be a healer and surgeon, but your skills with hammer and saw have as much worth to our enterprise, and probably more by the end to it. Each of us, I'm certain, will give as good as he gets."

"That's kindly to say, sir. I don't for a minute believe I'm equal to a doctor. I hope I'll be able to come to your aid."

"Truthfully, Josh, I hope not. Nor do I hope you will have need of my skills. I'm saying my prayers we all come through this in good stead," the doctor accorded, lifting his face symbolically, if not piously, heavenward.

Josh protested, "At least let me pay you for the medicine."

"With what, Josh? Should I take your dollar over the next rise and buy new suspenders from the Lakota?" He snapped his own for emphasis. "You keep your money for when you can spend it."

Josh was satisfied, but to himself, he vowed to help the doctor and his wife as best he could. "Say, Doc, I don't see your missus about. I'd like to pay my respects to her as well. She's not feelin' poorly, is she?"

"I sent her off when I saw you coming. She and some of the other women have worked themselves up over you and that Hampton girl being alone together overnight. Their Baptist minds have drummed that all up and are painting you two as fornicators without any more proof than their little minds require. I sent her off rather than chance her tongue getting the better of her manners. I expect she and some of the other women are tittering up a scandal as we speak."

Josh was appreciative that the doctor had prudently packed his wife off. He wasn't altogether sure that thanking the doctor would imply his guilt. He settled on a simple acknowledgement.

"That sounds like a good way to keep the peace." It sounded lame even as he spoke it.

"Son, I've no means to tell anyone their business, especially on a jaunt like this. If we can't cooperate, we'll be busted up certain. I'm just saying this matter won't just fade away. The more you see of the girl, the more likely it will come to a head. All I want to say is you two ought to watch your goings-on."

"I'll mind your words, sir. Thank you. We don't mean to stir up any trouble." Josh was abashed. Had they somehow been discovered? He excused himself and left to complete his collection rounds.

While he roamed from wagon to wagon, he felt everyone was judging him. Every man seemed to have a leer in his eyes, as though sharing his secret. Every woman seemed to stare through him accusingly. As much as he told himself it was just his own guilty imaginings, he couldn't shake the feeling. He had half talked himself out of visiting Elizabeth when he commenced arguing with himself it was none of their never mind. Soon,

132

he started to become resentful of the looks he imagined directed at him. By the time he had delivered his bundle and the tariffs to Gates, he was resolved to keep his evening assignation.

The company had retired. Only the couple of sentries who stared into the night were ostensibly awake as Josh found himself hoarsely whispering Elizabeth's name at her wagon tailboard. Her head and shoulders poked out of the tarp.

"Give me your hand and step smartly. If you keep serenading me, we'll draw an audience."

Josh disdained the offer and used both arms to boost himself up. He felt her arm tug at his belt to pull him up over the gate.

Elizabeth, on all fours, had backed up to give him landing room. As Josh looked up, he could see both of her breasts swinging free within the scooped neck of her cotton shift. Thin darkness or no, their soft shapes were clearly outlined against the darker background. He rolled to his back and gently pulled her head down to his, turning his head to better receive her kiss.

The kiss was ravenous. Like starved animals, they played their lips and mouths together. Before it was over, Josh had managed to pry his boots off his feet with his toes. They clunked loudly, too loudly, he thought, to the floorboards. Elizabeth withdrew from his embrace and raised herself up to her knees. Josh scrambled up after her and they fell together. She slid both hands down his rump and ground him into her. He, in turn, embraced her with one arm while his other caressed her breast through the threadbare cloth. He stroked the top slope and gently squeezed the nipple as it grew hard under his dandling. All the while, they kissed. From gentle wet pecking that progressed to the sucking of one another's lips into the mouth for exploration to delirious devouring of each other. Their breaths burned on their cheeks like the voice of a furnace. Josh brought his hands up to her shoulders and slipped the yoke down in an attempt to drag down her shift.

"No, Josh, you'll tear it." She crossed her arms below her hips and rocked on each knee back and forth to free the cloth under her. Looking at him in the dim light, her eyes glittered, not only with passion but also with an expression that she knew she was about to reveal to him a masterpiece. She lifted her arms over her head and shook her nakedness free before him.

Josh cursed the night. There was not even the added light of a single candle, but the hints of shape and curve and pale flesh were still overwhelming. He seemed to shiver from deep within and feared that he would unload himself unwillingly. Not being able to bear the thought of holding her with anything less than his own skin, he fairly leapt out of his shirt as Elizabeth fumbled with his belt and the buttons of his fly, all the while pressing against his turgid member with the heel of her hand.

Moments later, they were both feverishly naked and within the embrace of the other. They fell entwined on the makeshift bed as Josh rolled over to mount her.

"Josh, we can't! She put her hand on his hip and kept him at her side. Her fingers slid lightly down his shaft and firmly pinched the tip to stifle his ardor. "We'll make too much noise if we do it now."

"Don't you want to?" He almost shriveled at the rebuke.

"Oh God! Yes! I want you inside me again and again. We just can't now. I couldn't keep quiet. Nor you."

Taking his hand in hers, she placed it between her thighs. She raised her rear to adjust herself to his touch. Gently, she held her hand over his, cupping him tenderly against her vulva. As he began to sense her rhythm, she drew her fingers up to her mouth and replaced them wet between his fingers, exploring. Placing the tip of one finger against the back of his, she wiggled her bottom until she felt herself part so his finger, and hers, slipped within. Her hand captured another of his fingers and drew it to her dampness.

"Just touch me like that." She lifted her mouth to his and kissed him, immersed in her own selfish pleasure. He lay on his side next to her. Elizabeth draped one leg over his hips. The other lay slack, outturned, as she pulsed and rotated herself against his caress.

"Taste of me," she said. She took his hand and withdrew it from her swollen center and brought it to his mouth. He inhaled and tasted her slick musk, tentatively, then rising to a keen fervor. He kissed each of her fingers, replaced his hand within her, and resumed his task.

Elizabeth began to rock against his hand with a faster, more insistent rhythm. Her head lolled back and forth. Her breathing became shallow and rapid, almost a pant. She began to lightly gasp, then to whimper in a wordless quiet abandon. Lifting her mouth to his, they kissed wantonly.

As their mouths met, she came over the top and moaned into his kiss, his mouth covering hers so he could absorb her song into him. The seconds of her pleasure drew out, then gradually subsided. She took his hand away from her, the hand that moments before had brought her to ecstasy. Now she was too tender for human touch.

He could feel the flush of her body radiating him in the cool night. She breathed into his ear.

"And now, darling . . . let me do you."

Taking her fingertips, she traced the length of him from tip to root. Slowly, almost agonizingly, she encircled him and stroked him, just touching. His accumulation of passion had a mind of its own. Beyond his restraint and under her tender manipulation, he felt the irreversible spasm begin. His toes curled; his back arched. In the grip of his primal throes, he jetted himself into her fondling, across her fingers and onto her forearms.

Josh had choked back his own cries. When he opened his eyes, he saw he was gazing at Elizabeth, looking deeply back into his eyes. She seemed at peace and back in control. She dropped and kissed him, slowly resting her mouth against his as a substitute for the denied afterglow. Soon, she rose, took a cloth, and cleaned him up. In the shadows, he thought she had tasted of him too.

They dozed, but in the darkest part of the night she woke him and told him to dress and go to his own bed.

#
CHAPTER TEN
#

June 8, 1848

Dear Ned,

I am sending this back with a trader from Council Bluffs. I hope he sends it on. He seems like a reliable fellow, but how can you really tell? He charged everyone save me fifty cents for the mailing. That is because I collected from the camp.

I have much to tell of the journey, but first there is bad news to tell you. There was cholera after Fort Kearney and many people were afflicted, Ma and Pa among them, and despite all that could be done, they passed on. It was all so fast. They was fine one day, and the next they was gone. We buried them near a fine creek with trees on the bank. It was a very pretty and peaceful spot. The stream fed into the Vermilion River and was as fine a resting spot as any at home. I miss them terribly.

I wrote the sad news to Aunt Martha and Uncle Virgil, so maybe you heard already. If not, I am sorry to tell, but best you hear it from family. Elizabeth Hampton lost her folks and brother at the same time, and we have kind of hooked on together. They tried to send her back, but you know how fiery she gets when her skirt is tugged.

We are pushing on to Oregon, and I don't know when I will see you again so I hope you are doing well. They say the cholera come from up the Mississippi on the steamers, so maybe you ought to get a berth on a steamer to Mexico or somewhere else. Right now, we are in a place called Ash Hollow, which is just past the south fork of the Platte River. It is a fine place with good water nearby and many wildflowers and bushes of grapes and chokecherries. It is hard to leave after so many days of just grass and no trees. The captain of the train used to be a sheriff in Missouri to hear him tell. I think he might have been a constable or some such as he seems in over his head as captain here. There is a Frenchy name of Delacroix who is the guide, and he is a trapper and knows the way. Jubal is fine and always a help, like usual, though it feels peculiar being his boss. We are better than half to Fort Laramie and expect to see soon Chimney Rock like you may have seen in the Biddle Guidebook.

Your brother,

Josh

Dear Aunt and Uncle,

As I wrote earlier, I am continuing on alone. I miss my family something awful, but my grieving will make no difference. I am just now understanding how alone I am, though I treasure the thoughts of all of you at home.

I am well and in capable hands. We are traveling always west and are almost to Fort Laramie. There has been no Indian trouble, but we have met some Sioux. You shouldn't worry about me. I can take care of myself and will set up a business when I get to Oregon.

Your loving niece,

Elizabeth

Delacroix stood by his horse. One hand idly coiled a finger in and out of the mane. The other palmed the reins while the horse drank from a meager slough. He had found the slough two or three miles, he guessed, ahead of the train and had just descended from a knoll to refresh his horse before going on. He was anxious to move on but knew better than to overtax his mount. What prompted his excitement at going on was something he had spied from the top of the hill. A short distance away was what could be nothing else but buffalo wallows.

No animal but buffalo could cause the circular dusty depressions and the mangled grass. He anticipated what he would find upon his arrival and wanted badly to see how fresh the signs were. The sight or even the sign of the season's first bison was a thrill he never tired of. Fondly, he recalled his first visions of the mighty herds beginning their summer migration, and the first sighting each spring never failed to thrill him anew. Since he had started piloting, it was even more exciting to see the astonished faces of the pilgrims witnessing the shaggy, lumbering beasts for the first time. Even though he knew there would be a mad rush to see who could kill the first one, he still looked forward to the experience. Hell, he was anxious to draw down on one himself.

After he had explored the wallow, he would ride up to the next hillock. He seemed to recall the rise as the first from which you could spy the summit of Chimney Rock, which would be less than thirty miles ahead. What he was really hoping to see was perhaps a few stray dark smudges against the yellow-green background that would be one of the magnificent creatures. Even if he did see buffalo, he knew he must return to the train and lead them to the night's bivouac. They had been traveling well for the two days since leaving Ash Hollow, averaging close to fifteen miles in a day. The rest-over had been a good plan, allowing repairs and a chance for the tender hooves of the animals to harden up some in order to tough out the sandy terrain. If they continued to do well, he felt he could talk Metzger into an extended stay at the fort.

As well as they were doing, the DeKop group was making a race of it and were nowhere in sight. He had expected to overtake the heavily laden group but as yet had only seen the discards and the wide tracks of their freight wagons.

Leland Metzger was glad to be on the move again. People on the move were too busy to think up things to complain about and bicker over, and that suited his style just fine. The rest-up at Ash Hollow had been a good one, albeit one to which he and many others had been opposed to. The tragedy of the Donner party two years earlier was still fresh enough in people's minds to make them want to keep plugging away. The thought of being trapped in the snow was a hard pill to swallow in mid-June on this windswept prairie. He could see the sense in the rest stop now, what with the easier traveling. He didn't feel like he had just caved in to the scout's insistence of a few days' layover at the Hollow. The draft animals benefited from the stop, and he had to concede he was right about their feet. He'd noticed how their feet had become callused—if that were the right word for a mule or ox's foot. All had taken the time to tighten bolts, shim gaps in shrunken wood, and soak the wagon wheels so they swelled up tight on the iron tires. He sure noticed how much more tight and quiet his wagon rolled. It was peculiar how the little squeaks and rattles had appeared undetected and were now recognized only by their absence. The team was more tractable, too. Metzger told himself he must listen more to the Frenchy, though it rankled some. After all, he was the captain; it seemed to undermine his authority somehow.

All in all, it had been a fairly easy passage to this point. The road was well marked and he had traveled on worse traces in Missouri. If only someone had thought to include a few taverns where a body might take a dram or two.

Really, the only thing he regretted was hooking up with the Illinois people; safety in numbers and all. Their cholera had threatened to break them up, but the prospect of leaving friends and traveling in two or three small groups had held them together.

Truth be told, he was seriously considering resigning his captaincy, such as it was, when they reached the fort. It wasn't much of a bother keeping them all pointed in the right direction and moving. Being captain wasn't getting him to where he was going any faster. It was being called on to judge all the small town bickerings and dealing with the petty rivalries that raised his hackles. It was like he had left his old marshaling job and brought all the county's nuisances with him, without the solid authority to back himself up with the law.

His newest headache was that most of the womenfolk and some of the more hennish men were decrying the escapades of the Bonner boy and that Hampton girl. It was obvious he was creeping into her bed even amidst the whispered mutterings and complaints of adultery. He had taken the trouble to warn the boy, and his disregard of the warning began to rile him and make him bemoan his paper authority.

On the other hand, he remembered his own youth and how he had tracked about following his own rebellious knob. Damn! Elizabeth Hampton was surely a fine-looking woman and could probably bestir even toothless old Harlan Buell's withered pizzer. It was most likely half envy that put the other men up against Bonner. It seemed every hour some man would ride up, after his woman's pestering, to ask what he was going to do about them. Many wanted to turn them out, cast away like they were some wandering tribe of Israelites. Hell, maybe that's what they had become, no home behind them and none in sight ahead.

It wouldn't burden his conscience much to be rid of the Hampton girl. She was too damned independent by a sight and would probably be the ruination of young Bonner. He didn't want that. The boy had the guts and the brains of any three or four of the plodding farmers it was his trial to lead. Thoughts of freedom from leadership entertained him as he paced alongside his oxen, occasionally prompting them with a switch as the fancy came to him.

Josh was riding Natchez a little ways off from the left of the team but keeping abreast of the wagon. He was awaiting the crest of the next low rise, hoping for a glimpse of the peak of Chimney Rock. The guidebook indicted they were near enough to see it in the distance. Then there would only be twenty or thirty miles to its base. The passage would mark off another large chunk of the road west. More so, just seeing something different on the horizon would help convince him they were making some progress. He had to force himself not to press his knees in Natchez's flanks, urging him forward to the crest as it drew near. The steady, slow pace was a part of the game he played to pass the time. The anticipation and disappointment of raising another blank horizon was a part of the game as well.

There wasn't much chance of seeing the landmark till he walked into it, anyway. From his station in the middle of the line, there was a constant screen of yellow dust blowing across his vision, kicked up by the preceding wagons and the north wind. It could be worse. With a wind from the west, he would be choking down an acre or two of dirt and would be fortunate to see three wagons ahead.

How splendid it would be to be miles ahead of the train, scouting a clear and endless horizon for the train he was leading to the land of milk and honey. A dreamy smile crossed his face as he immersed himself in the new game.

While on the surface, Josh's mental game passed as an amusing diversion, a more subtle and meaningful debate dueled in his subconscious. The monotonous trudging carried him ever farther from the bonds tying him to Cairo, Illinois, and that orderly world.

Cairo, like an elastic band, was being stretched with every stride. In his subconscious, a point would be reached, a step taken, that would snap the past away, propelling him irrevocably forward into a vibrant if uncertain future. He was hoping the site of the famous sandstone tower might be the event that transformed him into the vaguely defined person he was daydreaming of. Each hour in the territories had lessened his fear of the unknown, made him more at ease in this new world of shallow rivers, Indians, and the natural course of things that daily sculpted his new life. It was hard to comprehend the courage of those who had first crossed this rough country, alone, in search of new vistas and the riches within. The natives, who claimed the land as their own, the explorers and trappers who poured from the East, lived lives beyond his own immature imaginings.

Custis Gresham was relentlessly trudging westward, too. His notions, while consumed in turmoil, carried no romantic notions as a part of his baggage. Thoughts of commerce and the sight of the wasted goods tossed recklessly or maliciously desecrated on the roadside burned at his soul. The thought he might have to part with some of his own possessions tore at him. He had paid good hard cash for his stores and intended to establish himself in the new land with these goods.

Gresham had started his career as a peddler, hawking notions and such to farms and backwoods hamlets. The clanking of his pots, kettles, and other wares was bringing back memories etched deep in his mind. He could hardly bear the sounds harkening of his wretched beginnings. The wanton wreckage, some fresh, and some bleached or rusted from seasons past, was hateful to his eyes. He wanted to peck through the discards, pull apart the overgrowth, and add to his own cache.

Back at the Hollow, everyone had lightened their loads, though grudgingly. He had seen tears as wives parted with some treasured memento of home. Men had grudgingly abandoned tools or food, almost always vandalizing their leavings. No face was more grim or mind so contrary as Custis Gresham's as he solemnly parted with a keg of nails and a crate of sewing notions, his token contribution to the offerings. It smacked to him of some pagan sacrifice to the gods of the trail.

Selfishly, he wanted more. Even more so, he wanted to keep his own. Perhaps some unfortunate wagon would be destroyed and he could buy the team at turnip prices, enabling him to keep a fresh team for his own precious goods. Better yet, maybe he could buy a nigger from one of the Missouri folks. It seemed unfair to him he hadn't been able to hold slaves at home while just across the river they were bought and sold every day. Wistfully, he recalled attending the auctions in Missouri, wishing he could have his own nigger twosome. It would be smart to have a young buck to lift and tote for his store and hotels. Better yet, to have a dusky and comely young Negress to take care of his home and his own baser needs when the occasion allowed. These were the thoughts that entertained Custis Gresham on the dusty crawl across the prairieland.

There were subtle changes in the trail at this point. No one had truly noted them and would not until the transition was complete. Then they would wonder how long the land had looked like it was. The terrain had begun to gradually surrender its soft, rolling face to become studded with higher and sharper bluffs. The effects of rain and wind were more pronounced here, creating escarpments where the smaller tributaries of the Platte sought its wide bed and joined the long slide to the Gulf of Mexico. The ground began to reveal large formations of marl and sandstone, protruding from the ground like the knuckles of tree roots exposed in a well-worn path.

The constant winds had carved the exposed rocks into varied and fantastic shapes, stirring the imaginations of the passing emigrants. Even the dullest plowman could envision cities and medieval citadels in the tumbled landscape, like a child gazing at clouds in a cumulus sky. Some might see a steam engine in the windblown jumbles; another might see a left-behind cookstove. Their visions were as varied as their experiences.

One, significantly, had a common recollection for all that passed. This was Chimney Rock, surrounded by a skirt of rubble that once formed its height and breadth. This limestone pinnacle, rising some five hundred feet from the Platte Valley floor, was separate and distinct from the tumbles and rock that were its neighbors. So precarious was its appearance that those who passed or bivouacked in its shadow carried no doubt it would soon, of its own accord, collapse to just another jumbled ruin of naked rocks.

About a dozen miles east of the Chimney were Courthouse and Jailhouse Rocks, formations named for some fanciful resemblance to the courthouse in St. Louis. Such was the romance of the road west; landmarks suffused in myths that enthralled migrants, who, in turn, created their own legends and mysteries of the road.

It was under the face of cliffs at Courthouse Rock that the Metzger party, if such it could be named, passed the night of June 17, 1848. The travel over the past week since had been monotonous but uneventful. The ground was deep with sand, and all were weary. Despite the reputed reason for its naming, its enormity lent a feeling of security to the tired travelers.

That evening, after the teams had been tended to, the meals cooked and eaten, and the children summoned back to their home fires, a groundswell of discord gained impetus. Dissent was first spoken by Mrs. Clark, who pestered the Reverend Clark to carry her voice of outrage to the men of the camp. The men relayed the message from campfire to campfire. Small groups gathered to concur or to plan a strategy.

Josh and Elizabeth were the reason for the conspiracy. Their trysting, as surreptitious as they thought they had been, had become common gossip throughout the camp. Besides being from across the Mississippi in Illinois, and therefore foreign to the Missouri core of the group, their obvious fornications were an affront to the Christian sensibilities of the company. A remedy, besides marooning, was sought and agreed upon. A delegation was selected and dispatched to confront the transgressors. Determined and consumed with moral competence, they approached the pair, who lazed about the fire after their evening meal.

Josh noticed the approach of the delegation, though it seemed like everyone in the train was there. This was unusual in itself as generally the enterprise of the train was carried out by the menfolk. He turned to Lizzy to see if she had seen the nearing crowd. She had.

He could see she was already bristling, almost eager for a confrontation. More than anything else about her, this was her most disturbing facet. She was so strong willed she could not accept any compromise with her own agenda. Her chin jutted out, her jaw locked, and her eyes stared, fixed upon the approaching company. Did she have some intuition that foretold a conflict, or was it just her nature to seek one? She had the look of someone who had just decided to charge headfirst through a wall and was about to do it. Elizabeth stood up, and Josh swore the approaching group hesitated collectively in half stride. This wasn't going to be pleasant. Nevertheless, he rose and stood by her side. He heard her greeting to the crowd.

"Good evening, neighbors. How nice of you all to come by." The sarcasm clotted her voice, and he shook his head. She certainly knew how to get off on the right foot.

"We didn't come to palaver, missy," thrust Wallace McCardle.

"No, we didn't," spoke up his wife, a hefty woman whose broad bosom heaved with indignation. Uncustomarily, she was in front of her husband. Murmurs of assent rose from the rest of the group.

Mrs. Bingham chimed in. "You two have been nothing but a trouble since you joined up." She strode forward.

Dr. Bingham leapt forward and restrained her by the elbow. "Now, Mother. We can settle this without hard words." He looked reproachfully at Josh with an "I warned you about this" look on his face.

"What is it needs to be settled?" Elizabeth spoke hotly.

Josh, in turn, took her by the elbow. He knew now what was in store.

Elizabeth flinched slightly at his touch, then looked first at his hand on her arm, then at his face, which was, he figured, pleading for her to back off. It seemed to work as her gaze remained on his and the tempest faded marginally from her eyes, her jaw unclenched.

Leland Metzger came to the front of the crowd and faced them, holding his palms up for silence.

"Now, people. Hold it down. We've talked this over and decided to let Reverend Clark speak for us." He turned to the wayward couple, looking directly at Josh. "I warned you twice before, son, and you chose not to listen. You'll have to listen up now. Reverend?"

Metzger motioned the bearded preacher to the front and retreated back to his wife.

Reverend Clark, as imposing a man as he was, loomed even larger now, stoked with rectitude. He stepped into the no-man's land between the antagonists.

"We all know of your fornication. No more than you can keep your sins from the eyes of the Lord can you keep your couplings from the eyes of your Christian neighbors. Do you deny it?" Clark charged them, pointing his finger at the pair accusingly. He lacked only the robes of an Old Testament prophet to complete the image.

Neither of the accused spoke. Nor did they hang their heads in the shame that the preacher's theatrics demanded. They both knew their silence was as equally a confession. At the same moment, they turned to each other, not knowing themselves whether the gesture was for comfort or for counsel. Josh was aware that this putting of their heads together must seem like plotting, but knew he must do something to head off Elizabeth before her tongue dug them both a pit to be cast into.

"Elizabeth, what do you want to do?"

Softly, she hissed her reply. "I want to tell that son of a bitch to rot in hell. We're none of his business."

He tried to reason with the thunderhead before him. "You can't do that. There'd be no backing down from there."

"Dammit, I know that! What do you want to do? Back down?" She looked at him scornfully.

144

Josh whispered back. "What do you want to do? Come up with a story and stick by it?"

Elizabeth caved in. "I don't know. I want to fight back, but I know it will only make matters worse."

"Let me try. You back up some. If we aren't together, it maybe will look better."

Elizabeth turned on her heels and retreated to where she could watch Josh yet be separate from him. Josh took a step forward to speak.

"What is it we are supposed to have done?"

Clark glared at him. "You have seduced this girl and now creep to her at night under our very eyes. Do you deny the truth?" The preacher repeated the charges.

Josh hoped he saw his escape. "Is this supposed to be some sort of a trial?" He didn't like the look of the crowd. They seemed to surge forward every time the reverend spoke. He looked through the faces for Mr. and Mrs. Gresham, the only other Illinois people. They were not there, but he found the long face of Henry Shearwood, whose countenance was drawn longer with concern for his friend. It held no reproach.

Metzger spoke. As captain he felt he had to make his authority known. "How do you plead? Guilty or no?"

Josh flashed indignance. "Sounds t'me that the trial's already over. Whichever way we speak ain't goin' to be nothin' more than a hog's squeal to the butcher. We may not be in the United States, but we're still in America and ought to have a trial, proper. I never seen a lynch mob, but I expect you all could pass for one."

It seemed like it might hold water. Righteousness seemed to fall at the crowd's feet, replaced by looks of doubt and chagrin. Maybe it was time to wax proper on the Bill of Rights. "Seems like I was taught in school—"

"Enough of your foorah! You are sinners and unrepentant ones at that."

It was Hattie Bingham. She seemed the most outraged. Perhaps because she had taken one of the sinners into her home, or at least trail home, she felt the most abused of the Christian ladies. Josh's impetus was lost.

Clark spoke again. "Son, you've a clever tongue in your head, but you can't turn us from our path." He pointed at the both of them. "You can travel with us as far as Fort Laramie, then you're to be cast out like Adam and Eve from the Garden."

Metzger added, "You're to stay at the end of the train till we make the fort."

This was worse than Josh had expected. Being left at Laramie meant they would have to turn back. Word would be spread around the fort, and they wouldn't be able to tag on with another expedition. In his head, he was chasing over a hundred possibilities when a calm voice from behind him struck his brain blank.

"Suppose we were to get married?"

He couldn't believe what he was hearing. Apparently, from the looks of those facing him, they couldn't, either. Every face he looked at was as dumbfounded as his own must appear.

For long moments, nothing was said as the proposal sank in. Husbands and wives began to group together, and murmurs began being passed from cluster to cluster.

Josh could almost see the crisis founder before him. Regaining a little of his wits, it was his turn to spin on his heel and gaze back at Elizabeth. Her look was one of absolute calm, certainly the only such face in this assemblage. Josh cocked his head and scrunched his face up in bewilderment. All he got in return was a plaintive and satisfied trace of a smile.

She spoke. "We've got Reverend Clark right here. He could marry us proper. I think that's the Christian and right way to be."

Josh strode up to face her. "'Lizabeth! What are you sayin'? We can't get married. We hardly know each other."

"P'shaw, Joshua Bonner. We've known each other forever. Besides, it's the only way we'll ever get to Oregon otherwise," she added. "You didn't seem to be winning anybody over. Don't you see that we have to?"

"'Lizabeth, I don't know—"

"Dammit!" She clenched at his arm. "We've got to or go back. What's more, we have to do it before we reach the fort or they might change their minds."

Josh glanced back at the still murmuring crowd. "I can't see as they've changed their minds yet. What are you getting us into?"

"I'm getting us out of something and on to Oregon. Besides, we can be together every night," she said sweetly and placed her hand on his neck.

"Now, propose to me. All they need is a kick in the pants to swing 'em. Make it good."

"'Lizabeth, I'm not—"

She leaned from behind him and called to the milling people. At the same time, she pressed on his shoulder, encouraging him to go to one knee. "Everybody, Josh has something to say. Please listen."

Josh assumed the position and took her hands in his. She stood demurely before him. The words came out of his mouth seemingly from nowhere.

"Elizabeth Hampton, I've loved you for as long as I can remember. I am asking you now, with all my heart. Will you marry me?"

He looked up at her, and after a befitting pause, heard her acceptance.

"Yes, Josh, I'd be honored to be your wife."

They regarded each other, neither daring to look at the throng about them. They waited for a reaction. Soon, while sharing their gaze, it began to seem their scheme was not from expedience, but to be what each wanted.

While the two betrothed stared longingly at each other, the rest of the company fidgeted amongst themselves. They felt somehow they were being hornswaggled. However, they felt almost like they wanted to be hornswaggled, much like the man in the medicine show with his card tricks and blarney. Acceptance was creeping, the toehold established.

First, there was a cautious putting together of heads, tentative and unsure at first, but gaining substance with each addition of heads. Husbands and wives looked at each other and quietly concurred.

Elizabeth and Josh heard the swelling approbation but dared not look up until a huzzah was raised. Josh recognized the slow voice of Henry Shearwood and silently thanked his new friend. Other voices raised the cheer, and Josh, unable to stand the suspense, twisted about to gaze in wonderment at the transformed throng. He still held her hands in his, and she pulled him to his feet and threw her arms about his neck. When they kissed, the crowd surged forward, hands thumping on his shoulders as they were separated by gender for congratulations and consultation.

He only saw Elizabeth for a few confused moments as the women hustled her off. Josh couldn't tell if her face radiated exhilaration, satisfaction, victory, or a combination of all. There was too much on his plate to consider Elizabeth's mood. He felt happiness, victory, relief, entrapment; but he was mostly overwhelmed by the swift event of his impending marriage, and at the quick turnabout of his neighbors. Muddled was probably a good summation for his feelings, and he decided to flow with the current, grateful mostly that it left him near speechless.

The men dragged Josh away, toasted him with flasks of brandy and whiskey, and offered clothes and shoes suitable for a wedding in case he had none of his own. Elizabeth was similarly feted by the women, albeit with more enthusiasm than their spouses.

Elizabeth, after the women left off their mooning and repaired to their own homes to make preparations for the nuptials, left her site to seek out Josh. As sudden as the idea had come to her, it had just poleaxed her new fiancé. He had gone along with the flow of the moment, and she knew she had to set at rest any doubts that might sway him away from marrying her.

She sauntered past the other firesides, acknowledging the salutations of the new well-wishers. Puzzling, she thought, how the mass of witch-burning righteous embraced her now that she was redeemed in their eyes. She had no respect for people who twisted in the wind with convictions of the moment. Still, she was grateful, in a manner, for their newfound support.

Nearing Josh's wagon, she discovered he was nowhere to be found. His hand, Jubal, was lying about, mending some utensil. When he saw Elizabeth approaching, he popped to his feet and snatched his broad-brimmed hat from his head. He knuckled his forehead and greeted the girl with a beaming grin.

"How do, Miss Hampton. I sure am pleased to hear the news—about you and Mr. Josh gettin' married. Best news t'come my way in a long spell."

"Thank you, Jubilee. I'm glad, too."

She was, too. Jubal had a nice smile, perhaps the most genuine she had seen since the episode earlier in the evening.

Jubal stood mutely before her, lost for word or gesture. He finally managed to shuffle his feet some, twisting his hat in his hands. Shyly, he eventually managed to look at her.

"I was hoping to speak to Josh. Is he about?" she asked.

"No ma'am. He's sittin' just away from camp, not far off," Jubal said as he pointed off into the gloaming. "I guess he's got some cogitatin' to do."

Elizabeth couldn't take the chance of wandering out into the night to find him. The hard feelings had been put to bed, and she wasn't about to give some snooping gossip an excuse to wake them afresh.

"Do you think you could fetch him for me, please, Jubal? I need to speak to him before we turn in." Perhaps not a wise choice of words.

Eager for an excuse to be away, Jubilee strode off on his errand, saying, "Yes, Miss Hampton. I'll fetch him, if'n he'll come."

Elizabeth was about to insist that he come, but Jubal had already fled to the shadows. She made herself comfortable on a keg and waited. Before many minutes had passed, Josh came into the circle of light. Jubal followed slowly and lingered back in the shadows, affording the couple some privacy.

"Evening, Josh," she opened, trying to gauge his mood.

"Hello, Elizabeth. How are you?" His tone was noncommittal but seemed resolute.

"I'm fine, Josh. We need to talk."

"Damned right, Elizabeth. We've got some words to chew." He didn't seem angry, just perplexed. He squatted down on the ground facing her and idly began pulling leaves of grass from the turf.

Elizabeth stated, "I'm sorry to spring my idea on you that way, sudden-like. Are you mad at me?"

He looked up. "No, I'm not mad, just feelin' caught up in somethin' I hadn't reckoned on." He shrugged a little as he finished speaking.

"Do you feel like I am trapping you into marrying?" she said, trying to keep any reproach from her voice.

"No, durn it. That ain't it, exactly."

"Then, what?"

Josh hesitated, sorting his words before he spoke. "You remember that big hill on your daddy's farm, the one we used to sled on when we was little?"

She nodded.

Josh continued, "I remember the first time I sat on my sled at the top, guess I was about five or six. Ned and his friends had already gone, and I was alone at the top. They were all callin' me down and watchin' to see what I would do. I'd watched them all go, and it looked like a good thing. I wanted to give myself a little push to start, but I was kind of wishin' I'd stayed t'home that day. Not that I was scared. I was just wondering how I wound up on that sled perched on the brink of the run."

He stopped talking and looked up at her, hoping to see her understanding how he felt.

"Did you go?"

"I went. I remember I started out slow and thinkin' it wasn't going to be so big a fuss. Next I recall, that sled was just a-flyin' down, and I knew I was just along for the ride, no matter what. I couldn't see nobody else, couldn't hear the yelling. I just remember watchin' the ground fly by, the sled leaping and bucking, and the snow flying up in my face so I could barely see. What I remember most is I wasn't scared. I liked the ride. I just didn't like not bein' able to do no more than hang on.

"Next I know, I was stopped and Ned and his friends was standing over me, cheering and laughing. I remember." Josh smiled and laughed. "Now I recollect that fool of a Hugh Duncan, with that horsey laugh of his, poundin' me on the top of the head like a drum."

Elizabeth looked at him, puzzled. "But you went down that hill many times. I remember."

"Sure, I did. Hundreds of times. Wasn't never the same, though, as that first shove." His face settled with fond remembrance.

She didn't speak.

"'Lizabeth, I guess what I'm saying is, I feel like I did when I was sitting on the edge there. I knew I was goin' to go. I just didn't recall how I got there."

"Josh, what are you saying? Do you want to back out? I'll understand if you want to."

"I'm not saying that. I just feel that someone else, not just you, but everybody, has kind of made up my mind for me."

She reached to him and took his hand, "I know what you're meaning. When I said it—getting married I mean—I don't know where it came from. It was like I heard the words, then realized it me that said them."

"'Lizabeth, marrying's a big thing." He looked deep into her eyes, a good sign. "It just seems there ought to be more to it than something that just pops into your head. It seems like we just haven't had the time to fall in love."

At the mention of love, his face flushed. He was mad at himself. He had lain naked with her, had been inside her. It didn't appear natural to get so riled just to say the word.

"Do you love me, Josh?"

"'Lizabeth, I can't say as I've ever been in love before. I don't know how I'm supposed to feel. I've never felt so powerful for anyone before as I do for you. I think about you all the time. I want you to be the last person I talk to before I go to sleep. When I wake up, I wonder how long before I'll see you again. I'm guessing that is love, and it's got hold of me real good."

Josh was amazed at himself, amazed he could talk for so long and so eloquently. Nor had he spoken to anyone about feelings like these. He was giddy from having said the words. Most of all, he wanted to ask her, to see if she loved him, also.

She could see in his eyes what he wanted to know. It would have been easy to just say, yes, she did love him. She wasn't certain herself, but she had to be honest with him.

"Josh, we're on our way to a new life, over a thousand miles from the world we knew. There's nobody else we can turn to, no kin or the friends we knew. We each have our own dreams and wishes we've made. We have to be together. There's no one else we can count on."

Elizabeth continued. "Oh, I'd planned my wedding in my mind for years. I dreamed of the prince I wished for, too. Every girl has since she the day she started wearing ribbons in her hair. But that is just a girl's fancy. What we've got now is real. I don't think either of us is ready to go it alone.

"Back home, I never would have thought of you as my prince. Since we've been together, you have shown me more of a man than anyone I've met before. You're no boy to me. I'll tell you this. What we have may be falling in lust," she blushed a bit in the face herself, "but I can feel there is more. I want to be with you, Josh. I am loving you."

Josh stood, all the while with her hands in his. He lifted her to stand before him.

"'Lizabeth, I guess we had ought to figure on getting married." He hesitated, chagrin on his features. "That felt more like a proposal than the flapdoodle before."

The two lovers pulled close and held each other in a fold that revealed their first real intimacy, more endearing than the carnal clutches they had practiced before. While entwined, she spoke of practical matters.

"You know we can't wait until we get to the fort to get married?"

Josh stopped smelling her hair.

"Why not?" he asked.

"If we wait until we get there, it will be easy for them to change their mind and abandon us. We'll have to hitch up with another train. The new train will want to know why we got left behind and might not take us. We would have to turn back."

Josh pulled back far enough to look at her directly.

"Are you afraid I'll change my mind?"

"I don't think so. Do you?" she replied.

The idea was still in the back of his mind, though it was a reluctant thought. As solemnly as he could, he replied, "No, I want to do it. We should be at Chimney Rock in a day or so. How about there?"

"We'll announce it in the morning." She placed her hands on his shoulders and kissed him longingly. "It will be fine, Josh. I'll be a good wife."

"I know you will. I love you."

"I love you, too."

The betrothed couple murmured together for a while before she departed.

Josh wandered over to Jubal, who had been pointedly ignoring the two, and pulled up a keg to sit on. Jubal looked over at Josh and started to smile a greeting. The young man appeared lost in thought. Josh was in no mood for his usual light talk with Jubilee, and his look must have conveyed his mood, for Jubal made no effort to speak more than a mumbled greeting. Josh managed a reply and fell silent. He needed to think.

Because of the announcement of the banns, the company did not make trail as easily as they were accustomed. The men, after breakfast, spent as much time visiting as readying their livestock. The women bustled back and forth, in twos and threes, congregating and breaking apart over and again with the exchange of plans and ideas. The kitchen chores, while ritual, were not completed with additional meals in mind.

All of the outrage and hostility present the day before was swept away on the froth of excitement the announcement generated. The weeks of drudgery, the difficult and unsatisfactory housekeeping, the boredom of meals and constant re-packing were forgotten. Something unique and exciting was going to happen. All the women wanted a share of the romance and the preparations that would put some shine onto their tedium.

Everyone seemed to have some secreted reservoir of fancy food or drink that had been preserved and hoarded for a special day. Most had thought the special day was to be when they crossed the Divide or when they first set foot upon the promised earth of their new Oregon home. However, as nothing is as hard to resist as temptation, the hidden victuals were declared, praised, and plans for their combination into pies and tarts were the subject of deep conspiracy.

The men, as was their nature, were of a simpler mind. Each remembered a small jug of brandy or whiskey whose consumption would lighten their wagon a bit. Men are such practical people.

It was within this spirit of festive revelry that Josh and Elizabeth announced they wanted to marry at the foot of Chimney Rock rather than wait until arriving at the fort. The proclamation elicited a repeat of the hubbub of well-wishing the day before. This time, the comments ran to the ribald, many centered on the symbolism of being married in the shadow of the upthrust spire. More confounding were the previously outraged womenfolk laughing right along at the bawdy jokes and adding not a few base quips of their own.

A practical consideration was finding fuel for the fires to cook the feast. There were virtually no trees or deadfall to be had. The processions of seasons past had reduced the occasional willow or cottonwood stands that grew near the riverbanks to stumps, and even many of these had been uprooted. The scrub brushes provided little more than kindling. There had been some experimentation with buffalo chips. These, as yet, were scarce in the region. Those few that could be found were damp from the recent rains.

After overcoming the initial distaste of using dung to cook their meals, a brisk competition for the choicest piles emerged. Women who would, at first, only handle the lumps with nervous fingers, now eagerly sought apronfulls. These they broke apart with unguarded enthusiasm. They marveled at the clean, hot flame the chips produced and at how evenly they burned. Old Mother Buell, who had at first refused to even eat a meal cooked over chips, now zealously declared them better than the peat she had cooked with as a young wife in Wales.

Fortunately, as Delacroix affirmed, they were entering one of the major grazing areas of the great herds. It was in this region that the native bluestem grass, commonly called buffalo grass, changed variety from the shorter strain of the East to the more luxuriant variant of the Western plains. Where not plundered by the passing migration of humans and their domestic herds, this variety would grow up higher than a cow's belly. It was these wavy bastions, caressed by the constant wind, that made the plains like a vast, dry ocean.

Delacroix, as scout, rode around the frontiers of the campsite, pointing out and notating discarded furniture and even broken wagons. Other sharp eyes spied combustible treasures across the river bottomland and scattered about to retrieve armfuls of scraps or to drag in larger pieces behind their mounts. The scout soon found he had his own hands full trying to keep the scavengers within site on the rolling plain.

A delegation of hopeful bridesmaids and best men accompanied the betrothed to seek the cooperation of Reverend Clark. After a few feeble protests at the haste of the proceedings, he consented to perform the ceremony at the designated time.

With the arrangements settled, the preparations for the day's march commenced. As the last utensils were packed away and the teams were hitched, Metzger and the scout rode amongst the throng, regimenting the day's march and shooing wandering children back to their respective wagons like loose chickens back to the coop.

154

It was near ten o'clock before the circle of wagons uncoiled itself and began its dusty way westward. The day proved to be temperate and, as yet, the northerly wind had not risen past a pleasant and stimulating breeze. The resumption of the creaks and clanks of wagons on the move lulled the emigrants into the familiar rote of marching and daydreaming their private fancies.

Josh, in his self-appointed capacity as scout, rode Natchez in a flanking position to the head of the train where Delacroix and Metzger had their heads together planning the advance. While the two leaders seemed not to be engaged in more than offhand conversation, he held Natchez back, not wishing to intrude on the deliberation. However, as he approached, both men turned and shaded their eyes to see who was coming up.

"*Bonjour, mon jeune ami.* Soon you are to go over the broomstick. You will be too tired to ride for a while, I think."

"More like a leap than a jump, it seems to me," retorted Josh. He doffed his hat and rode around to their right, out of the glare. "Bonjoor to you." He included Metzger with a nod and a smile.

"Good morning, Josh. Hope to make some miles today," Metzger paused, "lest you have some more surprises to announce."

"I do, too, Mr. Metzger," Josh replied. "How much farther till we reach Chimney Rock?"

Both men laughed.

Metzger offered. "Can't wait to get hitched up? Marry in haste, repent in leisure, I've heard it said."

"So it is in French," Delacroix spoke, raising a finger to emphasize the idiom's truth. "*Tel se marie à la hãte qui s'en repent à loiser.*"

"Truer words were never spoken. True the world over." Metzger rocked forward on his saddle horn with laughter.

Josh took his ribbing. "That wasn't why I was asking. I've been anxious now for two days to see it up close. I've been readin' about it in the guidebook."

"There may be better things to see this day. I have spied signs of the *buffle* ahead. We may come upon a *troupeau de buffles* today."

"Buffalo!" Josh piped up. "That'll be somethin', sure. How many is a 'troopo'?"

The scout smiled, amused at Josh's mangling of the French words. He had noticed how the Americans quickened the pronunciations of the French, Spanish, and Indian names rather than lingering over the flowing dialectic words.

"A troop, *mon ami,* can be any size, but not so large as a herd. *Buffle* will migrate together, but small groups may wander away from the parade, as the grazing takes them. I have seen signs, but it is unlikely we shall see more than a few together, and those not so close to the trail."

It was true. They had seen little game since entering the territories. Many emigrants had visions of plentiful meat to be hunted on the trail. The tales that came east portrayed an easy banquet, not only of bison but antelope and elk aplenty. Yarns of shooting dinner from the wagon boards prevailed, and all were disappointed at the scarcity of game. Antelope were plentiful but so easily disturbed they bounded out of range before even a skilled marksman could aim and fire. Even rabbits had become skittish and retreated from the approaching caravans. Only their sudden movement at the fringes of rifle range betrayed their presence. Some birds could be seen scattering at a train's approach.

The only animals glimpsed so far with regularity were the coyotes and wolves that scavenged along the trail. They announced their presence with a symphony of howling in the prenatal darkness. All had become accustomed to the nightly chorus.

"Will we have a chance to hunt?" asked Josh eagerly.

"If they are about, it will depend upon the wind not carrying our scent and sound to them. They do not see so well, and we may take some if we are fortunate."

Metzger spoke. "I hope so. I am as excited as the boy to see buffalo. I've seen robes and skins and horns and skulls. I'm shore looking forward to seeing one with all its parts on."

"So, too, am I. It has been a year since I tasted tongue or hump. I shall ride ahead. Why don't you two bring the wagons up?" instructed Delacroix. "There is a creek of clear water we may be able to reach today. A drink of water I don't have to chew would be as welcome as bison."

The trio parted, Delacroix on his quest for Smith Creek, the other two anxious to follow.

The emigrants made no noon stop this day but rolled on into the hot dazzle of the afternoon. The wind had backed some from the north, and the sun was firing the breeze as it gusted into the travelers' faces, raising dust so even those in the fore would occasionally shield their eyes from the assault.

The emigrants of 1848 were fortunate that the previous winter had been a dry one. The land had surrendered its moisture so that even a torrential day's rain was soaked deep into the earth. Had the ground been saturated, the loose upper layer of soil would have become a morass, nearly impossible to traverse. Wagons would have sunk to their hubs along the road in a wet year. Some days, the trail would yield only three or four exhausting miles to pioneers sore and lame from lifting their wagons from the quagmire.

The 1848 companies found the earth quickly absorbed the frequent deluges, drinking the rain and holding it to its bosom. The upper sandy layers could dry in a morning's wind and sun to turn its surface loose to the winds that played through the grasses. While the sand could make for a heavy passage, the extra mileage made a mouthful of grit seem a small price to pay.

As the Metzger train rolled toward Smith Creek, evidence of the buffalo became more evident. The passed the wallows that Delacroix had spotted the previous day. Not knowing what the trampled grass signified, most of the pioneers paid no attention to the signs of buffalo. Bleached skulls and scattered bones lay where the prairie scavengers who had disposed of carcasses carried them. Some skulls bore faint messages, written and left by previous seasons' emigrants, greetings or instructions for family and friends who followed. The writing was unreadable, worn by the winds and snows of winters past. Many of the travelers, Josh included, paused to scratch their names and the date on the empty skulls.

One of David Oroville's boys, Thomas, discovered a skull on a tripod of bones with a message from the DeKop party who had passed two days previously. The message, written in charcoal crayon, announced the sighting of buffalo at this site but none shot. Fresh droppings at the wallows verified the claim. Anticipation and excitement coursed through the train.

None before had seen the great beasts of the plains. Men checked their weapons and loads repeatedly. The women and children visualized mighty herds of the shaggy beasts, shaking the ground as they thundered past the plodding families. All peered through the dusty air hoping to be the first to raise the cry "Buffalo!" Mostly, they envisioned fresh meat and a respite from the tedium of their ritual fare.

As the afternoon wore on and the sun blazed overhead, a distant figure could be espied if a body used their hat to shield their eyes from the glare of the westering sun. It was the scout. He had found Smith Creek, a small freshet that tumbled clear over a pebbled bottom before being muddied at its confluence with the turbid Platte before its long journey to the Gulf of Mexico.

As the teams scented water on the wind, they lurched forward toward the stream. The travelers hurried, too. The vision of clear and cold water would seem like a glimpse of paradise itself. As each wagon raised the scout, he announced jubilantly, "Tomorrow, we eat fresh meat!"

#

CHAPTER ELEVEN

#

The balance of the afternoon and early evening was devoted to the preparations for the morrow's hunt. While there were still discussions and preparations for the upcoming wedding, the prospect of a fresh steak preoccupied everyone's attention. The air was heavy with the acrid smell of gun oil and the bitter tang of lead being melted and molded.

The men, like hunters everywhere, disassembled their weapons and exchanged lies of their hunting prowess. The variety of hunting stories was evenly matched by the variety and vintage of the assembled arsenal. Most prevalent was the Hawken rifle, heavy, with a large bore and able to take a wide range of charge. There were Pennsylvania and Kentucky long rifles. These were temperamental pieces, requiring a precise load of powder proportionate to the weight of the ball used. Too much could cause the shot to fly wild, too little and accuracy was diminished over shorter ranges. Only an individual's experience with a particular weapon could produce the wanted combination. The loading of such a personal weapon was a liturgy, superstitiously adhered. Most displayed the percussion cap models, either as manufactured or converted from the original flintlock.

Most of the party, being novice shooters, carried the Hawken. Though weighty, up to fifteen pounds, it was popular for its forgiving nature and oversize bore. Some shotguns were dug out, but Delacroix cautioned against their use as being ineffectual against the thick-hided bison.

The women of the train sharpened knives, eager for the slabs of meat to be brought to them for reduction to choicer, more manageable cuts. The young ones scavenged for twigs and buffalo chips, contesting for the least fragrant and driest "pies."

Elizabeth was helping Hattie Bingham unpack the varied contents of a large cauldron in which the surgeon's wife hoped to make a stock from the split bones she anticipated would be hers tomorrow. This stock, if time were plentiful, could be rendered to a paste that when mixed with water made a nutritious bullion. Elizabeth doubted there would be either time or fuel enough available for the project. However, she did as she was asked. The Binghams had no need to sharpen knives. As a "sawbones," the doctor kept all the medical and household cutlery implements superbly honed.

She was still a bit uncomfortable in Mrs. Bingham's company. She had been one of the most outraged at Elizabeth's premarital transgressions. Now that the wedding had been announced, she was easily the most enthusiastic promoter of the upcoming festivity. Elizabeth reckoned the matron just got bored and embraced any diversion from the monotony of being a physician's wife. Apparently, the cause for fervor didn't matter. Persecution or planning a wedding was all the same to her. She had evidently put yesterday's rancor behind her, and Elizabeth gave thanks for the older woman's capricious nature. Today, she was preparing to butcher meat, the next day, a wedding. She pursued each with a wholehearted, if fickle, enthusiasm.

"Day after tomorrow and you will be an old married lady like me," declared Hattie Bingham.

Elizabeth wondered if she was supposed to agree or offer that Mrs. Bingham wasn't an old lady at all. She chose a safer, middle ground.

"I just hope I'll be as happy with my marriage as you seem with yours."

"Well, dear. It takes a lot of work to make a marriage work. I'm thankful for what I have, though, I swear my doctor sometimes can be a flea in the ear. I've tried for years to get him to quit smoking in the house."

"If you love someone enough, things like that don't really matter."

"I suppose, when you are young and casting sheep eyes at one another. Nevertheless, as time passes, it's easier to pick a hole in someone's coat. Oh, dear, I'm not meaning to discourage you. I just mean to tell you that love 's first flush doesn't last forever. The difference between love and marriage is like a dog and a wolf. They are the same but different. You see?"

"Yes, of course," replied Elizabeth. "I guess I'm just nervous, not only about marrying but about this whole venture. How did you feel when your husband decided to light out for Oregon?"

"Land's sake, child! It was me that set our cap for Oregon. My doctor doesn't give a tinker's damn where he lives, long as he get to practice his medicine and dole out the nostrums."

"Back home in Odessa, he didn't seem to notice that Dr. Jonas was stealing his custom. Lord, and what custom it was. Mostly, we got paid in eggs, chickens, and such. When we decided to move on, it was up to me to collect all the receipts owed to us. That was how we paid for our gear."

"Do you think it will be better in Oregon?"

"Of course it will. We will have a hand in making a new land. My doctor and I will stick together, and so will you and your young man. He is a find, and you are a lucky girl. As long as you can keep buckle and belt together, you will be fine."

The next morning found Delacroix on the crest of a rise about a mile west of the camp. He had picketed his horse below the top of the ridge. He lay on his belly in the grass, surveying the scene ahead. He realized that the precaution of concealment was unnecessary. The locals well knew of their presence, but old habits became habits from repetition.

Through his glass, to the south he could see a large column of dust many miles distant. This would be the main herd of buffalo. It was as much likely that the cloud arose from their migration as from being stampeded by an Indian hunting party. It was safer to figure on the latter. Within his view were several smaller troops of animals, which led him to believe they had become separated from the main herd during previous days, perhaps by hunters.

From earlier encounters with buffalo, he knew that the men would drop everything to blast away at the herd. That was a given. Hell, he was anxious to blast away himself.

The nearest troop was about two more miles from his vantage point at the ridgeline. He must bring the emigrants past this point. It would be foolhardy to alert them now, as the hunting parties would be drawn too far away from the base, leaving the women and children exposed. Damn, it was certainly easier in some ways to travel on one's own, without the baggage and responsibilities of a scout. Scouting, however was what he was being paid for, and he had best do it well. It was unlikely that he could continue to make a living by trapping beaver.

Creeping backward down the slope to his horse, Delacroix concluded he wouldn't say anything about the bison and allow the train to come up. With the wind veered around to the northwest, he could bring the train up to within a mile of the animals without too much risk of alerting them by scent or sound. Buffalo didn't see well enough to be disturbed by the

161

approach of the wagons. Perhaps bringing the livestock ahead of the teams would help. In any event, it had looked to be a short passage today. As a bonus, the peak of Chimney Rock could be glimpsed from the top of the knoll.

Back at camp, the anticipation of the hunt invigorated the daily ceremony of breakfast and breaking camp. Yesterday's preparations were complete, guns oiled, knives sharpened keen as the travelers' appetites for fresh meat. They were already underway as Delacroix approached. He took his place at the head of the procession.

Leland Metzger raised his eyebrows in inquiry to the scout, leaning toward him conspiratorially. He was anticipating fresh buffalo roast like the rest. His theatrics revealed his yearnings. His ploy was futile. Delacroix would not fall. Frustrated, Metzger gave up.

"Well, what did you see?"

"You can see the top of Chimney Rock about a half hour ahead. Easy road, too," the scout answered evenly.

"But did you see any buffalo?"

"I found some real good signs. We'll see some soon. Perhaps we could move the livestock ahead of the wagons. We might be able to approach closer to any we see. *Buffle* don't have strong eyes. They might take us for more of their own if the wind is right."

The captain considered. "If eatin' a mouthful of dust will help me get some fresh meat, I'm willing." He turned and raised his arm to halt the wagons.

"I'll have 'em brought up."

Metzger rode back to the train, which was buzzing to hear any news he brought. The attention of the travelers was on Metzger's approach. Delacroix lifted the fender on his saddle and checked the prime on his Springfield musket, another old habit.

By the time the migration halted behind the screen of livestock and dust, they were within distant sight of the small throngs of buffalo. They had closed ranks somewhat and were migrating slowly to the west, perhaps seeking the main herd. This would mean a longer trek to keep downwind of their quarry. Still, they were able to approach to within a long mile of the grazing beasts without detection.

Stealth wasn't about to last as the bloodlust of the hunters, like its carnal cousin, built and built until containment was impossible. The climax was a scrambling for arms and horses as the signal to halt was given.

Josh was caught up in the melee. His rifle was in its scabbard on Natchez's saddle. His pockets were full of paper twists of powder and ball. He was adjusting the girth cinch and picturing a thunderous pursuit amidst maddened beasts when several successive events assaulted his brain.

First, to his left and rear, was the discharge of a weapon. At nearly the same moment there was a buzzing not unlike a horsefly, but noticeably faster and sharper.

Before the association was completed, he was aware of a solid whacking sound to his right. It sounded to him like what a ball might sound like as it burrowed into flesh. He looked that way first.

Wallace McCardle's horse was skittering about, wheeling to its left with nostrils flared. The bay's rider was struggling with one hand to stay astride the mount while waving his rifle about as though to balance himself.

"Gawd A'mighty! I've maimed myself."

The outrage and despair of the voice riveted everyone to its source.

Turning again, Josh was looking at Hollis Cooper. He was holding his right wrist with his left hand and surveying the wreckage of his right hand. A Kentucky long rifle's barrel protruded from the wagon bed.

Cooper's eyes were bulging agog as he gazed at the flow of his own blood and his now missing ring and little finger. Missing wasn't perhaps exactly true. They were still attached tenuously to the knuckles by mere strings of powder-blackened and bloody skin. Josh's first impression was that of a leg pulled almost loose from a Sunday chicken dinner.

Hollis's face was also powder blackened and speckled with gobbets of blood and gristle. There was no pain, only disbelief at the desecration of his hand. The fingers, not visible to the wounded man, jiggled like sausages on a stick with the trembling of the ruined hand. No one moved.

This was one of those life moments when events overtook time. For long seconds, there was no reaction to the tragedy, only the fixed attention of all present on the mangled fingers quivering before them. While it seemed like forever, only a few moments had passed before women cried out and men shouted.

Miriam Gresham was the first to rush to Cooper's aid. Her movement toward him broke his contemplation of a future without two fingers. He collapsed onto the seat of his pants, then keeled over backward. Mrs. Gresham tore off her kerchief and wrapped it tightly around the damaged hand. Within moments, it was dripping with blood. She looked about for Dr. Bingham.

Lemeul Bingham was no stranger to sudden mutilation. He had seen his share in the farming community of Odessa. During the frozen interlude, while everyone stared at the accident, Bingham had run to his wagon for his bag. Besides his normal bag of nostrums, he grabbed some surgical instruments and some opiate extract. Cooper was fortunate that he had brought along the painkiller.

When he returned to the accident scene, Hollis was sitting up, Mrs. Gresham was holding the bandage tight around the wound, and Metzger was standing around trying to look authoritative. The rest of the emigrants milled about some distance from the trio. Bingham barged past Metzger.

"Hollis, I want to give you some painkiller before it starts to hurt."

"Doc, it hurts plenty already. I could use some whiskey."

Bingham issued orders. "Metzger, could you find some brandy or some spirits? Mrs. Gresham, I'll need a bucket of water and some more bandages. Could you round some up, please?" Both rushed off to do his bidding.

Even with his past experience treating grave injuries, the surgeon always felt a touch of panic. The feeling passed, as it always did, as he started to organize the task before him.

"Hollis, can you stand?"

"I believe I can, if you will help me up."

Bingham crouched, placing the injured man's left arm over his shoulder. Metzger returned with a flask. Bingham suspected he didn't have to go farther than his back pocket to find the liquor.

"Give me a hand standing this man up. We need to get him to his wagon."

Metzger slid the flask into his pocket and stepped forward.

"Hollis, try to keep your right hand and arm still. We will help you up," Bingham ordered. Together, the two helped the wounded man to his feet and steered him to the back of his wagon. Cooper seemed to be more concerned with the condition of his living quarters than with his injured hand. He apologized as the two helped him to lie down on the improvised bed inside.

"I'm sorry it's such a mess. I haven't been m'self since I lost Amy and the young'uns to the cholera." He added sorrowfully, "I guess I'll never be the same again."

"Don't you worry about that. We will take care of you now, all of us," the doctor assured him. "How did this happen?"

"I was pulling the rifle out from under the seat to go hunt buffalo. I guess the hammer snagged on the brace and fired off. I must'a left the cap on the nipple when I was charging it. I'm a damn fool!"

Bingham wasn't really interested in the dismal circumstances. He just wanted to keep the man's attention diverted from his wound while he examined the damage. He opened his bag and took out the laudanum. The liquor Metzger brought would thin the syrup and help it go down a bit easier.

"Metzger, you have that flask handy? Pour some out in a cup."

Metzger was glad to have something to do besides stare at the blood-soaked bandage and cringe at the thought of what it concealed. He retrieved the flask and opened it.

"It's just strawberry brandy, but it was handy. Here's a cup."

Bingham raised the flask and the bottle of opium to eye level so he could apprise how much of the mix to make.

"Here, drink this down, but slow. I want it to stay down. Metzger, help him sit up."

While Cooper choked down the sedative, Bingham slowly unwrapped the bandages.

"This isn't going to be good. I am going to have to take these two off. The burns aren't bad and will heal without any real damage. I will wait until the opium takes away the pain. It shan't be long."

"Lordy, I hope so," Cooper forced out between clenched teeth. "The pain is comin' on fierce."

The doctor spent the next few minutes cleaning the wound and cutting away ragged pieces of flesh. Eventually, Cooper sagged into a drowsy trance. The amputation could proceed.

"Metzger, we will need some men to hold him still—and get my wife, she knows what to do."

Gratefully, the captain left the scene and soon returned with Hattie Bingham, Delacroix, and Henry Shearwood. Mrs. Bingham began to soak bandages and set out a tray for the instruments. The others stood about in the crowded wagon, awaiting orders.

Dr. Bingham was in his element. "Metzger, you hold his legs. Henry, you keep his shoulders down. Delacroix, you hold this arm still so's I can work."

With all his staff in place, the surgeon applied a tourniquet above the wrist and quickly cut away the flesh at the stumps, leaving a flap of skin to close with. Picking up a capital saw and testing its hone with his fingertip, he quickly sawed through the bone on the little finger. He then filed the bone to a rounded stump, tied the arteries and major vessels with silk thread, pulling the ends through the flap of skin. Next, he stitched the flap of skin over the rounded bone, tied the threads together, and proceeded to the ring finger. Within a half hour, he was finished, leaving a bandaged hand bound to Cooper's chest and two mangled fingers on the tray of bloodied tools.

"Good work, men. You too, Mother. If it doesn't get infected, he should be fine. We will keep him on the opium for a week or so, hopefully we'll see some laudable pus in a few days. If he can keep his arm clean and can stand to wiggle the stumps, he will soon learn to accommodate to his loss."

"There should be some salt pork put under the bandages, it will prevent blood poisoning," suggested Delacroix.

"I have heard that before," the surgeon replied. "I never found it to do much good except to replace one stink with another. I guess we can try it when we change bandages. Let's let the man rest. Mother, will you stay with him for a while?"

Hollis was out, stupefied by the opium draught. He probably would be for hours. The surgical team made their way back to their respective sites.

166

The accident had stolen the flair from the upcoming hunt. The curious or morbid strolled past the makeshift hospital, craning their necks to see anything there was to be reported. Eventually, with nothing to spy, anticipation for the hunt returned.

By the time Hollis Cooper was resting and dreaming of his missing fingers, most of the day had passed. The men were still eager to hunt but had no desire to butcher and haul carcasses at night on the prairie. The slaughter would wait for the morrow.

At daybreak, Delacroix departed to ascertain the location of the herd. He found it much the same as yesterday, with the smaller groups migrating a bit to the southwest of yesterday's grazing. He soon returned to camp with the news. The hunt was on. Men mounted up after an abbreviated breakfast washed down with coffee.

The hunting party separated into smaller groups, hoping to convince the buffalo they were being joined by others of their kind. Josh was in company with Wallace and Ethan McCardle and Henry Shearwood. Wallace's horse seemed no worse for wear after his wounding by Cooper's misfire. The damage appeared minor, just a plowing of the hide, now smeared with grease. Josh's team held the far left flank. Three other groups comprised the hunt, each with four or five determined, if novice, killers.

The exception was Delacroix, who rode with Metzger, the Orovilles, and Custis Gresham. The scout recognized that hunting was probably second nature to many of the men. The taking of a deer, a turkey, or a grouse was common fare for most tables. The killing of a fox or weasel to preserve chickens was part of farm life. The taking of buffalo, even from a stationary position, was far removed from any hunting experienced by the men around him. The road so far had yielded the occasional plover or pheasant shot from the grasses near their route. The occasional glimpse of pairs of wolves had invited some shots, and fleet antelope had been flushed by their passage. The antelope were far out of range before any weapon could be retrieved.

In four small encircling bands, the hunters were now trying to approach animals that were as large as their horses and weighed even more. Their horns and dispositions could be as fractious as breeding bulls. Delacroix doubted whether any of these men would approach a bull on horseback.

The buffalo appeared docile enough. Often a herd could be approached and picked off one at a time without so much as a nod from the brethren of the fallen. The scout didn't think today would be such an instance. These small groups had been separated from the main herd during an Indian hunt and would be wary. Delacroix was disturbed he could not spy any dust that might reveal the Indian hunting party's whereabouts. He almost regretted having steered the train toward the animals. It was far too late for regrets; besides, he wanted buffalo meat.

Scanning his company he noted that the crews were staying together and were working in a crescent to envelop their quarry. The wind had not shifted from yesterday, still blowing from the northwest. As long as they stayed behind and to the south, they would not bring scent to the beasts. That meant that he had best keep his eye on his right flank. If they drifted to the right too far, the animals might stampede back at the other hunting groups.

Delacroix raised his arm and signaled to the group on the right wing to swing slightly leftward, keeping their scent from the bison. He watched as they smartly wheeled and moved in the direction indicated. They apparently knew the reason for his signal and were complying. As a group, they realigned, keeping the herd upwind from them. Another couple of hundred yards and the hunters could commence their charge.

As the scout watched, the horses of the entire righthand crew bucked, sprang in the air, and headed off in confusion. The riders, gun hands waving in the air, held on for all their worth. Several of the horses broke uncontrollably back the way they had come. Delacroix, familiar as he was with the prairie, knew at once what had happened. The group had stumbled into a patch of pearblossom cactus. The spiny cactus grew low to the ground and could only be spotted amidst the grass by their pale yellow-white flowers. The horses had stepped into the patch as a body and had been spiked in their ankles and fetlocks.

Either the scent of the hunters had been carried to the buffalo, or the commotion set off a sudden rush of the scattered troops. They gathered into a single mass of about forty animals, bulls to the outside. They rushed in mass toward the left flank of the hunting party. Delacroix and the other groups not otherwise occupied trying to keep their mounts struck toward the panicked animals. The chase was on.

Josh and his friends, who had slowly been moving up into position, were transfixed by the sudden stampede. They had carefully been watching Delacroix direct the stalking and had been as startled as the scout by the abrupt bucking of the horses to their left. Now they stood in place, struggling with their own mounts as the rushing buffalo streamed toward their front. The battering of hooves on the earth began to cause the ground to resonate under their horses' feet. As the first buffalo crossed in front of them, they spurred their steeds forward.

The stampede was past them, so they fell in behind, choking on the dust thrown up. Josh could make out vaguely the shape of a rider to his right; the dust was too thick to see who it might have been. He dug his heels into Natchez's flanks, encouraging him to the pursuit.

Before he knew it, he was looking at the rumps of the fleeing animals. His intent was to approach from the outside of the pack, but soon he discovered animals all around him. Natchez did not flinch. Spotting a large bull just ahead, he slid over toward its flank. The animal jumped sideways a step and rudely pressed its flank against the horse's side, pinning Josh's leg momentarily between the two struggling beasts.

Josh unlimbered his Colt Walker and drew a bead between the bison's shoulder blades. Struggling to keep his aim as the animals veered and he was shaken with the galloping of his horse, he loosed his first shot. Nothing happened.

Damn, he thought. Had he done something wrong or accidentally wet his powder? Half cocking the pistol and rotating the cylinder, he saw that the nipple was empty. The percussion cap had fallen off.

Pulling the hammer to full cock, Josh again drew aim on his prey and fired. He swore that he had hit the bull square between the shoulders, but there wasn't even a twitch from the hurtling beast. Josh thought about drawing his rifle from the saddle scabbard but decided that he needed one hand to hold on to Natchez. He would try again with the Colt.

He fired again and was rewarded with what he thought was a flick of the mane behind the head. Again, there was no hesitation in the bull's stride. He quickly let off two more rounds. One certainly missed, but perhaps the second had struck home. Another shot had no effect.

By now, he was careening along in pace with the buffalo. Natchez had steadied, anticipating the sideways jolts of the buffalo. Josh felt enough confidence to use both hands on the pistol. He could now see blood coming from between the shoulders, oozing from at least one wound. Clutching the pistol, he leaned over as far as he dared and let loose with his last shot. Certainly, he had scored and the bison must stumble and fall.

Pacing along the wounded animal's flank, he looked for some sign of exhaustion. He was able to see the nostrils momentarily and hoped for blood, evidence of a mortal wound. The bull never slowed or even took much notice of him. Natchez was starting to wind and lather. Josh aborted his pursuit and cantered to a walk. The herd passed on, and he was left without his prize, his companions, and his bearings.

The chase had lasted no more than five minutes but had served to separate him from the rest of the hunters and left him with but a dusty glimpse of the departing rumps of the herd he had run with. As flat as the plain was, there were still contours. He had run over a slight rise and was alone except for a dusty haze to mark the scene. He could hear nothing of his companions, and the bison were now beyond earshot. There was no sound other than the buzzing of insects and the soughing of the wind as it caressed the crown of grasslands. Josh was turned about, confused from the pursuit and the thrill of the hunt.

The wind! He remembered that during the stalking the wind had been on his left cheek. Turning until the wind was on his cheek again, he realized that the train would be off to his right and forward. But just what angle should he take? He didn't know how far he had run and could possibly miss them. Of course, it was flat enough that he would see the camp, but he had no idea how far away they were. He could just make a right turn and hope to run into the other hunters. Or had they passed him while chasing the buffalo? He could easily be riding away from his friends if he turned right. It wasn't that he was worried much about not finding them. He just didn't want to run into the Indian hunting party first. He recalled his first encounter at the river, but that was with Delacroix. He didn't think he could maintain his aplomb in a solitary encounter.

Josh had decided against remaining where he was. That would make him feel like he was being rescued, and he certainly didn't feel any tangible concerns that warranted rescuing. No. Waiting was out of the question. He would split the difference from where he thought the train was and where he had last seen the other hunters. Hopefully, he would spot one or the other. He had just wheeled Natchez and spurred him to a canter when a voice from behind hailed to him. Stopping and turning over his shoulder, he spied Henry Shearwood coming up over a rise and waving his shapeless hat for attention. Josh was able to more easily recognize the hat than the rider. Henry approached and checked his mount, a painted Indian pony he had paid dearly for in St. Jo.

"I got one," he yelled breathlessly upon his arrival. "It's lyin' just over that ridge. Damn, that was somethin'."

Henry was more out of breath than his horse. The spotted horse, smaller than Natchez by three or four hands, wasn't even washy.

"That's great, Henry. I sure want to see it. But first, I would like to find everybody else. Was anybody with you?"

"Nope, Cheepah here ran right away from everyone else. Ran long after all the other horses gave it up."

"Cheepah? That's what you call him?"

"It's what he was called when I got him. Or close enough. I couldn't say the Indian words, so Cheepah it is."

Josh was glad to have both Henry and Cheepah's company, but he still wanted to find the other hunters. "I expect everyone is all strung out after chasin' the buf'. We are probably in the middle somewhere. What say we head back the way we come, then we'll come back for your kill?"

"Let's go find 'em. The bull I shot isn't going anywhere. Let's just mark where we are so we can get back to him before the buzzards peck him up."

The pair looked around for some sort of landmark and couldn't find anything distinguishable. They settled on riding with the wind on their left ears and counting the hills they went over. It was as good a means of tracking as they could devise. After just a few minutes' ride, they were joined by the McCardles and within fifteen minutes found the other hunters clustered around a fallen buffalo. They had already flayed it and were in the process of pulling off the hide by means of tying it off to a rope and using horsepower to peel it away from the carcass.

"Lew Petry, the McCardles' neighbor back home, waved his hat toward the newcomers and yelled, "Delacroix got one. Damn! Great shot, too. While the rest of us was decidin' whether to shit or go fiddle, he shot it right from his horse. Picked it off as it ran by, pretty as you please." Petry was as excited about the quality of the shot as much as the quality of the kill.

"Looky here," he continued, pointing at the wound. "Right through the ribs. It just rolled right over its head and kicked a couple of times. Damn!"

"I got one, too," Henry chimed. "No great shot, though. I had to put my muzzle right up behind the ear to make sure I didn't miss. Just as dead, though, I expect. It's lying a ways over yonder." He gestured with his carbine vaguely back the way they had come.

By now, all the hunters had gathered again. No one was hurt or had been thrown. Even though only Shearwood and Delacroix had brought down targets, the men were just as excited as if they had been the marksmen. No doubt as the tale was retold through the years, many would become the fortunate slayers of mighty bull buffalo on this day. Such was the way of men hunting.

Today however, the glory belonged to the scout and Henry. There was much backslapping and congratulations. Even the hunters that had run into the cactus patch shared their tales with enthusiasm. Just the thrill of being close to such magnificent beasts was thrill enough for all.

Both successful hunters basked in the praise of their comrades. Neither was very vain about their skills, and no one begrudged them their success. Henry gave more credit to his steady and swift mount than to his prowess as a marksman. The scout was busy dressing out the kill.

Delacroix had stripped off his shirt for the bloody work. While his arms and face were burnt brown, his lean upper body saw little sun. The pallor of his skin contrasted sharply with the gore he was soon immersed in. While his companions were busy with their tales, he quickly extracted the liver and held it up as a trophy. He loved *buffle* liver and wanted all to share in the delicacy.

"*Mes amis!* Come join me in one of the true pleasures of *le buffle*." He held the dripping treasure aloft and sank his teeth into the liver with gusto. As he chewed, he offered each man the gruesome prize.

Josh, too, well remembering the rattlesnake pie that the scout had prepared earlier, suspected that this was another ritual of initiation on the plains. Of course, liver was nothing new to any of the men. When butchering time came around at home, there wasn't much wasted. Liver was a delicacy, albeit cooked. None of the men were squeamish about the raw meat. It was a part of the hunt and a ceremony to be shared. By the time the dripping liver was passed to Josh, it had been bitten extensively. Each participant was obviously enjoying the treat. They tried to convey how good it was, even with their mouths full. Josh was anxious to join the circle of men with bloody chops and jubilant eyes.

As Josh accepted the prize and bit into it, he wasn't surprised by the texture. He was floored by the taste. It was far more than he expected.

The flavor was bold but not gamy, the flesh seemed to melt without chewing. His eyes lit up, and he passed the meat on gleefully.

Delacroix was enjoying his party but had not neglected his work. He had freed the hump and had extracted the sirloin behind the ribs. This he cut into manageable pieces and wrapped in an old piece of hide that he tied closed. He didn't clean himself up. There was still another animal to deal with.

"Some of you men stay here. Stretch out that hide and scrape the fat off." He unsheathed his blade and demonstrated how to flense the hide without cutting the skin. "There is more liver, and you can trim any other meat you want," he instructed. "We will dress out the other animal and return. We will leave the hide and the rest of the meat for our Indian hosts. Perhaps they will like our tribute. We can only hope."

With that, the scout mounted up and was joined by most of the others. Henry took the lead, cantering off to his own prize. Josh elected to wait where he was and to help with the work. He liked the liver enough to labor for some more.

Upon the return of the hunters, preparations were ready for the feast. The sharpened knives were once more whetted, the fires were stoked, and great kettles steamed. In the field, both bison had been cut up into quarters or sirloins and the back meat brought for further refinement. The women, familiar with dressing meat at home, cut up the prizes into steaks and chops and roasts. Each then proceeded to prepare a version of prairie banquet. Roasts and steaks, chops and skewered strips abounded. People moved from fire to fire, singing the praises of everything they sampled. No one even considered that just having fresh meat was feast enough. Even Hollis Cooper managed to enjoy himself, willing assistants cutting pieces for him. Everyone gorged. All agreed that bison was excellent fare and the star of the meal, despite the various side dishes and stews prepared with the remnants, potatoes, and onions. Whatever wasn't eaten in the first charge would end up in a stew or a pie. It was a race between the cooks and the gluttons to see if anything remained for additional meals.

The heroes of the hunt were toasted and invited to share at every campfire. Each was made to retell his account of the hunt over and over. Both Delacroix and Shearwood retained their modesty, and no amount of coaxing could get them to embellish their tales. Even after several potent toasts, their stories remained factual and disparaging of any valor. Certainly, though, they enjoyed the toasts and the varied preparations.

The feasting ran late into the evening. Late, considering the usual dawn-to-dusk routine. By nine o'clock, palates satisfied over and again, most had retired. Lethargy had overtaken the rest. Morning would find them asleep where they sat, albeit stiff and with stomachs full. Still, there was work to be done and more trail to break.

CHAPTER TWELVE

Chimney Rock was the next landmark, probably just a day or so away, no closer than when the emigrants had stopped to hunt two days ago. Within a half mile of the morning's walk, the crown of the spire could be seen. Probing nearly five hundred feet high, the distance was deceiving.

The train had been over gently rolling prairie for some time. Recently, they had encountered several rock formations sprouting from the plains. The unbroken grass ranges were no thinner and interspersed with rocky escarpments. There were no landmarks as prominent as the Chimney to this point. While the train had passed several large rock formations, none were so high or so isolated. Long ranges of crumbling bluffs had been encountered. These, however, spread out toward the horizon; none rose so spectacularly or singularly from the rolling grassland. At the end of the day, camp was made about a half mile from the base. It had been a good day's work.

The afternoon sun was passing behind the steeple of Chimney Rock. The appearance of the bright orb contrasting with the sandstone pillar was most striking. None of the emigrants had ever seen such a wild-looking sight. For many, the stark contrast of shapes in the sky brought home the reality that they were in wild and strange lands, and far from home. The wedding, scheduled for the next day, still remained as a link to lives led before embarking on their journey.

The bride and groom were naturally anxious about the events to transpire. The scout was anxious, but not for the same reasons. He sat alone by his small fire and considered the delays that had plagued the train over the past week. Normally, the road from the Hollow to the Chimney shouldn't be more than three or four days. With the confrontation with the girl, the rifle accident, the hunt and its feast, they had taken a week. Now, they would lose another day with the wedding and probably another week at Fort Laramie. It was hard to explain to people that they were racing snowstorms in the mountains when it was so fiercely hot and those mountains were just rumors in the distance.

Perhaps their road had been too easy so far. There had been no major accidents and, beyond adopting the remains of the Illinois expedition, no deaths. There had been adequate fodder, ample water, no really bad weather, and enough combustibles to afford cooking most nights. If there had been more hardship, then perhaps the desire to proceed faster might have quickened the pace.

Damn! Here he was cursing good fortune. Perhaps he should be congratulating himself on being such a capable scout. Perhaps he should just consider himself lucky to have such obedient emigrants in tow. He shuddered, remembering the Ohio party from '47. He had had to drag that group, kicking and screaming, along the road. Worse, their leader, Perkins, felt he knew more about the trail from his Fremont guidebook. Delacroix relaxed a bit, considering himself fortunate for the time being. He wouldn't look ahead any farther than anticipating the wedding and another feast. Thanks be that they were close to the fort. He was almost out of brandy.

"How long has it been since you have married anyone?" asked Abigail Clark.

"It's been some time. My calling was the saving of souls along the Mississippi River," replied the reverend. "I'm not sure I remember all the words."

"Now, Dayton Clark. I met you after my first husband died. You weren't near the river a'tall."

"I guess I had saved all those souls that were worth saving. Most of those that travel on the river aren't worth the prayers you say for them."

"I'm shocked. That's not a proper Christian way to think," chided his wife.

"Not near as shocking as the things I saw on the river. From St. Louis to New Orleans, I never saw people more in need of and more resistant to the Word. I guess I came inland for a spell just to be nearer to decent folk." Clark added with affection, "If I hadn't, I wouldn't have been so blessed as to find you."

"Glad I am that you found me. After my husband passed, I had just about given up. It was Providence that sent you to Odessa," Abigail offered. "I don't regret marrying you so soon after burying Charles."

"The last marrying I was at was ours. I was so nervous I only can remember our responses, not the preacher's part. I hope I will do well for the young couple."

"I don't mean to seem uncharitable, but those two should be grateful for any wedding they get, proper words or no. I can only imagine what has gone on between them."

Clark rose from his seat and took his wife by the hands. He led her toward their own wagon. "Come to the wagon with me, dear. I think we can revive your imagination."

Josh sat with Jubilee at their fireside. Scattered about them were several opened crates and portmanteaus. Josh had managed to piece together an acceptable wedding outfit. Jubilee was carefully brushing a claw hammer coat that had belonged to Josh's father. Josh was busily polishing up his "church" shoes for tomorrow's wear. The nervous energy he was expending resulted in an excellent shine. Some of the neighbor men had stopped by for last-minute consultations and advice. Their attempts at levity were lost on the young man, and the visitors soon left Josh to his reflections. The two continued their work without exchanging a word.

The nuptial preparations were enthusiastic on the bride's side of the camp. The women primped and preened over every detail of the bride's trousseau. Each button was tested, each pleat was pressed, each seam examined. Everyone had a part, and the bride relished the attention. Not surprisingly, Hattie Bingham competed with the others for mistress of the ceremony.

Elizabeth was sensing she would be up all night in order not to disturb the perfection of her ensemble. As enjoyable as the ministrations were, it was time she put a halt to them. She would be up all night otherwise.

"Let's try out a few things for your hair," encouraged Hattie Bingham. She approached, wielding brush and pins like her doctor husband would his lancets and clamps. "Just a few tricks I think you might like."

"Oh, Hattie! It's going to be so busy tomorrow. Let's not do any more tonight."

The remark had the desired effect. Mrs. Bingham stopped in her tracks, and the hubbub of the other ladies ceased. Someone remarked that the bride would need her rest. The bawdy remark received the expected titter. It was decided that tomorrow was time enough for the finishing touches, and Elizabeth was left alone with her thoughts. She must try to rest. No doubt all the ladies would return soon enough on the morrow.

Not surprisingly, Josh lay awake for most of the night. Staring up at the night sky, he watched the rising embers lift and seem to join with the myriad stars. The musings parading through his mind forbade any hope of sleeping. The degree of change in his life over the past year astounded him. From selling their river home and custom, the preparations for the trek with his family, the death of his parents, to the stark change in his daily life and responsibilities. And now he was to be married. How could everything, everything he had known, everyone he had loved, every aspect that was Josh Bonner in its entirety, be reshaped by events seemingly beyond his control? Fitfully, he sank in and out of sleep through the early morning hours.

Josh had been bathed, polished, and dressed since sunup. For most of the day he paced, sat, leaned, and walked around his wagonside. Mostly, it was a time to think. Actually, Josh reflected, the imagining about the wedding was more tiring than the wedding. He had spent most of two days ruminating on how he felt and decided finally that there was too much to think about all at once. The wedding was going to happen. He had better just enjoy the ride.

Jubal, after helping Josh get dressed for the big event, kept his own peace, tending to various chores. Finally, after watching his young companion fidget away most of the day, he had to speak.

"It's not goin' to be as much as you be makin' it, Josh."

Josh interrupted his pacing. He knew Jubal had said something but hadn't really heard.

"Did you say something?"

"I did. You makin' this day out bigger than it goin' t'be."

Jubal paused, knowing what he said wasn't clear. "I mean, a marryin' day is a big thing, but it's just one day. Actual, the marryin' ain't but a bit of a day. It's the bein' married after. And usually it mostly take care of its own way."

"You were married, weren't you, Jubal?"

"'Spect I still am. Just don't 'spect I'll see my woman anytime soon. Maybe never," said Jubilee. He couldn't help if a taste of bile appeared in his words.

"Where is your wife?

"Don't know. I ain't see'd her since we tried to cross the river to freedom. She's still alive. At least was last I knowed." Jubal didn't want to open an old wound. "I told you this all before."

"I know. You never told me about your gettin' married."

"What I was sayin'? When I got married up, I was the same way as you. Worryin' this and wonderin' that. When it came time, it was just over and done, real quick-like. There was a little dancin' and singin' after, then it was just life again, 'cept you had to think about someone else 'sides yourself." Jubal added, "Didn't even get much of that, not bein' a freedman or nothin'. Mebbe it be different for you, but I don't think much different."

Josh was astounded. While Jubilee was friendly enough, he didn't speak much. His speech was more than he had said in a month, all at once.

"How long was you married, Jubal?"

"Three years, three tolerable good years. Guess as good as years can get, tendin' another man's fields and pickin' his crops. All the time lookin' 'cross that river, thinkin' how it could be better. Then, we decided to run, she got caught, and that's the last I ever saw of her," Jubal recalled with sorrow.

"I'm sure you'll see her again."

"Don't know where she is, don't know where I am, don't know where I'm goin'. Can't figure how that will ever be."

"Jubal, I truly am sorry. I guess my worries seem pretty small to you."

"Josh, my troubles is long ago; yours is here right now."

"Don't know as they are troubles. Sure are here and now, though." Josh resumed his pacing.

True to form, the women had returned to Elizabeth's wagon soon after morning chores. Knife-sharp pleats were once again pressed, shoes given yet another buffing, and Elizabeth's hair was brushed, curled, and pinned in as many variations as women attending her. Finally, all agreed the preparations were complete. Turned out in the finest regalia that the

179

emigrants could muster, she was as stunning a flower that had ever adorned the Oregon Trail.

Josh finally figured it was time to go. Eventually, everyone had just meandered into the middle of the camp. No one had ever decided what time the wedding was to occur. The sun was past its zenith, both bride and groom were dressed and ready, the preacher had his book in one hand, his beard in the other. The guests, of their own accord, mingled around Reverend Clark. It appeared that marrying time had arrived.

Josh, as spruced up as he could manage, had left his site and had begun walking when he realized what he was lacking. He hadn't found or even asked anyone to be his best man. Impromptu, semi-shotgun, or otherwise, he figured that a best man was, beyond having a bride, at least a minimum requirement for a marriage. Damn! It was too late to just pull someone out of the crowd. He would just have to manage without. In his pocket, his hands twirled his mother's wedding ring. One last glance back toward Jubilee and he was off, a lamb to the slaughter. The idea of asking the black man to serve crossed briefly through his mind and was as quickly dismissed. He had been pushing his luck as it was. No sense in pouring oil on the smoldering embers of resentment that lurked behind this betrothal.

Elizabeth had much the same situation. As much as all the women had fussed over her trousseau, there had been no talk of maids of honor or other members of the wedding party. Doc Bingham had volunteered to give the bride away, giving some semblance of a civilized ritual. Any discussion as to other wedding party members ended right there. There was still the matter of her indiscretions that necessitated the marriage. No one was forgetting or wanted to be associated with those memories.

That was just fine with Elizabeth. This wasn't the wedding she and her friends had talked about and promised for each other when she was a child. This wedding was, however, the one that was going to take place this day and the one that allowed her the status of a married woman and continued association with the emigrants to Oregon. Any of the attendant foorah could be dispensed with as far as she concerned. She picked up her skirts and trudged to find the surgeon so he could do his duty.

By the time Josh reached the preacher, he had sweated through his shirt, grateful for the coat that concealed the puddles under his arms. Taking his handkerchief, he wiped the perspiration away as best he could. Resolved to the next words out of his mouth being "I do," he waited fretfully for his bride.

A hand touched his elbow. Nearly jumping out of his brogans, he turned to face the scout. "Looks like you could use some company," Delacroix offered to the most grateful face he had ever seen. "If you'll hand me the ring, I'll be proud to stand in your cause."

"Thank you. Why are you doing this?"

"I expect I will never get closer to a Christian wedding." The scout grinned. "Didn't want to waste such an opportunity."

Josh tried to express his relief and gratitude. "I appreciate this, I really do. I didn't know what I was going to do. Still don't, I guess."

"You just need to stand up there and say the words. I'll poke you in the ribs if you need it. Expect you will, at that."

Josh, with the scout in tow, made his way to the waiting congregation. The crowd parted where he entered, no groom's or bride's aisle. He endured some last minute backslapping and gentle hazing. Several of the women touched his sleeve and presented teary faces. For the first time since joining the Missouri party, he began to feel included and welcome. Grateful, he began to relax, at least a little.

Delacroix jogged ahead, taking his place at the preacher's left. He had replaced his worn jacket with a fringed buckskin shirt that hung below his waist. Resplendent with beading and obviously meticulously cared for, the scout wore it proudly, standing rigidly in attendance of his duties. Truthfully, he was more festively adorned than the drab attire of the groom.

Josh joined the two men, facing the preacher who loomed before him like an Old Testament prophet. Josh couldn't help but feel a bit intimidated. With his full frock coat, wide-brimmed hat, and freshly trimmed full beard, the preacher appeared even larger today than his usual imposing self. The big man's eyes glittered with the righteous authority of his position. Any relief Josh had garnered from the turnout of well-wishers vanished in his presence. It took all his effort not to squirm like a boy brought to task.

All that was needed was a bride, and soon a duet of fiddle and concertina announced her arrival with a scratchy rendition of "The

181

Wedding March." A hubbub of admiring whispers behind him alerted Josh to the direction of her entrance. He turned to his left and spied a primrose yellow veil peeking above the parting crowd. Though these people were generous and kind, no white wedding dress would be in order today.

Men doffed their hats and tugged at forelocks, the women peeked around their men to view the bride in her adornment. As the aisle formed itself, Josh had his first view of his betrothed. The sight stunned him so much that his fidgeting was forgotten instantly. She was gorgeous.

Beneath the pale yellow of her veil, Elizabeth's chestnut hair was pinned in a crown about her head, numerous tendrils of curls spun about her cheeks, setting off the heart shape of her face. Her hazel eyes seemed larger than usual, either from the excitement of the moment or through some cosmetic trickery that women possessed. Her lips and cheeks bloomed with a radiance that had no appearance of artificial contrivance.

The gown she wore was of the same pristine yellow as her headpiece, the sleeves, hem, and neckline trimmed in a green satiny ribbon. Another green ribbon adorned her long neck and accented the square yoke of her bodice. While the neckline was not immodest in any sense, there was no disguising the swell of her breasts beneath or the slim taper at the waist. The hem was cut low at her heels, the front cut shorter with snowy petticoats preventing any improper display of her legs. She wore high black shoes, polished to a rich glow and adorned with light green ribbon. The only minor flaw in her attire was a light coating of prairie dust on the toes of the shoes. Still, overall the effect was enchanting. The color scheme even complimented the natural grassland theater she marched through, her arm entwined with Doctor Bingham's. The doctor carried himself as proudly as if he we giving away his own daughter as bride rather than serving as surrogate.

Josh felt drab and colorless in her presence as she joined him before the preacher. When she stood next to him, all trepidation vanished. He was in awe that such a divine creature was soon to have her life joined irrevocably with his. He was in the presence of an angel. No, a queen was before him.

The congregation seemed to sense this. Perhaps it was the stark, barren environs; perhaps it was the majestic vision of this bride in the badlands that commanded instant and rapt attention. They were about to be a part of something solemn, joyous, and altogether thrilling. Each had been to weddings scores of times in their lives. This joining of two young people in this wild and spectacular cathedral of the plains was to be something special.

Josh stood with Delacroix at his back. Elizabeth and the surgeon stood to his left. It occurred to Josh she had no bridesmaids, and he felt singularly touched that she stood at the marriage altar on her own. His bride-to-be seemed not to notice.

Elizabeth was serenely calm, no concern of missing bridesmaids or other ceremonial trappings touching her repose. If marriage it takes to keep on the road to Oregon, then marriage it shall be, she thought. In a sense, it was a "shotgun" marriage, but nothing was to keep her from her goal. While she might not have chosen Josh Bonner for a mate, it was unlikely that she would find anyone so capable in the Dalles or anywhere else on the frontier. He was dependable, a known quantity, and an ardent lover. With her new status of wife assured, she looked forward to refining the physical joys of love. The stolen tastes she had experienced with Josh could be emboldened as much as they wanted now. From the way he looked at her in her wedding garb, there was no doubt of his continued devotion. She may have chosen in haste but, she felt, she had chosen well.

Neither of the betrothed noticed the cessation of the wedding march, lost in their own thoughts as they were. Preacher Clark, clearing his throat to commence the ceremony, finally intruded upon their musings. Embellishing from the Book, Clark spoke.

"Here, under the glorious canopy of God's sky, we are gathered, one and all, to witness the joining of two into one. This, through the holy sacrament of marriage.

"These two young people, Joshua and Elizabeth, have chosen each other, this time, and this place, to unite one with the other before God, before witnesses, and before this gathering. The vows they speak today are for time eternal. Let no man break their pact or strike asunder this marriage about to be."

With this last phrase as a challenge, he glowered over the heads of the congregation. There was, of course, no objection. There was, however, surprise that this otherwise dour preacher could speak so eloquently.

Clark continued, "Who gives this woman's hand in marriage?"

"I do," intoned Doctor Bingham. He strode forward, taking Elizabeth's hand and placing it into Josh's. Josh took her other hand as the surgeon retreated to his place. The vows began.

"Will you, Joshua, have Elizabeth to be your wife? Will you love her, comfort and keep her, and forsaking all others, remain true to her, as long as you both shall live?"

"I, Joshua, take thee, Elizabeth, to be my wife, and before God and these witnesses, I promise to be a faithful and true husband."

Turning to the bride, Clark repeated his intonation.

"Will you, Elizabeth, have Joshua to be your husband? Will you love him, comfort and keep him, and forsaking all others, remain true to him, as long as you both shall live?"

"I, Elizabeth, take thee, Joshua, to be my husband, and before God and these witnesses, I promise to be a faithful and true wife."

With those few words and an exchange of rings, the deed was done. The issue of husband and wife was put to rest with the declaration of their marriage and the invitation to kiss the new bride. It was over in moments, as Jubal had assured. They were now husband and wife.

They kissed demurely amidst the cheers and huzzahs of the crowd. Turning, the couple found their way down the impromptu aisle amidst more backslapping, handkerchief wringing, and joyful tears. The party was beginning.

Elizabeth couldn't help but notice the transformation of the people from the angry accusing mob of only a few days ago. Everyone was all smiles and congratulations. Not a few men stole a kiss when presenting their compliments and small gifts. The hypocrisy of the situation wasn't lost on her. All in all, it had worked out well. She was going to Oregon and had found a partner; from all indications, a good one.

Josh, still reeling from the onslaught of events, managed to wend his way through the well-wishers, the toasts, and the dances. After the ceremonial first dance with his bride, dance partners mobbed the couple. Josh had never measured himself as much of a dancer. Fortunately, none of his partners sought much more than enthusiasm as they reeled around the dirt dance floor. Josh exhibited enough verve to satisfy all comers. The constant toasting provided much of the incentive.

And so, the party continued. Like wedding receptions everywhere, children romped underfoot, dancers fell amid gleeful teasing, rousing toasts were made, and too much liquor passed too many lips. Even Reverend Clark and his wife, normally reticent, came out of their shells for a bit, the reverend spinning the young ladies about in dance and hoisting a few toasts too many.

Eventually, Josh was able to locate the scout apart from the crowd. He found him leaning against one of the wagon boards.

"I want to thank you for your help today. It meant a lot to me."

"I just wanted to be on hand if you started to stumble. No need, you did *splendide*."

Josh continued, "Still, I appreciate it. I felt a little strange that Elizabeth didn't have any of the women by her side."

"Can you blame any of them? Who would want to stand and be compared with such a beauty?" offered the scout. "Speaking of beauty, why are you here with me when your bride is wandering about? You should go." He dug into his shirt and pulled a small cameo on a wire chain from around his neck. "Please, take this small gift from me to your wife. It was my mother's. It should be around a neck far more graceful than mine." He pressed the cameo into the young groom's hand.

"Oh no. I couldn't accept something so personal from you."

The scout's face sharpened. "Why must you make the offering of a gift so *difficile*? I have a Crow wife, but it would not remind me of *mon mere* to have this around her neck. It is not valuable, but I would like to see that it stays with one of beauty."

Clasping both his hands, he closed Josh's around the trinket. "Take this to your bride. It would please me to see her wearing it."

How could Josh refuse such an offer? He could feel himself welling up with emotion. Rather than let the plainsman see how much he was affected by the gift, he hastily thanked him.

"Mr. Delacroix, I am certain she will wear it proudly. It appears that I am doubly grateful to you this day."

"I'll n'ya pa de quois."

The unfamiliar phrase stopped Josh in his tracks. "What was that?"

"Nothing, you are welcome. Now run along."

Taking his leave, Josh sought out his bride and soon found her, done dancing but still mingling amongst the celebrants. In order to avoid another round of toasts, he took her by the elbow and led her aside.

"Have you had enough of the reception?" he asked.

"Well, I'm a little bit tipsy," she replied. From her glittering eyes and slightly slurred speech, Josh saw that tipsy was just a memory for her.

"I'm borderin' on drunk myself," his slow tongue confirmed. "I have something for you. It's from the scout."

As they huddled together, he unfolded his hand and showed her the ivory carved necklace adornment. It was cleverly done with rich detail and obviously quite old.

Elizabeth held it up to better examine the carving. "It is lovely. I must thank him."

Josh cautioned, "Perhaps later. I got the feelin' he wanted to be alone right now."

"Well, whatever for?"

"I think he was too proud to show it, but I think he is missing his wife and thinking of his mother. Let's leave him be."

The celebrating continued through the rest of the afternoon. By four o'clock, everything that had or needed to be said had been, at least two times. Buoyed by drink and camaraderie, the party rolled of its own accord until the people separated into small groups of friends and past neighbors. People began to slip away to sleep off the alcohol or simply to rest up. Fortunately, the young couple was able to make their way to their wedding bed without an inordinate amount of teasing. Some ribald comments and barely hushed laughter followed them to Elizabeth's wagon. They could finally be alone.

Together they fell onto the bolsters and embraced. After a moment's thought, Josh arose to tie the bonnet ends closed for privacy. This was, of course, noted by the neighbors who added some final bawdyisms before abandoning the newlyweds to themselves.

Still a bit drunk, Josh fumbled with the petticoats, trying to clear his way to the groom's prize. Surprisingly, Elizabeth slapped at his hands and recoiled.

"Hold up there, husband. You are—I am—a bit drunk for this. It's still broad daylight, and I don't want to be putting on a show for the whole camp. Just lie down with me. We'll rest up." She smiled coyly at the deflated young man at the foot of her bed, "After all, we will have every night together now."

Crestfallen as he might have felt, Josh could see her point. Besides, a nap sounded awfully good. He collapsed next to her, drew her hips against his, and tenderly kissed his new wife. They kissed quietly until they fell asleep, anticipating the delights the night would bring.

Sunset didn't bring relief from the heat of the day. Elizabeth awoke, damp from her rest, her head still a bit foggy from the alcohol. Her once pristine wedding gown was mussed and twisted about her from tossing in her sleep. She lay back with her eyes closed, trying to shake the cobwebs from her brain. She could hear Josh breathing next to her, a trace of a snore on his exhale. Reflecting, she considered that she would be listening to his sleeping buzz for a long time to come. She rolled over and put her hand on his chest, feeling it slowly rise and fall. It was so much nicer having someone sleeping next to her than the solitude of the past months.

Sitting up and stretching her hands behind her head, she was able to undo enough buttons to slip the bodice of her dress down to her waist. Untying the sash and raising her bottom, she shed the cumbersome gown and its petticoats. Within moments she had stripped away the rest of her clothing and unpinned her hair. The air was still sticky but it felt so much better to be free of the clinging garments. Perhaps Josh would be more comfortable in his skin.

She rolled over and straddled his sleeping torso. Their earlier fumblings had left his shirt and trousers open, his boots had been tossed about somewhere. Elizabeth leaned forward, lightly stroking up from his stomach. Nothing stirred; he was dead to the world. Placing her fingers on his shoulders, she lightly massaged his muscles. She leaned forward until her breasts touched Josh's belly. Moving side to side, she tickled him by brushing his skin carelessly with her nipples. Eventually, her face was over his, her nipples resting delicately on his. She slowly moved, tracing patterns with her breasts, her hair hanging down, tickling his face.

Eventually, these delightful tricks finally seeped through into Josh's dreams. He first became aware of a tapping on his chin. He awoke to find that the cameo around Elizabeth's neck was the culprit. Of course, he was soon attracted to other diversions.

Elizabeth's naked form swayed above him, the failing light illuminating her skin with an orange cast crumbling to deep shadow. Each curve, each dimple, each gentle plane of her form was enchantingly highlighted by her other features. He could almost feel her smile as she realized the effect she was having upon him.

He had never become so instantly erect in his life. His member pushed back against her where she rested against him. As she felt his arousal, she ground herself along his manhood, then collapsed upon him, her mouth seeking his.

The kiss was no tender exploration. It started with lust and rushed headlong to abandon. The taste of the liquors consumed was exchanged and stoked the lovers' wanton fire.

Seizing his fingers, she guided his hand to where they ground against each other. Together, his member was guided into her folds as they picked up the other's rhythm. The initial blundering disappeared, and they moved to the other's pleasure.

In their prior forays, it had always been Josh who crawled atop. Elizabeth, now a wife, could indulge herself and was loving her mount. She sat up to better feel her man. The excitement of looking at where they joined was fabulous. Even more exciting was noticing her lover lifting his head to watch their union. She felt her climax build and ground her mouth to Josh's, smothering the ecstatic sobs that engulfed her. Before many moments passed, she was inhaling Josh's groans of pleasure.

They lay together, drained and slick with sweat from their exertion. Murmuring endearments that eased into mischievous suggestions and another round of exploring their marriage bed.

Spent, they then lay quietly, their thoughts turning to a future together and the many miles of the road ahead. A new chapter of their lives had begun.

CHAPTER THIRTEEN
\#

The next day began like the days and months gone by. A meal to fix, teams to tend to, camp to break, a train to form up. For Josh and Elizabeth, apart from the knowing smirks of their neighbors that acknowledged their trysts, the first day of married life was much like the days before. Within a few days, the bawdy remarks would cease and life could settle into the steady routine and parade.

For Jubal, life within the daily routine would be profoundly changed. The duties and the camp he had shared with Josh were now his alone. Josh would be tending to his bride's wagon and team. Jubal would be tending to Josh's gear and animals. He wasn't complaining. After all, taking care of Bonner property had been his job long before they set off on this trek.

The absence of Josh's company would be the hardest part. Not that he could blame the young man for spending time with his bride, especially one so attractive as Elizabeth. It was expected, but was not the concern of hired hands. Probably, after the new wore off, Josh and he would see more of each other. Eventually, there would be some conversation with Elizabeth. Jubal's concern was the enforced loneliness that would now be his daily fare.

Other than Josh, he had had no one to speak with. The scout came around sometimes, but he was so different than anyone he had known that most of the time was spent trying to figure if the scout was serious or just having fun with him. He remembered their encounter under the starlit sky.

Before, there would always be a few people stopping by, and their visits were enough to break up the monotony. The captain, Metzger, stopped almost daily. Usually, this was just to give the day's marching orders. None of Josh's acquaintances would be stopping by just to jabber with the colored hand.

It was possible, now he was on his own, that Ely and Dinah, the Clarks' slaves, might stop off for a spell. They weren't tending to Miss Hampton or her gear anymore. Now that Miss Hampton was Mrs. Bonner, they would get a little respite from the extra work assigned. Maybe they could spend some time of an evening.

Of course, it wasn't his place to ask. It might be that the reverend and his wife were scairt of having their people spending spare moments with a

189

free black. Free, at least, as a runaway could count himself. Probably they would just drift on over if and when they could. Mostly, white folk didn't pay much mind to what colored folk did once their day's work was done. Jubal kicked sand over the small embers that had boiled his morning coffee. No sense thinking about it. Wasn't much he could do if he wanted.

After breaking camp at Chimney Rock, the emigrants bore ever westward, loosely following the trace of the North Platte. The thick ocean of grass that had fed their stock for so long was thinner; the vivid green of spring was sere now from the building heat of the summer, taking on a yellowish cast. The ground was less sandy, interspersed with loose gravel. Myriad rock formations convulsed through the surface, perhaps indicating another Chimney Rock, all but its tip long buried under the turf. The slow undulation of the grassland verge was now spare. Crumbling rock ledges, like books tipped on a shelf, were piled along the trailside. Three days west of the Chimney lay the largest of these formations, Scott's Bluff.

The imposing monolith of weathered sandstone lay neatly across the direct path west. According to lore, the pile had been named for a trapper that had died, been murdered, or was buried there. The Indians named it *Me-apate*, "the hill hard to go around." For practical purposes, the Indian name was appropriate. Changing course to the north went away from the Platte, the only source of water. Worse, the northerly course was more arid, the fodder thinning in the increasingly alkaline soil. There was a pass to the south, but not an easy trek. The path was lumpy, rocky, and traversed over outcroppings of sandstone. In whole, a wagon breaker.

The travelers camped in the shadow of the Bluff after their advance from Chimney Rock. The afternoon's creeping shadows extended far from the base, providing an early twilight.

Delacroix stood up in his stirrups, stretched, and took in the view. It had been a long day and mostly tedious. A child could find their way from the Chimney to the Bluff. The tedium was navigating a path through the jumble of rocky escarpments that rose unexpectedly in your path. No problem for a man horsed, but difficult for wagons. He was forced to stop and direct his charges around tracks that could not be passed. Now, the sun was signaling the end to another day, and he could rest and let the Bluff remind him of earlier days and travels.

His first visit, years ago, was with the Bluff to his back. He had made a great circle on his quest for beaver and other pelts. After journeying up the Missouri River to its source, he had trapped along the Powder, Milk, and Yellowstone Rivers. Unlike the other *voyageurs,* he had not returned with the spring, but journeyed ever west, always wandering beyond the next range, mist-shrouded in the distance across some intriguing coulee or meandering vale.

He had to laugh to himself. How the years embellished his memories. He could now recollect his trek as wanderlust. At the time, it just seemed like a practical alternative to losing his hair. The Lakota and Arikira resented the white intruders and did their best to keep them out of their lands. True, they would trade pelts for goods but were just as likely to ambush the trading partner, take back the pelts, and trade them to the next unwary clutch of whites seeking their fortune in animal skins.

Eventually, he found himself wintering with a clan of Crow. After helping them to defend their winter camp from marauding Blackfoot, he had been welcomed into their lodges and had taken up with one of their women, Hidden Horse. He had stayed with the clan through several winters and was always welcomed back as a member of the family. They accepted him as the prodigal son who returned unheralded and assumed his place at meals, fire, and bedstead. There was no resentment of his periodic abandonment of Hidden Horse. He had always hunted for his extended family and always brought in far more than he and his woman consumed. When he left, she was always stocked with trade goods that she could barter for necessities. Hidden Horse always enthusiastically welcomed him back to her blankets, and her family accepted their informal union. Delacroix suspected that if their couplings had produced a child, there would have been expectations put upon him. A child had never come. In his younger days, the childless status was welcome. Now that he had aged some, he regretted not having sired any kin. Of course, it was still possible that when he arrived this fall there might be a child swaddled in skins and blankets that he could call his own. He welcomed the image, and a smile passed across his face. Time would tell.

Delacroix could see the wagonmaster coming up. There was no mistaking his bulk in the saddle. The scout was surprised that his horse hadn't broken under the strain. At least the man could pick a stout horse, probably learned from burying broken mounts.

The captain would be full of himself today. Delacroix had allowed Metzger to take the lead and tend to guiding the wagons. In Metzger's two months on the trail, he had convinced himself that he was a grizzled trail veteran, and this day of simple navigation simply reinforced the man's image of himself.

Metzger reined to a stop in order to talk to the scout. Delacroix noted he stopped upwind so his dust blew into the scout's face. No plainsman here, thought Delacroix, turning his face away.

"Sorry about the dust; I wasn't thinking," apologized Metzger.

Delacroix squinted back at him, holding his hat in front of his face. *"N'importe."*

"We made good distance today. Everybody's wagon's a bit creaky from the rocks, but no one had to stop."

The scout only nodded. He was more upset about the man interrupting his deliberations than in getting dusted by his careless riding.

Metzger sensed the other man's peevishness and apologized again.

"Durn! I said I was sorry."

"Again. I say it is not important." He didn't wish to discuss that he was upset more for the interruption. "You must learn this is not Missouri. While all may look peaceful, there is danger in what you cannot see. One careless act says you are not thinking of where you are and what is about."

Metzger stretched in the saddle, taking the opportunity to look for what he might not have seen.

"What? Is there something I should know about?"

"There is nothing here. I was just thinking of the last time I was here. You interrupted me." Delacroix hoped that would put the subject to rest.

"The Bluff, you mean? That's sure one damned big rock. Is it true it's named for a trapper got kilt here?"

Delacroix conceded to himself his moments of reflection were over.

"I have heard the stories, but I don't know as there is any truth. Places here have as many names and stories as people who have seen them."

"Looks like lots of people have camped here. Should I hold everyone up and make camp?"

"As good a place as any. Just make sure you pick a spot where the animals can graze," replied the scout. Surely he was competent enough to find an untrampled campsite.

Delacroix couldn't resist one more small jab. "Remember to keep your eyes open."

Leland had been feeling good about himself all day. The Frenchy was getting more moody the farther west they went. He recognized the last remark was intended to chafe him. Damn his eyes. He had done just as good a job leading the emigrants today as the huffy plainsmen. Making him feel small just for kicking up a little dust knocked the cap off the whole day. It wasn't like everyone weren't coated in dirt anyway.

The constable turned captain had hoped this migration to Oregon would turn a page in his life. A constable back home didn't have much authority and was relegated to tending drunks and defusing the fracases that were a part of small town life. Any real law enforcement and the county sheriff had to be called. As trail master, he had gained the respect of his neighbors. He was good at organizing things, and their relatively easy passage gave him more confidence in his stature every day. Little things like the scout's displeasure shouldn't bother him. Somehow, because it did, he felt a tinge of the disdain he was fleeing. What the hell! Tomorrow was another day. He would just stay away from the scout unless he needed to talk to him.

Metzger turned to the final task of the day and looked about for a flat place with plenty of forage. They could have stopped about anywhere except for Wallace and Ethan McCardle's traveling stockyard. He had thought them fools to bring all those cows with them. So far, they had done all right. Hardly any deaths and fewer deserters. If they got them all to the Dalles, they would have a healthy start to their homestead.

It looked to be a pretty fair pasture off to the north about a quarter mile. He loped off to check it over before signaling the approaching wagons. Delacroix's last remark came back irritably. Despite the prickliness it caused, he surveyed well ahead of his course. Damn that smelly old trapper!

The captain circled about the proposed site and declared to himself that it would serve. He signaled to the lead wagon, Shearwood's today, and watched as the routine of day's end was enacted once more in a strange locale. Eventually, all were settled, meals eaten, and the pioneers slept until the sun rose at their backs and the ritual of departure consumed the early morning.

Josh and Elizabeth had intentionally set up a discrete distance from the other wagons, or at least the others had left them a discrete distance away. As a result, they were quite close to the corral of animals. Being downwind from the herd, they suffered through the night from the animals' noises and emanations, but not enough to deter them from their now nightly pleasures. Both were feeling aromatic themselves as they were far enough from the river that water had become a treasure. Bathing was limited to wiping down with a wet towel. As a starving man dreams of banquets, they dreamed of plunging into deep, cool water. The demands of impending travel interrupted even those simple dreams.

"I think I should wander over and see how Jubal is handling things," Josh spoke, a tone of suggestion in his voice.

"Let's just sit a spell. It doesn't look like we're going to start off anytime soon," his bride replied. They sat huddled against one another. Elizabeth firmed up her embrace to emphasize her point and added, "Jubal knows what he's doing. No need to check up on him."

"I'm not checkin' on him. He just seems lonelier now. With me spendin' all m'time with you, he hardly has anyone to even talk to."

"We're supposed to spend all our time together, husband." Elizabeth had decided she liked saying "husband" as much as she liked having one. "Stay just a few more minutes, then go."

Josh settled back into her embrace, feeling her clinch release as they settled comfortably together.

"I suppose there is going to be some kind of meeting. That's all I can think of to keep us from starting out," Elizabeth suggested.

"I 'spect it's 'cause they haven't figured which way to go," Josh speculated.

Elizabeth leaned forward so she could look him in the face as she asked, "Which way, what do you mean?"

Her husband lifted his arm toward the sandstone monolith before them. "The Bluff, I mean. It's too tall to go over, and too hard to go through. We got t'go round."

Looking at the cliffs ahead, the rising light full on its face so each outcropping stood in sharp relief from the fissures still in shadow, Josh added, "You know what that thing reminds me of?"

"I can't imagine. It looks like an ant's view of a cow pie to me."

Josh could see her point and chuckled appreciatively. "Serious. To me, it looks like some big animal, a lion maybe. Like the *"Sfinx"* you see pictures of. You think it might be like that, some ancient people made it and now it's just wore away?"

Elizabeth's image of the cliffs changed momentarily, but she was already losing interest in the surroundings. Gently, she took his earlobe in her teeth and tugged him down where they lay spooned together. She cozied up like she was going to spend the rest of the day lying about like a tabby in a mote of sunshine.

Josh would have loved to lie about like this forever. He would have except he was out here in front of God and country. The public display, especially on a day set for travel, was too much for his sensibilities. He sat up and began loosening himself from his bride's enfolding.

"I best get over to see to Jubal and my wagon," he mumbled as an excuse.

She sighed and let her arms slip from his waist as he stood. "I suppose you better," she agreed but without much enthusiasm.

Jubal had yoked Banner and Flag in place of the mules today. He was checking the traces for about the third time when Josh came up.

"Mornin', Josh. I put the oxen in today. The ground's hard enough so they can pull together, and the mules could use a rest."

Josh immediately felt bad. Changing out the teams from mule to oxen involved switching out much of the tack, too. He should have been here.

"I should have been here to help. You should have come got me."

"Figured you was kinda in harness y'self. No bother, I needed somethin' t'do."

"Still—"

"Don't be thinkin' on it. I ain't got much to do but take care of m'self and the animals. And they take more care than I do."

"That's one of the reasons I came over. I worry 'bout you. You got nobody to talk to, now that I am over with 'Lizabeth."

Jubal wondered if he should admit to Josh he had had visitors. Immediately, he had no doubt. If there was anyone in the world he could trust, it was Josh Bonner.

"Well, that ain't rightly so. Dinah and Ely come by most ever' evenin'. We sits a spell and talks after chores." There, the cat was out.

Jubal was surprised that Josh didn't react at all. Either he was making much more of the slave couple spending time with a free man, or Josh was not as sharp as he had thought. He knew Josh had a head on his shoulders, so it must just be his own fears that made him jumpy. Still, he was going to ask.

"You don't think it's wrong. Slaves talkin' to me as they please. The Clarks don't seem to care."

"I wouldn't give it any mind. If the Clarks thought it was wrong, you would have had the parson over here like Moses after his people at the gold calf."

Jubal faintly recalled something about Moses in the Desert but wasn't sure about any gold calf. It didn't take much to imagine Reverend Clark fuming up if he saw something he didn't like in his own household.

It dawned on him that neither of his two premises was right. It was as he had thought before. White folk just didn't pay much attention to what black folk did once their work was done. He began to pick up gear and pack it away on the wagon.

Josh, more to appear busy than by need, checked the animals and tackle. He was conscious that Jubal was certainly competent at his task, and any serious scrutiny might give offense to his friend. On the other hand, just standing about made him feel irresponsible. He strolled about, giving a tug on a strap here and there and stroking the placid animals. He was just crouching down to examine Banner's hooves when, from under the animal's belly, he spied Delacroix's boots coming to camp.

"I just left your pretty young wife. She said you would be here," announced the scout. "I wonder why you would rather look at ox legs than hers," he added as a friendly jest.

Josh didn't need any reminders of his divided duties. Best to get right to the meat of the matter.

"What brings you about this mornin'?"

"Come up to Metzger's rig. We're having a palaver."

Josh enjoyed the scout's colorful language but stuck to his course. "Are we meetin' about which way to go? What do you think?"

"That's what we're meeting about, and I only want to lay this out but once. So come along and you'll here what I got to say."

Josh bid good-bye to Jubal and strolled up to Metzger's while the scout continued his rounds.

He found the men in small groups speculating on the reason for meeting. Lew Petry, as was typical, stood off by himself.

"Good mornin', Mr. Petry. Hope all is well."

"Me and the kids are doing fine. The missus is complaining 'bout a few trifles, but that's her way." Ever'thing fine with you?"

"All's well with me. I don't see Metzger."

"His highness will show when he's good and ready. I wish t'hell I knew what this was about."

Josh was a little surprised Petry hadn't grasped why they had been called together. Listening in on some of the conversations, he found most of the men speculating on the reason for meeting.

"I'm thinkin' we're gonna talk about whether to head north or south around the Bluff," said Josh.

"Probably right. I don't know why we got to decide. That's what we're payin' the Frenchy for."

Josh was formulating a defense of the scout when Metzger appeared, Delacroix in tow. He raised his arms and demanded the crowd's attention.

"If you haven't figgered out what we're doin' here, we've got to talk about which way we're going to head off. Delacroix and I talked it over, but I think you better hear it from him. I've pretty much made up my mind, but I want to hear what you all think."

He motioned the scout up to address the crowd.

"You have to make a choice today about our route. We can go north around the Bluff or south around it. There's good and bad reasons for going either way.

"If we go to the south we stay close enough to the river to get to water. There is a pass that way, but it isn't easy going. South's rockier than the gullies we have had for the past days, and it's a bit longer than the northern way.

"The northern route is about half a day shorter, but it's dry. There are no springs, no creeks to get water from. It's harder on the animals, and it will take most of the way to Laramie to get back to any water at all. Think first about how much water you have."

"Precious little," shouted out Ethan McCardle. "Our herd can't go north."

The debate was on.

"We can't be always holdin' ourselves up for your cows. I vote north," said a voice from the back.

"I've barely water for my team," said another. "I can't go north."

"My wagon's shakin' to pieces now. Go north."

"A half day's extra march through them rocks might turn out to be two days. North, I say."

Metzger let the debate rage for a few minutes before shouting out, "Enough. I'm thinkin' south, and I'll tell you why. I'm carrying two kegs on my wagon. One's empty and so dry it wouldn't hold water anyway. The second's almost full but it won't last if we went north. How's the water holdin' up for the rest of you? You got enough to last three or four days? If we stay south, we can send someone off to refill at the river. It's why I say south."

Everyone agreed they were short of water, but still some voted for the north, fearing the extra strain the rocky way would put on their wagons and stock. Eventually, it was concluded to go south and to send someone for water if it got desperate.

As the crowd broke up and set off for their camps, Lew Petry commented to Josh and anyone else close enough to overhear, "If he'd already made up his mind for us, why bother to call us all up to argue about it? We could already have made three or four miles."

Scattered grumblings concurred with Petry.

Josh thought a lot of grief could have been avoided if they had just headed off south. Most of the men hadn't even realized there was an alternate route. Starting up a debate was probably not the best plan as everybody's nerves were on edge. They had been too long thinking about Fort Laramie, and delays of any kind rode sore on their hides.

And south it was, the mule-drawn wagons off first to blaze a trail. Next, went the slower oxen teams followed by the loose stock. This arrangement would separate Josh's and Elizabeth's wagons. Soon after breaking trail, the road ascended, eventually leaving even the brittle hardpan of the valley behind. The path entered a pass that climbed along the south of the Bluff with rock formations piled to the left. The climb was steady and wound about many heaved up rocky ledges. There was no chance of wandering off the path at this point. No false passages lured the migrants into dead ends forcing retreat. There was often room for two or even three wagons, but the true path was obvious, the rocks scarred and rutted by the wagon tires of past seasons. The pass soon had the wagons spread along its trace. Slower teams like Josh's often had to halt while wagons ahead were manhandled over the rough terrain. Metzger and Delacroix constantly rode the length of the expedition, trying in vain to keep the wagons bunched closer together. It was difficult even to find a flat enough space to halt and rest the teams for a moment. Brakes had to be set and wheels chocked, lest any advantage be surrendered.

As the teams, mule and oxen alike, began to tire, it became harder to maintain an even pace. The wagons moved in humps and jerks across the lumpy ground, wheels often jolting off the bumps, jarring wagon and passengers. The bolts and pegs that held the wagons together, already dry, began to work from their beds. Constant wedging and tightening had to be done on the move. Each pounding drop, even if only a few inches, threatened to part the boards or relieve a wheel of its iron tire. A halt was called at about two in the afternoon. Everyone was sore from the ride and the struggle to assist the wagons. The women and children had descended from the wagons, electing to walk rather than risk further loosening of their teeth. The men, stripped to the waist, were soon scorched pink, adding another contrast to the tanning of their arms and face with the pastiness usually covered by their shirts. All were parched with the dust and exertion. Water was precious. The few gulps taken washed away the dust but only increased the desire for more. The draft animals were rationed a ladle at a time.

Jubal, stripped like many of the men, felt the effects of the sun on his dark skin, particularly on his back and shoulders. Recalling trains being watered from a tower, he pictured himself under a sloughing flow of cool water. He watched Banner and Flag slurp from the dipper he offered.

"How are the oxen holding up?" Josh said as he approached.

"Those are fine, strong animals there. They're still a-pullin' steady. Gots to admit my knees is getting as creaky as the wagon."

"It's my feet that are killin' me. I think if I take m'boots off, my feet would swell like melons. Damn! Now I'm gonna be thinkin' of melons for the rest of the day."

"Mebbe you could try one of these little cactus. They look like little melons with prickers all over 'em," Jubal replied with a laugh as he pictured trying to eat one of the formidable plants.

"I wonder how they even find a place to grow. Nothin' here but rocks. Even the dirt gave up on this place," Josh observed.

"I've seen some big goats, or at least glimpses of 'em. Big white ones with horns that wrap all around their heads. 'Spect they must eat the cactus."

"Mebbe that's what I keep getting a peek at. I keep seein' things movin', but when I look, there's nothing there. Guess I'm skittish of Indians. Spread out like this, we're easy pickings," said Josh, adding, "Guess they eat the goats."

"Ever'thin' finds its way."

Josh was about to ask his friend about the curious statement when the scout appeared coming down the trail.

"There's water ahead. Not that it will do the animals any good. It's down in a gorge, but we can get a few bucketfuls. We're gatherin' up some boys to climb down and fill buckets we can haul up. It's good water, but don't take more than a bucket or two for your kegs."

"How much is there?" asked Josh.

"There's a spring out of the side of the mountain and just a small pool leaking into the rocks. We'll take what we can, but there's precious little at that."

"How's McCardle's herd doing for water?"

"I guess going dry makes you inquisitive," Delacroix replied. "They're doing better than the rest of us. They got nothin' to haul but their own sorry hides. You best worry about your own animals."

Without another word, the scout spurred away to spread the news about the spring. Perhaps his short attitude was a reflection of concern about the choice of trails.

"Guess I better get up to the wagon; looks like we'll be moving out."

"Don't you worry about us back here. We're doin' jist fine."

Josh had no worries about Jubal and the gear. He clapped him on the shoulder and assured him of his confidence, then began the trudge up the hill. He hadn't gone halfway to the wagon when the two oldest of Wallace and Ethan McCardle's boys sprinted past him with bucket and rope. Josh couldn't remember their names, but there was no mistaking the McCardle lineage in the two boys. He speculated that his concern for the McCardle stock was unfounded. As last in the train, they would claim the final dregs of the spring water.

When Josh arrived back at the wagon, he found Elizabeth up on the wagon seat.

"How are you holding up, darlin'?"

"I don't know which hurts more, my rear or my feet. I climbed up here so I could try to make a fair choice." At least her spirits were still high.

Elizabeth added, "Hear all the hubbub ahead. The spring is just around the bend. Thinking about a cool drink is keeping me going."

"Want me to run ahead and get you a dipper?"

"Thanks, but no. We'll be moving up soon, and the anticipation is almost as welcome as the water itself. I'm already tasting it."

The mule team was already sampling the water on the breeze and fidgeting in their harness, apparently not content to picture the cool relief in their dim imaginations.

Within just a few minutes, the procession had restarted. As they rounded the bend, the team, without any prodding, picked up the pace.

The young couple spied the water splashed on the rocky trail. Just the sight of water glistening on the rocks in this parched clime was enough to set their mouths to wanting. Five or six boys were enthusiastically hauling buckets up the wall of the gorge thirty or so feet below. Each was soaked to the skin and enjoying every minute of their chore. Half a dozen full buckets stood by the roadside.

One of the boys—Josh thought it was Lew Petry's son Caleb—jogged over and tugged at his forelock. He handed Josh an oak bucket.

"Captain Metzger says only three buckets a wagon, two for your keg and one for your animals. 'Course, I guess you could spread it out any way you like," he added. A grin spread across his freckled cheeks as he sprinted back to help haul up more buckets.

Josh halted the team, braced the wheels, and helped Elizabeth down from her seat. The temptation was to pour a bucket over his head. It would have felt like heaven. Elizabeth instead handed him a dipper she had brought. Josh plunged it into the still sloshing bucket and began to bring it to his lips. He stopped, thinking of his bride, and held it out for her to drink from. He hoped she hadn't noticed his selfish act.

If she had, any regard was forgotten instantly as the water passed her dried lips and leaked away at the corners of her mouth, the liquid cutting tracks in the dust of her face and neck.

"My God! That's the coldest, most delicious thing I've ever tasted. Again," she beckoned. The second dipper brought an icy stab to her head and made her teeth seem to rattle in her jaw. She didn't care about the momentary pain other than to slightly slow her greedy desire to slake her thirst. It was so good. When she finished the second dipper, she motioned Josh to partake.

"I don't know if it's the wanting or if this is just the best water I've ever had. It's colder and sweeter than any well water I've ever tasted."

It wasn't like Josh needed any encouragement to drink. Just watching his wife pour the icy liquid down had brought on a near panic of ravenous thirst. He wasn't disappointed as he mimed Elizabeth's devouring of the magic tonic, even to the grimace at the ice pick sensation in his brain. His whole insides seemed to soak up the water and swell like a sponge left in the sun, then dipped. He bent over and poured a third dipper over his neck, shivering with an invigoration that almost made him dizzy. He shook his head, flinging droplets over his bride. Her face was spotted as the drops cut through the trail dust.

She laughed with delight. "Let me try."

Taking a ladle but wanting a bucket, she poured the water deliciously over the crown of her head and relished the icicles coursing over her scalp and down her blouse.

Josh was enjoying Elizabeth's shivering cascade as much as she was when he noticed the group of boys at the gorge's edge had ceased their hauling and were openly gawking at them. The boys had probably watched the same scene with every wagon. What had made them all stop and stare? Josh knew it wasn't him, and he recalled how Elizabeth would turn all the male heads back in Cairo. It came to him again how fortune had smiled to send him such a beauty. *Too bad, world, she's with me!*

Josh's gloating over his blessing came to an abrupt end as he felt himself being nudged toward the gorge's precipice. It was the mule team he had ignored in his celebration. Instantly, he felt a fool and wondered if the boys had been staring at his irresponsibility. While he had been indulging himself, the team had wandered toward the cliff face and was peering longingly at the water beyond their reach. Actually, they appeared ready to make the descent, and the lead pair was scratching tentatively at the rocky ledge, perhaps considering a leap of faith, a leap that would doom the mules, the wagon, and the boys below. Josh quickly came to his senses and seized the bit, trying to divert their attention.

"'Lizabeth, give me a bucket, quick!"

She had already seen what was about to transpire and had a bucket at the ready. She held it under the closest mule's snout and swept a palm full of water at it, quickly diverting its attention to the wet relief at hand.

If the mule team experienced the same sensations as the two humans, they weren't saying. Greedily, each dove at the bucket Josh offered in turn. So enthusiastically did they pursue the drink that Josh struggled to keep the bucket in his grip. The last mule enjoyed being served as Josh upended the bucket and poured into the animal's upturned mouth. Satisfied or not, the single bucket would have to do. The remaining two were poured into the keg mounted on the wagon side to be rationed until they returned to the river.

And so the train passed the small spring, the final seepage soaked up by shirts and wrung into buckets. All received some as they stopped for their ration, with the McCardle herd taking the last drops. Fortune had smiled in providing the small fountain, unexpected and gratefully received.

It took until suppertime for the bulk of the expedition to reach the summit and consider the equally perilous descent. Summer had stretched the daylight hours, but not enough sun remained to attempt the journey down. A path as rocky and contentious as the road up lay before them, the grade not steep, but long and twisting. Recalling the spectacle of DeKop's draft wagon careening down Windlass Hill, no one was willing to chance the trek with tired teams and looming nightfall. They would camp at the summit, rocks and wind for bed and kindling. No fires would heat a meal or brew coffee. Cold camp and biscuits would serve. The weary travelers did not complain. Most crawled into wagons before the sun had dipped behind the distant Laramie Mountains.

Not until dawn cast long shadows over the land did the travelers take note of the spectacular perch upon which they had rested. A panorama, stretching perhaps a hundred miles, greeted the early riser, stretching and gaping from their bed.

Toward the east, the sun had crested the plain, rising from its purple bedclothes to shower the sky with shades of red and orange, dispelling the indigo night. Chimney Rock appeared a dark spire against the sunrise. The horizon revealed was so vast many imagined seeing the curve of the planet unveiled before them. To the north, the rumpled crest of Scott's Bluff lay at their feet. Shadows hiding in the folds made the protrusions appear to float without binding to the earth. Turning to the west, toward their goal, a plain of shadows painted the floor of the basin; a faint glimmering on distant water marked the trace of the Laramie River. On the far horizon, the Laramie Mountains lay shrouded with distance and indistinct in the faint light. On the mountain's northwest shoulder, a gathering storm hung, a gloom the rising sun would not penetrate. To the south, morning light made the Platte a brilliant yellow ribbon spilled on the shifting prairie.

There was no chore to starting out. No fires had been built, for there was no forage of kindling. People and animals were watered, and the descent began. The wagons had been punished with the jolting climb. The road down was as rocky as the ascent. The emigrants had long ago learned how to up and down hills. Because the wagons were so fragile and held together mostly from habit, extra care was employed. Each wagon couldn't have been driven so deliberately had it contained explosives. Fortunately, the road was as much worn as the trail had been uphill. No wreckage of broken wagons shaken and jolted to death marked the trailside. If any earlier travelers had lost their gear, it had been picked up for firewood by scavenging pioneers. By afternoon, the level plain had been reached. Sandstone escarpments still protruded from the scrub brush and hardpan, but in comparison, the way seemed as smooth as any plank road in the East.

The train bore southwest, trying to regain the Platte. The spring, an unexpected salvation, had kept the trek over the pass from becoming a dry ordeal. Each of the wagons still carried kegs that sloshed pleasantly as they made their way. The wagons had to get back to the river for a soaking. The wagons, many of them new only a few months ago, now seemed like relics from a misused farm. Boards newly joined and painted were loose, the surfaces scaly open sores where the sapwood had dried. Gaps between planks appeared. The wagons now looked like they had been built with old fence boards. Even the harnesses, kept limber with saddle soap and tallow, were starting to bleach white, the finish flecking away. While the deterioration caused concern, the wagon bodies and tackle could be repaired. The great anxiety was for the wheels and tires. Spokes, once polished smooth, were becoming like old axe handles with lifted grain to splinter the user's hand. The iron tires were wobbling on the rims, threatening to slide off and roll away like a child's hoop. Baling wire had been wrapped around suspect spokes and carefully bound around the tires in hopes it would hold the parts together until either water was met or the wire wore through. Man and animal with cracked lips and gummy mouths would make it only with discomfort. The wagons carried not just possessions but the hopes and dreams for a new life.

The train moved slowly back to the North Platte. Every ear was tuned, awaiting the sound of catastrophe, the sudden crack of wood or crash of a wagon losing a wheel. All knew how close they were to water yet how agonizingly slowly they must proceed. Not more than a couple of hours would bring them to the shallows where they could revive their gear.

The day had been hot, but not oppressive. A constant wind had built with the rising of the sun, carrying the dry air over already parched skins. Those who let their attention stray from the quest for the river and looked to the sky saw the great tempest building to the northwest. Cumulus clouds piled and stacked over a purple-gray anvil of thunderhead, arranged like pancakes reaching high to the heavens and spreading out over the western horizon. By the time the train had reached the river, the wind had died. The air lay still in anticipation of the oncoming weather. The sun had moved behind the anvil; the shadow of twilight fell over the plains in mid-afternoon.

By the time the emigrants reached the Platte shallows, the storm had seemingly stalled. A curtain of rain lay under the clouds, and only the distant flicker of lightning and the grumbling of thunder gave evidence of the deluge creeping their way. A soaking was coming, but the weary travelers would take the one that lay at their feet.

As anxious as they were to drive into the river, the many crossings behind them had taught the need to probe a stream before entering lest they sink to hub of wagon and belly of beast. If you found pebbles under your wheels, it was a safe bet to drive across or perch upon.

Exhausted, the people fell into the shallow. They sat with their clothes pillowed with trapped air as their skin soaked up moisture as gratefully as their wind-stiffened clothing. Sighs of relief escaped past chapped lips. If animal or inanimate wagon could sigh, their voices would have joined the chorus.

Josh and Elizabeth sat in water up to their necks. Upon their heads sat hats recently soaked and now cooling tired brows. Only a scant few inches between brim of hat and chins remained above water. Neither spoke or moved; the sensation of cool water carried on gentle currents too good a feeling to be spoiled with words. Had they taken the effort to look around, they would have found no person standing. All their neighbors had as much of their bodies as possible under water. Even the somber Reverend Clark could not be seen except for the toes of his boots and a bristle of beard floating on the surface of the river.

What normally would have been a chore, soaking the wagons to revive the tired wood, was today a melee of thrown buckets of water and dousing of neighbors. Children and dogs frolicked in the stream. Probably the task was unnecessary as the storm over their shoulders was slowly approaching and promised a night of heavy rain. The deliverance of reaching the river sustained the people as they soaked everything in sight. Each, as they left the river, sent an expedition upstream to refill kegs with water not clouded by the festival going on in the river.

Metzger and Delacroix loafed in their saddles as their horses drank from the river. Neither of the two had joined in the wet free-for-all celebration. Much as they may have wanted to, their positions as the leaders could not allow it.

"That pass wasn't as bad as I thought. Good to find the little spring," Metzger remarked.

"I've been through that way four or five times and never seen it before. But you are right. It was a good thing to find."

"They sure are carrying on. You'd think they had been through hell itself 'stead of just being away from the river for a day or so. It's not even that hot," said Metzger derisively.

"It will be hotter, the more west we go. A lot dryer, too," the scout added.

A sudden gust whistled at their backs, almost knocking off both their hats. The pair turned, reminded of the storm bearing down.

"We better get 'em moving, *mon Capitaine*. Time for circling up."

"You think it'll be a bad 'un?"

"It is already a bad one, just not here yet."

Full night found the wagons formed in a corral with the herd penned inside. Riding stock was kept fettered to each wagon, handy if the need arose. Mule, horse, ox, or cow, all turned their rump to the broadside of wind and huddled together as best they could for shelter.

The wagons, rocking with the force of the gale, sheltered people who climbed into beds and ventured out only for as long as it took to stuff a rag where the wind had breached the canvas. Those that peeked out witnessed a duel of lightning in the clouds and waited as the claps of thunder boomed ever closer.

When the rain finally arrived, it was like a river levee breaking. It didn't just drum on the wagon covers or pound the hardpan to instant mire, the heavens were draining like a plug pulled from a barrel. Anyone foolish enough to venture out would have been astonished to find even drawing a full breath was honest work. How could clouds hold so much water and how long could the storm sustain itself? No such questions were voiced. The noise was so intense, so constant that conversation wasn't worth the effort. Many reflected how peculiar it was that on that very morning they had been worried about how dry their equipment was. Others wondered how long it would last and if they had moved to safe ground.

The effort it had taken to move the train from the river to what high ground could be attained had been worth it. Nearly half a mile from the

Platte and they hadn't gained much more than five or six feet above the river. It would have to make do. There wasn't anything higher without retreating up the pass again, and there was no chance now of moving anything through the morass about them.

Eventually, in the shank of the night, the storm either passed on or ran out of rain. By then, the emigrant corral had become an island that was fast shrinking away. There was no telling whether they were on the banks of the river or were now in the river. Driftwood, carried down from the Sweetwater Mountains, floated like a lost fleet and would lie scattered along the road for the next forty miles.

"Marooned. We might as well be marooned, like some pirate in a story," Elizabeth said as she pulled her feet loose from the muck. "Look at this. You can barely take a step without sinking to your ankles. I'm amazed the wagon is still above ground."

"You should have seen the McCardles this morning. Guess they lost some cows in the storm. They tried to follow them, and their horses got mired. They almost had to crawl on their bellies back to their wagons," offered Josh. "Either their cows didn't get very far or they're drowned. Even if they found some alive, they couldn't drag 'em back," he added.

Elizabeth couldn't care a whit about some lost cows. She was poking about in the larder, hoping to find something dry enough to eat. The storm had invaded through cracks in the canvas and boards. Every box of hard biscuit was sodden or at best, damp. Maybe it could be fried up with some fat, but there was nothing dry enough to burn.

Surveying the camp Josh found everybody else was more or less in the same fix. No way to move, no way to cook, and nothing much to do but arrange for drying or salvaging what possessions they could. They were going to be stopped here until the ground got firm enough to roll over. Fort Laramie was only two days away, but it might have been across an ocean, even if that ocean were mud.

#

CHAPTER FOURTEEN

#

It ended up taking six days to reach the fort. After two days of being stuck, a few wagons experimentally ventured forth. The experiment ended in mere yards as the wheels sank into the mire. The rest of the second day was spent retrieving the adventurous cattle and placing them back in the corral. The third day was spent in speculation about how quickly the sun would firm up the ground sufficient for travel.

When they finally set out, the going was ponderously slow. The wheels picked up muck that almost filled the spokes. Shoes and boots were caked so each step was a labor of picking up and putting down. The hems of skirts and cuffs of pants caked with mud at each step. It was a sorry looking lot as reached the bank of Laramie Creek and prepared to cross.

Even nearly a week after the storm had devastated eastern Wyoming, Laramie Creek was still swollen and turgid. Carrying down silt from the mountains, it poured into the Platte, the confluence of the two a collection of sandbars and eddies of muddy water and debris.

The residents of the fort were not ones to miss an opportunity to eke out a dollar or two from the emigrant trains. Within two days of the storm, a rope ferry and flatboat had been rigged across the torrent. The barge had spent its former days as a collection of wagons, broken and abandoned by travelers who elected to pack up the steep trail to the Continental Divide. After the ferry business lost its charm, the flatboat would end up dispersed around the fort, wood being a marketable commodity. For the time being, the ferrymen would listen patiently to their customers lamenting the toll. The only response from the enterprising ferry owners was to spit an occasional wad of tobacco, more to show they were paying attention than considering negotiations. Eventually, they knew, the toll would be paid, the freight would be hauled, and a few silver coins would go in their pocket.

"Eight dollar for a wagon and fifty cents for a horse! You're robbing us," Custis Gresham protested.

"Horse, mule, or ox. They's all a half dollar," informed the ferry owner. A stain of tobacco juice bisected his chin and spotted his shirt. "If you don't like it, you can check prices at the other ferry."

"There is no damned other ferry! You should be ashamed," wailed Gresham.

"There used t'be, but he went out of business 'cause his prices was too cheap. Couldn't cover his costs," came the practiced reply from the proprietor of the only water conveyance for several hundred miles. "You can pay or you can swim. What'll it be?"

"I'll pay, damn your eyes and damn your boat."

"You look like a man who's squeezed a nickel or two before. That'll be eleven dollars. Wagon, team, and both horses. You and your missus can ride fer free if you're not walkin'."

Josh listened to the exchange and was amused to see the storekeeper, who had indeed pinched a few nickels in Cairo, get his comeuppance. Not many made a sharper trade than Custis Gresham, and it was fun to see a crude teamster get the better of him, especially with the smug knowledge of who was calling the shots.

By the next morning, the only members who hadn't crossed were the McCardles. Nothing could convince them to part with the coin necessary to transport fifty or sixty head of cattle by barge. Figuring the water would recede, they, with their wagons, would wait out the crest. Josh left Banner and Flag in their care rather than part with the toll. Two wagons and eight mules were dear enough fare.

The reality of Fort Laramie caused the emigrants to rethink their idea of frontier forts. Expecting to encounter something similar to the limestone fortifications present along the eastern rivers or even the wooden palisades left over from earlier Indian wars, Laramie had to be a disappointment.

Originally built as a trading post by the American Fur Company, there had been no fort at all until the army had shown a lukewarm interest in protecting the fur industry from British intrusion. As yet, there was no permanent garrison. A company of troopers used the outpost as a base for patrols and escort of commerce along the Platte. As cavalry were wont to do, building walls and shoveling mud was reserved for punishment details. The results were slow and of a quality as might be expected from such unwilling artisans. Now that the deluge had passed on, the penitents of the fort were busy. Being constructed of mud, the wall had settled some and its edges had softened. Men, stripped to the waist, carried buckets of mud and slung double handfuls against the walls where clumps had melted or sloughed away.

The hewn wooden gates swung on leather hinges between two turrets providing crossfire to anyone attempting to breach the portal. Attacking this outpost would not be easy as the walls could be easily manned. Scaling the walls would be the only reasonable means to gain entry. At least the illusion was maintained from the front. Fort Laramie was not complete. Beyond the turrets at the corners, the walls were still under construction, only partially enclosing the buildings. The buildings, ramshackle as they were, comprised the balance of the fortifications.

Ramshackle was a befitting description for the denizens of the outpost, too. No soldiers drilled or flashed colorful guidons on the parade grounds. Those not stripped to their trousers sat about in the shade or leaned along the rough walls of the buildings, leaving some doubt as to whether they were leaning against or supporting the buildings themselves. Rough traders, trappers, and skinners milled about with no apparent task or direction other than to assure an even disbursement of aroma throughout the enclosure. Hides, staked out on the ground, provided odors for any corners neglected by the residents. A few Indians, come to trade pelts for whiskey and other trinkets, passed in and out of the gates, alternating their procurement of rotgut with the consumption and consequences of their enterprise. The only visible sign of industry was the sound of a blacksmith's hammer ringing out its challenge to iron hot from the forge. Elsewhere, hidden from sight, honest work was probably being performed. If so, it was well disguised by the general air of lethargy that abounded.

Those emigrants, hungry for new faces, striding eagerly through the wooden gates, found themselves maundering about near the entrance, averse to explore this lost outpost of modern civilization. Other than the sight of buildings, no sign of the civilization they had left behind was evident. Laramie was simply a place of commerce, built without any comfort or nicety that didn't promise to pay its keep.

Only those with a pressing need for commerce continued in, seeking what appeared, by its display of goods, to be the sutler's store. These unfortunates were confronted with prices for common staples ten or twelve times what they had paid at the outset of their journey. Items that were to be replaced as necessities soon were categorized as unobtainable luxuries. Perhaps a square deal could be made if the travelers had pelts or hides to trade. Other than fur, their hoarded coins were the only custom here. There was no need for the household items they might have negotiated with. Most of what they offered to trade was lying on the trail and could be had for the picking. There was not even market enough to warrant an expedition to replenish stock.

Josh and Elizabeth found themselves amongst the crowd standing about in what would be the parade ground of a regularly garrisoned fort. The trappers and traders lazing around were about the scruffiest lot of people they had ever seen. The soldiers didn't seem much of a cut above the rest. It seemed almost the greater threat to life and limb was inside the fort rather than outside its wall.

"This place looks rougher than a cob," said Josh. "Reminds me of the bag end of Cincinnati."

"I don't know what it reminds me of. It certainly isn't what I expected," replied Elizabeth.

"This is one of those places that once you are in, you wish you was out."

"Well, in any event, it's all there is. Let's look around," resolved Elizabeth, taking her husband's hand in hers.

As the couple set forth, they took some other hesitant people in tow. No one felt comfortable exploring on their own.

It was obvious the residents hadn't seen many white women, especially so rare a beauty as Mrs. Bonner. All those with nothing to do, which was most everyone, gravitated toward the couple. The visitors strode toward what must be the store. At least the display of boxed and barreled goods gave that impression.

Surprisingly, the oddest sensation for the new arrivals was walking into a building. Even the shortest ducked their heads as they passed the doorway. If they had given it any thought, it might not have been such an amazement. This was the first any of them had been indoors for two months. No lamps were lit, and the few small windows lent a dim ambience to the wares on display. The recent rains and leaking exterior left a promise of mildew in the air. Mixed with the musty smell of old dry goods and the fragrance of ripe hides, the store did not invite lingering. Everything for sale was dusty and shopworn. Even new goods quickly took on the look of ultimate neglect. No prices were marked; apparently, they were as flexible as the customer's ability to pay.

A man, with the look of the proprietor, leaned on a broom. Together, they gave the appearance of a couple whose dance had been interrupted. The man was tall and thin, a perfect dance partner for the cornstraw broom. He set his partner to rest against the plank counter and came to greet the half dozen or so new prospects that wandered into his establishment.

Sporting the deep bronze of an outdoorsman and a mop of salt-and-pepper hair, his identity as the storekeeper came from the bib apron that seemed to wrap several times around his lanky frame. He extended a long hand, rough with hard work, to Elizabeth.

"Howdy, I'm John Tutt. Welcome to Fort Laramie, paradise on the Platte." He managed a genuine laugh at what must have been a tired line. "Look around. I've probably got what you need." He didn't offer to relinquish Elizabeth's hand.

Josh stuck his out in rescue. "I'm Josh Bonner. This is my wife. We're happy to have made it this far. Feels strange, jist bein' inside."

"Most people feel that way when they first arrive. Once you've spent a winter here, you won't be so sure this is inside." He gestured with his free hand, taking in the whole establishment.

Elizabeth finally had to wring her hand away from the sutler. He didn't seem to mind his prize being wrested away.

Taking in the other loafers in the store, she had to concede that at least Tutt's hand was clean. The thought of touching any of the trappers and skinners made her shrivel up a bit. She closed up to Josh. He put his arm on her waist possessively.

"We'll just browse a bit, might find something we can't do without," said Josh to be polite.

Tutt ducked behind the two and began his song and dance with Lew Petry, his wife, and boy. "Hello, I'm John Tutt. I own this place."

Josh and Elizabeth had wandered away and were more enjoying the sensation of a real roof and walls than examining any of the wares being offered. There was really nothing they needed, though Josh reminded himself to check his gunpowder to see if it had been wet by the storm.

By now, many of their friends had come into the store and were strolling about, examining the goods under the studious eye of the sutler. All knew anything they selected would come dearly. No one touched anything, fearing that showing any interest would cause the storeowner to descend. Tutt hovered nearby, hands clasped behind his back, rocking slowly on his heels. The similarity to a scavenger lingering until its meal quit squirming wasn't lost on the travelers.

Before the negotiations began in earnest, The Bonners slipped away, only to be greeted at the doorway by some of the malingerers who had cozied up to review the fresh visitors. This appeared to be some sort of ritual. The travelers, unfortunately, were not privy to the intricacies of the observance. And an observance it was. The residents just looked over each person, occasionally muttering some comment about dress or appearance to one another. There was nothing inherently unfriendly about their attentions. It was patently curious, almost shy. These men had been living in the wild for much of the year, or years. Being at Laramie was just as novel for them as for the wagon trains that stopped for rest and replenishment.

Living in hardship had eroded away any social skills that might have ventured west with the collection of trappers and skinners. Most were barely acquainted with others of their trade. The trappers spent months at a time with no human contact. Their graces were as worn as the stiffened hide breeches and shirts they lived in. They had become inured to their solitary pursuits and gun-shy of their fellow man.

In this remote outpost, there was a paucity of white women. Not many came overland, and few so comely as Elizabeth. The inmates could not recall when, if indeed they ever had seen such a beautiful creature. By degrees, they all were in awe, in love, or in lust with her. Those that had spied her from across the parade grounds were determined to speak to her but were struck dumb as stumps once close by.

Elizabeth, being no fool and well attuned to the attentions of men, was cognizant of the effect she had upon them. Her native instincts almost got the better of her before she recalled she was married. To yield would be to disrespect her husband. Demurely, she adhered to him, exhibiting the modesty a newly minted wife should possess.

The scrutiny his wife received was like a concussion to Josh. He knew the effect Elizabeth had on men. In Cairo, he many times had seen how his bride left men stammering. In the last few months of travel, the men of their party had become familiar with her and were less flummoxed. What they were experiencing now was a shock. The men of the fort weren't leering at her. Their reaction was enhanced by the lack of any women. To be exposed now to a rare beauty was more than their systems could take at a single gulp. Worse was the realization he was going to have to absorb the stares of strange men gawking at his wife for a long time. His feelings were a mixture of pride and satisfaction, tempered with anger for all men and their blatant exhibitions of want.

"Goddamn, she's just a girl. There'd be plenty more to look at if you wasn't livin' all in the middle of nowheres."

Stupefied that their ambitions had been spoken, the men fell silent. Their gaze dropped to their feet. A group of schoolboys caught truant was an apt impression of the scene.

Finally, one spoke. "Are there more trains behind you?"

Josh, perplexed at how quickly his outburst had changed the men's demeanor, replied, "I 'spose, but we haven't seen any since a group led by a Dutchman from Ohio passed us up." He added, "They've been here, haven't they?"

A smaller man dressed in buckskin pants and an oversized cotton shirt replied.

"DeKop, you mean. He tried to buy animals. The ones he had were hard used. There was none to be had, so they pushed on after a couple of days."

Well, the ice was broken. The group pushed in asking questions. It was still apparent that none had the gumption to speak to Elizabeth directly. Talking at her husband gave them an excuse to stay near the girl.

One, a gaunt specimen pocked with smallpox scars thrust out a hand. "I'm Aaron Patch. Signed on as scout fer the army. Been trappin' out here since I left Kentucky eight years back." His grin was sincere but missing some lowers in the front.

Josh took the hand. "I'm Josh Bonner. This is my wife, Elizabeth. We're from Illinois, headed to Oregon."

"Pleased to meet ya," Patch replied. He nodded at Elizabeth shyly, touching his cap. He retained Josh's handshake, keeping the couple captive. The others hung near, appointing Patch spokesman.

"Good to meet you, too. What do you do for the army?" Josh asked.

"Mostly I keep track of the Injuns and look for buffalo. 'Course, if you find the buffalo, you usually find the locals, too."

"The rest of you fellas work for the army, too?"

"Those that can, do," said Patch. "The rest are skinners waitin' for pelts to take east. What's left is hunters fixin' to settle up for the hides they brought in."

Josh wrested his hand away and looked for a polite way to depart.

"Will you be stayin' on long?" the scout inquired, unwilling to release his captives.

"No," Josh replied. "We'll just stay long enough to rest up and make repairs. Thanks be we won't have to buy anything. Those prices are dear."

"Oh, Tutt's not so bad. He just bought the place, and he trades square if you got hides or furs. Don't trade when yer drunk. He'll skin ya then."

Josh could feel Elizabeth tugging at him. He tried another avenue of escape.

"Do you know where we can find the commander? We'd better see if there's a place we can stay."

As reply, most of the hangers-on gestured generally toward a pair of frame buildings near the gate. None offered a spoken direction.

"He'll probably put you up in the new officers' quarters." Patch pointed to a framed and partially closed building under construction. "That's it. Best roof around, though there's no insides yet. Looks right comfortable."

Handshakes all around, and the couple strolled away. Patch caught up with them and leaned in to divulge a confidence.

"You folks be careful around here. Most of these boys is all right, but there's some hard cases about. Watch out for the short, bald man with the notch in his ear. Him and his crowd ain't much better'n animals," the scout whispered. "Sweeney's his name. It makes my mouth sour just to speak it." He spit lustily for emphasis.

"I've seen bad types before, livin' on the Big Muddy," Josh assured with more confidence in his voice than he felt.

"You ain't run across bad like this bunch. They came west to avoid the noose or got left out here by those smart enough to maroon 'em. Sweeney, Clement, Thibeault, and the rest. They stay mostly out of the fort. Captain Brennan won't have 'em around."

"We'll keep our eyes open; tell the rest of our folks, too," Josh assured. "Thanks for the warning." Thanking Patch, they made for the offices.

Elizabeth spoke. "You think we should tell Metzger?"

"I'm fixin' to. Better he should know there might be trouble about."

"I guess we should. We should have asked what the others looked like."

"From what the trapper said, if you find the bald one, you find the rest of his crowd. Let's look about for Metzger."

They didn't find the captain, but they found his horse and Delacroix's fettered before the clapboard sheathed building. They decided to wait; the office had an official look.

Not much time had passed before the duo emerged accompanied by an army officer.

The officer was young, maybe thirty; his clean-shaven face enhanced his youth. A battered black hat was pulled down tight on his head. His uniform was so dusty dirt cakes drifted off him as he strode the board porch. He was still talking to Metzger and Delacroix when he spotted Elizabeth.

"Welcome to Fort Laramie, miss. I'm Captain Matthew Brennan, Fifth Cavalry."

Elizabeth dipped politely. "I'm Elizabeth Bonner. This is my husband, Josh."

Brennan tugged at the brim of his hat, dislodging more dust. He stripped away his glove, offering his hand. "Pleased to make your acquaintance." His attention returned to the woman.

"Excuse my dust, ma'am. We've been out on patrol to the north."

"It's good to know the army is taking over the fort," she replied graciously.

"It won't be official for a year or so. In the meantime, we are just keeping an eye on things. I am going to have some of my men clean out the officers' quarters we are building. There will be room enough for the women in your party to sleep indoors," offered Brennan.

Metzger jumped into the exchange. "We'll be keeping the wagons near the gate while we are here. We're thinkin' it best with all the Indians camped about."

Elizabeth looked solicitously at Josh and then at the three leaders. "We have been told there are some vile characters hanging about. Is that just talk to rattle newcomers?"

"You must mean Sweeney and his crowd. They are a vicious bunch. I'd have them in jail if we had one. We keep an eye on them as best we can. You will be all right if you stay with your people."

Josh listened to the exchange, grateful his young wife had brought up the warning from Patch. Complaining about some men he hadn't even seen would have been callow in his estimation. As soon as the thought was borne, he felt like he was hiding behind his wife's skirts. The next thought was that the dashing officer paying attention to his wife was ignoring him.

"Captain, are all these Indians camped about any trouble?" asked Josh.

"They come mostly to visit with each other. Other than a little whiskey trading, they keep pretty much to themselves, John."

Josh decided to let the gaffe lie. "Are they Cheyenne Indians?" he asked, thinking of the crew he had met at the river crossing.

"I expect mostly. Some Sioux and Arapaho get mixed in. To tell the truth, I have to depend on my scouts to tell me. I've only been on the plains for a few months."

Josh turned to Delacroix. "Are there any of the people you lived with here?"

"Not likely," Delacroix replied. "The Crow are sworn enemies of the Oglala and their allies. Crow and Nez-Perce are north and west of here. You'll have to make do with what's here."

For some reason, Josh sensed the older men were patronizing him, making him feel like a boy. It was particularly irksome to have the scout join in the mood.

Delacroix sensed he had offended his young friend. He tried to make amends. "Perhaps if we meet some of my clan farther on, I will introduce you, show you how to tell the difference between tribes."

Delacroix could see Josh visibly brighten at the prospect. The four emigrants left the officer to his duties and headed back to camp.

"We'll keep circled up, away from the Indian camps and whatever renegades might be about," Metzger decided. "The animals will have to graze farther north. The grass is 'bout chewed down near the river," he added.

"Guards will have to be put out," the scout advised. "Indians covet horses more than anything."

Josh volunteered. "Jubal and I will take the first watch. Elizabeth, why don't you gather up things and stay inside, mebbe take a bath."

"Are you suggesting I need a bath?" his wife asked in mock indignation. It was too easy to fluster her beau.

"No, 'course not. I just meant, well, you know. It would be nice," Josh fumbled in reply.

The two older men, walking behind the couple, exchanged a look of amusement at the young man's bumbling.

Back at camp, Jubal and the stock were missing. He had unhitched the animals and escorted them all nearer the riverbank where they could water and nibble at the nubs of grass left behind by other herds. Josh traipsed out after them.

"We're goin' to move the stock up north of the fort. They can find pasture there. Captain says to set a guard. I volunteered us for first watch."

"That's fine with me, long as I can get a bite afore we go."

"We should have time. I asked for the first watch so we could ride Natchez and one of the mules back. They'll have eaten their fill by then, and we can keep them safe by the wagons."

"Mebbe we can bring 'em all back," suggested Jubal.

"I don't feel easy about herdin' em all at night, through other camps, and such. Tell you what. We'll bring a pair back, the brindled grays. I think them two is kin, anyways," Josh compromised.

It was getting on dusk when the two left camp, Jubal on foot leading the teams and Josh riding flank on Natchez. As they passed the Indian enclaves, it seemed every man's eye was turned on them, each eye covetous and plotting against their stock. The whites tried not to stare but were understandably curious about the Indian camps. Both had seen pictures of tipis and Indian camps, but this was right up close, a stone's pitch away. Substituting the tipis for wagons, any of the encampments looked much like their own. Women were preparing meals or doing home chores, the children were gathering and toting, cookfires drifted smoke about the peaks of the tents. Reflecting, Josh realized that unlike the wagon camps, these villages were the homes of the plains nomads, not just stops made en route to another destination.

Unlike the white society, the menfolk clustered together and relaxed. Some were obviously drunk, a few even passed out in front of their shelters. It was obvious the men dominated the society. Their skills at hunting and protecting the clan relieved them from the mundane work of running a household. If providing for the home included running off the animals of visiting whites, Josh thought, he had better be vigilant during his watch. While the Indian women and children paid no heed to their passage, the men gravitated nearer to the pilgrims, drawn by the herd, no doubt picturing a village-wide feast.

Certainly, they wouldn't try anything so close to the fort. They couldn't be that brazen. Still, even from a distance, this crowd didn't have the dominating, confident demeanor of the crew encountered back at the river. These seemed more accustomed to finding a meal close to home, secured by the easiest means available.

Later that evening, despite his oath of vigilance, Josh found himself drowsing in the saddle. He cursed himself for each brief moment he caught himself jerking awake, lulled by the monotony of the crickets around the herd. Each time he snapped to, he looked about for Jubal. No good to be caught out shirking his duty. Each time he found the dark man, he was walking amongst the herd, stroking flanks or assuring some animal spooked by who knew what.

How could this happen, he wondered? Over the past months, he had spent hours under a blinking canopy of stars, attentive to his charge as guardian for his sleeping neighbors. Each noise or call of a night animal would rouse his attention to the threat that might be approaching, perhaps bearing harm to his fellows. Now, with a potential threat known and within a sprint of this very spot, he couldn't keep his eyes open.

There was more sound, enough that there was no silence to be broken by the scurrying of some night foraging mouse or swoop of owl, seeking the mouse for his meal. From the fort, there was a constant undercurrent of sound, voices raised in revelry, doors closing, boots scuffling along. From the Indian villages, there was only the occasional sound of dogs roaming about. No sound of people escaped. No forms eerily revealed by firelight or crackle of burning wood. Other than the faintest orange of a banked fire and the dim silhouettes of tipis, there was no visual sign that the camps were inhabited.

Josh glanced at the lantern-lit wagons near his own camp, punctuating again the difference between their transient camp and the lifestyle of the native residents. Looking again toward the Indian camp, *"not a creature was stirring, not even a mouse"* crossed his imagination. Peculiar, he thought. He realized once more he was beginning to doze. Jerking awake again, he peered around for Jubal.

Life abounded all around the fort. Insects and small animals stalked or stood frozen in fear, depending upon their nature. Owls hovered and bats flicked in a night illuminated only by the distant stars. Predator and prey in the everlasting dance played out to an audience of oblivious men.

In truth, many men were mindful of the night's secret activities. Those that lived in and depended upon the natural world possessed dexterity more akin to intuition. The trappers and scouts, and to a lesser degree some few of the teamsters and soldiers, knew their lives could depend upon observation of the lands and life they moved within. The keenest of skills belonged to the Indians who lay quietly among the tufts of grass and watched the drowsy herd and its guardians. Stealth and sensitivity to nature kept their clan alive, fed, and sheltered. These were no interlopers, rather a fabric of the dance. Their opportunity would come.

Within the hour, the watchers noted the approach of two men, traipsing clumsily through the tufted prairie grasses. The pair cursed quietly when their missteps sent them lurching forward. Be assured that their cursing would have been louder had they known how close they came to stepping amongst the silent red-skinned observers of their passage. Henry Shearwood and Lewis Petry came to relieve the sentries.

Josh, drowsy as he was, marked their approach from over a hundred yards. He stared toward their sound until he could discern their shapes emerging from the gloom. Starlight limned the pale features of their faces a yellow-gray.

"You boys weren't practicing sneakin' up on us, now, were you?" Josh said in greeting.

"Damn near broke my ankle gettin' here," complained Petry. "Ground's as lumpy as my wife's gravy."

"Was easy findin' you, though. You're a pretty good target up on that horse," commented Henry.

Josh hadn't even considered how visible he was. He was disgusted with himself for revealing his lack of knowledge. It wouldn't happen again.

"I'm still here, so I guess there's nobody out here tryin' to get me."

"Where's your boy?" asked Petry.

"He's not my boy. He's a freedman. And I think he's standing right behind you."

Josh was as amazed as the other men were by Jubal's presence. He hadn't seen or heard him at all.

Petry tried to recover his shock. "What're you doin', sneakin' up on me?"

Jubal answered quietly. "I wasn't doin' no sneakin'. You walked right past me, standin' between these two mules."

"Still . . ." sputtered Petry.

"Sorry, Mr. Petry. I didn't mean no harm."

Josh wanted to drop the subject. Shearwood came to his rescue.

"Guess it's been pretty quiet?"

"I've heard some voices from the fort and from some drunks over t'the east. My guess is it's Sweeney and his bunch."

"How about the Indian camps?" asked Petry.

"Nothing. Haven't even heard their dogs bark," Josh replied. "Did you see anything, Jubal?"

"No, suh," he commented. "Jist mules and cows."

Josh noted that Jubal seemed to dummy up around the other whites. Probably just being careful. Most of them were Missourians, accustomed to slavery.

Petry spoke. "Well, cain't be too careful. We'll take over now. You'll see camp when you get near. It's lit up pretty good."

To Josh's ears, sweeter words were never spoken. He couldn't wait to flop into bed. He bade good night to the relief party and pointed Natchez toward home, Jubal breaking trail as he walked between the gray pair of mules. Having spent the last hours in the black night, his vision was acute enough to avoid the tufts of weeds the relief watch had cursed. Josh, in trail, let Natchez navigate.

Arriving at camp, Josh noticed a covered pot warming at the edge of the banked fire. Elizabeth had apparently been able to fix a meal from their damp pantry. Josh's drowsiness hadn't left him. He was too tired to eat. He removed the pot from the heat and climbed wearily into the wagon. His bride was awake and turned up the wick on the lantern above their bed.

"I fixed up some bacon and biscuit. It's probably still warm."

"I'm tuckered out for some reason. Don't know why. It was quiet all night. I'll eat in the mornin'."

Josh sat on the edge of the bolsters and pulled off his boots and socks. The thoughts of a full night's rest enticing him. He retrieved his nightshirt and moved to turn down the lamp. As he stretched out to do so, he felt Elizabeth's hand cup his balls. As tired as he was, he felt his sap begin to rise.

"Darlin', I'm so tired. I don't think I can."

"Not all of you is tired," she countered. She flattened her hand out, rolling his marbles up against his willful member, her finger lightly sliding down its length, garnering the proper response.

"Sweetheart, m'pecker may be the only part of me that's not tired out. My brain just wants to rest." As he reached to extinguish the lamp, he caught sight of his wife, her skin cast in the dim orange of the light, her breasts barely concealed by her nightdress. He could see her erect nipples through the cloth. What was the matter with him? Normally, he would have been on her in a moment. He was just so tired.

Gently, he removed her hand and turned the lantern off. Collapsing into the mattress, he regretfully declined her advance. He spooned up to her, as much to subdue her ardor as for comfort. He felt his half-hard erection against her flank and began to regret his refusal.

Elizabeth had been awake since Josh had left camp. Even while fixing the evening meal, she had been entertaining wicked thoughts that would become real once her man had returned from his duty. Her passion had built with each passing hour of his absence, and she would not be deterred.

223

Moving from his embrace slightly, she raised the hem of her nightdress, exposing her buttocks. Slowly, she pressed back against him only to feel him mostly withered, only a trace of chubby hardness remaining. This would not do.

After wetting her fingertips with spit, she reached behind her and found the velvety soft tip of his penis. She caressed and rolled her fingers around and achieved the expected results. Josh groaned quietly but she couldn't tell whether from her ministrations or from resignation. Certainly, she could revive him.

By moving her buttocks gently against him, she succeeded in not only resurrecting the erect penis she wanted but assured herself that Josh's thoughts of sleep had vanished. He was fully erect. She could feel the arch in his shaft. Pressing down, she positioned him between her legs and pressed him against her soon to be welcoming opening. Her passion had been brimming over all evening, and she could have manipulated him inside her at a touch. The sensation of rubbing him against her, between her lips but not inside, was remarkable. She felt herself approaching climax without him even being inside. Finally, she pushed him just inside and instantly felt the surge of her own coming and heard her own whimpering from deep in her throat. She was almost vibrating with pleasure as her man gave two or three short thrusts at her as his own release overtook him. He gasped into her ear as his convulsions spilled him into her. She shifted so she could feel him plunge into her. She left her fingers at their joining, reveling in the sensation of her own touch. Again, she felt the release of her orgasm and let it overtake her.

They lay joined until Josh fell away. He was already asleep, but she felt him slowly being released from her clutch. She wiped herself with her nightdress and settled against him. He probably wouldn't be so tired in the morning. Not many minutes passed before she, too, fell asleep, contented in the arms of her man.

#

CHAPTER FIFTEEN

#

The lover's had anticipated awakening languidly and contented in the other's embrace. As they fell asleep, they looked forward to waking slowly and renewing the rutting of the evening before, perhaps at a more leisurely pace. That was not to be.

Just as the stars were fading in the east, the couple awoke with a start. People were skittering about outside the wagon. Shouting voices carrying orders and asking questions competed with the scurrying of footsteps. Josh and Elizabeth looked at each other with the realization that something was amiss. They were fully alert and scrambling to get dressed as a knock on the wagon announced someone.

"Josh, Miz Hampton—you awake?" It was Jubal. He was shaken enough not to remember it was now Miz Bonner. The agitation in his voice was apparent.

Still pulling on his pants, Josh stuck his head out the rear flaps.

"What's going on? What's the ruckus about?"

"Indians! They stole the horses and mules."

Josh leaned out as far as he could, looking for Natchez, who he had left hitched to the front wheel. "Did they get Natchez? I didn't hear nothin' a'tall."

"He's right here. The gray pair, too. The ones got stole is from the herd. Appears they came after we left. No one missed any of 'em till this mornin'."

Josh felt himself being caught up in the hysteria spreading through camp. Collecting himself, he jumped to the ground and peered through the pre-dawn toward where the herd had been.

"Did they get them all?"

"No," Jubal replied. "Banner and Flag and t'other cattle is all there. Just the horses and some mules." He then fell silent. Josh recognized bad tidings.

"What is it?"

"Miz Hampton's . . . I mean Miz Bonner's whole team is gone. The other pair of yours. Stole, too."

225

"Goddammit! Who was on guard when it happened?" Josh was prepared to be enraged at the sentry's carelessness, and then he realized they might have been hurt, maybe killed. "Damn! Are they all right?"

"It was Mr. Fisher and Mr. Dawes. They ain't hurt or nothin'." Josh recalled the two men as steady hands. He didn't know them well, just enough to say hello and to respect them as conscientious family men.

Jubal continued. "They said they didn't even notice the stock was gone till they was bein' relieved. They ran back to camp to tell right away."

"Them scoundrels must have been sneakin' animals off, one at a time, all night. I didn't see a damned thing," Josh acknowledged.

"What I came to tell you was everyone's meetin' to figure what to do. You're 'sposed to come along right away."

"I'm coming. Saddle up Natchez for me, will you?"

Josh grabbed his boots and started for Metzger's wagon and the meeting. He had just started off when Delacroix and the McCardle brothers reined up their horses before him.

"Grab your horse and gun. You're going with us. You're one of the few with a mount left," the scout ordered.

Josh looked up at the grim faces.

"Won't be a minute," he said, turning for home, where he dived over the wagon board. He found Elizabeth dressed and waiting for him.

"I heard Jubal and you talking. I know about the thieves. Do you really have to go?" Elizabeth handed him a bedroll. "There's some food and a change of clothes in there." She knew he was compelled to chase the stolen stock.

"You know I have to," Josh replied. He was assembling cap, ball, powder, and patches for the Colt Walker. He also picked up a bag of shot.

"Dig out that shotgun for me. Be careful, it's loaded."

Fully armed, he made to depart. At last thought, he grabbed his hat and coat.

"Oh, Josh, be careful. Come back safely."

He kissed his bride good-bye. "'Course I will." He descended, ready to go. Jubal was waiting with Natchez's reins in hand.

"I filled the saddlebags with some biscuit and a hunk of ham. There's a little grain for the horse."

"Thanks." Josh thrust the shotgun into its scabbard. "You take care of things till I get back." He wheeled away and caught up to Delacroix and the McCardle brothers.

"How much of a start do they have?" asked Josh.

"Maybe two, three hours," answered Delacroix.

From the fort, two riders were approaching. Captain Brennan had released two scouts to come along, providing local knowledge. They veered into the group. Josh was pleased to see it was the gaunt Patch. He recognized his newest companion from the group at the store, recalling the decrepit hat he wore mashed down to his eyebrows more than the face. They slowed to a walk as introductions were made. The second scout was a Mexican skinner named Robles. He had volunteered just for something to do.

"Any idea which way they headed?" asked Delacroix.

"North, then east to Laramie Creek," replied Patch. "They'll try to hide their track in the water. When we find where they left the water, we'll have a better idea where they're headed."

"How's that?" Ethan McCardle asked.

"If them thieves was Cheyenne or *Brulé* Sioux, they'll head off to the northeast, maybe as far as the Rosebud," the scout considered. "If they was Arapaho, they'll make for the Sweetwater range. We'll know more when we find which side of the crick they leave."

The six horsemen reached where the herd had grazed during the night. The trail of the stolen animals was easy to pick up. Even Josh could discern the deeper imprints of animals on the move. The path disappeared over the ridge of a tufted hillock and slanted off toward Laramie Creek. The trackers followed until they came to the banks of the stream. There they split into two groups, Josh, Patch, and Robles crossing over to search the east bank for where the plundered herd exited the current.

The pursuit was on. Noon came and went without any sign being found. Josh was anxious about the head start the thieves had. He grew concerned they might have overridden the mark.

227

"Could we have missed where they came out?" Finally, he had to ask.

"No," Patch replied. "One rider might have slipped out. This bunch is drivin' animals, and they'll have to stick close to the herd."

"That's good for us," he added. "It's slower goin' in the stream than followin' alongside. They ain't gainin' on us."

It was true. They were keeping a good pace.

Still, the scout didn't have anything to lose if he failed. The loss of more than half of their pulling power would be insurmountable to the emigrants. The whole train would be without horses, as well. They had to get the missing animals back. It would probably mean a fight, a fight they had to win.

Elizabeth had collected all of their everyday clothes and put them in pillow covers to be laundered. She assembled some small personal items in a hand basket. It was finally a hefty load she lugged to the fort. Despite the concern for the missing animals, a laundry day was planned, and all the other women bore similar burdens. Besides, the chores and the company would take their mind off the trouble. Afterward, they would set up housekeeping in the partially finished barracks. Everyone was looking forward to the respite from the monotony of life on the trail. The theft and the pursuit was all anyone spoke of.

As the women drew near the fort, they noticed a quartet of men observing their progress. As they got closer to the gate, it became apparent the four were gloriously drunk at nine in the morning. The men began calling out to the women and commenting in blustering voices about the features and charms of all that passed. None of their commentary was welcome as it consisted of appraisals of the beauty or figures of all, from the oldest grandmother to the young women. Elizabeth felt her grip tighten as the men leaned in toward their victims, attempting to grope their breasts and buttocks. Where were the soldiers?

Even accustomed to the attentions of strange men, Elizabeth was outraged at the coarse behavior. These must be Sweeney and some of his lackeys. As she crossed before them, one swept off his cap and mimicked an exaggerated bow. His performance revealed a deeply sunburned bald dome, coursed with a pale, ugly scar that ran from his crown and cut through his left eyebrow.

228

"Mornin', missy. Give you a hand with those clothes," he spoke. His friends, drunk as they were, exploded with laughter at the clumsy foray. She chose to ignore them.

The big one, a swarthy man who could have been deemed handsome had it not been for the cruelty etched in his face, stumbled forward, attempting to snare her butt in his graceless clutch.

"Let's see if that ass feels as firm as it looks," he shouted for his friends' entertainment. She sidestepped his advance, almost stumbling under her burden.

Unphased, he continued his torrent of insults.

"A saucy one. Perhaps she would like to try a man for a change."

She was stunned by the thought that these ruffians had been watching them and must know Josh had left in pursuit of the horse thieves.

"A man wouldn't be drunk in the morning and making a fool of himself tormenting a bunch of women." She couldn't resist striking out.

"Come here, sweet stuff. Maybe you would like to be tormented with this," was the swarthy man's reaction. He fumbled at his pants, freeing his penis, which he wagged at her. His friends giggled at how clever he was.

"Why, it looks like a dick, only smaller," said Elizabeth, to the amusement of the other women.

He was knocked speechless. The big man stood there with his cock in his hand, not knowing what to say or what to do with the offending appendage. His friends screamed hilariously at the jape their friend had suffered.

"She got you there, Jack. I always said you had a small wanger," pealed the bald one.

"Fuck you, whore. I'll have you begging for this someday." He waggled his thing at her as she strode past. The sight of the big man flipping his flaccid penis at Elizabeth's departing back sent his companions into new howls of delight at his expense.

"And fuck you, too, Joe. I didn't know you spent time talking about Gentle Pierre." Again, he waggled his thing. He put himself back in his pants and swung at his friend, finally losing his balance, pitching on his face.

While the hooligans were being diverted by the trials of their companions, the women scampered into the fort and the dubious safety of the post. Fortunately, they were met by a corporal, who escorted them to the officers' quarters under construction. The women would be quartered here until their party took to the trail again.

The building was just a shell. In places, there was not even clapboard sheathing, leaving the interior to be scourged by the elements. Fortunately, it had been swept by the troops and at least offered a semblance of shelter to the grateful women.

A procession of fort denizens was bringing wood to the building, dropping it into a pile near the stone chimney. The wood had been gathered together, scrounged from the deserted wagons scattered about. The hastily gathered pile may well have contained the ferries that had transported them over the Laramie River only a few days before. The corporal let them know the work of the residents was not just for goodwill. Although they were too reticent to speak, there was a tacit agreement to launder clothes in exchange for the fuel. The pioneer women considered this a fair exchange. Quickly, they sent for more kettles and strung additional clotheslines outside. They immediately set up housekeeping. They divided up the interior with clotheslines, each staking out a cubicle of privacy by draping tarpaulin or blankets over the suspended lines.

Soon, water was boiling, soap was being shaved from the cakes, and dripping clothes were hung to flap dry in the constant breeze carrying over the plains. The smell of clean filled the temporary home of the emigrants. The women, grown accustomed to doing their wash in the chill water of a convenient stream, reveled in the luxury of hot water and plenty of soap. The congeniality of the circumstances made the work more of a social event than a chore. The incident at the gate was replayed with great delight, reliving Elizabeth's skilful disarming of the situation. Soon, the unpleasant encounter was set aside and old topics were resumed. Lively conversations lessened the drudgery of the task. All things being considered, it was turning into a passable day.

Most of the men who had brought the firewood owned no other clothes than those they stood up in. Stripped, the locals disappeared into various shelters or made for the river to pass the time. Delegates brought heaps of absolutely filthy shirts, pants, and underclothes to be laundered. They were told to dump their burdens on the floor. This turned out to be not such a good plan. Fleas and other vermin were soon abandoning the clothes, seeking warm bodies for shelter and food.

The filthy clothing instantly became a priority. Hesitant to handle the rags, sticks were employed to hook and pitch the clothes into steaming cauldrons. Brooms swept out the offending vermin, and scalding water spread on the floor did for the rest.

The wash water instantly clouded to a dirty gray. The waiting teamsters, hunters, and scouts were summoned to fetch more water from the river. The task was assigned to those who still had clothes on, much to the delight of the naked men huddled together. After several changes of water, the clothes ceased to stain the wash and could be fished out and hung to dry. It was several hours before the bartered laundry was done and the laundering of their own clothing could commence. The cauldrons were scoured first. Many of the women complained they had received the short end of the trade.

The hours of laundry, the sweeping, and the constant breeze through the building left it with an air of cleanliness that hadn't been enjoyed in several months. The women settled into their designated cubicles or gathered into small groups. Elizabeth sat with Wallace McCardle's wife, Virginia, his sister-in-law, Pearl Callahan, and Ethan McCardle's wife, Tasmin. As relatives of the men pursuing the thieves, they had more at risk than the loss of some mules or horses.

The two sisters certainly bore a family resemblance. Both were lean in the face with prominent wrist and elbow bones protruding at the joints. Each could be and probably were attractive. The hard life of a woman on a Missouri farm had worn away the youth from their features and left them scoured by work and time. Tasmin McCardle had led the same life but retained a chubbiness in her features and a livelier outlook on life. Her normally cheery disposition sagged with concern for her husband and the other men. Elizabeth couldn't help but reflect that the women's attitudes were much like the men they shared their lives with.

"I haven't been able to think of anything but the boys," said Tasmin. "I wish we could have just let the Indians take the horses and go on."

"Wallace and Ethan shouldn't have gone at all; it wasn't any of our herd was stolen," piped up Virginia. She didn't fail to cast a glance at Elizabeth, as though it were somehow her fault the men were absent.

"Now, Ginny, they had to go," replied her sister. "They were the only ones with horses left."

"They could have lent the horses to someone else. Our herd was still across the river. No one came over to steal from us," countered Virginia.

"That's just an accident. If we hadn't been waiting for the current to slow, the herds would have been together, like we always have. We just were lucky this time," said Tasmin.

"Yes, and now we have to bring our herd over before we wanted to. Worse, we have to do it with just us and the young'uns," countered Virginia. "They'll probably get run off, too," she added.

"The thieves went with the animals they stole," said Elizabeth. "Besides, we're keeping the herd inside the wagon circle now."

"Ever heard the expression 'locking the barn after the horse is gone'?" Virginia tartly replied.

Elizabeth's nerves were just as tightly strung as the other women, but she was having a hard time with Virginia McCardle. She had to say something.

"Of course, but we couldn't just leave the animals out there and risk more getting run off."

"Your man was one of the guards last night, and it was your mules got taken. He ought to be going after 'em", said Virginia.

"Ginny, be fair. No one knows when they were run off. The scout said they probably stole them one at a time," her sister granted. "Besides, no one had to ask Josh twice."

"Someone older should have gone. He's too young."

It was apparent Virginia wasn't accustomed to not getting the last word. Elizabeth vowed to try.

"Josh would have gone even if it hadn't been our mules. He's never shied away from doing his part, and more."

Virginia was ready. "I still say he's too young. Come along, girls. We got a herd to move."

Elizabeth was sorry, despite the caustic Virginia, to be left to worry all on her own.

Watching them depart, she decided to retrieve a bolster to sleep on and some other personal items. Her laundry should be dry by the time she got back.

Patch, Robles, and Josh had been traveling in single file for most of the day. On the other bank, the McCardles rode side by side behind Delacroix. Between the six of them, they watched the bank for tracks and scanned the horizon for a dust cloud or some other sign of their quarry.

It was discouraging. They had been watching the embankments for some sign the stolen herd had left the water. He was certain that when they did, the track would be obvious. It had been so long now and they were traveling so slowly. He couldn't help but feel they had somehow missed the mark and were dawdling along while the thieves escaped. He began to doubt his companions' motivation, thinking that only his animals had been stolen. The McCardles and the scouts had nothing to gain but a fight with Indians on their home range. Every time these doubts flummoxed his brain, he was instantly ashamed. He knew in his heart at least Delacroix wouldn't let him down. He began to wonder if the Indians had even gone to the river to hide their tracks. Then he would remember their trail entering the water so many hours ago and knew they must be on the right track. It was just so damned discouraging not to be making any discovery.

Just as Josh was trying to shake away the doubts, Robles cried out.

"There, just ahead. Before the bend." Robles spurred his horse ahead and whistled to the trio across the river.

Patch peered ahead and then turned to Josh. "Glad we picked up the trail. I was beginning to wonder whether I had missed the mark." He threw a lopsided grin at Josh and trotted off.

By the time Josh reached the other two, Delacroix and the brothers had splashed across the shallow stream. Josh felt foolish thinking they had overrun the track. The deep indents at the water's edge and the scuffed embankment were so conspicuous they might as well have been signaled with a road sign. The scouts didn't even bother to dismount in order to read the spoor.

"I count five ponies," said Delacroix.

"Reckon so, might be six," ventured Patch. "No more'n that."

"They don't seem to be much in a hurry. Probably think they slipped us," guessed Robles.

"What tribe do you think they are?" asked Josh.

"Cheyenne, *Brulé*. It don't make much difference. We're going after 'em. Now, we got a trail to follow," replied Delacroix.

Patch gauged the sun and the length of the shadows. "We still got three or four hours of daylight. We ought to pick up the pace. We could lose the trail if we get any more of a wind."

The group took up the pursuit, three watching the trail and three watching the sky for any dust cloud on the horizon. Ethan McCardle rode next to Josh.

"Don't fret, Josh. They'll like as make for the next water. The scouts know that, and we'll get your mules back. We'll get everythin' they stole."

His brother leaned around from his brother's left and added, "Teach the thievin' red bastards a lesson, too. Won't we, Ethan?"

"I'd be pleased to get back with the animals and without any holes in my hide," replied Ethan.

"I don't think six of them will run from six of us. We're probably in for a fight," Josh ventured.

"Reckon so," both brothers conceded.

They followed along for several hours, frequently halting for some few moments while the scouts interpreted the signs on the ground. While Josh could see markings in the dirt and broken twigs, he couldn't discern anything useful from the trace, other than it was still there. The scouts discussed their findings and apparently concurred. The trail ran straight, whether to water or other Indians, or both, was a guess the scouts kept to themselves.

The sun had just touched the distant mountaintops when they once more halted and Patch dismounted, squatted on the ground, and announced, "Looks like one of the ponies has broken off here." He pointed to the north without looking up.

"You think he's lookin' for some of his friends?"

"I think he's circling back. See if anyone's coming after them," suggested Delacroix.

"'Spect you could be right about that one," said Patch. "Robles, you ride trail and watch our backside."

"He picked a good place to separate," said the Mexican. "It's rocky enough that his trail would be hard to find without full sun."

Delacroix pointed to a small rise about two miles to the northeast.

"We'll make a cold camp up there. Might see something when the sun rises."

"What say we put a post out, to the north?" suggested the lanky Kentuckian. "Mebbe we can spot the one on our trail when he tries to join up with his friends."

"It would be worth knowing," Delacroix concurred. "If he joins up with his friends, then we'll know we've been spotted. I'll take the first watch, Josh here the second. You, Robles, and the McCardles can split up the rest as you please."

A cold camp on a prairie hillside was a miserable place to spend an evening. They placed themselves on the backside of the knoll so as not to cast silhouettes that might be spotted. The ground was hard and scattered with thorns dropped by the scrubs surrounding the campers. The only redeeming feature of their bivouac was that the hill sheltered them somewhat from the gusty wind that had veered to the northeast. The *voyageur* immediately set out into the scrub to stand watch, leaving Josh with his two new companions and the McCardle brothers. Ethan and Wallace were asleep as soon as they finished eating. Neither of the other two was very talkative. After a brief recap of the day's ride, the conversation ceased. Other than the occasional sound of a man shifting about and an occasional rumbling of a cleared throat, Josh might have been alone. The wind kept the bugs away and masked all but the whisper of drifting sand tumbling across the scrabbly ground. Sapless brush crackled and rattled as it bent to the breeze.

Dinner had been a biscuit and a salty piece of ham, washed down with tepid water. The meal was only sustenance, something to chew and swallow. Josh, anticipating his own stint isolated from his companions, had to force down the lump in his mouth. The food may as well have been dough rolled in sand. Knowing he would be sequestered in hostile country with only his vivid imaginings for company was paralyzing. Unable to sleep, he awaited Delacroix's return. One of his companions muttered a phrase from a dream.

He slipped a few yards away from the sleepers, hoping that he could better hear, perhaps being able to pick out the steps of the returning scout. Under the starlight and by the faint light of a new moon, he could discern shapes. Sitting with his arms about his knees, he held the Colt Walker in restless hands that perspired despite the chill night. Trusting his senses, he felt certain he would be able to see anyone approaching or hear steps, at least from upwind. He sat quietly, only occasionally shifting his hips to relieve the discomfort.

After sitting for about an hour, a loud whisper carried on the breeze alerted him.

"Halloo, the camp. It's Claude, coming in."

About fifty yards away, a clump of bushes stood up and walked with arms outstretched. Before the scout had revealed himself, Josh had detected no movement, no sound.

"I see you. Come in."

Even with the scout exposed, he could only faintly detect the sound of his moccasins as he climbed the grade.

"I thought it best to hail before walking in. Even over the wind, I could hear you rolling the cylinder in your revolver. Thought you might be jumpy."

Josh confessed he had been rotating the cylinder of his pistol and hadn't been conscious of it. Once more he had been proven the buckwheater.

"Grab a blanket and I'll show you where I hid out. You can see a long ways and still be out of the wind."

The two slunk over the landscape to a stand of tamarisk. Delacroix showed Josh where he had hollowed out a shallow depression that let him look out from under the branches.

"Keep your eyes open, and nobody will slip by you this way." The scout waved his arm in an arc from north to east. "One of the McCardles will be out in a couple of hours. Be watching for him."

Delacroix melted into dark obscurity, and Josh commenced his lonely vigil.

Away from the camp, the night's normal sounds became threatening, the familiar now seeming ominous. Many nights he had spent under his wagon, wrapped in a robe and listening to identical sounds. On post, the isolation of four or five hundred yards from camp, the noise seemed to surround, to creep up on him. Knowing that the threat was mostly in his imaginings brought no solace. He had constantly to keep reminding himself of the fact. There was always the chance that the next crack of branch or slip of pebble would herald an Indian creeping up to slaughter him at his watch.

Eventually, the anxiety gave way to tedium. Nothing disturbed the scene in front of him. Not an owl, a coyote, or even a night bird passed before him. His butt and his knees went numb. His neck was stiff, and his back protested the inaction. Josh resisted the temptation to gape and stretch lest he reveal his position to some lurking assassin. Before long, his bladder began to sing. Its tune could not be ignored. Josh was not about to piss near his lair, nor would he want the next sentry to have to suffer from his leavings. Taking a last cautious sweep of the landscape, he stood and slipped cautiously sideways from the tamarisk stand. Peering at reference points on the horizon, Josh tried to establish bearings so he could find his way back. Crouching, he counted off one hundred carefully placed steps before he stopped to water the ground. Kneeling so as not to make a silhouette, he unbuttoned and let the water flow.

When he was done, he reflected on his surroundings. Free from the confines of the hidden bushes, he could see in all directions. Above, the moon was near setting, its light too weak to offer a shadow. The stars swept across the sky like sparkling quartz cast on an indigo background. His previous dread was replaced by a feeling of calm solitude. The canopy above was placid, its limits overwhelming the concerns of any single individual. While still alert, his anxiety fell away like the shedding a cloak. Returning to his lair, he was able to pick it out within just a few steps. He settled in and scanned the night landscape.

Soon, the moon had set, the stars providing only the faintest illumination. Josh heard steps behind him. His first thought was of his imaginary stalker. The steps seemed to proceed for a few feet, stop and head off in another direction, only to halt once more. It could only be his relief, trying to find the hideout.

Still, just to be cautious, and on the off chance that it might be the illusive Indian adversary, Josh moved as quietly as he could from under his protection. The sounds were still behind him. He wheeled and cautiously peeked through the upper branches. There was no mistaking Wallace McCardle for a stealthy Sioux warrior.

"McCardle, to your right," hissed Josh.

McCardle jerked away from the sound of Josh's voice.

"Sorry, I meant your left," he said, raising his voice to a stage whisper.

"Where the hell are you?" he replied.

Josh could see, as the man swung to the sound of his voice, that he was carrying a shotgun at the ready. As Josh was now standing up, he wondered just how skittish his relief was. Moving slowly, he crouched down.

"Take your finger off the trigger of that scattergun and I'll show you."

He stood, exposing himself.

"I'm stumbling around here blind. Can't see a blasted thing."

"Your eyes get used to it. I'll come get you."

Venturing out, he retrieved the new watchman and showed him the burrow under the tamarisk.

"Why didn't Delacroix come with you, show you where t'go?"

"'Cause he's asleep. The Mex is up. He pointed the way but didn't feel like gettin' out of his bedroll."

"I'm goin' to get into mine."

"Have you seen anything?"

"Nothing. Not a bird, bat, or bug. At first, it's a little . . ." Josh was about to say "scary," but he thought it childish, ". . . unnerving. It's so quiet. After a while, it got real peaceful."

"As long as I got my shotgun, I don't figger to be rattled by anything."

Josh realized the elder McCardle brother was all bluster. He was just as afraid as Josh had been. Josh, having endured the nerves, felt more confidence in his own abilities, more assurance in his bearing.

Back on the hillside, Josh found Robles sitting up, smoking a *cigarillo* he had cupped in his hands for concealment. The *vaquero* nodded at Josh.

"You couldn't sleep?" Josh asked.

"*La noche es muy hermosa, así que pacífico.*"

Josh shrugged. "I don't understand."

"The sky, the stars. It is beauty. It brings me peace."

"It sounds nice, the way you said it in Mexican," replied Josh. Robles nodded.

"I know what you mean. It's almost like you are the only person on earth."

"It makes me think of Mexico," said Robles.

Josh granted the Mexican was a long way from home. "What made you leave Mexico?"

"I sailed on a boat to California to work on a *rancho del ganado*, a cattle ranch. I just wandered around after I got tired of the work."

Josh was enjoying his talk with the Mexican roustabout. He was just going to ask him about California and tell him that his brother, Ned, was a sailor when they heard a ruckus from the direction of the outpost. McCardle was making his way back, blundering over bushes in his haste. He clamored noisily up the short grade, starting small pebble avalanches.

"I seen him. He rode by bold as you please," he exclaimed breathlessly.

McCardle's return had awakened everyone.

"Which way was he riding? Was he riding hard?" Patch asked.

"He was headed east, same as us. He came by me not fifty feet away, ridin' easy." McCardle turned to Josh. "It was right after you left, not two minutes. I stayed put until he was out of sight. Damn!"

Josh saw how rattled the older man was. It was easy to feel superior, seeing how frightened he was. Josh couldn't help but wonder how he would have reacted. Probably the same if he had come by when Josh first got there. Now, after spending a watch alone, he was not so certain.

"You don't think he spotted you?" asked Ethan, scrambling from his bedroll.

"No, he didn't even look my way."

Delacroix was up. "I don't think they picked up our trail. He would have been *plus prudent*, trying to find us. He wouldn't have been riding so plain."

"Let's get after 'em," said the younger McCardle.

"They're not tryin' to put miles behind 'em. Prob'ly just headed to water," said Patch.

"Do you know where they are headed, then?" asked Delacroix.

Patch thought a moment. "They be springs pop out all through these hills. Most you can't depend on." He thought some more. "There is one, near a full day's ride at Horse Thief Coulee. That'd be my guess."

"Well named, I say," spoke Ethan.

"Well, hell," said Patch. We're all up, so's we might as well get started. It's prob'ly not more than three hours to sunup."

The inhospitable camp was soon gathered and packed. The chase party rode out, picking their way east through the dim starlight.

While Josh was standing his watch under the tamarisk bush, Elizabeth was staring at the ceiling of the unfinished barracks. She had, over the course of the day and with Jubal's help, carried some bolsters and other creature comforts to her little space. Surrounding her were similar cubicles populated by families enjoying a respite from the cramped wagons. Possibly the biggest treat was having a ceiling to look at and a window to look from. It had been months since there had been a roof over her head and a place to just relax and reflect.

How often the most innocuous of choices turned out to have the most monumental results. She tried to remember when her father and mother first began to talk about selling off and settling in the Oregon territories. It may have been the book of Captain Fremont's adventures that first stirred the longing to see the vast western expanse. Elizabeth recalled conversations at the supper table where her father cajoled her mother with prospects of riches and virgin land in the newly opened expanses. Her brother would chime in with tales of adventure from Fremont's narrative. To him, in his imaginings, it was almost as if they had already set off.

Never, she remembered, did she give any credence to the talk or the possibility that they might actually pick up stakes. Left to her own devices, she would have gone to Cincinnati. She imagined the glory and romance of the bustling river town. Fancy haberdasheries, luxurious homes, riverboats, and fancily dressed men and women in watered silk dresses who never had to haul water or wood were her dreams. Given her druthers, that's where she would have headed.

Instead, she let herself be swept up in her parents' grand scheme. It seemed the idea of packing up all their possessions and hiking west had just, of its own accord, rolled up her life and carted it into the wild lands.

Now her family was gone, buried with only a wooden marker next to a creek presuming to call itself a river; their dreams and schemes never to amount to more than the first steps of the long journey. Now, she found herself married to a man to whom she had never paid any attention, the marriage coming about in an impulsive moment of declaration.

The thought just popped into her head. *Why had she done that?* Contemplating, she understood her parents' dream had passed on to her. She wanted the new land. She wanted the chance to manage her own affairs. Fanciful dreams of luxury diminished to vanity before the chance to build from nothing a new existence. Fancy men in top hats and vests seemed callow compared to the strength she had discovered in the shy boy from Cairo. Their lives were their own; their fate cast two into one.

Yesterday, fortune had tried to trample their dream. Indians, through a chance opportunity, stole their means of transport and could maroon them here at this collection of rude huts and ruder men. Without the animals' safe return, they could not travel. Josh had to prevail.

Where, she wondered, could he be? They'd headed off toward the north, tracking thieves that may have run in any direction. No one at the fort seemed to give a second thought to the fate of the pursuers. No one except the families of the missing even seemed to consider where or how far the chase might lead. All but Josh were at least experienced horsemen. Here he was, a boat mechanic, wandering an ocean of scrub and scrabble. He could be futilely pursuing a quarry that vanished into the rocky hills or perhaps had lain in wait to ambush their trackers.

The thought shocked her. Losing the animals would be a dire hardship. Losing her new husband would be a tragedy, the second cataclysm in near as many months. Picturing herself without her companion set her eyes to weeping. She couldn't withstand such a loss. The first few sobs were of self-pity as she played out the melodrama in her mind. As soon as she realized she was crying over a scenario she had created for her own torment, she quit the playacting and ceased becoming an audience for her own dire predictions. It was just damned foolish, she thought.

Her musings were interrupted by the sound of creaking floorboards from outside. It was long past nightfall, and the settlers were all turned in. Someone was creeping about outside her window. Her first thought was the drunken Thibeault, or perhaps another of Sweeney's crowd. She hadn't seen any sign of them all day despite being on the lookout during her several trips from wagon to fort. They had been pointedly scarce.

There were no lamps lit inside the building to help any peeper to see in. The starlight gave only enough light to pick out what and where things were. Elizabeth rolled quietly to the floor and dared a glimpse at the window. There was no face leering in, but she could still detect the sound of footsteps outside. She slid under the hanging blanket that was her wall and found herself in a deserted corridor of blankets. It looked like washing hung out overnight. She crept to the doorstep and listened for the intruder. Faintly, she could hear someone step off the porch and walk along the back side of the building.

Pressing her back against the wall, she was determined to steal a glance at the intruder. Other than screaming, she had no means of defense, and she would be poxed before she would resort to that kind of hysterics. Certainly, she could see without being seen. Stooping, she slipped her face past the jamb.

The figure walking by startled her. The form had been passing just as she was able to catch sight of the prowler. No mistaking the man who had been lurking.

"Jubal," she whispered. Loud enough to be heard, but not enough, hopefully, to disturb her neighbors.

"Yes'm. It's me all right," came the familiar voice from the shadows.

"What are you doing out there? People might get the wrong idea if they found you prowling around here."

"Lordy, Miz 'Lizabeth. That's about all I been thinkin' on since I got here," confessed Jubal.

"Then what are you doing out there? Come up here into the light."

"Josh. He asked afore he left that I keep a watchful eye on you. He don't trust some of the folks here."

"Well, I can see his point," admitted Elizabeth. "I want you to go back to the camp. I'm perfectly all right here, and it's far too perilous for you to take a chance being seen near the women's quarters."

Jubal protested. "Mr. Josh said I gots to watch you."

"I know, and you both mean well. Just the same, I can take care of myself. You just run along. I am more concerned with our property left in the wagons."

242

Elizabeth was immediately reminded of her cache of money hidden in the flour barrel. The price of commodities at the fort was such that even regular staples were worth stealing. It was easy for her mind to picture the barrel being wrested away from the wagon and rolled away by thieves. She imagined the fiends' delight as they discovered the unexpected plum. The pictures in her mind created enough anxiety that she became desperate to get Jubal on his way.

"Go, Jubal. Get along." For emphasis, she stamped her foot down on the wooden porch. Immediately, she felt foolish for her display.

Jubal must have been astonished at her actions. While he left immediately, he couldn't help but look at her as though she had lost her head.

Elizabeth watched him depart and went back to her little cubicle. Worry over her husband and the success of his mission assured a restless night. As she disappeared inside, unfriendly eyes peered after her. Unfriendly ears had heard all.

Despite having broken camp by moonlight, the pursuers were certain they were on the right trail. Patch was confident the thieves were headed to the aptly named Horse Thief Coulee. Surely, their suspicions would be confirmed when they picked out tracks after sunrise.

At dawn, signs of the driven herd were found. Almost immediately, any doubt about whether they were on the right trail was dispelled by a grim and disheartening discovery. Vultures were picking away at the stiffening body of a mule.

The posse drove away the carrion hunters and rode circle around the carcass. Its throat had been slit and the meat behind the ribs, as well as both rear haunches, had been harvested. Josh recognized the carcass as one of his own animals, marked by two notches cut in the ear on the day it was purchased in St. Joseph.

Down in a gully, hidden from the casual traveler, were the remains of a campfire and suggestions that the mule had provided both the evening meal and had been dressed out for future provisions.

"He must have come up lame," surmised Robles.

"I 'spect so. Either that or they were low on grub," said Patch.

"More important, they took the time to dress out the meat. That means they think they're in the clear," added Delacroix.

Josh had been listening to the exchange of speculations without speaking. The others had been speaking of possibilities and gave no consideration that the dead mule was more than a source of conjecture. The mutilated body was one of the animals that were supposed to pull his belongings through to Oregon. Without it, and more so, without the recovery of the balance of draft animals, Elizabeth, Jubal, and he would be marooned at the fort.

The casual manner in which his property had been stolen, killed, butchered, and eaten tore at his guts. The more he thought of how an impulsive theft by strangers had endangered all his dreams churned like poison. With black determination, he vowed that his tormentors would be punished. He longed to pursue, to corner, and wreak havoc upon his prey. It was how he now thought of them, not as people, but as objects of a growing hatred. He'd forego adding to the speculations of his *compadres*.

"Let's git on with it. I've seen enough dead mule," he interrupted.

Josh's change of mood caught everyone's attention. None were more caught off guard than Delacroix and the McCardle brothers. Their familiarity with the easygoing young man made the transition even more remarkable. No one moved.

"I want my animals afore they cut up any more. If you think they are headed for this coulee, then let's move out," Josh urged, wheeling Natchez's head toward the east.

The pursuit had turned grim. No longer were they chasing animals, they were chasing men. Any recovery of animals would include a harsh lesson for the thieves. Perhaps now that was the purpose of the chase.

Delacroix rode just behind Josh. Even from the back, he could see the change that had overcome his young companion. Josh was normally not a talkative man. Now his silence hung on him like a shroud. Josh sat his saddle with savage purpose. The scout didn't want his anger to cause him to be careless. He approached.

"We'll get your animals back."

"I aim to, and I mean to make certain they think it over before stealing anything else," Josh said darkly.

"Stealing horses is the way of the red man. It is how they count their worth, by how many horses they can steal," the scout tried to explain.

"They didn't steal from you. They stole and et my animal—the one that was going to draw my wagon to a new home. It's not a damned game."

Delacroix had perhaps underestimated Bonner. Josh had the look of a man who had decided to run his head through a brick wall and was about to do it. Still, he was green. The scout was determined to keep him out of trouble.

The pursuers rode throughout the morning and into the early afternoon. They were closing and took their nourishment in the saddle. All were traveling with more caution now. They paused before cresting any hills to spy out the land in front of them.

Patch had halted them around noontime to dismount. He got on all fours and examined the tracks so closely he appeared to be smelling them. The trail was freshly cut and true toward Horse Thief Coulee, a few hours ahead. They would reach the draw long before dark.

It was maddening to Josh to slow and stop the pursuit now that they were so close. Every time they stopped, he fretted in the saddle, anxious to be off again. His companions were frightened by the young man's intensity. Part of their fear was that he would do something rash, endangering them all. They didn't know exactly how many men they were pursuing and weren't certain if the outrider had detected them the night before as he rode backtrail.

Soon, they were near the coulee and its spring. The horses could smell the water, and after a long ride without relief, they seemed as anxious as Josh. It was going to be difficult to keep them quiet.

Patch drew up into a gully and halted. Once more, he dismounted and crept up to the top of the draw. Even he seemed more wary now, taking care not to raise any dust on his ascent. At the crest, he removed his hat and peered under a stand of mulefat. He seemed to lie there motionless forever before slithering slowly back to the group.

"If I recollect true, two over is Horse Thief. I been here before, and I'm sure that's it."

"Did you see anything?" asked Ethan McCardle.

"I cain't see over to the coulee proper. Didn't see anyone lookin' back. If they are there, then we got 'em," said Patch.

"We can't wait for dark," said Robles. "It's too long and they might hear us. We got to get a better look."

To Josh, it looked like it was going to be another palaver. The time was over for talk. If they were there and didn't know they were about to be attacked, there was no point in thinking about doing. It was time to do.

The first thing the others knew about Josh's plan was the sound of him breaking open his shotgun and checking the caps under the hammers. He turned his mount and trotted slowly out of the draw toward his quarry.

Uncertain of what to do, they followed to the tail slope of the hill to see what his plan was. What they saw unnerved them. He slowly increased his speed to a slow canter. It was obvious he was going to bolt around the last concealment and have it out with whoever was on the other side.

"What the hell's he doin'? He don't even know where in the coulee they would camp," exclaimed Patch.

"I'm pretty sure he aims to find out," replied Delacroix, checking the caps on his pistol and carbine. He didn't wait for any rejoinder but sprung out of the draw to back up his friend. The others exchanged glances and followed.

Josh wasn't sure what he expected to find as drove into the coulee. Something in his mental core said he was acting the fool. He didn't listen. His blood was up. He was looking for retribution.

Horse Thief Coulee fanned out at its entrance but quickly narrowed to a draw between steep, crumbling rock bluffs. Even in the afternoon, the light was subdued as the gully narrowed. It was wide enough only for about six horsemen to ride abreast. Josh, a couple of hundred yards ahead of the others, entered alone. Loose rock that had cascaded to the floor checked his headlong charge. Moving in at a quick trot, he hoped to maintain the element of surprise, if ever he had had it.

Josh dropped the reins and spurred Natchez onward. The shotgun was at the ready, both hammers cocked. As the horse picked his way over the rubbled ground, the shotgun would be his only chance of hitting a target. Together, horse and rider moved farther forward toward a gentle bend in the narrowing gorge.

Delacroix and the others were coming up behind. The McCardles were clumsily trying to check their weapons and hang on to their mounts. Robles and Patch followed the other scout. As a result of the scattered start, they were riding in file, surrendering the impact of a united attack. If their quarry was awaiting them, they could be riding under hostile guns like ducks in a row.

Josh felt focused, never more so before in his life. Without flinching, he scanned the ground and steep slopes for movement. He was not conscious of being afraid, savage intent driving him toward the confrontation. His breath was shallow and quick, seeming to pulse in his ears. He heard running water. The tail of the coulee was just around a sharp bend.

Rising Wolf had been dozing after his long night ride. In his sleep, he heard the pounding of his horse's hooves as he thundered across the plains. In his dream, he smelled the sweat of his horse and felt the wind in his hair. Like all dreamers, he soon realized the air was still, the sound of horse's feet had punctured his dream.

Looking down into the coulee, he spotted the white man. It was the young one who had walked by their camp with the sun-blackened man. At first Rising Wolf thought he had been seen. There was a shotgun pointed toward him. His sleep washed away as he recognized the white man had the weapon pointed at the sky, ready to swing from side to side.

Rising Wolf dug at the pouch on his belt for a cap to prime his weapon. Thinking to be cautious, he had left the musket unprimed to prevent an accidental discharge. Plucking one between his fingers, he stood up, bringing the hammer to half cock. He was just slipping the brass cap onto the nipple when he was punched hard under his ribs, knocking the breath from his body. He fell hard onto his knees, then toppled over. The musket lay on his chest, forgotten. The tiny brass cap rolled from between his fingers. Rising Wolf once again left this world, perhaps to resume his dream.

Chasing into the coulee behind Josh, Delacroix was shocked to find Josh was far ahead of him, nowhere to be seen. *Le fichu jeune idiot* had perhaps galloped off to his death. He must find him before it was too late.

Just as Delacroix was about to urge his mount to a gallop, he spotted a sentry standing and loading a musket. The scout swung his carbine, took aim, and fired. Through the smoke, he was able to see he had struck true. The sentry collapsed. Delacroix sprang forward.

Josh had not heard Rising Wolf cocking his musket. He was too intent on his pursuit. He did hear the crack of a carbine, not knowing if the shot was aimed at him. Knowing any chance at surprise would be lost if he did not act, he sprang forward and into the herd of stolen horses and mules.

The shot had come as a surprise to the remaining five Indians. They had slept soundly, secure in the certainty that they had eluded any pursuit. They had spent the day drinking popskull whiskey and snapped painfully awake at the gun's discharge.

Turning to where Rising Wolf had been, they saw his body lying face up, his left foot twitching. Realizing they had been discovered, the choice became fight or run. Three chose flight while two charged to their weapons.

Josh's gallant assault was halted when he ran into and amongst the stolen herd. Understanding that if he did nothing he would soon be a target, isolated above the backs of the animals, he spied one man running toward the ponies and fired one barrel of the shotgun. The shotgun's boom scattered the already startled herd but accomplished little else. Josh had inadvertently aimed high, concerned for the animals. His target disappeared in the melee of panicked animals.

Already another Indian was running toward his mount in an attempt to flee past him. Rotating around in the saddle, Josh let fly with another burst of shot. His target managed three more rubbery steps before colliding face first with the flank of his pony and collapsing into the dust. The animals scattered at the noise. Josh dug in his heels and Natchez leaped into the open.

Josh attempted to sheath the empty scattergun, but in his haste, only slid the barrel down the outside of the scabbard. He let it drop and drew the Colt Walker.

Natchez bolted when Josh kicked his flanks and swung toward one of the thieves nocking an arrow to his bow. Josh pointed and pulled the trigger of the revolver. The canyon walls echoed with the crack of the pistol. Quickly, Josh snapped off two more rounds.

Emerging from the acrid cloud of gunsmoke, he found his assassin crumpled beside his bow. The arrow was gone, perhaps dropped or perhaps loosed at the rampaging horseman. Josh sought more targets.

With three of his companions down and two more fleeing, Camps in the Mountains found himself alone, confronted with a madman. There might be more coming, and he decided to take his last clear chance to run for it. He slung his ancient, rusty musket over his shoulder and leaped onto his pony. Immediately, the madman fired a shot after him. He heeled the pony to a run and ducked for cover behind the pony's flanks. Another shot he was certain would have scored, zinged past where he had been sitting. His last sight of the wild man was of him wheeling the big horse around to torment his escape. A last shot slammed into the rocks to his right as he rounded the protection of the bend in the gully. Ahead were a string of white men. He must get beyond them to safety. There was no sign of his friends. Perhaps they had already fallen victim?

Delacroix was reloading when the first two riders galloped past him. The escaping Indians blew past Patch, Robles, and the McCardle brothers before they had even come into the coulee. The Indians whipped the ponies cross buck and soon diminished into the scrub. All the hunting party had convened at the entrance and was cautiously advancing to the sound of the guns. It was hard to tell how many shots had been fired due to the repeating echoes from the walls.

It was easy, however, to tell that the firing was back in the canyon. They could only guess what the outcome was and whether their young friend still drew breath.

Suddenly, they heard the sound of pounding hooves and flattened themselves against the rocks as a bullet buzzed threateningly over their heads. Camps in the Mountains and most of the other animals then came hurtling past. He was hanging on to his horse for dear life and was fleeing without any concern for the rocks in his path. All of the pursuers were so startled they only watched, their weapons not even brought to bear. Soon, that Indian, too, was lost in the confusion of his flight and the clattering of horses' hooves catapulting to the mouth of the canyon.

As the first of the animals appeared, the crew spread out to contain their flight. There wasn't enough room to maneuver and turn their heads. Their only hope was to block the entrance until the stampede could be slowed. Fortunately, they had just begun their sprint and were only gaining momentum. The canyon, restricted as it was, also served the cause by keeping the animals strung out. Once the first couple of animals could be brought up, the rest found themselves rushing toward a stalled herd.

Delacroix and Patch, ever vigilant, pressed past the animals to gain the back of the coulee. They surveyed possible hiding places but felt the single sentry dispatched earlier was the only Indian left. Once they rounded the last bend, they found Josh, his furor depleted.

He was clutching Natchez's reins, restraining him from joining the departing herd. He circled, looking for adversaries or fleeing targets. The two scouts held back, not sure if, in his turmoil, Josh would lash out at them.

The fury that fueled Josh's reckless charge and directed his fury toward his enemies still coursed through him. His arms and legs began to tremble uncontrollably, the muscles anxious for direction. There was nothing left to be done, the trembling absorbing the excitement that had pumped through his system. His brain was sharp. His senses attuned to every detail around him. Contrary to his companions' perceptions, his charge was not the blind rampage they had witnessed. Far from being blunted, his thoughts were keenly aware of what he had done. Even now, as the excitement drained away, he felt exalted, satiated. The powerful charge within his body turned to a rubbery exhaustion. He sat as still as he could, regaining his composure. The rest of the men rounded up the strays strung out over the course of the narrow defile. The work done, Patch and Delacroix ventured over to the young warrior.

"My Gawd, man! I hope you never get mad at me. I never seen the like," marveled the Kentuckian. "Gawd A'mighty."

"You must have had the devil on your shoulders, young Josh," added Delacroix. "You must learn to be afraid."

"I'm plenty afraid now. Look at me. I'm shakin' so much I can barely keep t'the saddle."

The two scouts laughed appreciatively. Delacroix leaned over to embrace Josh, either for his heroism or for his idiocy.

"That, *mon ami*, is normal after a tight scrape. *Fortunate*, scrapes this tight don't come along very often. You did well."

The other riders had completed the round up and rode over to add their congratulations and exclaim about his heroics. Ethan McCardle had retrieved Josh's shotgun. Josh accepted their accolades without comment. Truly he just felt tired and wished he could dismount and sleep for about two days.

Several miles away, Camps in the Mountains joined up with the other two survivors. They, too, were shedding the last of their jittery charge and wished to sleep. The thought of being pursued by the madman and his friends told them they must continue to put distance between them and the threat that had cornered them and decimated their ranks.

As they collected their thoughts and rested, they talked of the boy who had looked so foolish at the camp and had been transformed into a wolverine over a few stolen horses. They wondered how he could keep shooting his weapon, how he had charged into the unknown. When they rejoined their clan, they would tell the tale of the man who would henceforth carry the name of Gun Always Loaded.

#

CHAPTER SIXTEEN

#

The Fourth of July was approaching, and relations at Fort Laramie between the emigrants and the denizens of the fort had warmed considerably from the initial first wariness. Natural human curiosity, the success of the laundry day, and the approaching Independence Day celebration had overcome any reservations the settlers had about the motley collection at the fort. The foreboding starting with the scandalous charges for the ferry service and the exorbitant prices being charged by the sutler had resolved into an exchange of services that became the form of custom between the two groups.

Spontaneously, preparations for the Fourth began. Proposed was a home-cooked meal for the crew at the fort in exchange for enough armfuls of firewood to both cook a meal and to heat water for baths. The plentiful supply of driftwood washed down from the mountains had provided a means of exchange. The bartering would provide untoward luxuries for both groups.

While a hot bath wasn't a priority with the hunters and scouts at the fort, they rejoiced at the idea of a meal that wasn't dried, salted, or seared just enough to scorch away the hair. The settlers, in return, would gain the luxury of steaming in a bath that didn't have a rock bottom and wasn't icy cold or clouded with mud. It was a fair exchange, anticipated by all.

Elizabeth, like the other women, had retrieved jars of preserves and broken out, with some reservation, china plates that had been stored in barrels of flour or grain. The menfolk dug out jugs of flavored brandies or bonded whiskey, a treat for the men accustomed to trade whiskey adulterated with who knows what.

The fort's hunters, more skilled than the emigrants, managed to bring down some pronghorn antelope and prairie hens. These were being carefully dressed out for a proper preparation. Usually, such meats, even if the extra effort to harvest them was expended, would just be hacked into convenient hunks and seared over an open fire. Others spread out over the floodplain gathering heaps of driftwood that were piled neatly behind the unfinished barracks. Their talk was of meals eaten and of homes long left behind.

Of course, not everybody joined in the preparations. Some of the trappers and hunters had no fond memories of civilization and family. Many of these were fugitives and criminals whose path into the territories was hastened by the pursuit of law or the fear of retribution by those they had wronged. Out of shame or just cussedness, this group lingered in sullen contemplation of the preparations going on around them.

Chief among the sullen was Joe Sweeney and his band of thugs. Others of their ilk, who generally avoided Sweeney's mob for safety's sake, gravitated toward the other outcasts. They spent their time drinking and generally deriding the efforts of the now friendly groups. They no longer hurled disparaging remarks, painfully aware that any comment would only emphasize their outcast status. Their ridicule was confined to gestures and closely held comments evoking laughter from the other conspirators.

What was most troubling to Elizabeth was the tendency the ruffians had of seeming to disappear frequently and almost instantly. On her route from wagon camp to the fort, she would see the group of them gathered in various postures, drinking, arguing amongst themselves, or grousing about their exclusion. Just moments later, they would have dispersed, vanishing without notice or trail. Only a few minutes would go by and she would spot them leaning against another one of the buildings, their arguments, drinking, and lazing about simply resumed at a new stand.

Always she would find Thibeault staring after her; his humiliation seemed revived each time he spied her. Whatever he might be doing, he would stop and devote his vile attentions toward her until she had passed. It was difficult to ignore him. His staring was lewd and infused with a menace she had never experienced. It confounded Elizabeth's nature to let his attentions go without once again demeaning him before his fellows.

Never before had she felt threatened by a man's gaze. Realizing she should not provoke him, she struggled to ignore him. Thankfully, he did no more than balefully stare after her. Had he called out some insult, she would have been after him like a terrier. It worried her that she knew, and despite whatever misgivings she felt, she would have been powerless to suffer his catcall without reprisal. It frightened her he might recognize this and be biding his time until he felt that the time or place was to his advantage. Worse, the longer he was held at bay, the more vicious he might become. She had no doubt his capacity for violence was intuitive and unrestrained.

Jack Thibeault watched the bitch parade past. He made a point of
letting her know he was watching. She could pretend not to notice, but she
knew he had his eye on her. More than anything he wanted to her to know
he hadn't forgotten the incident at the gate. It would have been easy to call
out to her, assuring her that there was a reckoning coming. That he didn't
call out infuriated him, too. Much as he would have loved to bray out
some obscenity, he was afraid she would once again get the best of him. It
was hateful to be bested by a woman. Had she been a man, the
confrontation would have ended in the dirt before the fort. It was so much
more direct to deal with a man.

Had her pup of a husband been there, he could have dealt with him
instead of the bitch. Even if her nigger had come to her aid there would
have been some satisfaction in carving up his black hide. Thibeault's
fingers instinctively caressed the hilt of the knife sheathed handily across
his lower back. How nice it would be.

Thibeault's seething anger was nothing new to his drinking crowd.
None credited his brooding silence to deep contemplation. It was obvious
he still stung from his earlier disgrace. They knew he only lacked a nudge
to send him lashing out of control. None wanted any part of him.

Even Sweeney, whose own ferocity kept even Thibeault at bay, saw
no need to provoke him. He had seen the trapper's temper step past all
reason. Once he was off, only blood would sate his fury. They were all on
thin ice at the fort and didn't need to provoke the army captain into
banishing them. On the other hand, it was going to be annoying, spending
the day trying to step around the big fool's temper.

As Sweeney saw it, he could either get the man drunk enough to pass
out, let him stew, or find a convenient outlet for him to vent upon. The
first option would use up whiskey hard to come by. The second meant
spending the day skulking around to avoid him. The third option looked
best if he could find a convenient foil to absorb his wrath. For lack of any
other entertainment, it might be fun to let Thibeault jump on some
unsuspecting fool. Perhaps Moon, the half-breed, would do? He was none
too bright and wasn't familiar with Thibeault's moods.

Sweeney nudged Clement and winked to clue him of the impending
entertainment. He sidled up to Moon, who was drunk enough to be
swaying slowly in place.

"Hey, Moon," he whispered. "Jack sure can't take his eyes off that red-haired girl. You'd think he would lay off after she twisted his tail."

"Sure, he looks riled up. I think he's up to no good."

"Mebbe she lost interest after seeing Gentle Pierre."

The reference to Thibeault's manhood had the desired result. Moon brayed drunkenly and Sweeney joined in, but more discreetly.

Thibeault overheard the laughter behind his back and swiveled around, instantly enraged. Since Sweeney was one of the offending duo, he singled out the smaller Moon for his abuse.

"What are you laughin' at, ya filthy half-breed?"

Moon's mouth snapped shut like one of his own leg-hold traps. He was too drunk to respond further and simply stared stupidly at his antagonist. Sweeney had backed away, abandoning Moon to Thibeault's rage.

"What's so damned funny, runt?" The big man accented his inquiry by shoving Moon squarely in the face, sending him sprawling.

Moon might have been a runt, but he was not about to stomach such abuse. Drunk or no, he sprang to his feet and charged headfirst into Thibeault's mid-section. The big man absorbed the charge like a cushion. He joined his fists together and struck down on Moon's back.

Sweeney had his desired results. He and the rest of the drunks roared and began to cheer for the out-matched Moon. Thibeault was no one's favorite.

The upheaval caught the attention of passersby, including Elizabeth. She had turned at the noise just in time to see Moon struck to the ground and leap up once more, groping for the blade he kept in his boot. Thibeault reached behind him for his own knife. The drunks who had been cheering fell silent as their spectacle turned deadly.

Elizabeth and the other settlers who had been passing studiously avoided looking at the rabble. When the cheering started, they couldn't help but look. When the fight progressed to knives, they were entranced as raptly as any of the drunken mob. Murmurs of disgust and concern for the combatants stirred through the crowd of onlookers.

Elizabeth watched the little man get pushed down and come up with a skinning knife. Thibeault jumped back and, reaching behind him, whipped out a wicked-looking blade. The two parried and circled each other. As drunk as he was, the little man was still quick. Several times, he slipped around the bigger man and thrust in a short arc. Thibeault was even quicker. Deftly, he avoided the little man's attacks, slipping and ducking the blows. Once more, Moon slipped in to strike. Thibeault stepped into the arc of the blow and countered with a slicing motion.

He caught Moon on the forehead, either by design or luck. The blade was so sharp and so quick the wound did not immediately bleed. Within seconds, though, Moon was blinded by the sheet of blood flowing into his eyes. He tried to staunch the bleeding with his free hand. He was swinging blindly with the knife, trying to keep Thibeault at a distance. Moon was essentially helpless, and Thibeault was stalking him, a cat toying with a mouse.

Sweeney had seen enough. He knew Thibeault. He had seen this tactic before and knew he would move in, striking when and where he wished. The fight was over. Only the torment remained.

Joe Sweeney could ill afford to lose Moon to death or serious wounding. He was the best trapper he had and was far more valuable than Thibeault's dumb strength. The confrontation Sweeney himself initiated had rapidly gone beyond entertainment. It was threatening his livelihood. He drew his pistol, put it onto half cock, and advanced to separate the pair.

The combatants were ringed by spectators as Sweeney pushed himself into the impromptu arena. Knowing it was unwise to step between them, he slipped up behind Thibeault, who was concentrating on his next sortie, and pushed him sharply in his back. His fury, systematically being assuaged, was born anew. Thibeault swung to confront the new assailant. He found himself looking down the black bore of a pistol, Sweeney's steely eyes lining the sights upon him.

"That's enough. You're done!" threatened Sweeney.

Thibeault's mouth moved. He was thinking of some retort, but no words came, his blade hand frozen in the air. He made a halfhearted lunge. Sweeney's arm leaped forward, slapping the barrel down hard on Thibeault's wrist. The knife fell in the dust.

With Thibeault reeling from the pain in his wrist, Sweeney stepped close and grabbed a handful of hair. The barrel of the pistol pressed up under his jaw. He thumbed it to full cock.

"I'm pretty certain you heard me the first time," Sweeney stated in mock civility.

Thibeault, familiar with his partner's capabilities, visibly sagged, as a supplicant before a bishop.

"You heard him laughin' at me," he countered weakly.

"I did. Now I am going to have to stitch up your handiwork," said the scar-faced leader.

No comment.

"Pick up your knife and go sleep it off," ordered Sweeney.

There was no argument from Thibeault as he departed. He pushed his way roughly through the crowd with the cheap arrogance of the defeated bully. Sweeney turned his attentions to Moon. He paid no more attention to Thibeault. He knew he wouldn't retaliate.

"Well, pard. I hope you got some whiskey left. I'd rather you was passed out before we truss you up."

"If I hadn't a been drinkin', I woulda knowed to stay away from that bastard," replied Moon. He sat in the dust, puzzling over the drenching he had taken in his own blood.

The emigrant spectators, even those accustomed to the rough ways of backcountry or river towns, were appalled at the capricious display of violence. Without Sweeney's intervention, they were certain the bigger man would have methodically slashed his blinded victim to ribbons and left him to leak his life away into the dust. Sweeney gained some admiration for his actions among the spectators. None were aware he had instigated the fight for his own amusement or had stopped it to protect the more valuable of his assets.

Many of the women were holding hankies to their faces. They daubed at the tears of pity evoked by the brutality they had witnessed. One or two stepped forward to minister to the injured man. Someone rushed off to find Doc Bingham.

Elizabeth was strangely unmoved by Moon's thrashing or by Thibeault's dressing down at the hands of the man she perceived as only another, tougher cur. Curs. That was an apt portrayal. She felt no more for the men than for mongrels snarling and snapping at each other in the dusty streets of Cairo. Back home, dogs fighting in the streets brought

257

loafers out from the shade and drunks out from the saloons. Decent people crossed the street as much to avoid the revelers as the dogs themselves. Her sensibilities, roughened as they were by the cross-country odyssey, still reserved enough refinement to hold the whole scene in contempt. She continued on to the bunkhouse, where chores awaited. Perhaps she would find an opportunity and the privacy to properly bathe before the festivities got underway.

The other men left Josh alone even after his frenzy had subsided. The transformation they had witnessed left them so confounded they couldn't aptly find ways to speak to him. Eventually, they hoped, he would return to the affable young man they had broken trail with two days ago. Discovering the banshee that lived so near to his skin made them all nervous. Delacroix and the McCardle brothers were almost in shock. Patch and Robles were astounded but, having no familiarity with Josh in his normal skin, only marveled at his foolish courage.

"That boy's quite a wildcat," commented Patch. He, with the others, was lying about the campfire they had liberated. "Never seen anything like it."

"I was thinking, when we left the fort, that tracking hostiles was no such good work for one so young," Robles threw in.

"I think, if we had left him behind, he would have followed," said Delacroix. "There were, after all, some of his animals taken."

"It was damned crazy, chargin' in like that. He couldn't have knowed what was ahead of him," said Patch.

"We all must be crazy, too," added Ethan McCardle. "We all followed him, didn't we?"

"Such courage should inspire men to follow," Robles reflected.

"Hell," said Patch. "I jist wanted to see what was goin' t'happen."

Patch's comment started a round of laughter. Even as they enjoyed the jest, they were uneasy, wondering how much of the Mexican's observation was true. Later, left alone with their thoughts, each would reflect on why they had followed a madman into the cauldron.

Josh was squatting against the embankment near the body of the first Indian he had slain. He was contemplating the destruction he had wrought when he heard the men laugh. Cringing, Josh wondered if the laughter was at his expense. If it was, he deserved it. Delacroix and Patch would undoubtedly have come up with a plan of attack if he hadn't given in to his furor and run into the coulee like a fool. He was lucky they all hadn't been killed by his impetuosity. He didn't deserve to sit with them.

He felt wretched enough for having killed a man—more accurately, two men. The victim at his feet was the one he had shotgunned trying to flee. He had turned a man, in an instant, from a living being into this corpse lying in the dust. Remorse would not take away the blood caking in the dirt or stop the flies from crawling over the cold skin.

Regret at taking another's life was not the root of Josh's wretched state. The turmoil conflicting him, berating him, was the lack of anguish he felt at his own barbarism. He had killed. The taking of life, even justifying it as avenging a theft that jeopardized his own life, should instill some sense of penitence. Yet here he sat, contemplating a death he had willfully inflicted. Why didn't he feel wicked?

He couldn't join the others at the fire. He couldn't face their contempt. Never could he expect them to accept a murderer into their circle.

Since they had broken camp that morning, he had eaten only a dry biscuit and coffee. He was ravenous but could not make himself join the others. What would the others think of a man who could kill two human beings and then sit down to a meal? What disgrace awaited him when they returned to the fort?

The attack had apparently interrupted the victims' meal. His companions were enjoying the spoils around the appropriated campfire. It was more of Josh's own mule that was providing dinner for his friends. He guessed he couldn't blame the others for eating the rest of the meat. It would just have gone to waste, and practical men wouldn't let that happen. Still, it just didn't seem right. He couldn't help but feel vexed, resentful at the men who were eating his mules, at the Indians that stole them, and even at the mule itself for being singled out to be eaten. Only the anger kept him from wallowing in self-pity. The irony of eating the mule he had come to rescue was not lost on him.

"You ought to get something to eat." Delacroix had come to visit him in his solitude.

"'Spect I wouldn't enjoy eatin' my own mule as much as you seem to be."

259

Mules were not what the scout had come to talk about.

"It is good you are angry. Anger is better than feeling guilty over the men killed today." He strode over to the body, still lying sprawled where it fell. He prodded the stiffening legs.

"I take it that it was not easy to deliver the *coup mortal*?"

"If you mean, was it easy to kill them? I guess I was out of my head for a while. Now it's all over, I don't know how I should feel."

"I killed a man today, as did you," Delacroix said. "I will not lose any sleep over him."

"You shot to save my life. That's different."

"Pas si très différent. Losing your animals may have cost you your life. It still might." He shrugged. "*Possible*, you may be able to trade for more."

"Are you saying we shouldn't have come after 'em?"

"*Non.* I am saying that you acted from anger. We might have been able to steal them back."

Josh considered his point. "I'm sorry for losin' my head, but I can't say that I feel sorry for what I done. Trouble is, I don't feel much of anything."

The scout nodded toward the body on the hill. "He was not the first I have killed. I believe I felt much as you do when first I took a life."

Josh realized that this man had been living perilously for years. It shouldn't have come as a surprise.

"What happened that first time?" Josh asked.

"*Cela n'est pas important.* It is enough to know that what you feel is not *particulier*, not different."

"I feel different."

"Ah, I have a hard time saying what I mean. You will always now be different from men who have not been in battle. You will now be like those men who have heard death whisper to them. You will be all right."

Josh kind of understood what he meant. "Thank you, friend. And thank you for saving my life today."

The scout did not want to talk of gratitude. "Rest. Tomorrow we return to the fort."

Long after sundown, Patch was standing sentry on top of the bluff. He didn't expect the Indians to return for another round, but there were more dangers than just Indians about. Perhaps one of the dangers sat in the gully across from him.

For several hours, he watched the young man quietly sitting by his kill. Patch felt better when Josh lay down and curled up to sleep.

As it turned out, they discovered not all the animals had been recovered. Either some had slipped away from the Indians or had gotten by them in the stampede out of the coulee. Sorting through the herd, they could not tell how many were gone. They did not see Preacher Clark's black-stockinged dun, and it was discovered another of Josh's mules was missing.

Josh had awoken in a better frame than when he slipped off to sleep. Then, finding the other notched-ear mule gone, that sent him into a sullen funk. He was no better off than if he had just waved good-bye to the thieves and gone back to bed. The only advantage he could discern, if advantage it could be called, was that he was now an experienced man-killer.

True, the posse had recaptured the animals. Without their success, many of the settlers either could not have gone on or would have to severely lighten their loads. That prospect was a reality for the Bonners, and it set heavily upon the shoulders of a young man with already much to bear.

Josh was still not certain if the men would accept him. They had seemed friendly enough at breakfast. Wallace McCardle and Patch made some feeble attempts at humor, trying to get Josh to eat some of the mule meat. The attempt fell flat and further conversation was limited to the practical. At least there was no attempt to shun him.

As the nature of riding herd kept the men apart, Josh remained unsure of his status. In a way, he was relieved to be riding trail. Despite the dust, he was content to be alone with his thoughts.

On the practical side, he tried to work out how he could combine the remaining two of his own mules, four of Elizabeth's team, and his two oxen to pull two wagons. Elizabeth's was no problem. She could use her original team. The quandary arose trying to imagine how to pull his wagon with only two mules and the oxen. They could not be teamed, so they would have to pull in pairs. The only solution he foresaw was to drastically lighten the load. Perhaps half of all he had would have to go. He tried to recall his inventory and, mentally calculating weight and bulk, decide what could go and what was indispensable.

He supposed that most of the furniture could go. After all, Elizabeth had a wagonload of furniture, and they were carrying an extra bed, dresser, table, chairs, and the like. He hated the thought of discarding the familiar items he had grown up with. They were a last link to his old life and seemed somehow like family. The thought of shedding these last mementos of home almost brought him to tears. Another good reason to be riding alone. Perhaps Elizabeth could discard some of her family items.

Elizabeth was his biggest concern. What would she think of him, leaving as a husband on a perilous quest and returning a husband with blood on his hands? How could she accept such a man? What would the other men tell of his recklessness and his brutal attack? Disquieting thoughts accompanied Josh as he plodded along, trailing the herd.

They traveled through the rest of the day eating dust and moving the animals slowly to the southwest. The work left little opportunity for talk, and a reticent mood prevailed throughout the evening. What little exchange there was revolved around the utilities of the task ahead. The reluctance to intrude upon Josh's dour attitude was contagious. Quietly, the men cycled through sleep and watch duties. The milling sound of the picketed animals was all that disturbed the night.

Perhaps a quiet evening was all the men needed. For the past few days, they had been in hot pursuit. Their depleted systems would rejuvenate with some rest and the certain knowledge that the next day would bring a return to family and more mundane chores.

The day broke clear and warm. The wind had backed, so the dust they kicked up dispersed in front of them. Spirits, including Josh's, brightened, and the men frequently called out to each other, bantering lightly among themselves. Josh even managed to smile a bit at the exchanges. High spirits were returning to the men. They looked forward to rejoining their kin and family. The anticipation of returning as victors lay lightly upon them.

By late afternoon, they were approaching the flats along Laramie Creek. After the crossing, they could anticipate one more night afield before returning to the fort. As they descended toward the creek, they spotted a pall of dust lifting on the warm breeze, a haze of pink suspended in pale blue marking the progress of other travelers.

It was a band of Indians on the move. Delacroix and Patch weren't certain, but, from the direction they were approaching, they thought the clan was one of those that had been camped at the fort. As they got closer, the two scouts concluded that they were indeed *Brulé*. It would only be speculation as to whether they had encountered this bunch before. The thieves they had cornered were Sioux. If the survivors had hooked on with this clan, there could be trouble.

The tribe was strung out over the plain. Women and children walked in file. Horses and even dogs trailed *travois* loaded with the various household possessions. They did not appear to be traveling in haste. Had the surviving Indians rejoined this troupe, then the men would be the only ones presented. The women and children would have been hustled off to where they could be sheltered. This encounter should simply be two bands of travelers passing along the trail.

Still, the whites were far outnumbered and a long way from any assistance. Josh and the McCardles were particularly apprehensive, having so little experience with the Indians. Josh recalled the warriors he had met at the Platte River crossing. The image of scalps dripping fresh blood onto a pony's flank stood clearly in his mind. Mindful of the dire warnings in the guidebooks set them to clenching their teeth. After all, honorable men like Fremont and Bonneville wouldn't have described dangers just to embellish their tales.

Delacroix, Patch, and Robles saw little threat from the band of travelers. The indicators of a leisurely migration to better ground were reassuring. Still, they had to keep their wits about them.

As the two parties neared each other, some commotion was stirring in the Indian camp. As back at the fort, the whites were attracting attention, particularly from the men. The mounted warriors moved in a protective salient around their families. Still, it seemed it was just curiosity that brought the men forward. Slowly, the two groups paralleled each other, each pausing to take the other's measure, both keeping an eye out for some treachery.

This surely was one of the encampments from Fort Laramie. The men seemed to be gesturing toward the herd. They must be aware that animals had been stolen and that men from the fort had taken off in pursuit. Now the pursuers and the animals were returning. They had to be curious as to the fate of those who had seized the animals as prizes. If, indeed this were the same clan, then some of their menfolk would not be reuniting with their families. There were no gestures of greeting or other exchange between the two groups. The two processions were passing with studied disregard. It was difficult to discern whether the encounter would remain uneventful.

Reflexively, Josh reached for the butt of his pistol. His hand recoiled like he had touched a hot stove as soon as he realized what he was doing. Had he tactlessly put them in peril? He looked to Delacroix to see if he had marked his gaffe. The scout glowered back at him.

Delacroix and Patch rode with their rifles casually laid across the saddle pommels. The rifles had been unsheathed when the Indians were first spotted. Thus, the weapons were at the ready without the necessity of making a display of drawing them. Another sign of their experienced that Josh marked.

The two groups passed within a hundred yards of each other, close enough for mutual acknowledgement, but not so close as to appear threatening. At the nearest point, Patch lifted his slouch hat and slowly waved to the Indians. It must have been one of the few times he removed the crushed relic. His forehead was pale, a distinct demarcation between sunburn and skin that never saw sunlight. A few of the Indians lifted their lances casually in acknowledgement of the greeting. Josh prayed this would be the limit of any exchange. If the Indians rode over for a palaver, the subject of why they were out on the plains with a mixed herd would have to come up.

The passage was made without incident. The Indians resumed their march. The whites continued on in studied nonchalance. Josh, riding trail, had to force a casual air. He could almost feel Indians lurking behind him, but he would be damned before he turned to look. It seemed hours before he figured they were out of danger and he dared to look back. Other than the hovering pall of red dust, there was nothing to see. They rode on.

The Independence Day preparations were nearly complete. After a day of laundry, cooking what delicacies could be fashioned from their meager larders, and adding those festive touches as could be improvised, the rest of the afternoon was free from toil.

The women retired as a group to bathe and dress for the party. Once the celebration commenced, they would find little time to relax. An interlude of attending to each other's hair, dresses, and accessories would be more refreshing than the party itself.

Of course, no one had packed the family bathtub when they embarked. Indeed, not many had even owned a bathtub back home. Washtubs were plentiful, and after rinsing the laundry, the galvanized tubs would do as splendidly as any porcelain tub in the finest hotel. To bathe in hot water with attendants was a luxury beyond compensation. Soon, a regimen of heating water, bathing, and keeping the fires stoked was underway.

The young girls and women went first. Undoubtedly, they felt privileged to take the first baths. Soon they understood the opportunity to go first meant they inherited the job of keeping the operation going. Those that went last were the fortunate ones, a privilege reserved for the mothers and grandmothers.

If having women at the usually all male fort was a novelty, then the knowledge that the half-finished officers' quarters harbored naked women dazzled the inhabitants. Of course the women, knowing the nature of men, took every precaution to ensure their modesty. A section of the bunkhouse was cordoned off; the bathers were surrounded and jealously protected by the women. Sentries, armed only with malevolent stares, kept the female-deprived men at bay.

Most of the men, despite their burning desire to catch a glimpse of undraped women, kept a respectable distance. This didn't mean that every scurrilous effort to outwit the guards wasn't contemplated, attempted, and foiled. The women effortlessly frustrated the amateurish tricks devised. The men had to satisfy their curiosity, as men will do, with speculations of what was going on at the baths. Bald-faced lies about successful strategies and tactics spawned renewed attempts carried out with elaborate attentions. As each attempt was foiled, the lies about their successes grew.

The most baleful and malevolent stares from the women bastioning their sisters were reserved for those coarse men whose efforts to gaze on the naked women were blatant. Joe Sweeney and his bunch overtly tried to peer into the windows from as close as they could get without actually going into the building. Even they were not that bold. They rode their horses past, standing in the saddle to garner a better view. They tried mounting the roofs of adjoining buildings hoping to see inside. They even made an attempt to enter the crawlspace under the barracks before being rebuked by a defense of boiling water and strategically applied broom

handles. It was still a game to the ruffians long after it had become a
resigned drudgery for the women.

Jack Thibeault abandoned his fellow voyeurs early on in the
enterprise. Still smarting over his humiliation at the hands of the bitch and
the rancor of his fellows over the injuring of Moon, he slipped away,
sitting in the shade of the eastern palisade. Idly, he sipped at a bottle of
sutler's whiskey. An occasional pull maintained his hangover at a low
throb. Besides, he had other plans for the evening than bullying his way
into the festivities.

Sweeney's boys, knowing they wouldn't be welcome at the party,
intended to intimidate their way in. They didn't expect much trouble from
the emigrants, and experience had taught them the soldiers and their
soldier-boy captain, Brennan, wouldn't offer much resistance. They could
do pretty much as they pleased. While Jack would attend long enough to
fill his belly and cadge whatever liquor he could, Thibeault had his own
agenda. Joe and the boys would provide enough diversion. That would let
him attend to his reckoning with the bitch.

Elizabeth had just finished her bath and had slipped into a faded
muslin shift. The sun was low on the horizon, and she had yet to do her
hair and slip into her dress. The cycle of baths was not complete yet. She
still had to do her stint as charwoman.

Elizabeth had never thought of herself as inhibited, but the experience
of bathing with all the other women was something she would happily
forego in the future. Surprisingly, she was uncomfortable in the presence
of so much frank, female flesh on display. The women, usually encased
from head to toe in high-necked dresses, bonnets, and button top shoes,
made the most of the afternoon of unfettered socializing. Elizabeth had
seen quite enough stringy thighs, deflated breasts, and blue veins for a
lifetime. It made her laugh to think of the men, going through all sorts of
gyrations to glimpse some female skin. Had the women thrown open the
doors to the public bath, the men would probably have fled in horror from
the nearest exit. It had made Elizabeth comprehend how fleeting was a
woman's beauty. Seeing the gamut of female development, from the
unblemished skin and flat chests of the young ones to the desiccated bodies
and sagging flesh of the grandmothers was a sobering revelation. The

years allotted to savor youth's vibrancy were stolen by time, labor, and childbearing. She was all the more determined to enjoy what she had and to resist the ravages God subjected women to.

Recalling the pleasures of the marriage bed evoked a longing for her man's swift return. She couldn't wait to feel him inside her and to satisfy him in kind. Provocative visions of lovemaking made her feel all loose inside and caused her nipples to become erect. Thankfully, she had thrown on enough clothes that the others couldn't detect her arousal. Regrettably, she put such thoughts out of her mind. She told herself he would be back soon despite the nagging worry she consigned to a dark cupboard in her mind. Suppose he didn't come back, or came back wounded?

The sun was setting, and it was all coming together. There were still final preparations for the feast demanding attention. Tables had been stacked with dishes and cutlery, plates of breads, cheeses, and other delicacies awaiting sampling. The main courses were cooked and being kept warm prior to being served. Everything that could be covered had been in order to protect it from the grit sifted from the constant wind and from the ever present flies, bees, and hornets.

The men, of course, had already commenced celebrating and were standing around, waiting to be served. Elizabeth, wiping off some plates with a damp towel before covering them with a weighted tablecloth, was able to hear the clinking of bottles on the rims of short glasses. The men would be half in the bag by the dinner's end and crawling off to sleep away their hangovers before nine o'clock, leaving the women to clean up their messes. At least the women could sleep in peace in the bunkhouse without having their husbands crawling on top of them when they finally turned in for the night.

Elizabeth had put on a primrose off-the-shoulder dress with several stiff crinoline petticoats, wildly out of place in the surroundings. Most of the women had taken the opportunity to put on some finery despite the locale. Mrs. Clark's slave, Dinah, worked her fingers nearly bloody drawing up corsets and whalebone stays. Even on the prairie, the dictates of fashion would outweigh comfort.

The emigrant men had taken the opportunity to brush out their coats and shine their shoes. Reverend Clark had pulled out his ceremony coat, a claw hammer of heavy wool. With his vest, wide-brimmed preacher hat, and his imposing size, he dominated the crowd. The soldiers, recalling a vague memory of spit and polish, made some attempt at a gallant, soldierly

267

appearance. The young officers pulled it off with some accomplishment. The scouts, hunters, and teamsters donned their freshly laundered togs with pride. To their credit, they seemed to be the only ones enjoying the evening in comfort.

By dusk, most of the men were passing around jugs. The more enthusiastic drinkers drank directly from their mouths, the ritual of the glass forgotten. Many of the soldiers and single men from the fort were boisterously drunk. Even Reverend Clark was nursing a pony of blackberry brandy. After all, it was Independence Day. The victuals had been well laid into. Most of the roasted wild game was in tatters. Empty jars of preserves and jellies lay tipped over on the tables or had been requisitioned for drinking glasses.

The holiday had inspired the concoction of impromptu fireworks, proudly sent skyward to pop in the night sky. While gunpowder was a precious commodity, this was a special occasion, and blank charges were fired into the air from a variety of firearms.

It was during this fusillade that Sweeney and his cronies made their unwelcome foray. They sauntered, as a pack, into the midst of the celebrants. They went unnoted for the most part. Only the bulk of men moving as a group attracted any notice.

The day was a special enough occasion that Jubal, Dinah, and Ely were in attendance, quietly socializing amongst themselves. Mrs. Clark had just brought them cups of cider when the louts bowled past them, announcing both their entrance and intentions. They crowded past, and but for a timely intervention by Ely, would have knocked the gentle woman to the ground. Jeering laughter returned her scowl.

Sweeney and his crew rolled along shoulder to shoulder, formidable as a
Roman phalanx. The challenge was palpable. They expected no resistance. Despite their menace, they clung together until they could ascertain no one would rise to confront them.

All eyes turned to Captain Brennan. After all, he was the official authority at the fort. Rather than assume leadership, his sole act of defiance was an exposition of dignified outrage. Without the willingness to exercise his station, his posturing gave all the appearances of a recalcitrant schoolboy awaiting an audience with a harsh headmaster. His puffed-out chest and upthrust chin was but bluster. At that moment, all realized he would do nothing. His status as commander of the troops was lost in that single moment of inaction. He would never command, all could see that truth but Brennan, who continued to pose with his hand on the hilt of his dress sword.

The decent folk would either have to stand for themselves or surrender their dignity and their party to Sweeney and his ruffians. Those that didn't know Leland Metzger from Monroe County looked to the constable turned wagon train captain. Those familiar with him looked but expected nothing more than they realized. Metzger was overfed and overdrunk. Swaying like a performing bear, he made no move. He might as well have slunk away. The emigrants were adrift on a sea of cowardice.

Reverend Clark moved his bulk in front of Sweeney. Alone, if necessary, he would defend his wife's honor. If he defended his fellows as part of the bargain, so much to the good. With arms crossed over his chest and his feet spread for balance, he defied the bareheaded trapper.

With his cronies behind him, Sweeney advanced upon the preacher man. He resembled nothing so much as a malevolent troll, squat and dangerous. His place, having already been diminished by Thibeault's earlier humiliation, required reconstitution. He couldn't afford to let some bumpkin preacher challenge him, no matter how imposing the man's presence. He had humbled bigger and meaner men in his day. Sweeney's mind turned over ways to insult a preacher. This would be too easy.

He never got the chance. Reverend Clark could not let the affront to his wife stand. He clasped Sweeney's throat, squeezing his windpipe and drawing the troll close. He bent over so Sweeney's chin was scratching against the preacher's beard.

"Thou art like a worm that crawls from the earth," he growled at his captive.

Sweeney's response was restricted to something between gargling and retching. Clark had hoisted him so his heels were off the ground. Sweeney's hands twisted on the preacher's forearm to no avail. He was a prisoner and edging toward panic as his chest burned and his vision began to fade.

Clark cast him away. Sweeney was able to remain standing but leaned over, wheezing. He blew air like a ragged bellows. Struggling for breath, he shook a wavering fist at Clark and choked out, "You son of a bitch." His original planned insults weren't even a memory.

269

Clark advanced toward him, announcing, "The evil man pours out his evil words without a thought." As he closed, he leaned in to whisper a confidence to his recent victim.

"I'd pay to see a fight between us, it would be a good'un. This doesn't look like a payin' crowd, though. Maybe we can get together another time."

Joe Sweeney wasn't a stupid man. The life he lived and the people he lived it with wouldn't abide stupidity. Prudence and a knowledge of his surroundings had kept him alive these many years. He had managed to prosper when others starved by paying attention to what was going on around him. Something was amiss here, and worse, he hadn't seen it coming.

He never should have been caught off step by the preacher. He had been anticipating taking some of the strut from the self-righteous bastard when his windpipe had been squeezed and his vision had tunneled in on a pair of pitiless eyes. This Bible pounder looked like he had spent some time with his feet up on the devil's hearth. There was more to him than met the eye.

"Reverend, please accept—" Sweeney hesitated for a moment and rumbled his throat clear. His windpipe was still recovering from Clark's caress.

"Please accept our apologies. We might have come on a mite strong, but we was just anxious to join the fun. We'll behave ourselves. Won't we, fellas?"

Clement, Thibeault, Moon, and the rest wondered what was going on. The boss should have laid into the big man as soon as he was dropped. Maybe he had something up his sleeve and was asking them to go along. They all mumbled their assent.

"You almost knocked Mrs. Clark to the ground," reminded the preacher.

Sweeney was in a fix. He couldn't abide having his stature undermined before his cronies. They must never doubt his resolve or his authority. He couldn't be seen as groveling before the bigger man, yet he didn't think a confrontation with him would be in his best interests, either.

"We was jist tryin' to get through the niggers. Guess we didn't see her standin' there."

"Those people are a part of my household. You have offended my house as well as my wife."

Damn, thought Sweeney, this son of a bitch just won't let it go. There had to be a way out of this.

"Preacher, we didn't mean any offense to your home or your wife. I guess we get to be a pretty rough crowd, living out in the wilds. Not used to civilized folk and all. Please accept my apologies for me and all my boys." Sweeney snatched his hat off his head and turned in supplication to Mrs. Clark. His manner seemed to mollify her, at least a bit.

"Now, Dayton. The man's trying to apologize. Try to show a little charity to those who may have strayed," suggested Mrs. Clark. It was obvious she didn't feel much charity herself but was doing her best to avoid a public confrontation.

With that, the tension seemed to dissipate. Both Sweeney and Clark visibly deflated. Brennan, Metzger, and the others sensed a crisis was past. Slowly but with some renewed vigor, the festivities resumed. Sweeney's men were even offered some refreshment. At least the intruders would be tolerated, if not welcomed.

Eventually, their group broke up and they began to circulate amongst the citizens and soldiers. Separately, they didn't seem so threatening. Sweeney's crew stepped warily through the crowd, constantly seeking out their *compadres* for reassurance and succor.

The evening passed on, the festival atmosphere declining in proportion to the amount and variety of alcohol consumed. Another Independence Day had dwindled to its final hours. While the few children present still ran excitedly amongst the forest of adults, even their efforts at sustaining the event became forced. As predicted, most of the men were in their cups, bed looking more attractive all the time.

Elizabeth was helping to clear up the remains of the meal. Crusted dishes, silverware, and scattered glasses were collected to soak until morning. She had refrained from drinking more than a few token toasts. She had never liked the taste of strong drink, though she had sneaked a taste or two during fests at home. Mostly she disliked the effects it had on men and the debilitations John Barleycorn exacted on his devotees.

There was a more pressing detraction for her this evening than celebrating the birthday of her country. Again, she had found the despicable Thibeault staring holes through her. He seemed to be making certain she caught his eye at every opportunity. The look on his face was a mixture of amusement and menace that was unmistakable. No one else seemed to notice his fixation on her. Repeatedly, she told herself she was letting her imagination run away. A persistent inner voice assured her she was not fabricating concerns for nothing.

Wallace McCardle's son, Jesse, one of those who helped gather water from the Scott's Bluff spring, was playing some sort of juvenile flirting game with one of the girls. It appeared to be Emily Petry, daughter of Daniel and Sarah. Elizabeth thought they were some kind of cousins, but that didn't seem to hamper their enthusiasm for the game they played. They were engaged in a version of tag, using the mingling adults as a playing field. Emily was hiding behind one of the men, peeking out and dodging Jesse's attempts to corral her. Jesse danced back and forth in front of the man, hoping to catch Emily out of step. They had picked the wrong spot to cavort.

It was one of Sweeney's confederates, the brooding and silent Clement. The horsing around of the youngsters was challenging his surly attitude.

"Get away from me, you fleas," he yelled

Emily scurried away. Jesse, startled at the outburst, stared up stupidly at the enraged drunk. His reward was a push on the top of his head that sent him sprawling onto his butt. Drink had soured Clement's already dark humor. He aimed a kick at the boy, who, coming to his senses, easily scurried out of harm's way.

Daniel and Sarah Petry hadn't seen the incident, but it hadn't escaped the attentions of those in the immediate vicinity. One of the fort's corporals, perhaps missing family at home, spoke up.

"They's just kids doin' what kids do." He put his hand on Clement's shoulder to add emphasis to his protest. That was a mistake.

Clement turned into the man's reach and swung a clubhouse right hand at the corporal's head. The soldier, perhaps not as drunk as Clement, stepped into the punch. The fist missed its target, only the forearm making its mark. The soldier retaliated with a blind uppercut that only grazed the other man's cheek. The combatants clutched each other and staggered in their dance. The confrontation all had been avoiding was underway, fueled no doubt by several jolts of potent drink. Together ,they crashed against the table Elizabeth was clearing, spattering her with all manner of leftovers. The two managed to keep their feet and struggled for advantage.

They grunted and cursed, seeking both to keep their enemy close and yet free their own fist for a telling blow.

Leland Metzger, as drunk as any man there, saw an opportunity to redeem his place. The humiliation of not taking any action when Sweeney's crew barged in stung. He had years of experience dealing with Saturday night rowdies back in Monroe County. He pushed his way through the circle of spectators that invariably gravitated to fistfights. Without a fare-thee-well, he clapped the two men's heads together. The corporal, being the recipient of his dominant right hand, collapsed like a steer poleaxed on slaughtering day. Clement, stunned but upright, received an open-handed clap on the side of the head as reward for his failure to succumb to the initial knock. He fell heavily into the table, taking the checked tablecloth and much of the tableware to the ground with him. Both men lay at his feet. The whole fight hadn't lasted thirty seconds. Leland stood over the two men in case they needed a reminder. A smattering of applause and tribute gladdened his heart.

"Back home, we got a real comfortable jail for birds like these. I expect the army has accommodations, too." He was speaking to Captain Brennan.

The young captain had already stepped up. He saw his chance to save face and wasn't about to let it slip away.

"Sergeant Tolliver! Take these two to the stockade. Keep them where they can't see each other when they come to. And I'll want to see Corporal Plough when he's cleaned up and sober."

The sergeant volunteered four soldiers to remove the late adversaries to their evening quarters. Still stunned, the two could walk but offered no objection to the escort.

"Thank you for your quick intervention, Captain Metzger. You show a practiced hand in such matters," lauded the young officer. Metzger fairly glowed in the praise and particularly in the recognition of his "rank." As men and women stepped forward for some well-deserved backslapping, he felt justly redeemed. It didn't bother the former constable a whit to share the stage with the cavalry officer.

Brennan swept the crowd for Sweeney's face and barked out, "Sweeney, I thought you promised there would be no trouble."

The bald troll was not about to kowtow so easily.

"Clement ain't under my *command*." His emphasis on the last word was executed perfectly to undermine Brennan's position. "Besides, it takes two to fight, and your corp'ral was right in the thick of it."

"I'll tend to Corporal Plough. I expected you to control your men."

"My friends ain't so'jers. I don't give them no orders. If they do what I say, then it's 'cause they respect me." He couldn't help but get in another dig.

The crowd was quiet but obviously enjoying the exchange.

"I've a mind to prefer charges and mete out punishment for that lummox," retaliated Brennan.

"You do with him as you want. You'll probably be easier on him than I will. We just came up here to join the fun. I can't help it if Clement don't become a shower of light when the drink is on him," countered Sweeney.

Brennan was anxious to end the exchange. "In the morning, we can work out something suitable to both our tastes. Agreed?"

Sweeney figured he had come out on top in the exchange. He nodded his assent.

While most of the people were enjoying the verbal sparring between the soldier and the trapper, several of the women were attending to Elizabeth's dishevelment. The front and bodice of her dress were speckled with an assortment of stains no amount of blotting or rinsing promised to fix.

Elizabeth was thinking that this was a typical finish to an evening sustained by thirsty men with unlimited access to jugs of spirits. She wanted nothing more than to get out of the clammy clothes and away from the scene of her spectacle. She never thought to look about for Thibeault. It wouldn't have done any good, anyway. He had slipped away as soon as the fight had ended.

Jubal was standing about on the gate palisade, content to reflect upon the evening. The solitude was welcome after the ongoing tension of the celebration of Independence Day. He had a number of things that needed contemplation

His own independence was high on the list. It seemed damned peculiar to be participating, even at the periphery, of an Independence Day celebration when his own freedom was in question. The farther he got from the United States, the freer and more independent he felt. Figuring he would finally be safe in Oregon, the delay at Fort Laramie seemed intolerable. Peculiar also that Dinah and Ely seemed so content being the property of another, even one so conscientious as Mrs. Clark. Other than Josh, the slave couple were the only people he could count on as friends. Even with Josh, the matter of his escape from slavery remained largely unspoken. With the couple in bondage, it was by now understood that a black man's freedom was not a subject open for discussion. If only they could get on the move again.

Above, the moon was waxing through the new quarter, the circle around it prominent. There was just enough light to reflect off the riffles of the river downslope from the gate. To the west and north of the fort, outlines from the Indian camps could just be seen, the hides of the tipis showing as pale cones protruding from the gray and black background. If you looked close, you could see the small orange glows of banked fires before some of the cones. Since Josh had left to chase the horse thieves, two of the Indian encampments had departed, trailing everything they owned on makeshift drags.

South and west of the fort was the wagon camp, mostly dark now but with just a couple of wagons illuminated dimly by trimmed lamps within. The rest of the wagons shown in the moonlight just like the Indian tents. They looked like loaves on the prairie instead of cones.

Jubal was glad he hadn't been tagged for guard duty. Despite the Fourth being a white man's holiday, he had enjoyed most of the activities, particularly the fireworks. The McCardle women, with their men absent, had brought their herd across Laramie Creek and had gathered the animals near the protection of the loosely bivouacked wagons. They and some of their kids had elected to forego the party in order to protect their animals. He wondered if there were any grown men standing guard. If there were, it probably wasn't anyone sober.

Jubal noted a solitary lantern making its way from the fort to the encampment. The party was breaking up and some of the men, not having the benefit of the barracks to sleep in, were returning to lonely beds. Jubal was glad he had strayed away after the rough men had arrived. It was much more peaceful up here on the gate. He supposed he had better check up on Elizabeth one more time before turning in.

Elizabeth was having a hard time keeping the hem of her dress out of the dust and holding the lantern up high enough to cast enough light to watch where she stepped. The dress was probably ruined, anyway. Hiking up the hem was surely a wasted effort. She would put it to soak before she turned in. Meanwhile, she'd have to rummage out something to wear before returning to the fort and her private little space at the barracks. So much for an evening of relaxation. Now she was going to have to dig out yet more clean clothes. She reached the wagon, set the lantern on the seat and stepped up. She was pulled violently back down by her waist. She reached for a handhold but only succeeded in sending the lantern crashing to the dirt.

Jubal had gone back to the party scene and, upon inquiring, found out Elizabeth had trooped back to her wagon to change her soiled clothes. He was shocked into action. He vividly recalled Josh's admonition to keep on eye on his bride. Now she had wandered off and was on her own. He hadn't really expected her to tell him where she was going, but it would have been nice.

Thibeault threw the girl down and pounced upon her, intent on keeping her quiet. Instead, she sprang up. He was just as quick and pinned her against the flour barrel hung on the side of the wagon. She made an effort to bite the hand that covered her mouth. The callused palm almost snuffed off all her breath.

He could tell what she was trying and wasn't about to suffer any wounding from the bitch. Quickly, he drew his hand away and delivered a concussing slap that sent her reeling and stung his palm with great satisfaction. It was time for her comeuppance.

While she was still stunned, he dragged her off into the scrub, then mounted her.

She reached behind him trying to fend him off and felt the hilt of the knife he carried on his belt. It was held in its sheath by a slit in the leather thong that popped over a stud. She slipped the tab away and pulled the shank free. Thibeault felt the woman's meddling with his weapon. His hand sprang backward, but was too late.

Elizabeth pulled the blade free, gathered a bit of momentum, and struck him low in the left side. Her attacker jerked away, ripping the knife from her grip but causing the blade to arc further into his vitals. She wasn't certain how deeply she had cut him, but it was sufficient to make him retreat.

Thibeault's reaction might not best be termed a retreat. His focus was on subduing the girl so he could punish her insubordination. As soon as he realized the fumbling of her hand behind him involved freeing his blade, he knew he was in trouble. He had been cut before, and most woundings produced a quick, sharp pain that quickly subsided. Usually, the more serious the infliction, the less actual pain there was. The body protected itself that way. Not this time.

The shrieking jolt he felt as the steel entered his back was more like having an appendage crushed. He shrieked loudly and snapped upright. This swung the blade through his muscle and opened a small, neat grin in his left kidney. His short, protesting shriek was instantly snuffed as the breath was torn from his lungs. Involuntarily, his back arched. He was able to pull the knife free before he collapsed onto his back. He lay there, seemingly paralyzed, breathing shallowly.

Running from the fort, Jubal thought he could tell in the dark which was Josh's wagon. Just as he was certain of his identification, the light near it flashed out. Miss Elizabeth might be in trouble. Josh would never forgive him if he let something happen to her. He stretched his steps, all the time wondering what he was to do. He had nothing to defend either the girl or himself with.

As he arrived, Elizabeth had just managed to sit up. Her head still was swimming from Thibeault's stunning slap. Already her cheek had swollen her eye mostly shut and a dark mouse was curled up on her cheek. Even her ear was swollen.

Jubal slid to a stop, almost toppling over her crumpled form.

"Miz 'Lizabeth, what happened?" He caught site of her swollen features. "Oh, Lord. You been hurt."

She seemed to recognize him but didn't respond. She just sat in the dirt with her pale yellow dress puffed up around her. Jubal sped around her, looking into the dark for either her assailant or for help. Neither could be said to have their wits about them.

"What happened?" Jubal repeated.

Elizabeth didn't respond. Instead, she held out her arms, asking to be helped to her feet. Jubal lifted her up and supported her by the elbows. He was beside himself that she didn't answer. Then he noticed the slick, wet sheen on her arm and splattered over her dress. Even in the dark he could tell it was blood.

"Ma'am, you gots to sit down till we find where you be cut."

Elizabeth gazed at her bloody forearm. Absently, she wiped her hand on the ruined dress. She stepped away from Jubal's support and peered out into the brush.

"I'm all right, Jubal. I think," she added the disclaimer.

"Miz 'Lizabeth, tell me what happened here." His outcries were beginning to attract attention.

"It was that Thibeault. He followed me and tried to attack me. I stuck him with his own knife."

"Lord, Lord, Lord. Mr. Josh, he's gonna have my hide. I was s'posed to be watchin' over you," he lamented.

Either Elizabeth didn't believe his protestations or wasn't paying attention. She continued to look in the brush.

"I don't know how much I hurt him. He might still be around. You'd better get a pistol from the wagon."

The thought that a wounded Thibeault might be lurking about penetrated Jubal's lament.

"Where do you keep it?"

"Never mind. I think I found him." She motioned for Jubal to come over and see.

Jubal saw the moccasin-soled feet sticking up before he heard the shallow breathing. Thibeault's arm lay in the scrub, moving weakly and crackling the brush.

Together, they crept closer, cautious this might be a ruse. Thibeault looked directly at them. His look appeared calm. There was no fear or rancor. He was just staring upward. He tried to speak but still hadn't recovered his wind.

"I guess we had better get Dr. Bingham." Elizabeth had regained her composure, though her words came out thickly. Whether from being disoriented or from the swelling to her face, Jubal couldn't tell.

"I'm here," spoke a voice. The commotion had attracted some of the other campers. Dr. Bingham was one of several that materialized out of the dark to see what the ruckus was about.

"Let me take a look," said the doctor, sliding his way between them. As he stooped over the wounded man, he found the knife lying by his side. Gingerly, with a fingertip on the point, he stood the offending weapon on its hilt. He looked over his shoulder quizzically at Jubal and Elizabeth. He slid his hand under Thibeault's back, inquiring with a physician's touch. His palm came away bloody.

"What went on here?" he demanded. He then seemed to notice Elizabeth's swollen face for the first time. Even the night couldn't hide the discoloration blooming around her eye.

"My God, girl! Are you all right?" He stood, seeming to forget the prostrate man.

"He came after me. I was able to get hold of his knife and get him first," Elizabeth replied. Still visibly shaken, she was doing her best not to break down in tears. "You had better look after him. I think he's hurt bad."

Bingham judged the girl wasn't seriously damaged and returned to Thibeault, now his patient.

"Can you speak?" he asked.

Thibeault had been able to capture enough wind to resume a semblance of normal breathing.

"I think I'm hurt bad." He was glad there was no blood in his speech. From the loss of breath, he thought he had been cut in the lungs. He knew that to be a sentence of death.

Bingham tried to reassure him. "You're cut. Many times, it looks worse than it really is. I don't suppose you can roll over?"

A heavy groan proved he could not.

Bingham was in his element. "Jubal, take the tailboard off the wagon. We'll carry him to the fort. Henry, Custis. Lend a hand," he ordered.

Jubal was helping Elizabeth to the wagon. She appeared on the verge of collapse, whether from shock or injury it couldn't be said. He lowered the gate and helped her up.

"Miz 'Lizabeth, you climb up here and rest. I'll tell the womenfolk you need some help." He received a squeeze on the shoulder as affirmation; then she lay back.

Thibeault had been manhandled on the rude litter to the fort. He now lay facedown on a table. The same outdoor table had earlier held part of the holiday feast.

Thibeault had passed out on the journey, to his good fortune. Bingham was probing deeply in the wound, trying to staunch the persistent, steady flow of blood. His wife sponged so he could see and handed him the keen tools of his trade. They were a practiced duo, having done similar duty on similar tables before. Jubal held a lamp and moved it as the doctor directed.

"Miz Bonner. Is she goin' be all right?" he asked.

"She took a hard knock, and she's had a bad shock to the system. This man's bleeding to death. Move that light a little closer and keep it steady."

Jubal was leery of questioning so august a personage as Doctor Bingham.

"She could be hurt bad, too. I seen people get bad hurt and not bleed a bit. 'Sides, this is the man who hurt her," he pleaded.

Bingham paused in his grim work.

"This is the second piece of human trash I've stitched up in two days. This one will be lucky if he lives. I am a doctor. I have to help where I can. At least, with wounds, you feel, as a doctor, you can do something. When someone is hurt and you can't tell why . . . well . . . then doctors can't do much to help."

Jubal was stunned, thinking there was something terribly wrong with his young charge. Hattie Bingham tried to relieve his concern.

"I'm sure she is all right. She needs rest more than anything else. Help the doctor, then we'll look in on her." She went back to sponging for her husband. Jubal held the lamp and thought about Elizabeth and what he would tell his friend when he returned.

It seemed like the only time she could think was when she was alone in the confines of her wagon. Tonight, she was alone but didn't feel much like thinking. Either the blow to her head or the shock of being jumped had left her muddle-headed. She was content to just lie with her eyes closed and endure the ache of her swollen features. Disconnected thoughts

280

ran through her brain like starlings flitting through rays of light in a winter barn. It was dreamily unreal and, truth be told, not entirely unpleasant.

She considered the mind must protect itself this way. When something was so awful, you just tucked it away somewhere and covered it up. Her attention darted away on starling's wings. Next, she thought it was just from being struck. She had never been hit so hard in her life. Once, her mother had slapped her. She couldn't recall right now just why. That had been just to get her attention. Thibeault's blow had been thrown to knock her senseless. It was remarkable she had been able to recover, and even more remarkable that now all she wanted to do was to sleep. It's just what she did, and that's just how Jubal and Hattie Bingham found her. The doctor's wife changed the damp compress and left. Jubal stayed by the wagon, ashamed the girl had been hurt by his inattention.

#

CHAPTER SEVENTEEN

#

Only a few more hours and they would be home. Delacroix and Patch decided they would travel at night. The last day had been so hot that the herd was suffering. Next water would be Laramie Creek, and that crossing was only a few miles from the fort. They encamped in the afternoon, sought what respite from the shade they could find, and started up again at dusk. It was harder to keep the animals together, but the trek was so slow with exhausted animals that there didn't seem much risk of losing any more.

Now the animals smelled water, and without prompting, picked up the pace. The men, at least those with loved ones waiting for them, imagined they could detect the scent of home. Even if home was just a wagon, the promise of returning was like the scent of water to the animals. A few more hours would bring the dawn and reunion.

Though the men had largely accepted Josh's rampage, he still was anxious about the reunion with his wife. He was a changed man, a killer. He felt like it must show on his face like the scars of smallpox.

He had seen soldiers home from the war with Mexico. They appeared the same as they had when they left to cheering crowds. They didn't look at all the same when you looked them in the eye. The eyes said they had seen things, things they couldn't, or wouldn't, describe. They might return to their old work. They might rejoin the bosom of their families, but there was no mistaking them for the same men who had departed. Would it be the same with him? He feared so.

Sweeney and his crew mingled despondently by Thibeault's pallet. He had been moved into the back of the sutler's store, the fort lacking anything resembling a hospital. It had been fortunate Bingham was at the fort to attend to him. Otherwise, he would have been left to the ministrations of whosoever volunteered to stitch him up.

Thibeault was conscious and making light of his wound. He even managed to kid about being stuck by a woman. Even though his jokes fell flat, reprisal being a constant theme, his friends still managed to laugh. It was morose laughter at best. The big man, who none really liked, was gravely injured. He was weak, his features sunken, and his complexion gray from the loss of blood. No amount of gallows jest could allay that fact. He was still seeping blood past the stitching, soaking the sackcloth that served as sheets. The room smelled of blood and sour bodies.

Bingham had carefully sewn his way out of Thibeault's back, starting with the violated kidney and working outward through muscle and skin. The stitches would hold and the wounds would heal. Infection and sepsis were the real danger. Bingham looked in from time to time. He would check his work and sniff quizzically at the bandages and at the wound. The surgeon had cleaned the scraps of shirt and twigs and dirt that had invaded the wound, but you could never be certain. It hadn't even been a full day. If infection were going to appear, it would still take some time. From there, the sepsis would grow and finally kill him.

Sweeney had seen men die from sepsis before. They would lie in their own stink, the wound becoming swollen and tender. Each time the boil was lanced to relieve the pressure, the reek of the pus pouring out would choke a vulture. It would have been kinder to let him bleed out.

Sweeney added to the banter, laughing at the right times and reliving with Thibeault some of the good times and places they had been. Thibeault undoubtedly knew he had perhaps received a mortal injury. He was also aware of the prospects of infection. They would be damned if they were going to remind him.

"I guess I still know how to pick the lively ones, don't I?" Thibeault joked weakly. "This one really touched me."

"Better you should stick with the ugly ones, Jack. They don't put up as much of a bother," responded Moon, their differences set aside.

"Lest they stick you," Sweeney added, sparking another round of forced mirth. It was obvious none of the men wanted to be in the sickroom. It smelled horribly, and being with the grievously injured man reminded them how tenuous a hold man had on life in these wild places. The doctor came to their rescue.

The sutler had escorted him into what had been his storeroom. It had only been an hour or so since he had last probed his handiwork.

"Let this man rest. He's not going to get any better without some rest," the physician commanded. His tone was unnecessary as the onlookers needed little prompting to excuse themselves. They filed out quietly. Sweeney lingered a moment to query the doctor.

"Is he going to be all right?"

Bingham put his hand on his back and ushered him out. He closed the door behind him.

"It's not likely he will bleed to death, though it will take some time to stop. Still," he reflected, "he's lost a lot of blood."

"I've seen men die when they seem like their cuts are healing. Is that going to happen?"

"I won't lie. He has as good a chance of dying as pulling through. If his kidney quits working or if the wound infects, there is little anyone can do. I took a lot of dirt out of him. There were rags from his shirt and probably some horseshit in there, too. You can never be certain of getting it all, even after sluicing with liquor. I just don't know."

"Ol' Jack. He didn't deserve this," said Sweeney.

The comment stopped the doctor in his tracks. He glared at the rough man. Although older and smaller than the trapper, he had no hesitation in retorting.

"He brought this on himself, he did. He followed that girl from the fort and attacked a helpless woman, another man's wife."

"Turns out she wasn't so helpless, was she?"

"That girl has more spunk than almost any man here. Don't delude yourself. It wasn't luck let her get the best of him."

Bingham wouldn't admit that he was tempted to just let Jack Thibeault bleed out on the ground. After he found out what had happened, he would have been justified. Silently, he said a quick prayer that his medical training saved him from committing an egregious sin.

"I know Jack. He wasn't going to hurt her. Just wanted to give her some comeuppance for playing around with him."

"I don't know him, but I have seen a peck of men like him. Men like you, too." The doctor's outrage was getting the best of him. "You are a pack of bullies and ruffians, not fit to be around decent folk."

Sweeney could barely contain himself. It was people like the doctor who had driven him away from St. Louis. People who were so self-righteous they wanted the furs he traded but didn't want him or his kind.

"Decent folk like you, ya mean?"

Bingham knew he was pressing it. "Let him sleep. I've done all I can for him. Now I have other things to attend to."

Sweeney spat on the floor, narrowly missing Bingham's pant leg. He assumed his extra polite tone.

"What do I owe you for your services, doctor?"

"I don't want anything from you or from him. Now, let me pass."

Sweeney put his palm on the doctor's chest.

"He had better not die," he threatened.

"It's up to Providence, not me. I hope to be a long way from here before God makes his choice." He sidestepped and walked away. Possibly, he regretted not letting the would-be rapist die, but he kept his own counsel.

"Dear, it must have been just frightful," said Abigail Clark. "The Lord was watching over you, as always." She and several other women were attending to Elizabeth's injuries. Mostly, it was just an opportunity for the women to gather and quiz their sister for details of the attack.

Elizabeth was losing patience with the hen session. How many more times could they change a compress, she thought. Their excited chattering as they projected themselves into the scene was maddening. At first, Elizabeth had been grateful for the company. It was thoughtful of them to care, but her injuries would heal, and she wished they would leave her be.

True, her face was a fright. Looking in a hand mirror in the daylight had shocked her as she surveyed the swath of damage. Her cheek was swollen and red and the mouse had spread down to her mouth. The rough shape of a handprint was apparent in shades of purple and yellow. The cut to the inside of her cheek stung, and she would spit pink for a couple of days. It would all heal, but it hurt like blazes today. She hoped it would subside before her husband returned.

Bingham peeked over the tailboard. He was still fuming from his exchange with Sweeney, and now he was going to have to deal with a

285

flock of chattering women. He thanked Providence his own wife had enough sense to have done what she could and retired.

"Ladies." He tipped his hat to the gathering. Many still wore their dresses from the evening before. Had they been there all night? "Let the poor girl rest. She's soaked to the skin from you messing with the compress."

"She needs the company of other women," said Virginia McCardle. She had taken time out from watching her animals. She had been on guard last night and was the first woman to arrive at the scene. Probably, she had been up all night. Unlike the other women, she was dressed in work clothes, appropriate for tending animals. "Just thinking what might have happened scares me near to death."

"Rest is what she needs. Sleep will do her more good than sitting around in a nightdress." He was still mad and trying hard not to lash out at the women. "How are you doing, child?" he asked Elizabeth.

If her face weren't so sore, she would have kissed the kindly doctor. Sleep was what she wanted, and he had come to her rescue. She managed a grateful smile instead.

"I expect you are right. It hurts some to talk, and some sleep will do me good. Is Jubal out there?

"I'm right here, Miz Bonner," Jubal responded. "Do you need anything?"

"A drink of water might be nice. Perhaps you and the doctor could assist the ladies from the wagon." Bless the doctor for his timely appearance.

Begrudgingly, the women were handed down. They would regroup in the shade somewhere to continue their tittering. Elizabeth thanked them for their concern as they departed. The doctor poked a bit at her cheek. The injury was proud, but nothing was broken. Jubal brought her a tin of cool water. She took a sip and set it by the bedside. They left her alone, and she was soon at rest.

If the doctor was still fuming, Sweeney was furious. It had taken all his restraint to keep from knocking the old fool to the ground. He would have, but he still might need him if Jack took a bad turn. If the sepsis came on, there wasn't much the old sawbones could do, but Jack deserved a fighting chance.

Damn Jack, anyway! His constant bullyragging had brought all this on. From the first confrontation with the redhead, then the go-round with the preacher, and finally Jack's getting stabbed with his own knife, his authority had been undermined. Every effort he made to cement his hold over his men had been thwarted. There had to be a way to set things right. His ability to command was at stake. All because of some tart that had caught Jack's eye.

He could push Brennan for some action. Unfortunately, he had effectively cowed the young officer, making him so spineless he couldn't count on him when he needed him. He couldn't go after the girl directly. She had the sympathy of the soldiers and the settlers. Whatever plan he landed on, he would have to neutralize the preacher. There was something he was missing about that fellow, something he didn't like.

Maybe he could come down on the nigger. He had been there when Jack had been stabbed. He could lay the claim it was the slave who had jumped Jack, not the girl. If he could raise some stink, he might convince them to let them flog the coon, or worse. It didn't seem likely anybody would risk their own hides to save the nigger. He would have to make sure the preacher didn't stick his nose in.

Jubal was sitting in the shade of the wagon. It was brutal hot, and the night's breeze was but a memory. He didn't see how Miss Elizabeth could sleep inside. Maybe she was worse hurt than the doctor thought. He recalled how the doctor said when a person was hurt inside there wasn't much anyone could do.

He rose to get a dipper of water. Removing his hat, he drizzled water over his neck, relishing the cool tingle as it ran down his back. It would be good to go lie in the river, but he couldn't leave his post. He had done enough damage through his inattention already.

When he stood back up, he marked Sweeney and his troop advancing toward the wagon. They were spread out several paces apart. A little farther apart and they would resemble a line of hunters flushing birds from their roost. A chill ran down his spine. This rivulet of cold was quite unlike the one from the water. Panic shivered him momentarily. They were out for trouble again. He turned around, seeking help.

"Don't you move, boy," barked Sweeney.

Jubal's fear almost got the best of him. His legs seemed poised to run off with the rest of him attached. He couldn't leave Miss Elizabeth again. He knew they wanted revenge for their friend. Jubal stood his ground, hoping his trembling knees didn't give him away.

Sweeney's crew fanned out, moving to cut off any retreat.

"You've got to answer for backstabbing our partner," accused their leader.

Jubal's fear slid another notch toward terror. He had seen what happened when a black man was made to answer for some slight to a white. Free or slave, it made no difference. The black was going to settle up, either with a flogging or kicking at the end of a length of hemp rope. He clutched his hat with both hands, placing it over his chest in supplication, perhaps resignation.

"Suh, I didn't hurt nobody."

"We been talking it over. There is no way that slip of a girl got the better of Jack Thibeault. It had to be a sneakin' coon stabbing him with his own knife. Probably, you kilt him, too."

How could he answer? The truth would look like he was trying to blame a white woman. If he didn't deny it, he was as good as dead.

"Mister Sweeney, I never hurt Mister Thibeault," he repeated.

His denials, of course, found no sympathy from his accusers. By now, the commotion had attracted people from the camp. As Sweeney had calculated, they all stood within the half corral his men had formed. From the right, the reverend came, holding his flat hat down on his head.

This was going just as he planned. Torrance and Crabb, who he had dispatched earlier, came up behind the preacher. By now, Clark had a pistol in his back and had been warned to keep his business to himself. It was time to start selling the crowd.

"Folks, we been talking this out. It could only be this darkie that stuck our friend. We figure the two of them were fighting and the girl got in the way. She got hit by accident trying to break them up. When she did, the nigger grabbed Jack's knife and stuck him in the back."

Metzger was there, but Sweeney didn't figure to get much sass out of him. Metzger piped up. "By God's thunder! That's not the way we hear it told, Sweeney."

"She's just covering for him. No sense losing your property if you can help it."

"He's not anybody's property." Elizabeth appeared at the back of the wagon. Her face was still swollen and mottled, but her outrage was obvious.

"That son of a bitch tried to rape me. I was lucky to get a blade in him. I wish I had been able to kill him."

Sweeney tipped his hat. "Ma'am. It's a shame you got hurt, getting mixed up in a brawl. Nobody's going to think the worse of you for sticking up for your boy. But you can't expect people to believe that you got the better of Jack."

"Bring him over. I'll stick him again if you don't believe me."

"I'm sorry to hear you speak like that. He is probably going to die." Sweeney put, he thought, just the right touch of reverence in his tone. "It's only right you should try to protect the boy, but he is going to have to answer for his crime."

Sweeney and Clement stepped forward as though to take charge of Jubal. The others closed in, more to keep the crowd from interfering.

"Come with me, boy. We're going to see Captain Brennan and find out what really went on."

There was no one present who presumed Sweeney's intent was to have Brennan mete out justice. No one stepped into the fray. Jubal gazed, his face a mask of appeal. Instead, he found a Hawken rifle being pressed into his hands. Without thinking, he accepted the weapon and swung it toward his aggressors. The rifle offered him some protection, but playing a weapon toward a white man would be fatal for him regardless. Nevertheless, he thumbed back the hammer.

"Boy! You put that gun right down," ordered Sweeney.

Jubal seemed as perplexed to be holding the weapon as Sweeney was to be facing it. "Suh, I don't want nobody to get shot. I ain't done nothin', and I don't want no bad thing to happen," he pleaded.

Sweeney's voice was calm, but his hand moved toward the butt of the pistol in his belt. "No one will get hurt. You just set that thing down, real gentle-like."

"You keep the gun, Jubal," Elizabeth commanded. She stood in the canvas portal of the wagon. Her hands held a pistol, cocked and beaded on Joe Sweeney.

In the past three days, Joe had had guns in his face three times, more than in the past three years. He was getting damned tired of it.

"Missy, you know you can't shoot anyone. Put that thing down."

He was right. Elizabeth wasn't going to be shooting anyone. Not because she wouldn't, but because she noted there was no cap on the nipple.

"You are right. Nor did I stab your friend. Why don't you just step up here and I'll hand it to you," she proposed.

It had all the appearances of a standoff. The participants looked about for help from the crowd. Elizabeth saw the two men stationed behind Reverend Clark. She had sought him out first as the most likely to intercede without provoking violence. Mrs. Clark wrung her hands before her face. She had seen the black barrel of the gun poking her husband's ribs.

Sweeney's friends still felt they had the upper hand. None of the settlers appeared ready to back up the two. All of Sweeney's boys were armed. Perhaps one of them could get off a shot before either of the two reacted. Not a one of them wanted to be the one to first try. The result was a measured advance upon the defiant girl and the darkie.

Elizabeth was hoping they were more transfixed on her intentions than on the fact there was no way to fire the gun. She was the only one that knew they were in a bluff, not a standoff.

"Little lady, we can't stand here like this all day. I am going to come over there. I don't think even a fierce one like you would shoot an unarmed man down," said Sweeney. He raised his hands and waved them disarmingly. He stepped forward.

"I don't think she will, either. But I'll have a go," said a voice, punctuated by the ratchet of a cocked hammer. Josh had returned.

"Oh! You're back," exclaimed Elizabeth. The timbre of her voice conveyed the solace she felt at his return.

Sweeney was hoping the young man would be befuddled by his wife's outcry, it turned out he was the one to be distracted.

A scrabbling from his right showed Crabb laid out on the ground. The French scout held a skinning knife under Torrance's throat; a bright bead of blood trickled through beard stubble onto his dirty collar. Clark was embracing his wife, no longer a hostage to Sweeney's stooges. Patch, Robles, and the McCardles had posted themselves strategically around the scene.

"You damned young pup!" challenged Sweeney, outraged to be facing yet another gun. "You don't even know what's going on here."

"I know you and your bunch are threatening my wife and my friend. That's plenty enough for me."

"He ain't no pup, Sweeney," chimed in Patch. "I see'd him charge into a camp of *Brulé* and kill two of 'em afore they knowed he was there."

Sweeney knew when he was licked. He started to point an intimidating finger at his tormentors but didn't know whom to single out. The finger waggled in frustration before him. Sweeney made a fist, either in anger or frustration.

"You haven't heard the last of this," he threatened through clenched teeth. "Jack deserves better than this."

As he retreated, his men closed about him, scurrying for the sanctuary of the group. For this day, a confrontation had been averted.

Josh rode toward his wife. The tears that stained her cheeks were relief at his return and from deliverance from a dicey situation. She fairly leaped into his arms, nearly dragging Josh from his mount.

"You're back, you're back. It has been so awful. Don't ever leave again." She fairly squeezed his head off his shoulders with her embrace.

"Looks like I got back just in the nick. What has been going on here?"

"I'll tell you later. For now, just hold me." Josh was half falling from Natchez's back. The sorrel was prancing in a small circle, trying to cope with the awkwardly balanced load. Josh had to find a way to set her down without being pulled from the saddle. Clark came to his rescue, supporting her at the waist.

"Let me help you down, missy. You'll squeeze that man of yours in half if you hang on so."

Elizabeth's eyes streamed as she gazed up at her man. She was about to break down and blubber. Wiping her nose and eyes on her sleeve like a little girl, she held his pant leg and wouldn't release him. After he dismounted, she clung so tenaciously he was thoroughly embarrassed. Between kisses, he asked, "I recognize that bald one. What business has he got with you that needed an unprimed pistol?"

"I had to do something. They were going to take Jubal. Whip him. Maybe worse." Through sobs of joy, she relayed her tale of confrontation, assault, and mayhem. All of the anxiety she had bottled up over the past few days abruptly came to the fore. Finally, with Josh's return, she could cope with all that had happened in the past days.

The scouts and the McCardle brothers were transfixing the crowd with the tale of their pursuit as Josh dismounted and slipped away with Elizabeth down to the riverbank.

"You're trembling," said Josh. Actually, she was shivering like a puppy pulled from broken ice.

"I can't help it. This is all too much for a body to bear. If that man had taken another step, I fear I might have fainted."

"Faint? I've a hard time picturing that," he replied. "You're tougher than a bar of iron."

"You would like to think so. I'm just a person, and a person can only take so much before they fall apart like a cheap toy." Elizabeth hadn't relinquished her hold. She needed the comfort that came from his physical contact.

"It will be better now. It's all over." Josh patted her back in reassurance.

"It is not over. Suppose they come back? And quit patting me on the back. I'm not a pet spaniel."

"I get a feeling you're getting some spunk back," grinned Josh. He held her at arm's length. His smile slipped away as he looked at her tear-streaked face. It was the first good look he had at her swollen, mottled face.

"Was it that Thibeault fellow did it?" he asked. A tornado of fury swirled behind his eyes.

"Of course it was him. But what can you do to him that I already haven't?" she replied.

"I guess you hurt him pretty bad?"

"There's a good chance he will die."

"If he does, he dug his own grave," Josh judged.

"I suppose so. I still will feel awful if he does. I never imagined anything like this happening."

Josh supposed this was as good a time as any to reveal what he had become. She might not judge him so harshly as she might soon be a killer, too. It was an awful way to describe his wife, even if only in a private thought.

"You know, I won't think any less of you if he does die," he offered.

"What do you mean? I had no choice but to defend myself."

"Guess I was just lookin' for a way to tell you what happened while I was gone."

"What?"

"I kilt two Indians, ones that stole our mules."

"Oh, Josh, don't feel awful. You were just after your stolen property. It couldn't be helped." Perhaps she was seeking a means of defending her own violence. "Just like I was defending myself."

"Mebbe, mebbe not. You didn't have any choice. Me, I just went into a rage. We might have been able to get our herd back without shootin'. I just went crazy and rode in lookin' for trouble."

It was out. He peered into her eyes, seeking a clue. He had confessed badly. Listening to his own words, he sounded like a cold killer. If she flinched, he would just break down.

There was no flinching on her part. She simply threw herself against him, grateful just to have him near. He felt her tears soak through his dusty shirt. At least she had stopped shivering. Wordlessly, she tried to communicate her relief to him.

What the hell was he thinking? Here his wife had been through hell since he had left her. He shouldn't even have gone. His pride had made him go off, seeking adventure more than recovered horseflesh. He was a married man and had no business running off after hostiles.

Worse, he thought, he was trying to use her distress and guilt over injuring her assailant to assuage his own guilt, to manipulate her into accepting him after killing two men. He clenched his teeth, despising himself for being so thoughtless and for trying to exploit her vulnerability.

Never again, he vowed. Never again! He held her closely until his own eyes welled with tender emotion.

They walked awkwardly in each other's embrace back to their wagon home. As he walked, he waved away those who came to console his wife and to congratulate him for his valor. Knowing why they were sought out made him want to declare that she was the valorous one, and she alone could console him in his shame.

Tenderly, they retired to the privacy of the wagon. Despite the heat, they slept soundly, nestled as spoons in a drawer. As the evening cooled the land, they woke, kissed, and, as tenderly as they had slept, made love.

#

CHAPTER EIGHTEEN

#

Tomorrow, they would be on the trail again. It had been two days since Josh's return. The time had not been spent lolling away in each other's arms. There was work to be done.

The couple, now short a pair of mules, were trying to rearrange their belongings to accommodate the reduced pulling power. Everything they owned was piled between the wagons. In order to lighten the burden Josh had elected to turn his wagon into a cart. A long day's work had moved the larger rear wheels to the front. As the large wheels restricted the turning, he had to lock the axis of the front tree. He had removed, through trial and test, enough of the rear end of the wagon to balance the load on the remaining two wheels. Elizabeth was cutting and re-stitching the canvas cover.

The problem before him now was sorting out and deciding what could be kept and how to pack the remaining inventory. A scattering of the furniture he had grown up with lay on the ground, left to fall apart in the harsh climate or, more likely, to be chopped up for firewood. The thought of leaving his parents' belongings to such an ignoble fate brought tears to his eyes. The pile of discards grew as he tried to adjust the freight.

"I can barely bring myself to leave these things behind," he said.

"I wish we could bring that sideboy. I remember how much store your mother set by it."

"T'wouldn't do any good to bring it. Ever'thing she kept in it is piled here on the ground." His hand fanned over a litter of plates, tablecloths, napkins, and crockery. The everyday items of his family and home lay on the ground, already coated with dust sifted from the everlasting wind. All of the furniture would go excepting his mother's rocker and its bolsters. His memories of his mother, gently rocking in the front room as she performed the little tasks of housekeeping, or read her Bible, could not be left heaped by the roadside. Her Bible, the pillows, and the chair, now knocked down and tied in a bundle, would continue their westward way.

The tools that had been his father's would forge west. The wooden handles and the iron grips of his father's trade and his own, worn smooth from the craftsman's grip, carried more than memories. They were his tools, his vocation, his chance in a new land. Even still, some of these, the ones he could have replaced at a smithy, would lie in the dust along the

295

Laramie River, soon to rust into junk. The weight was just too much. If he relented to sentiment, it would kill his team. His choice must be swift and certain. Any error in judgment must be on the side of prudence.

The clothes. He couldn't imagine they had packed so many clothes. Between the two families, they had seemingly carried enough wardrobe to supply a store. Loose garments and tightly tied bundles lay strewn on the ground, soon to be weather-stiffened rags.

Josh had saved two changes of clothes and a couple of extra shirts and underwear. Elizabeth kept only two dresses, one for everyday and one for special occasions. For the days on the trail, she had appropriated some of her father's woolen and cotton pants, shirts, and his broad-brimmed felt hat. Her choice to wear men's clothes was more than practical. Discarding women's trappings symbolized she was no longer just extra cargo on the trail. She was now a part of the team that would push these animals to Oregon. Whether the work was cooking, cleaning, or mending harness, her attire declaimed her will, her intent.

When picking through the pile of clothes, she willed herself not to recall Mother and Father as they dressed in life. She was able to keep her emotions in check, despite the memories the clothing evoked. When she came across a store of her departed brother's clothes, she could no longer be stoic. Slumping to the ground, she clutched the fabric dreams of what might have been. The patched pants and darned elbows of what never would be lay as shrouds upon her vision. Some she must keep. At least a part of them would travel west, even if their wearers' shrouded remains now lay buried in the shade of a tree near the Big Sandy.

"Hello, there." It was the Reverend, come to visit.

Josh wiped his eyes on his sleeve and tugged at the bill of his cap. "Afternoon, sir."

Elizabeth almost curtsied, then stopped, visualizing how absurd the gesture would appear, dressed in oversized men's attire. She wondered if she should tug her cap, too. The thought was droll, almost bringing the hint of a smile to her lips. Clark evidently wasn't amused by her transformation. His consternation was palpable from the way the scolding words rolled in his mouth, fighting to get out. Admirably, he controlled himself. Elizabeth stifled a laugh at his consternation. Tugging at the bill, she reckoned the hat hid her face. There were more advantages to dressing like a man to be discovered.

Her husband realized what was going on and deftly came to her rescue.

"What can I do for you, Reverend?"

"Just came by to see how your rig was coming along."

"It's comin' together. I can't seem to get it to balance right."

"It certain is a shame, having to leave all of this behind. If only your mules hadn't been stolen," Clark sympathized.

"They wasn't just stole, they was et," said Josh, a little caustically. "Your dun was taken, too. I'm sorry we couldn't get him back."

"A shame. He was a good mount, though he had a tendency to bite. I hope his new owner has discovered that trait."

Josh laughed. "I guess its good you can joke about it."

"God worketh all things after the counsel of His own will."

"I suppose he does. Still, it's too bad he was lost."

"The scout tells that you were quite the hero."

Josh soured a bit inside. It was hard enough coming to grips with his actions without people reminding him of what he considered as shameful. Clark seemed to read his mood and dropped the topic.

He seemed hesitant to continue, clearing his throat before speaking. "The loss of my mount is something else I wanted to talk to you about."

Hell, thought Josh. I've already twice said I was sorry. He started to apologize a third time before Clark interrupted.

"No need for regret. I know you all did your best. The fact remains I am left on foot. I was wondering if we could talk about your selling me a horse."

Josh was taken aback at the man's gall. It was obvious the only horse he owned was Natchez. If the Reverend thought he was going to use his station or play on Josh's guilt to wheedle his horse away, he was headed down the wrong trail. Before he replied with something smart, Josh held back and said stonily, "He's not for sale."

"I'll pay hard cash."

This was too much. "Then I could listen to it jingle in my pocket while I walked to Oregon?"

"No, of course not," Clark replied as reasonably as he could muster. "You could ride one of your mules. I would offer to buy one of the mules, but it wouldn't look right for a man of the cloth to be riding a mule."

"But it would be just fine for me to ride a mule, then?" Josh was steaming in his boots. Elizabeth spoke up before Josh had a chance to retort further.

"They aren't for sale. We will need them to pull the wagons. There must be a horse for sale at the fort?"

Maintaining with some difficulty a reasonable tone, Clark told his tale of woe.

"Horseflesh in these parts is pretty dear. I asked Hollis Cooper as he was going to stay on at the fort. He appears to have gotten work as a teamster for the army. I guess the loss of a couple of fingers doesn't stop a man from driving a team. In any event, he won't sell."

"Nor will we. I said I'm sorry for not getting your dun back, but we are going to need what we have."

"Then how about selling me your darkie's horse?" suggested Clark.

Josh replied icily. "He's not my darkie. His horse is his horse, and I'd be damned surprised if he would sell it to you or anybody." Technically, the nag Jubal rode was a Bonner horse, but there was no need to pass that tidbit on. "You'd better keep looking. I got work to do." He turned his back on the preacher, ending the conversation before he went too far.

"I was simply hoping you might have some more respect for a man of God," Clark said before turning to leave. He strode away like a storm cloud on two feet.

Elizabeth called after him.

"What does Doctor Bingham say about Thibeault?"

"He says the man is turning for the worst. It appears you managed to kill him, after all." Clark had responded casually without turning around, hoping to get in a jab before he left.

Never one to let the last word go unsaid, Elizabeth called after him.

"You had better go ask. Looks like there might be a horse for sale, after all."

The walking storm cloud froze for a moment and pronounced, "The woman shall not wear that which pertaineth unto a man, for all that do so are abomination unto the Lord thy God," then stomped off on its way. She could almost imagine lightning bolts roiling about his head.

Elizabeth knew she shouldn't antagonize Clark. Despite the kindness he and his wife had extended to her, he had no call to almost insist they part with their animals so he could save face. Besides, getting that little jibe in had cheered her up immensely.

"Is that buggy going to be able to travel tomorrow?"

Delacroix had approached as they had watched Clark storm away. Undoubtedly, he had witnessed the scene with the preacher. The amused look on his face almost assured he had.

"I . . . we'll be ready," confirmed Josh.

"If you can carry some of this for a week," he said, indicating the goods strewn about, "you can sell them to the Mormons at the Last Crossing."

"We've tried at the fort. They offered to trade for bacon, but we are trying to save weight," Josh explained. "We would be in the same bind with the Mormons."

"I said sell, not trade. The Mormons will pay cash, especially for clothes. You wouldn't have any trouble carrying a few silver coins, would you?"

"Where would they come up with cash?" Elizabeth asked.

"They run the ferry at the Crossing. They will trade for passage, but most of their business is cash money. They trade square, too. Not like these American Fur Company robbers." He spat for emphasis.

"I would rather give it to them than see it go to rags on the ground. We'll take your advice, with gratitude," replied Elizabeth.

Delacroix looked at Josh.

"We'll be ready," replied Josh, anticipating the scout's next comment.

That evening, Thibeault died. Though he was pissing blood, the wound to his kidney had healed properly. The infection from the filth that couldn't be removed from his wound had gone septic. Despite repeated lancings to release the pus from his swollen back, the infection just got worse. The loss of blood and the damaged kidney were too weak to offset

the poison growing inside him. At the end, he had to lie on his stomach.
His skin was so puffy and hard, even the slightest contact with the
bedclothes sent spasms of pain through his body. He died cursing the girl
who had brought him to this wretched end. His friends wrapped him in the
burlap sacking that had been his last bed and buried him before the sun got
too high and made the work too hot.

That next morning, the emigrants departed Fort Laramie. Rested and
well fed, they set out once again. The wagons were in single file as they
departed, with the herd loosely trailing behind like a knot at the end of a
rope. Soldiers, teamsters, and trappers came down to wish them well as
they left. Patch and Robles rode along in company with Delacroix, their
bond that of men with a mutual trade and shared experience. Captain
Metzger at first rode with the trio, then dropped back and rode alone.
Excluded by their common bond, he withdrew.

Jubal drove the cart Josh had fashioned over the past couple of days.
Josh, watching from behind, was proud of his work. Not having the
convenience of a workshop seemed not to have been detrimental to the
final design. It appeared to be balanced and to drive well. Josh walked
apace of Elizabeth's wagon, Natchez hitched to the rear. Banner and Flag
were in company of the herd trailing the expedition.

To Josh's right were the Clarks. Mrs. Clark sat calmly in the wagon.
Ely was driving, with Dinah behind Mrs. Clark in the wagon. Dinah was
keeping up a lively conversation. She had learned that as long as she could
entertain the mistress, the longer she and Ely could ride instead of taking
shank's mare. The reverend took up his station at the side of the wagon.
He was riding a gray mare with dappling across the shoulders and black
stockings. It was a handsome horse and well cared for. He had apparently
been able to strike a deal with Thibeault or his executors.

Not all watching the procession depart exuded good will to the
pioneers. Sweeney and his boys, the dirt from their friend's grave still
under their nails, sullenly watched them roll westward. Joe Sweeney,
never one to forget a slight, debated whether to pursue them. Nothing
would suit him better to strike back at the people who had sabotaged his
stature. His companions offered some comment, but sensing his mood,
watched in silence as their leader brooded and perhaps schemed.

Well, the story is moving along now. Both Josh and Elizabeth are "blooded," and neither seems much the worse for it. In the next segment, they meet up with someone who, with a simple trade, will send the young couple off their path and change the course of their lives. Sometimes, it's the small things that change everything. Hope you are enjoying this as much as I enjoyed writing it. Many thanks for signing up for the journey. If you might take a few minutes and leave a kind comment where you bought this, I would really appreciate it. Independent authors rely on reviews to compete with the publishing houses. Thanks in advance.

The next segment <u>The Platte River Waltz, The Growler Brigade</u> is available as an e-book on Amazon.com or as a Createspace.com print on demand.

PRAISE FOR

The Platte River Waltz, The Growler Brigade

"I loved Volume One (Orphans), and I loved this one as well. It is rare that I hate a book to end. BRING ON THE NEXT ONE . . . PLEASE! Great historical fiction, and main characters I can care about . . . what more can I ask for?"

~As reviewed on Amazon

I couldn't stop reading the first book and started reading this one as soon as I finished the first. It is a well-written page-turner, and I am eagerly awaiting and hoping for a third book.

~As reviewed on Amazon

This entire series is exiting and realistic. The background has been well researched for the westward travel. There is happiness, hardship, celebration and death - all just as in real life. The characters have a depth that made me want to follow them and be a part of what was happening - at least most of the time. Really great story, but you have to read the entire series as these are not good stand alone books.

~As reviewed on Amazon

Volume 2 of the tale of Josh and Elizabeth continues the challenge of an 18 year old taking on a man's responsibility trekking across the Great Basin and the Sierra Nevada. Just two years after the Donner Party, the Bonner Party heads for Donner Pass. Ute and Piute object, water is undeniable, and members are fractious. Jubal grows into his own and Elizabeth develops mature techniques to keep her beloved on an even keel.

The adventure became my own. I recommend this story to those who like historical fiction, westerners or adventures. Consaul enriches with fascinating detail the trail to the Gold Rush.

~As reviewed on Amazon

Made in the USA
Coppell, TX
21 May 2022

78038756R00167